JOHN MICHAEL CURLOVICH

the LOVES of the ARGONAUTS

For more information contact:
Riverdale Avenue Books
5676 Riverdale Avenue
Riverdale, NY 10471
www.riverdaleavebooks.com

Design by www.formatting4U.com
Cover by Scott Carpenter
Digital ISBN: 978-1-62601-310-0
Print ISBN: 978-1-62601-311-7
First edition, September 2016

Author's Note

It was a given in the classical world that male love superseded the love of man for woman. That is implicit in virtually all ancient writers, from Homer and Hesiod to the last of them in the fourth century, when Christianity finally laid classical culture to rest. It was widely accepted, for instance, that Achilles' love for Patroclus motivated his behavior in the *Iliad*. Hercules and Hylas were universally understood to be lovers, and one variant of the legend of Hercules held that he performed his famous 12 Labors for no other reason than to please King Eurystheus of Argos, who was his lover (and that one of Hercules' sons became Eurystheus' heir and successor on the throne!).

Scores more examples could be cited, and I am hardly alone in recognizing and emphasizing it. Reviving, or re-emphasizing, the homoeroticism of the ancient world was part of the driving ethos of Sergei Diaghilev's Ballet Russes, a century ago, for instance. The same could be observed about Szymanowski's opera *King Roger*, and on and on.

Nor was it strictly a matter of sex between older men and boys, as is so often claimed. Alexander and Hephaestion were both adult males, as were the playwrights Euripides and Agathon and the philosophers Zeno of Elea and Parmenides. Aristogeiton and Harmodius, the lovers who brought democracy to Athens, were indisputably both adults. It is recorded that Marc Antony, the great heterosexual lover in popular history, had a lover named Dellius who was also one of his generals. Anyone familiar with classical history and culture can cite many more examples.

This factor—almost always omitted from modern accounts of the ancient stories, explains a great deal that is otherwise rather puzzling. Jason's attraction to men, for example, provides a plausible explanation for the tragic failure of his marriage to Medea. And a homocentric culture goes a long way to explain the story of the murderous Lemnian women.

* * *

My hero is Acastus, son of the usurper Pelias. He is usually cast as a villain, and frequently as a gay, or gay-ish, one. In the wonderful Ray Harryhausen film *Jason and the Argonauts*, for instance, he is not exactly played gay, but he's not exactly played straight, either.

As for Jason, the classical accounts hardly portray him as the good, selfless hero so dear to Hollywood. He was instead depicted as crafty and ambitious, much more akin to the Biblical thief Laban or to Odysseus in Homer's epics. This was hardly regarded as a negative character trait in the ancient world. Even the god Hermes was portrayed as an admirably sly thief. It is quite a different matter in modern eyes, of course.

* * *

While bringing out the culture of male love that pervaded the ancient world and ancient literature, I have tried, to the extent possible, to be faithful to the legends of the Argonauts and the Golden Fleece as laid down by the ancients, particularly Apollonius Rhodius in his epic *The Voyage of Argo*. The conventions of modern storytelling and modern sensibilities have not always made this possible, but I hope I will be given credit for making a good effort.

Johm Michael Curlovich
September, 2016

Chapter One
In My Father's House.

There is a long tradition that someone telling a story like mine should invoke the Muses, to help him tell his story well, to give him the art he needs. And there is so much to tell: The death of my city, Iolcus, which in its day had been one of the glories of Greece. The company of Argonauts, heroes in so many ways, heroes in their love for one another. The Golden Fleece and the Hydra. Jason and his love for Idmon, the seer, and the way he betrayed him to marry Medea. And my own love for Kalais, the winged man, the beautiful man who carried me to the heavens and loved me there.

But it is not the Muses I call on now. Our love was the gift of the goddess, and I know I could never describe it well without her inspiring my words. May she give me the fire I need to tell my story.

* * *

Our dynasty was founded a hundred years before I was born by King Athamas, the younger son of the king of Corinth. What became of the previous ruler is not recorded; the official story is that Athamas took the throne peacefully. But the final kings of old dynasties tend not to have happy fates. When I was older I tried to find some record of what had happened; but our family had been much too efficient in hiding the truth, whatever it might have been.

At any rate, on the day Athamas took the throne there was a huge public celebration. The new king rode in procession before his people accompanied by his wife Nephele, who was pregnant, and his young son and heir Phrixus, and Helle, the boy's twin sister. They were eight years old, and by all accounts they were beautiful children.

1

At the height of the festivities in the main square of the city, and seemingly from nowhere, a ram appeared, the largest ram anyone could remember seeing, the size of a young bull. And its fleece was the color of gold, which was quite unheard of. This was taken as a blessing on the new royal house, a gift from Zeus, who had always been Athamas's patron. It may actually have been staged, of course, but one way or the other, no sensible king could have missed such a ripe opportunity for propaganda. The appearance of the ram was heralded throughout Greece as a sign from the god.

But the blessing turned into a curse, and the reign of Athamas was not happy. Hoping to build on the promising beginning of his reign, and amid much fanfare, he made the journey to the great oracle of Zeus at Dodona, to sacrifice and ensure the god's continued blessing. Young Phrixus and Helle remained in Iolcus with the queen, who was nearing her term.

The priests of Zeus made him welcome. The great oracular oak, which was said to be the oldest living thing in the world, stood magnificently at the center of the sacred precinct. Athamas sacrificed five unblemished ewes to the god. Then when the rites were completed and the moment came for supplication, he asked the oracle, "What must I do to ensure my line will be a long one?"

Everyone waited, quite still. Then the divine wind came, and as it rustled through the leaves of the sacred oak, the voice of the god could be heard whispering, "Your children must die."

"No!" Athamas cried out. "No!"

The wind went calm. The voice of the god went silent. To dispute the words of the oracle was sacrilege. The indignant priests refused any further assistance or hospitality. Sad, apprehensive, the king returned home, only to learn that in his absence the queen had miscarried and bled to death.

For Athamas to murder his children would bring a curse on him. To refuse and let them live would bring ruin to his house. The oracle seemed to have left him no option that would not cause anguish. But the god's word had been clear enough. Phrixus and Helle, the king decided, would have to die for the continuance of the royal house.

But that was the kind of thing that could only be done in secret. He led them into the forest behind the city, to a little shrine of the goddess Hecate, and attacked them with a ceremonial knife of bronze. They struggled, but they were children and he was a strong, accomplished warrior. They were cut; their blood splattered him.

But before he could strike them dead the golden ram appeared again. Seeing it made the king hesitate. And in that moment the children climbed frantically onto the ram's back. It leaped into the sky and vanished with them. The king was left there, gaping at the place where his children had been, polluted with their blood.

Athamas remarried, hoping for more sons, but his second wife proved barren. The throne of Iolcus passed to his nephew Colophon, a devotee of Poseidon, from whom we all were descended. The god's promise of a long dynasty proved true.

That at least was the official story. I was never certain how much of it to believe.

* * *

When I was born, my mother dedicated me in the temple of the Muses, and my temperament had always inclined toward the arts and learning, not to war and government. But I was enough of a political creature to recognize the official story as effective propaganda: a sign from Zeus to bless the new royal house; then its miraculous disappearance, so that no one could ask inconveniently to inspect it. But I never quite understood why my ancestors had infused the official myth with the taint of child-killing. Even if it was horribly true, why blot the city and the children of the family by dwelling on it?

* * *

My earliest memory is of walking outside the city walls with my nurse Anticleia, exploring the surrounding hills. Sometimes my sisters Callimache and Cleito went with us, but on that day we were alone. It was a brilliant summer afternoon, the sun was blindingly bright, and the world was greener than seemed possible. I was seven, maybe eight years old; I wore a linen tunic and went barefoot. Anticleia, though she could not have been more than 40 years old, wore heavy black robes, like an elderly widow, or a witch.

Iolcus had always seemed to me the fairest imaginable place.

3

Our palace sat on the top of a broad hill overlooking the bay, with the city stretched out below it. The water was deep and blue and teeming with fish, the harbor was busy even in winter, and there nearly always seemed to be dolphins. A lighthouse guarded the harbor entrance, a magnificent bronze colossus of Aphrodite, the patron goddess of the city, dressed in swirling robes, crowned with a circlet of stars, holding a lantern aloft. It had been made by the famous sculptor Phraxis. On bright days it seemed to gleam almost as brightly as the sun; at night it bathed the harbor in a rich orange glow.

The walls of the city, as if in deliberate contrast, were of heavy black stone, massive, almost cyclopean; I remember believing only the giants could have built them.

Our metalsmiths made bronze weapons and ornaments for export, and merchants from all over the Mediterranean came to Iolcus to trade. The countryside around us was lush, abounding in every kind of food. There were groves of olive trees, rich orchards, vineyards full of plump red grapes, beehives producing the sweetest honey. Autumns were vibrant, winters white and beautiful. Best of all, it was a time of unaccustomed peace and even harmony among the Greek cities. When my tutors told me that Iolcus was blessed, it seemed to me they were only stating the obvious.

But that day it began to change for me. We had been walking in the hills, stepping carefully over the little rivulets that abounded. The paths were familiar; I made Anticleia take me there often, and as we walked she made me recite the stories of the nymphs and tree sprites of the various streams and groves, which always seemed to matter more to her than they did to me. At one point there were apple trees; Anticleia held me up to one and I picked two apples, one for each of us. We drank cool water from a nearby spring.

Then, just as she told me it was time for us to return home, a beautiful green and brown butterfly flew past us. Anticleia took the opportunity to remind me what I knew perfectly well, that the word for butterfly was identical to the word for the human mind: *psyche*. The insect was so beautiful; it flew so lightly. I wanted it; I chased it.

"Acastus! Come back here!"

It was my first act of defiance. I looked back at her, paused for a moment to weigh the consequences, then kept chasing the butterfly. Anticleia followed me, but in her heavy robes she had trouble keeping up. Before long, I had lost her. The butterfly flitted to the top of a low hill, then down the other side, and I followed gleefully, not really caring if I caught it but enjoying the chase. This was farther from home than I had ever been, and at least for the moment I was on my own.

"Acastus!" Her voice was comfortably distant. I kept running.

The butterfly landed on the side of a tree, flapped its wings twice slowly and was still. I walked gingerly up to it and lifted it carefully from the bark, and it sat calmly in the palm of my hand. Its forewings were iridescent green; the rear ones were tawny brown. Its eyes were black and huge and, it seemed, quite oblivious to me. I watched it, fascinated. Despite its name it did not seem to have anything obvious in common with my mind. In my hand it seemed to weigh nothing.

For an instant I felt a boyish impulse to crush it. But that passed. I turned my hand and studied the insect. Its antennae vibrated; the scales of its wings shimmered. It remained quite still.

"Acastus!"

She was coming closer. The sound of her voice made me start, and the butterfly, alarmed, flapped its wings and flew straight up, beyond my reach. I watched as it vanished into the treetops.

Treetops: I had been so intent on pursuing it that, without my realizing it, I had entered a little grove. The trees were dense; there were enough of them—alders, sacred to the goddess—to blot out most of the sky. The ground was covered with dead leaves. There were also a great many tiny bones littering the forest floor; some predator hunted there, or brought its prey there to eat. Somewhere nearby foxes were barking, two or three of them, and I knew that they must be the hunters.

This was farther from home than I had ever been, it was a landscape not quite like any I had known, and I was alone. But I was not afraid.

Between the foxes' barks there was another sound. Someone or something was calling out. Or more precisely crying out. I could not quite tell where it was coming from, but I had to see. I looked around. The ground sloped upward; the trees thinned a bit; there was more open space. There was still the crying. At the top of the hill I could see a little shrine of the goddess.

Then partway behind a tree I saw it. Something was lying on the ground, wriggling or kicking. It was a child, a baby, a newborn in fact; there was no mistaking the sound of its cries. What on earth could it be doing there? I looked around for its parents, but there was no one in sight. The little thing wailed and rolled on the ground; even from a distance I could see that it was covered in dirt and leaves. I had to see it, touch it, help it, there was no one else.

The infant was naked. A boy. Its eyes were large and dark and it had the olive complexion so common in Greece. Where its right arm should have been there was a withered stump, not much more than a thick cord, dangling uselessly. The child seemed to notice me for a moment, then directed its gaze into the sky and continued crying.

30 yards away a fox came out from behind a tree and stared at me. It barked shrilly, yapped at me, then turned tail and disappeared again.

The baby cried. I got down on one knee to examine him. He seemed so small and helpless lying there. I touched the side of his face with a fingertip, but he seemed not to feel it, he continued his bawling.

I looked around again. There was no one else in sight. I touched the child again, pressed the flat of my hand to his face. And this time he responded. His eyes looked in my direction; I could see that he was trying to focus them. Carefully, not certain I could manage him, I slid a hand under him and lifted him up. He squirmed in my arms and kept on crying; then, after a moment, he seemed to calm down a bit. I brushed some of the dirt off of him.

From behind me I heard Anticleia's voice. "Acastus! Don't! Don't touch it!" She came lumbering up the slope toward me, holding onto the trees for support.

I looked down at the infant in my arms. It seemed strong and healthy enough, except for its bad arm.

"Put it down!" Panting heavily, she reached me.

Something in her manner made me hold the child more tightly. "He needs someone to take care of him till his mother comes back."

She stood still. I could tell that she was reminding herself she was my nurse, that she had to be patient with me. "Its mother will not come back. Please, Acastus, do as I say and put it back on the ground."

"Why?"

"That child is not our concern."

"No, I mean why won't his mother come back?"

She was still out of breath. "Look at where you are. Can't you see?"

I had no idea what she meant. There were the trees, there was that little shrine above us. From somewhere in the woods came a growl, I presumed from the fox.

"That baby is misshapen, Acastus." She scowled and pointed a finger at the stump of his arm. "You mustn't handle it. That kind of ill fortune can be catching."

Like most of the women of mother's household, Anticleia was a devout believer in magic and luck; I had long since learned, in any unfamiliar situation, to expect superstition from her. "He was born this way. I'm already formed."

"Acastus, I am telling you to put that infant down." Her tone was stern, almost threatening; I had not heard her talk that way often, and it made me suddenly unsure of myself.

"Will you tell me where we are, Anticleia?"

Finally she had begun to breathe steadily. She extended a hand and pointed up to the hilltop; heavy black cloth draped down from her arm. "That shrine is sacred to the goddess Hecate, the wanderer in the night, the Queen of Hell. She is the one who takes the souls of children to the underworld."

I had not expected it. "The—?"

"To hell. Yes."

"But—but this little boy isn't dead."

"He will be soon enough, when the foxes have their way with him."

It was an awful thought. "No!"

"Look around yourself, Acastus."

I looked. There were the trees, the shrine, the little bones littering the ground... And then I understood. "No!" I held the little baby even tighter, and he began to cry again, and I felt tears coming to my own eyes. "No!"

"What would you do with this deformed thing, then?" She said *thing* as if it was the filthiest word she knew.

I looked at the baby in my arms and tried to think of a way to comfort him. "Maybe if I take him home and feed him and keep him warm, he'll grow up to love me."

"It would hate you for making it live in such a wretched state."

7

"No."

"The city would hate you for saddling it with another beggar." Suddenly, unexpectedly, she lunged forward and caught hold of my ear. "Drop the child. Drop it!"

She twisted my ear, and I shrieked with pain and, without wanting to, let go of the infant. It fell heavily to the ground and screamed out in fright and pain.

"There are too many misshapen creatures in Iolcus already. More are born every year. This is all that can be done with them." She caught me by the collar of my tunic and pulled me away from the baby. "Come home now. Leave it to the foxes, Acastus."

Of course she was stronger than I was. I struggled against her, but there wasn't really any point, and I knew it. She led me by the collar back down through the woods, back to places that were more than familiar. Behind us I heard the foxes barking happily.

Once, I had been in the stables when one of the mares foaled. The colt only had rear legs, no front ones, and its eye sockets were empty. The groom ushered me quickly out, and I never knew what had happened to the colt. But this… This was the first time I had encountered human deformity. And human cruelty. It was the day I began to realize things were not right in Iolcus.

That night my sleep was disturbed by a dream. I was in a narrow valley. It was filled with the bones of children, deep with them, they covered me up to my shoulders. I was sinking, being drawn under. But I woke before I could vanish beneath them. I still remember that dream so vividly. It had the sharpness and the clarity that only dreams have, never reality.

* * *

Not long after that, my mother died giving birth to my youngest sister, who was named Creusa after her. I don't have many memories of mother. She wore black all the time, like most of the women of our household. She had a parrot, an ill tempered grey thing she had bought from an African merchant. I remember it biting me once, and drawing blood. She taught it to speak the ancient Pelasgian language, which only the priestesses of Hecate ever spoke. After she died the parrot refused to eat or let anyone take care of it; it died not long after mother.

As for my father Pelias, he would never have much to do with me. The earliest thing I remember about him is that he stood me up once before the guests at a drunken dinner and told them I would never make a fit king. "My lady wife insisted he be dedicated to the Muses instead of the gods proper to manly things." He pushed a fistful of flowers down the front of my tunic. It was so humiliating.

He had had too much wine, but then he nearly always had more wine than he should. There always seemed to be cuts and bruises on him, from his drunken stumbling about the palace. He only managed to stay sober and clear minded when there was official business to be conducted, and not always then. Such prosperity as the city enjoyed, it enjoyed despite its king.

Pelias was troubled by nightmares, frequent ones. He would awaken, screaming, and his screams would echo though the halls of the palace. When the priests and priestesses who served the various gods would ask him what he dreamed and offer to interpret, he would tell them sullenly that he could not remember. I don't think anyone ever believed that.

But a great many nights, as I sat in my candle lit room reading or writing, or trying to learn the art of carving, his cries would reach me, and I would smile and think that sometimes, at least, the gods were just.

Then there were my sisters. They were totally spoiled. Pelias ignored them, too, claiming they reminded him too much of mother. And so the household witches raised them, and they grew into selfish, domineering terrors. Creusa was still an infant, but a completely disagreeable one, always crying, always demanding attention. Callimache and Cleito, the two older ones, fancied themselves adepts of the goddess and dressed in black like their teachers. Father used to call them his three Fates. I learned early to avoid them as much as I could.

Anticleia was a good nurse, I suppose, but I never had much trouble slipping away from her when I wanted to. Perhaps she let me; I don't know. But those moments of freedom were the times I really felt alive.

Just below the palace were the barracks and the broad field where our soldiers drilled. We didn't have a large army; I was lucky to grow up during a time of relative peace in Greece. Only the

Spartans made much trouble, and they were off in the Peloponnese, far enough away to seem no threat.

Still, our soldiers drilled every day. They stripped naked and jousted, wrestled, fenced. There were times when I sat and watched them; their bodies were so beautiful.

A great many of them were lovers, which is common enough among soldiers. Sometimes I listened outside the barracks to the sounds of their lovemaking. And sometimes I imagined them asking me to join them: my first erotic fantasies. When I was 12, some of them invited me to join in. That was the way I learned about sex.

But not love. The undercurrent of aggression that ran through their games and even their sex play repulsed me. Most of the boys in the Greek royal houses wanted to be warriors. Leading an army, after all, was the surest road to kingship. Pelias seldom let me forget that. But it was not for me. Despite my father's constant prodding, I resisted his every effort to make me a soldier.

Instead, I would steal my way down to the harbor, which was always the most fascinating part of the city. Iolcus had a small navy, which was kept anchored at the farther part of the bay. I avoided that. There were too many more interesting things to see. Trading ships, fishing vessels from all over the Aegean, royal embassies from other cities and even other lands... And I must admit that the seamen themselves attracted me, too. Their bodies were almost as beautiful as the soldiers'.

One thing that drew me was the lighthouse, which seemed to me the most magnificent thing in the world. The gleaming bronze goddess stood tall and solemn, her gaze fixed on the distant sea. Everything about her, her pose, the serenity in her features, her place on the edge of the sea, spoke to me of timelessness. I remember sitting on the breakwater for hours at a time, watching her watch the Aegean, trying to understand her promise of a world elsewhere. That she was the goddess of love only made it more tantalizing.

The lighthouse was tended by a retired sea captain named Epiphanes. He was no more than middle aged but for some reason he had given up seafaring. Rumor had it that, in their youth, he and Pelias had been lovers, but I didn't believe it; *love* and *Pelias* were not connected words in my mind.

But for whatever reason Epiphanes seemed to like me. He used to let me help him as he lovingly polished the bronze, and even now and then to climb up through the hollow inside of the statue, up to the lantern with him at sundown and light the fire.

But it wasn't only sex and the lighthouse that drew me to the harbor. The sailors who lived and worked there were my friends. They looked after me, gave me little presents, were concerned when I seemed unwell or unhappy.

They told me stories of their voyages, strange dangerous places, fantastic creatures, dragons, griffins, sphinxes. I never quite believed them; the stories sounded too much like Anticleia's water nymphs and wood pixies. As I grew older they tempered the fantasy in their tales. But a few of them always insisted to me that if you travel far enough you will find amazing things.

One man in particular, Brygus, the captain of a fishing boat, seemed to take a special interest in me. He lived on the island of Chios in the Aegean, did his fishing, then came to Iolcus to sell what he'd caught. The sea was fertile; I saw a lot of him. I remember asking him once why he didn't simply move to Iolcus. He seemed not to want to talk about it, but I pressed him.

He scowled at me. "You're too young to realize what kind of place this city is."

"What do you mean?" I was completely lost.

"This city isn't healthy."

That was completely unexpected; it stirred memories of the shrine of Hecate and the foxes.

"I have a wife and two sons back home. I won't bring them here. Iolcan women die giving birth. Iolcan children—" He left he thought unfinished, but I understood what he meant.

"Athamas tried to kill his children." I whispered, looking for connections. None seemed logical.

"There's more blood than that in this city's past. Do you know that your father killed his brother to take the throne?"

I had never heard it. It chilled me. But it did not much clash with my perceptions of my family. "I didn't know."

"Yes. His brother Aeson was the king then. He had a son named Jason, a beautiful, sweet natured, red-haired boy everyone loved."

"Don't they love me?"

"Of course. But you are Pelias' son. He murdered Aeson and his wife. There's a story that Jason's nurse spirited him away before he could be killed too. But people believe that because they want to. Pelias could hardly have let the boy escape." Brygus smiled a gentle smile at me. "Not even if he was drunk."

"So I'm not really the prince?"

"You are now." He put a hand on my shoulder. "And you'll make a better king than your father."

"I don't want to be a king. I want to be a fisherman like you."

Brygus laughed and hugged me. "Be whatever you want to be, Acastus."

The conversation left me more than mildly disturbed. I had that dream again, the valley and the children's bones. But Brygus, uniquely among the people I knew, had been honest with me.

Another reason I went to the harbor was that I loved to swim. Stripped naked, I would dive into the deep blue water and swim for hours at a time. I never seemed to tire of it. By the time I entered adolescence I was one of the best swimmers in the country. Sometimes I swam and played with the dolphins in the harbor, and swimming with them made me an even fitter athlete.

* * *

I did not confine my explorations to the harbor. There was also the main square of Iolcus, smack in the center of the city, and it always seemed enormous to me. The temples of the gods lined it. And one corner was taken up with the marketplace, where there was wonderful food to be had. The merchants seemed to enjoy looking after me almost as much as the sailors did. People called me "little prince," which annoyed me, but I knew they meant it affectionately.

At one end of the square there was a sculpture of King Athamas. He stood, larger than life size, over his cowering children, knife raised, about to strike. It was an old statue, carved in soft red stone that had begun to crumble, and the workmanship was crude; but even so it was possible to see the terror in their faces, the cuts already inflicted on their little bodies. The sculptor had had at least that much art.

In the daylight, when the marketplace was full of people, the sculpture was effectively hidden, lost in the crowd. But at night

Iolcans, except for the ones who frequented the taverns along the waterfront, tended to stay in their homes. And so at night, when the square was empty or nearly so, the statue of Athamas dominated it. It was the king and his children, not the temples around them, that drew the eye. When the moon lit the figures they looked like rough hewn ghosts. I often wondered why any city would erect such a monument to its own awful past, but there it was.

By day, at least, the marketplace was a place for learning. We had visitors from Phoenicia, Egypt, Crete. Men from Africa with wonderful black skins told me stories about fantastic animals. One of them brought a baby elephant for sale, once. I wanted it. But Pelias refused. A representative of the king of Thebes bought it. I heard that it died as they were taking it there.

Once a merchant from a distant place called the Land of Ch'in stopped to trade. He had rich yellow skin and dark eyes shaped like almonds, and I found him quite beautiful. He wore an astonishing red robe that shimmered like woven light, and on it was embroidered a dragon. I asked him if such creatures really existed. "They certainly do, little prince," he told me, "at least in the Land of Ch'in."

The rest of the square was lined with the temples. Apollo, the Muses, Ares, Aphrodite, Poseidon of course, the Fates—there were more than a dozen of them. They weren't large, but they were built of fine stone, and they'd been built by the best architects. No one much ever went inside them, really, except on the days of festivals. Iolcus was much too worldly a city.

But I did.

It was in the temple of Apollo that I first felt the spark of the divine. It was the smallest temple in the city; the god of learning and light was hardly appreciated in a city as commercial as Iolcus. Most of the time when I was there, I was the only one in the temple; not even the god's priests seemed to spend much time there. The temple had a library. I went to read and learn things beyond the state myths my tutors drilled me in day after day.

And I went to see the god: At the head of the sanctuary stood the statue of Apollo. It was just over life size, mounted on a white marble base; the statue itself was carved from black marble richly veined with purple and green. The god stood naked but for a cloak, one knee bent casually, one hand extended, as if he was offering something to me, or perhaps beckoning to me. And the lines of his body were so perfectly sensual. Even when I was quite a small boy, I would stand in a dark corner of the sanctuary and stare at it, as I stared at the bodies of the soldiers, wanting it to be real, to be alive, and to hold me.

I was fourteen when I finally had the nerve to walk up and touch it. The stone was warm. I caressed the muscles of Apollo's leg, felt the rippling contours, ran my hand up his thigh. How I wanted him to be doing that to me.

I wanted to touch all of him but I wasn't tall enough. Behind the statue was a chest of some dark wood, elaborately carved. I pulled it around and climbed onto it and put my hand flat on the god's stomach.

Then suddenly there was a voice. "You're Prince Acastus, aren't you?"

I turned in alarm. Predictably, the priest had come in; I recognized him from the festivals. He was a man in his thirties with a beautiful black beard; he was dressed for the street, not the temple. I felt as if I'd been caught committing a sin. But I faced him. "Yes."

"It's a beautiful statue, isn't it? I often run my hands over it myself. The idea that cold hard stone can be made so lovely and sensual—it always seems like sorcery to me."

I was still perched absurdly on my box. The situation seemed unreal. His casual intimacy was the last thing I expected.

"Feel the muscles in his arms." The priest smiled and took a step toward me. "Just here. There are times I could swear the skin gives under my fingers."

He lifted me and I felt the stone again. "Why is it warm?" I asked. "Stone should be cold."

"I don't know. I wish I understood. I imagine there's a mystery in it." He smiled at me. "You don't know how I wish I had the art to make something as beautiful as this."

I ran a hand over its chest. Let my finger rest on its nipple. "Who was the sculptor?"

"My father. Here. This muscle in the thigh. It's so—so—" He took my hand in his and moved it down the god's leg. And it excited me. Gently he put me back down on the wooden box.

I looked into his eyes. "What is your name?"

"My father was Phraxis."

14

"The one who made the lighthouse?"

"He sculpted the statues of the Muses too. You've been to their sanctuary?"

I nodded.

"I think he was quite brilliant. I wish I could be half the sculptor he was."

"I thought you were the priest."

He laughed. "It's hardly a full time job. Not in Iolcus. The gods of trade get worshipped here. No, my position is more of a civic honor than an occupation. If that. My name's Cleanthus."

For a moment we looked into one another's eyes. There was desire, at least on my part. We were in the temple of Apollo. Then he remembered himself. "Not many people come here. It's good to have a member of the royal house remember the gods."

"I'm not much of a prince. Not to hear my father tell it."

Again he laughed. "That's what fathers do. Phraxis never stopped belittling my own carvings."

"You really are a sculptor, then?"

He nodded. "I have a little workshop off the square. I do a brisk business in funerary steles for dead wives."

By then it never surprised me to hear people say things like that. "The Iolcan curse."

"Everything human is cursed. And blessed." He hesitated for a moment. "You are a beautiful boy, Acastus."

It caught me off guard. No one had ever told me so before. Cleanthus was a handsome man, and I told him so.

He took my hand again, pressed it hard against Apollo's thigh. "Cold statue, warm god, one and the same. I've always thought the city should have a temple to Ganymede."

It took me a moment to realize what he was telling me. And, quite at the same instant, we put our arms around each other. His were strong—a sculptor's arms. I felt so good, warm and safe. He held me there in front of the god for what seemed eternity.

We never actually became lovers, Cleanthus and I. I was too young, I was not ready for love, not real love; if I had been just a bit more mature…

* * *

15

Our relationship developed into one of master and pupil, leavened with a deep friendship. I told him I had often wanted to try my hand at carving; I had even made some halting efforts; but there was no one at the palace who could teach me. And so Cleanthus took me to his workshop and began to train me in the sculptor's art. Taught me how to hold the bronze tools properly, how to find the grain of the wood or the stone, how to feel the life in it and begin to bring it to the surface. He gave me tools, his old ones, worn down but with use still left in them.

I practiced first on hardwood; then when I was ready he gave me bits of marble. I worked late every night in my room, by the candlelight. Pelias would hardly approve of such an unmanly pursuit, after all.

Now and then, when his nightmares made him cry out, the sound would startle me, the knife or chisel would slip, and I would ruin whatever piece I was working on. At times the sound was quite furious, as if he was throwing things around his room. But in time I learned to keep working, keep my mind focused and my hand steady, despite the sounds of fear and anger in the night.

My first completed piece was a group, carved in olive wood: the Three Fates. Cleanthus studied it, pointed out the faults, praised the good things. I had tried to give them my sisters' faces, but they were not recognizable. He took my hand in his and guided the knife, showed me how to refine the lines. He taught me with love; I worked with love. And he praised me every time my work showed improvement.

Pelias, perhaps in an effort to allay his nightmares, decided to build a new temple, dedicated to the Furies. Cleanthus received the commission for the sanctuary statue, and he let me work on it with him. He modeled Alecto and Tisiphone; I sculpted Megaera, and I gave her my mother's features, as I remembered them. I even gave her a familiar owl, but I made it look as much like a parrot as possible. It was the first work of mine to be seen in public. Cleanthus told me I was the best apprentice he had ever had.

And so I began, by steps, to live the life I wanted. I swam, solitary exercise; I sculpted, as alone as any artist. The things that gave me satisfaction had less and less to do with my family and the city, more and more to do with myself.

* * *

My younger sister Creusa had a defective mind. From the time she was old enough to walk she ran riot through the palace halls, screaming obscene things, smearing walls with urine and excrement. When anyone tried to calm her she would bite them savagely, then laughingly lick up the spilled blood. Her nurses, trying to dress her, would be spit upon, or worse. Once she took a brooch and drove the pin through a woman's hand. In the end Pelias had to have her confined in a distant wing of the palace, under guard.

Pelias married again, hoping for more children, or at least for more sons, or to be accurate, more *manly* sons. I don't think he meant it to hurt me, but it did.

His wife was a local widow, still young, quite wealthy, and there was a great deal of gossip about her fortune and what the king might do with it. She became pregnant pretty quickly. But when she delivered it was twin daughters, joined horribly at the head. they were exposed at the shrine of Hecate. The woman herself went mad, raving through the palace and at times even the city itself, begging everyone she met to help her find her lost daughters. Pelias had no choice but to confine her, too, in the same wing where Creusa was imprisoned.

From time to time we would have word from the countryside of animals born deformed. It seemed to happen more and more often. An entire herd of sheep proved sterile. And at the same time the population of Iolcus began to decline. It was the awful number of stillbirths and deformed children left in the hills by their parents, and women dead in labor. And with the people, the city's economic prosperity was beginning to go. I used to spend long days in the palace library, and in the libraries of the various temples, reading the old chronicles, trying to understand if it was merely the force of history that was killing Iolcus, changing tides and fortunes, or if it was something darker.

When I was fifteen a block of marble shifted in Cleanthus' workshop, falling on him and crushing his legs. I was not there when it happened but one of his assistants came to get me. When we reached him he was dead. Rather than live crippled he had drunk poison. There was awful pain in his face; I wanted to know if it was from the accident or what he had drunk. And the artist in me studied his expression; some day I might be able to use it.

He received a civic funeral; priests are public officials, after all. Everyone attended, even Pelias. I carved the stele for his tomb, a low relief of Zeus and Ganymede, in rose red granite from Egypt. People praised it, wondered who the sculptor had been, but no one knew and I kept silent, not yet bold enough to declare publicly my defiance of Pelias' military ambitions for me. It was good, the best thing I had done, but it was a long way from the master work he deserved. But it was done with love, and I suppose that showed.

One afternoon in autumn a boy ran into the town square crying excitedly that there were centaurs in the hills nearby. The town emptied; everyone wanted to see the miraculous creatures. But of course there were none. Angry, disappointed townspeople talked about stoning the child who had started it all, but cooler heads prevailed.

* * *

In the winter of my sixteenth year the threat of war came to Iolcus. The Spartans, who had 'til then been content to ravage the Peloponnese, began to extend their ambitions. Their forces moved north and east and soon all of Greece was threatened. Famously, their army was composed of pairs of lovers, which is what accounted for its fierce efficiency—no man wants to be defeated in front of his lover—and it moved with mechanical determination across the face of Greece. Making war in winter was unheard of, but the cold weather did not seem to faze the Spartans. Snow filled the vacant eyes of the war dead.

By then my path in life was set, and it was neither a military life nor a political one. I had achieved some fame as a swimmer, even winning the laurels in the funeral games for the King of Euboea, who had been crushed under a chariot. I had begun acknowledging my sculpture publicly, and it had attracted a certain measure of attention. I was especially skilled at rendering women; and I had managed to capture some of the naturalness of the work of Phraxis, which caught people's eyes. No less a personage than the king of Argos had commissioned an Aphrodite from me, making specific mention of how sensuous my women were. With his payment he sent a letter saying the figure was so real he had to restrain himself from wanting to make love to it. It was foolish exaggeration, of course, the sort of thing politicians say to their clients. But I was flattered. And the problems of government, particularly of the government of a city as troubled as Iolcus, interested me less and less. When Pelias conferred with his advisors in the palace library, I never attended.

Late one night I was working by torchlight in my studio, an unused storeroom at the rear of the palace. I had acquired a piece of porphyry, the purple marble from Asia Minor; it was new to me, and I was testing its properties. It hardly seemed soft enough, yielding enough under my chisel; I thought it would be a better material for architecture than for sculpture.

A cry cut through the air. Pelias was having his troubled dreams again. But his cry was louder and more anguished than I had heard before. I waited to see if there would be more, but the night remained silent and I went back to my stone.

Then there were footsteps, soft ones. When I looked up Pelias was standing in my doorway, his hair disarrayed, his robe open, feet bare. He went and stood beside one of the torches, glaring at me all the time. The torchlight made the lines of his face seem even more stark than usual.

For a moment we stared at each other. Then he spoke. "You're no son." There was a skin of wine in his hand. He was drunk, as always.

I rolled my chisel casually between my fingertips. I was long past the time when Pelias could intimidate me. "I beg your pardon?"

"I said you're no son."

I laughed at him. "You haven't exactly been much of a father. And I'm the only son you have."

"Swimming." He snorted. "Women swim. Nymphs and fish swim. Men take up arms."

"If it helps you to think of me as a woman, be my guest." I went on studying the stone.

"You were bred to be a king." He staggered and grabbed at the shaft of a torch for support. But it wasn't anchored, only resting against a box, and he tottered and nearly fell.

I couldn't help smiling. "A king like you?"

"A king."

I put my tools aside and sat down on the stone block. "I don't want to be a king. It doesn't look to me as if the family business has brought us anything but suffering. The women all dead or mad, you drunk all the time... How many sons did my mother bear you before me, deformed things you had to leave for the foxes?"

"I'm not drunk."

"Call it what you will, it comes to the same thing. And I've had enough of it. There's a lively market for art in Argos. I could make a good living there."

He gaped at me.

"Don't worry, I'll change my name if you like. No one will know that a prince of the house of Athamas has deserted his city."

"The city." He seemed to have trouble focusing. "The city is cursed. Every year there are fewer children born healthy."

"Pelias, I know it."

"Iolcus needs you."

Again I laughed. "For what? Do you think I can stop the Spartans with my chisel? Do you think your army would even follow me, if it comes to that?"

"No. You're too much a woman."

"Do you think the gods I sculpt can make babies come whole and women stop hemorrhaging? If the Spartans level the city, at least we'll all be out of our misery. What do you say, let's leave the gates open for them."

"The people love you. Heaven knows why, but the people love you."

I stared at him and shrugged.

He looked away from me. "All right, then. I need you."

"A moment ago I was no son."

"No, you're not. But bad blood runs in our family. Athamas tried to slaughter his children. I killed my own brother for the throne. Your betrayal is nothing next to that. And as you said yourself, you're the only son I have."

Again I shrugged. "There is no betrayal here. I'm being true to myself. It's as uncomplicated as that."

Abruptly he sat down on the floor. His eyes seemed to go empty; he stared fixedly at a place on the floor in front of him and began to tremble. The wineskin fell beside him.

"Pelias?"

He seemed not to hear me. He began waving at the air, as if he saw something threatening him. Then it passed.

"Pelias!" I had never seen him in such a state. He remained lost. I crossed the room and shook him by his shoulders. "Pelias, what do you see?"

"Hm?" Almost at once he was himself. He looked around for his fallen wineskin, picked it up and drank.

But I took it out of his hands. "You've had enough wine."

"No!" He made a grab for it, but I was too quick for him. "Give me my wineskin, Acastus."

I walked back to the marble and sat again. "What do you see? These nightmares of yours, what are they about?"

"They are not mere nightmares."

That was unexpected. "What on earth do you mean?"

"There is a ghost."

"A ghost." I didn't try to hide my disbelief. "And is it a large ghost or a small one?"

But he ignored my sarcasm. "It is the ghost of Phrixus."

"The son of King Athamas? The boy who disappeared with the golden ram?"

He nodded. "His ghost comes to me when I'm asleep and begs me to help him find rest."

"Help him? How? Help him with what?"

"I don't know. When I tell him I don't understand what he wants, he turns violent, beats me, claws at me, bites me. Look at these bruises." He held out his arms, which were covered with welts and cuts. He reached up and touched a large bruise on the side of his forehead. "He's the one who has cursed the city."

I found it pathetic. "If you'd walk around sober, those bruises wouldn't happen."

"There is a ghost. The city can't be healthy when the royal house is haunted."

"Of course."

He fell silent. I wanted him to be gone, so I could work. There was marble dust on the back of my tunic, where I had sat. I brushed it off and turned my attention back to the stone. With luck Pelias would simply leave.

But he wasn't done with me. "For a prince of the royal blood to practice a trade or a craft is not seemly."

"No, I suppose it isn't." I took up my mallet and chisel. "Leave me alone, will you?"

"I murdered my brother Aeson and took the throne. He comes to me in dreams, too, seeking revenge. The knife went through his eye

21

and into his brain. His blood polluted me." He looked me up and down. "It occurs to me that you might be his revenge."

"One of the priests can purify you easily enough." I casually struck a chip off the stone.

"No. I've tried that."

I turned and looked at him. "Then?"

"Aeson had a son."

"Jason. I've always assumed you did away with him as well. Dynastic murder isn't worth much if it isn't thorough."

"Yes, there was a boy, a little son, named Jason. He is the true heir to the throne of Iolcus."

"He can have it."

"I don't know where he is."

"How surprising."

"I would make him king and bypass you, if I could. He has to have bigger balls."

I laughed at him. "There's no use trying to hurt me, old man. My hide grew too thick for that years ago. So your dead brother haunts your dreams."

"Yes."

I had to say it. "Good."

"Acastus, I did it for you."

I gaped at him. "Be serious."

"I mean it."

"Did I ask you to? When I was a child, did I climb on your knee and beg you for the crown? You've never done a thing for anyone but yourself. And maybe your wine seller."

"You should be married by now. Or at least betrothed."

"There isn't a chance of that." I placed my chisel at the top of the stone and struck it as hard as I could. Part of it shattered. But most of it remained intact.

"Acastus, there's a ghost. Help me rid myself of it. You're the only one I have."

"And I'm no son. Go find yourself a priest, Pelias. Leave me to my marble."

Finally he seemed to run out of the energy to fight with me. "I thought—" He climbed slowly to his feet. "I only thought—"

"Don't." I glared at him.

22

"Oh." He shuffled heavily to the door. Stood and stared at me for a moment. Then, leaving the wineskin, he turned and left.

I should have gone back to work. There were commissions to be filled. But I had lost my taste for it. I took a long drink of his wine, extinguished the torches, all but one, and went back to my own bedroom.

Sleep came slowly. Something made me keep a light burning. Late in the night Pelias began to cry out again, and it woke me. The air was filled with violent sounds. I wished it would stop.

* * *

Winter dragged on. There were heavy snows, violent storms. Trade all over the Aegean slowed, and Iolcus felt it, though there was still a bit of traffic. Hungry people came to the palace, begging for food. Pelias turned them away.

During an uncharacteristic warm spell I saw my friend Brygus' boat moored in the harbor. He had come to Iolcus less and less often over the years; markets elsewhere had become more lucrative. But there was a particular tavern he had always been fond of, and that was where I went, looking for him.

He was drinking wine at a table off in a dark corner, and he was alone. I smiled and said hello.

"Acastus." He took my hand. "I was in Argos. I saw the statue you carved. It's quite beautiful."

"Thanks. It's good to see you." I sat down at his table.

"There were rumors you'd left Iolcus."

"I've thought about it often enough."

"Then—?"

I shrugged. "I imagine it's inertia. Or some benighted sense of home and family, some vague feeling that if I stay here I'll find what I've always needed and never had." I laughed. "But someday I'll go."

He drank. "My wife died last year."

"Oh. I'm sorry."

"I thought I had what *I* needed."

It took me a moment to realize his point. I did not want to think about it. "The Spartans are on the move. The cities between them and us are putting up good fights, or they'd have been here by now. For once, Iolcus is lucky."

"For once." He had had a good bit of wine; it was showing. "Any other city would think itself lucky to have a prince like you."

"Don't be naive, Brygus. It's the warriors people adore. I'm a son of the Muses."

He stared at me. "Do you actually believe in the gods?"

It was a question no one ever asked. It startled me. "As much as anyone else does, I suppose."

"That isn't an answer."

"No, it isn't. Give me a drink of your wine."

He asked the innkeeper for another cup and we saluted each other's health. But he was not to be shaken from his question. "I asked if you believe in the gods."

"Not with my mind, no." I drank.

He raised an eyebrow.

"But we're not all mind, are we, Brygus? When I'm sculpting, that's when the gods are at work. Every night when I begin work—"

"You work at night?"

"Yes."

"I thought artists preferred the light."

I shrugged. "When I start to work each night, the first thing I do is spend some time studying what I've already done. And it always surprises me. There, in the stone, I'll find the most wonderful line— the curve of a lip, the graceful drape of a cloak—and I'll have no recollection of carving it. And they're the lines that give my work life. Where do they come from?"

"From the Muses?" His tone was wry, but I think he knew I was being serious.

"I haven't been able to think of a better explanation."

"And Iolcus. Do you think the gods have cursed the city?"

I took a long swallow. The wine was much too sweet. "How can anyone know? At times, I think there must be a simpler explanation. Poison in the earth or the water. Disease brought on the wind from foreign places. People are on edge; the city has been so tense for so long now, and the threat of the Spartans is making it worse. I'm frightened of this city and yet I can't bring myself to leave. Why is that, Brygus?"

He watched me from a corner of his eye without answering. We fell into silence. We drank. At one point I reached across the table and touched his hand, but he pulled away from me.

I was beginning to feel the wine. "Pelias never stops tearing me down. I should be a soldier. I should want to be king. But when I sculpt I feel the hand of god. It isn't possible to give that up."

"Do both."

"No."

"Oh." The wine had made him sad.

"Pelias says the ghost of Phrixus is haunting him, haunting the royal house, haunting the city."

He drank. "Who knows? Maybe it's true."

"It can't be."

"Of course not."

"He's making excuses for himself."

"Of course he is. The gods touch you but not him."

I stared at him. Absurd as it was, and drunk as he was, what he said unsettled me. We talked for a while more, but I was careful to change the subject and keep it neutral. It was only small talk, the sea, the weather, the markets, gossip about his old crewmen.

Finally, I had had enough wine to let my guard down completely. "Brygus, I pray to Aphrodite for a lover. She never sends one."

"You can't be as inexperienced as all that."

"Not sex, not copulation—love. I go with the soldiers now and then, when I need to. I've had affairs with a few of the other young artists in the city. But not love. Never love."

"I had love, Acastus." He took one long, final drink. "And the gods took it away. Who can say why they do what they do?"

Later that day he returned to his boat and put out to sea. I never saw him again. A rumor went around that his boat had gone down in a storm, but no one really knew.

* * *

The night after that, very late, the moon was dark. Clouds built and it began to rain heavily, a cold winter rain; I could hear the downpour through the stone palace walls. There were cries in the air, as always: Pelias. I could not sleep. I went to see.

His room was much larger than mine, almost cavernous, the king's bedchamber. But huge as it was there was only one candle

25

burning, off in a far corner. Pelias slept, wrapped in a blanket, tossing fitfully, letting out little moans.

There was a sudden sound, like a shriek. I thought it must be Pelias, but it seemed to come from somewhere else in the room—or from everywhere. The candle trembled in its holder and the flame danced. Pelias moaned.

Then above the candle I saw something like a purple glow, formless, transparent, hovering. It drifted across the room to the king and seemed to settle on him. And he screamed. "Stop! Please!"

Something made me run to him. I caught him by an arm and shook. "Pelias, wake up, wake up. You're dreaming again."

From nowhere there came a gust of wind; the candle went out. A cloak, hanging on the wall, billowed as if there was something alive inside it. A map blew off a table. The purple mist vanished with the candlelight. The only light was faint, from the hallway outside.

The king opened his eyes and stared at me. "Acastus." There was a fresh bruise on the side of his face, bleeding slightly.

I was lost for anything to say. My being there was so uncharacteristic. I avoided looking at the bruise, avoided thinking about what it might mean.

"Did you see him? Did you see Phrixus? He was here." He took hold of my arm like the frightened man he was.

"There was no one here but me and you. The candle light played tricks in the darkness, that's all."

"No. He was here."

"Pelias, go back to sleep." I pulled free of his grip.

I had to leave before the oddness of my presence there struck him and he said something about it. I could hardly explain it; it didn't really make any sense at all that I should have gone to his room. Without saying another word I turned and went. He would ask about it in the morning, but by then I would have some story. I couldn't sleep, I would tell him, I went for a walk, I heard a sound…

But back in my room sleep would not come. And the darkness bothered me. I went to the kitchen for a fire and lit a dozen candles around my bed. There could not have been A purple glow in the king's chamber, it had to have been a trick of the light. There could not be a ghost. That could not be possible.

* * *

After that one relatively warm spell, the winter turned savage again. There was heavy snow and the fiercest wind anyone could remember.

My sister Creusa escaped from the rooms of her confinement and made her way, somehow, down into the city, in the middle of a furious snowstorm. She threw herself onto a little boy and sank her teeth into his throat. His blood sprayed the snow on the ground. The townspeople, the few who were out in the storm, caught her, and she struggled furiously, laughing all the while. But they lashed her to a post and began sifting through the snow to find stones. A woman, presumably the boy's mother, rushed to him and tried to stanch the flow.

Just at that moment I entered the square, following a contingent of the palace guard, looking for her. When the guards realized what was about to happen they rushed to release her. But the people formed a wall and would not move. Everyone's clothing billowed wildly in the wind.

The captain of the guard ordered them to disperse.

"No." A fruit merchant, a man I knew, spoke for them. "The house of Athamas has brought nothing but evil to this city. Look at that poor boy on the ground there, look at the blood. It's time they begin to pay." He tossed a stone casually in his hand, seeming to relish its heft.

The soldiers drew their swords. The people closed ranks. Creusa screamed and struggled to free herself of the ropes that held her. The snow was falling more and more thickly; there was more wind. I had left the palace without a cloak, and I felt myself shivering; I hoped it didn't show.

I had to try and intervene. If the people killed her, even a king as dissolute as Pelias would send the whole army, not just a few guards, to exact a terrible revenge. I stepped out between the two groups.

"Please, all of you. Don't let this happen."

Everyone gaped at me. I saw knives in the hands of some of the people. The soldiers, from their expressions, seemed to think me a fool.

But I went on. "Iolcus has seen so much needless death."

"Then one more won't hurt." The merchant sneered.

27

"I don't understand this. You've always made me welcome among you."

"You don't assault children." "But—"

"Stand aside, Acastus. We don't want to hurt you."

It was hopeless. There seemed no way I could control what was about to happen.

A sudden, blinding squall of snow blew up. When it passed, a man had stepped out of the crowd and stood beside me, at the center of it all. He smiled. "Excuse me, Prince Acastus."

The effect was so strange; he seemed almost to have materialized out of the snowstorm. I didn't recognize him; I had the impression no one else did, either.

The man was seven, eight, maybe ten years older than me. He was not very tall but his body was perfectly formed, the body of a gymnast or a boxer. Despite the cold and the storm he wore only a short leather tunic, boots and a red cloak, which was open, showing off his form. His hair was pale red-blond, very un-Greek; even his eyelashes were the color of sunlit bronze. And his eyes were the iridescent green of malachite. I found him quite strikingly beautiful.

He held up a hand, and something in his manner made everyone be still. "This is no way for Iolcans to behave." Looking at the people he said, "The gods have seen fit to hamstring this girl's reason. Do you really want to add to her misery? If you shed her blood, will it help the city" Before any of them could say anything he turned to the guard. "And you, do you really want to shed the blood of your fellow Iolcans? Nothing good could come of that, and you know it."

He took a step toward the crowd. "Let me talk to the girl. Let me see if I can calm her."

Not certain what else to do, the people parted for him. He walked to Creusa and held up a hand to touch her cheek. She snapped at it. But he took her face forcibly between his hands and made her look at him. Her eyes were wild with rage.

"Listen to me, girl. You don't want to be like this. You don't want to hurt other children. You want to be good." He paused, then went on in a voice so soft it was almost a whisper. "Don't you?"

Improbably, she reacted to this. It seemed not to be his hands but his calm voice and manner that affected her. He kept on talking. And gradually her body relaxed. He stroked her cheek, and she let him.

When finally he untied her, she took his hand docilely. "There, now, let me return you where you belong." To the merchant he said, "Take the boy she attacked to a good physician. I'll pay the fee if need be."

The merchant seemed uncertain what to do. "May we ask who you are, sir?"

"Of course." He smiled. And he made a dramatic pause, like an actor working an audience. Then he told us, "I am Prince Jason."

There was a wild flurry of surprise. Then the wind blew even more fiercely and, despite their obvious curiosity, the people began to disperse. They went quickly; this news had to be spread.

Jason told the soldiers to return to the palace; Creusa would go with them quietly, now.

After a few moments he and I were alone in the square. He smiled at me, and his smile made him even more beautiful. "Will you show me to the palace, Acastus?"

I stammered; I felt like a fool.

"You don't have a cloak on, Acastus. Here."

He enfolded me in his own cloak. Our bodies touched, and he was so warm. I felt his arm go round my shoulder.

"Here," I said, "this way. The palace is over here."

We walked, very close together.

Our thighs pressed together.

I was seventeen years old, you understand, and I had never had a lover, not a proper one. But Jason...he was as beautiful as any man I'd ever seen. I wanted him to be the one.

Chapter Two
Jason and I

"It's such a beautiful city. You're lucky to have lived your life here."

We were on the roof of the palace, Jason and I. The night was cold, but despite it he only wore his leather tunic, his boots, and his red cloak; I was in heavier things. The full moon shone brightly through breaks in the clouds; there were occasional flurries of snow, and the air had the tang of frost. Our breath was smoke. The fire in the lighthouse torch danced.

"I've never felt especially lucky." It wasn't easy to keep the bitterness out of my voice. I found Jason beautiful, and I hoped I wasn't staring at him too pointedly.

He was at the edge of the roof, leaning slightly forward over the battlements. He looked from the city below us to me, then back again. I moved to his side. The moonlight outlined everything in silver. The flame in the lighthouse was the only thing not glistening white. There was not much wind but for some reason the surface of the water was turbulent.

"You've had a home, Acastus. That's more than I did."

"You have one now." There was no irony in what I said. The story of him calming Creusa had spread through the city, and the people had welcomed him as if he was a savior. Pelias, once he was certain that Jason hadn't come for a vendetta, had embraced him as a son, or at least a nephew. I had a vague sense that I should be jealous, but all I felt was a sense of relief. Jason could have the government of the city if he wanted it. I wanted to work at my art. And I wanted...I wanted...well, I wanted him.

He turned his back on the city and faced out across the roof to the hills. Like everything else they were moonlit; but the dark places among them were quite black. "I keep telling myself I should remember things. The city, the harbor. If nothing else, you'd think the lighthouse would stand in memory. It's so magnificent. But nearly everything's a blank."

"What do you remember?"

"Not much."

"Where did you grow up?"

He laughed softly. "Let's just say I was raised by the centaurs."

It was not the first time I had asked him. But he was always evasive about his life. Everyone had accepted him so easily, the people, Pelias, myself; no one had many questions for him, it seemed. And the few that were asked, he avoided. We needed him to be Prince Jason, it was that uncomplicated; everyone in the city needed that.

The story of Aeson's son escaping from Iolcus was widely known, and it would have been so easy for an impostor to capitalize on it…

But I had never had anyone to believe in. And he was so beautiful. "Centaurs, Jason?"

"Yes. Exactly like Hercules." He smiled.

Everyone knew that the famous warrior claimed to have been reared by the horse men. It was such a convenient way to cover up humble origins. "Have you ever actually met Hercules?"

"No." There was a sudden gust of wind, and it carried a cloud of snowflakes. They glittered like gems in the air.

"Neither have I. I doubt if Iolcus would be exciting enough for his taste."

"They say he's gone mad, you know. Killed his wife and his children and lost all reason."

I stood in front of Jason and looked pointedly into his eyes. "Should I believe in heroes?"

"No." He touched my cheek. "Of course not."

"Of course not." I mimicked him. "You're supposed to be the one who saves the city."

"It's worth saving. I've never seen a place so lovely."

A pair of birds flew over our heads; it was too dark to make out if they were the kind that carried omens. The wind kicked up, then died again. The fire in the lighthouse swirled.

"You'll have your chance to save it soon enough. They say the Spartans are on the move again."

"They can be dealt with."

I found his confidence so odd, so unlike anything I had ever known myself. Except when I was sculpting, or swimming. "How do you think you can deal with them?"

He shifted his weight, put a foot on the battlements. "No one knows if they're actually going to come here. They could easily turn north, toward Argos. I think they'll do that."

"Argos is a larger and stronger city than Iolcus. They'd have an easier time here."

"I know it, Acastus. But Iolcus is on the sea. We have ships. They can't cut us off and starve us. All their experience is for land warfare. Siege warfare."

It hadn't occurred to me. Not for the first time, I realized how little aptitude I had for military matters. "You haven't seen our navy, have you?"

"No."

"It isn't very large. And the ships are old."

"They float, don't they?"

"Just barely. I can't remember the last time they put out to sea."

"Oh." He seemed not to have expected it. With surprising animation he turned back to face the harbor again. "Where are they moored?"

"There, at the far end of the harbor." I pointed. "Out of everyone's way. Iolcus is a commercial power, not a military one."

"Then it's time we became one. Do you feel like taking a walk?"

"Where to?"

"There. I want to have a look at the fleet."

"Now?" I was in the mood for lovemaking, not naval architecture.

"Why not?" He smiled and touched my cheek again.

In only a moment we had made our way down through the palace and were walking down the hill to the city. Jason kept close to me. The clouds were thicker; the moon was a luminous patch behind them. Foxes barked in the hills. His cloak billowed in occasional bursts of wind.

"Your father goes to bed so early. Very unkinglike."

"He doesn't sleep well."

"Oh. Is it...?" Whatever question he had in mind, he backed away from it.

"The wine he drinks gives him evil dreams."

"Evil?"

"Yes, Jason." It was the last thing I wanted to be talking about. "Your father dogs him."

"Oh."

"I think he thinks making you welcome will end the dreams. But he still drinks."

"He must know I don't bear him any ill will."

"Tradition says the murder of a relative has to be avenged. Nearly everyone expects you to try it. I'm not certain why you haven't. Iolcus could be yours again."

"He says he's going to give it to me anyway. Why should I have to kill him for it?"

I have no idea what made me ask it. "Do you really want a haunted city?"

But Jason stopped walking and stared at me. "Haunted?"

"Yes. Surely you've begun to realize the kind of place Iolcus is. You must have heard the rumors by now."

"No. Not so far." He seemed genuinely puzzled. I had to remind myself he had not been in the city very long. "Suppose you tell me."

But I was not anxious to talk about it. "Pelias says it isn't only dreams. He claims there's a ghost, too. The ghost of Phrixus comes." I did not try to keep the sarcasm out of my voice. "It torments him in the night. Not a dream, mind you, a ghost."

A hare, a very large one, ran across our path and disappeared into some bushes.

"Do you believe him?"

I didn't know what to say. I had seen that purple mist in Pelias' room by dim candlelight. But my mental state that night had been so strange. It could have been anything, or nothing. "Of course not."

We were in the city now, heading toward the marketplace. The wind kicked up, billowing Jason's cape, showing me again his legs and his arms. The clouds above us were thickening more and more, hiding the moon then revealing it again. The streets were deserted; lights showed in a few windows but most of the houses were dark. Above everything towered the lighthouse. Jason moved closer to me, I presumed for a bit of warmth.

"This whole business of vengeance, of blood feud, within cities, within families…" Jason stared at the lighthouse flame for a moment, then looked at me. "I lived in Palestine for a time. At the court of King David. You've heard of him?"

"Of course. Traders from his ports come here all the time."

"There's a legend among the people there about a killer named Cain. He murdered his brother. There are a lot of variations on the story, but in all of them he's a fratricide. In the traditional way of settling these things, that would mean that someone in the family would have to kill him in turn, to avenge the first murder. But no one was willing to do it; Cain was one of them, too, after all, and for a kinsman to murder him would only require still another vendetta. Instead of killing him they drove him into exile. He was branded with a mark on his forehead so that no one, however distantly related to the family, might kill him accidentally and start the whole awful cycle of revenge again. And so the bloodletting ended. The family was free of pollution." He paused and took a long breath. "The Hebrews consider that the beginning of civilization."

We had reached the square. Even in the diffuse moonlight it was bright. The lighthouse loomed in the distance, taller than anything else, its flame jumping in the wind. There was no one around, and the only sound was the wind. At the far end of the square the stone Athamas held his knife aloft, frozen in the moment of his infanticide.

Jason turned and looked at me. "I've always thought that the story of Cain is the essence of what government should be. I want to rule Iolcus like that." He had been talking quite seriously; then he broke into an unexpected smile. "So your father doesn't have a thing to worry about. Not with me, at least."

"Have you told him about that?"

"No."

The obvious question would have been, why haven't you? But something made me hold back. We stopped walking near the entrance to the temple of Poseidon and sat side by side on the steps. For a moment we were still, and silent. Then, quite unexpectedly, Jason reached over and touched my cheek still again, very gently. "When the time comes for me to rule here, I'll need people I can trust." He smiled, then made his face a blank. "Like any king." The tip of his finger moved close to my lips.

It excited me. He was so beautiful. I stood up and took a step away from him. "You're not Pelias's heir yet. And you've hardly been here a week. How do you know you will be?"

"I know. He says so." He stood and followed me; reached out and took my hand; held it for a long moment. "You haven't changed your mind, have you? I mean, everyone says you have no interest in the throne."

Once again, despite the excitement I was feeling, I backed away from him. "No. Of course not. I'm a sculptor, not a politician. It just seems to me that you're being a bit—" I groped for the word. "—presumptuous?"

"You have no idea what it means to have found my family, even if there's a bit of rot on the family tree." He had no intention of answering me. I had made a show of not letting him get too close to me, but he ignored it and planted himself directly in front of me. "To have found someone like you, who I know I can count on."

He was trying to seduce me, not just physically. Part of me resented it. Part of me wanted it. I let myself lean into him, let my cheek touch his. "I've been planning to leave Iolcus."

"No you mustn't do that." His lips were near mine. I wondered if I should let him kiss me; wondered if he knew that I was aware he was trying to manipulate me. Or did he think me a boy, and a foolish, pliable one at that?

I looked into his eyes. Even in pale moonlight they were vibrant green. I opened my lips.

Suddenly something moved near us. We jumped apart. There had been a beggar sitting beside the temple steps; I had taken him for nothing more than a heap of rags. But suddenly he—she?—scuttled up the steps and into the sanctuary. Arms and legs were stumps; movement was awkward, beetle-like. Jason, startled, backed away and drew his knife. He gaped at the figure as it disappeared inside the temple.

For a moment there was silence. Jason looked at me, then again at Poseidon's house.

"There are a lot of them." I tried to sound offhand. "You'll get used to it."

"It was deformed."

"Yes."

"In most places a creature like that would be exposed at birth."

It was difficult to know what to say. He had not yet realized the unpleasant truth about his new city, and I didn't want to be the one to tell him. I could still feel the warmth of his touch. "There are more like that. A great many. The foxes can only eat so much."

His puzzlement was obvious.

"You won't be needing that knife, Jason."

Still looking flustered, he sheathed it again.

But beggars were not what I wanted to be talking about. "They say that David is a great king."

"He is, yes." He was still staring at the entrance to the temple.

"They say he has—they say he loves a man named Jonathan, and that their love is honored by everyone in the country. And that Jonathan is the son of the previous king." It was my turn to tease.

But Jason's mind was elsewhere. "I want to talk to that man." He began to climb the steps. Not much wanting to, I followed.

In a moment we were inside. There was near darkness. A votive flame burned in a lamp before the statue of the god, outlining it in bronze light; otherwise the sanctuary was quite black. Our footsteps echoed softly. There was movement in the darkness; I knew what it was, which put me one-up over Jason.

"Hello?" Jason peered into the black chamber, trying to find the beggar.

There was something moving, but there was no answer; there was not a sound.

"Hello?"

Nothing.

Then suddenly Jason jumped and let out a little shout. He turned and looked at me. "Something touched me. Something grabbed at my legs."

"And such nice legs, at that."

"I'm telling you there's something here."

I laughed. "There are cats here, Jason. Temple cats. You'd think they'd be living in Hecate's temple, wouldn't you? They're sacred to her, after all. But for some reason they prefer Poseidon. There are dozens of them."

"Cats." He stared at me blankly.

"Yes. The priests feed them."

"Oh." He pretended to arrange his cloak. "Where could that man have gone?"

36

I shrugged. "To the bosom of the god?"

"Don't be foolish, Acastus."

"Maybe the cats ate him."

"Will you stop it?"

"Then he must have gone out the back door."

"Oh." He looked a bit sheepish. "Why would he have run away from us?"

"Wouldn't you?"

He stared, not seeming to understand. "He was a beggar, wasn't he? Why didn't he ask us for...?" For some reason he did not finish the thought.

One of the cats brushed against my leg, then another. The lamplight flickered on the god's statue; it seemed almost to be moving. It was one of the oldest temples in the city; the workmanship in the statue was crude. Staring at it, Jason took a step toward it. "I've always wondered why people believe the god of the sea is the one who brings earthquakes." He turned to me. "Does that make any sense to you?"

"No. But we were on our way to the harbor, remember?"

"You're right." Playfully he slapped me on the backside. "Let's go."

We left the temple, ran down the steps and across the marketplace, like two boys playing. Jason's cloak billowed behind him. We headed for the waterfront.

* * *

And there she was, the goddess of love towering over us, 60 feet tall, tall enough for a proper god even though she was only bronze, bathing us in the warm glow of her fire despite the cold night. Jason stood very close to me; our shoulders touched. He was trying to seduce me again, I knew, for reasons that had to do with politics, not love; and he was as beautiful as any man I had ever seen.

But even I, of all our family, was enough of a politician to understand the situation. I had never been outside of Greece, and I certainly couldn't claim to have been raised by centaurs, but I was determined to beat him at his own game.

Waves splashed against the breakwater. I inched closer to him.

"There are usually porpoises playing at the mouth of the harbor. The water must be too rough for them tonight."

"They're supposed to be a sign of good luck."

"Maybe they know something about Iolcus you don't, Jason. Maybe that's why they're gone."

He grunted and walked ahead of me.

The moon was almost completely obscured now; the wind kicked up. "The ships are moored down there, at the end of the harbor."

There were ten of them, bobbing heavily on the waves. No one seemed to be manning or tending them. Jason walked back and forth on the pier, inspecting them. "When was the last time they put out to sea?"

"Three summers ago, I think. Just for a few exercises."

"How old are they?"

"God knows. Older than me, anyway."

"And the crews?"

"We don't have many full time sailors. Mostly it's fishermen who need extra work."

"I see." He did not look pleased. "And how much of a budget is there for upkeep?"

"You'd have to ask Pelias."

He paced back and forth once again. Then he jumped across from the dock to one of the ships, the *Nereid*; he caught the rail, climbed up onto the deck and began looking around. After a moment he disappeared below.

When he reappeared, he was frowning. "This won't do. These ships are as old as the hills. This one looks like it's ready to come apart at its seams." He held out a hand to me. "Why don't you come over here?"

I reached out and took it, and he pulled me up. I had never actually boarded one of them before.

Jason stared at me, then smiled widely, as if having me beside him on the ship was the most delightful thing he could imagine. "I'm think I'm going to have to send for Argus."

"Argus?" He was the most famous shipbuilder in Greece, almost legendary for the strength and fleetness of his craft. Even I knew his reputation. "You know him?"

"Of course." He smiled, pleased with himself.

"He's old, isn't he? Retired?" The deck rose and fell; I caught the rail to steady myself.

He nodded. "He's nearly 60. But he'll come for me."

"Stop sounding so smug."

"I want to make love to you." He took a sudden step toward me and put a hand on my waist. "You are a beautiful young man."

Only Cleanthus had ever told me so before. I wondered if it was true. "So are you."

"Then—?"

He was very close. I kissed him. The rolling of the deck left me feeling a bit disoriented. And he kissed me back, very hard. And my determination to play hard-to-get vanished like that beggar in the temple had.

Above us, Aphrodite's light danced in the wind; I closed my eyes. He was better than anyone I had ever kissed. I felt his arms close around me, felt his hand slide down my side and take hold of my cock under my tunic.

"Acastus." He whispered it, then kissed me again.

We stood there for a long time, holding each other, kissing. Then we went below and found an empty cabin and made love. Jason wanted to take the top, I could tell, but I maneuvered him onto the bottom, and it was very satisfying. It was the older man who always took the top. Not with us, not that night. When we finished we fell asleep in each other's arms.

Not for long, though. It was very late when we headed back to the palace, almost dawn; the sky in the east was just beginning to lighten. There was a cold stiff wind. We walked along the waterfront hand in hand. There were fisherman readying their boats. Some of them stared at us, obviously wondering about our relationship. Some of them called greetings to one or the other of us, or both. "Jason! Acastus!" Seeing us together like lovers seemed to surprise and please them.

In the square, vendors were preparing their wares, and early shoppers were busily inspecting produce, hens, suckling pigs, bolts of cloth. Again people smiled and greeted us. It hardly seemed possible that the atmosphere of the city had changed so quickly. There was a bit of magic about Jason, even if the magic was a confidence trick, which I suspected. I found myself wanting to kiss him again.

Soldiers were drilling in the Camp of Ares, just below the palace. We watched them. Their naked bodies were magnificent. I found myself wondering, if the army of an unmilitary city like Iolcus is so splendid, what must the Spartans be like? Jason wanted to go and exercise with them. The eastern sky held the faintest tinge of red.

Then an earsplitting scram came from the palace, just above us. Everyone froze. Jason and I looked at one another, then rushed to see what it was.

And it was Pelias. We found him in his chamber, surrounded by servants, cowering and gibbering in a corner. His clothes and his bed were stained with wine. When he saw us he pushed his way through the servants to us and threw his arms madly around Jason. "My god, you're here!"

Jason looked from him to me, plainly puzzled.

"It's the ghost, Jason," I whispered. Pelias was trembling. "The ghost of Phrixus. He's here."

I looked around. Disbelief showed on every face in the room.

"Phrixus." Jason smiled and tried to calm him.

"He's here."

"And what does he want, Pelias?"

"He wants peace. He says he wants rest."

"Is he here now?"

The king looked around apprehensively. "It's dawn. You know ghosts hate the sun."

Jason glanced at me from the corner of his eye. "Then you can sleep now, Pelias."

It seemed to come as a new thought, an unexpected one. Stupidly he echoed, "Sleep?"

"Yes. Get some rest. We can talk about this later."

"Later?" He was still shaking; I felt almost sorry for him.

"Later, Pelias." Jason put an arm around his shoulder and guided him to the bed. The king lay down and let his nephew cover him with a blanket. But his eyes were wide open. Clearly his dreams were getting worse.

Slowly, quietly the servants began to leave. Pelias, for some reason, stared at me. Jason went around extinguishing the lights. In a moment the room was empty but for the three of us. In a faint voice, almost a whimper, Pelias said, "Make him leave me alone."

Jason crossed to the bed, bent down and kissed him on the forehead. "We will. We'll see to it that you get the peace you deserve. Sleep now." He nodded to me and we walked out of the room.

Not for the first time, I found myself admiring Jason's way with people. "I wish I could do that."

"Do what?"

"Calm people like that. Move their emotions the way I want them to go. I still remember the way you soothed Creusa, that first day."

"Oh." He looked a bit sheepish. "That was easy."

"You can't mean it."

He nodded. "I have an ointment, a narcotic. I smeared some on my hand. And when she bit me, she swallowed it. It could have pacified a bull." It was his first acknowledged bit of fraud.

"Oh." I didn't know whether to admire his cleverness or dislike his duplicity. "Everyone thought it was just...just you. The force of your personality."

"Personality only goes so far."

So I was beginning to realize. "Well, you certainly have what it takes to be a king." I didn't necessarily mean it as a compliment.

But he took it as one, and thanked me.

We walked in silence for a few moments. When we reached his room he kissed me again. "Good night. Or rather, good morning. We'll need to talk later. We have to get to the bottom of Pelias and his ghost."

"It can't be a real ghost."

"As long as he believes it is, what difference does that make?" He smiled. "Besides, you haven't traveled. You have no idea what a strange place the world can be."

"That's the kind of thing the sailors used to tell me when I was a boy."

"They had a point."

"Of course."

He kissed me lightly on the cheek and turned to go into his room.

"Jason?"

"Hm?" He looked back over his shoulder.

I knew it was pointless to ask, but I had to do it anyway. "Are you really who you say you are?"

He grinned. "If I told you I am, would you believe me?"

"I don't know."

"And if I told you I'm not, would you believe that?"

It was the last question I expected. "I don't know."

The smile disappeared from his lips. "Good."

"But—"

"You've just had your first lesson in diplomacy."

He went into his room and I went to mine. Tired as I was, sleep was a long time coming. I was preoccupied wondering whether I had really been the one on top, after all. But when I finally slept, I dreamed of Jason and me, intense, erotic dreams.

* * *

"What's holding them together?"

We were at the harbor. Argus, newly arrived in the city, paced back and forth, busily inspecting our fleet, or what passed for it, and the look of disapproval on his face grew steadily more pronounced. He was in his sixties if not older, tall and thin, with bright silver hair. His eyes were black, like a bird's, and they were constantly in motion, taking everything in, missing nothing. For a man of his age, he was remarkably lively.

Jason and I stood back and watched him beside the *Nereid*, the same ship where we'd first made love. It was high noon, and the sunlight glistened brilliantly, almost blindingly, on the waves. The colossal Aphrodite was the color of Jason's hair; she might have been made of divine fire.

"Give me a hand, will you?" Argus held out his hands to us and we boosted him up and across the gap between the pier and the ship. Steadying himself against the rail, he looked around the deck.

Pelias had initially resisted Jason's plan to send for him. But after days of discussion, Jason finally convinced him. The Spartans were laying siege to Pagasae, a few miles to the west of us. We would be next. And Iolcus could never hope to defeat them on land. We were, however tentatively, a sea power; geography made it the natural thing for us, and it seemed our only hope. Finally, reluctantly, his eye jealously on the contents of the royal treasury, the king let himself be persuaded.

It had not taken Argus long to arrive; it seems he had been living in comfortable, even voluptuary retirement in a suburb of Argos. Within a week he had joined us, apparently pleased to be at work again, busily consulting with Jason about our situation. He even gave Jason some ideas for speeding up repairs on the city walls. The fact that a man of his reputation came so quickly when Jason sent for him impressed everyone, even me.

I looked up at him on the deck. "Should we join you?"

"I don't think this wreck would hold all three of us."

I jumped up beside him. "It's not that I don't appreciate a sense of the dramatic, but—"

"Look, Acastus. Look at how rotten these timbers are. When we get below, I'll bet we find all the beams in the same sorry condition. Or worse. We'd do better with a fleet of bathtubs."

I looked. He was right.

"How could any city let its fleet decay like this?"

"We're a commercial power." I knew it sounded lame. "Or at least we used to be. The world came to us, not the reverse."

"Even so. What would you do if someone blockaded your trade routes? Or the harbor itself? How could you hope to fight back?"

"It's never happened." I tried to sound offhand.

"My wife never died. Until last year."

His point was perfectly valid and I knew it. Obviously enough, the fleet had been new once; it might even have been formidable, at least for a city that wasn't really a military power. Its current sorry condition was one more sign that Iolcus was a city in decline; it was as simple as that.

But I couldn't make myself say those words to him. Not that he wouldn't have noticed it anyway, but...

He put a hand on my shoulder. "Let's go below and see how bad it is." He called down to Jason, who was still on the pier, "Are you coming?"

"No, I think I'll wait here. You two get to know each other." He smiled and strolled off in the direction of the lighthouse.

Argus and I climbed down a ladder into one of the holds. There was a lot of dust. I heard the sound of waves lapping gently on the gunwales. Despite the sunlight streaming in through the hatch, we were in almost total darkness. It took my eyes a moment to adjust.

But Argus seemed to have no trouble seeing; almost at once he began rooting around, tapping on the beams and the hull; at one point he seemed to be sniffing the air for something.

I went and stood behind him, looking over his shoulder, trying to see what he was up to. But I had no clue.

Then, suddenly, he interrupted his tapping and sniffing to look up into my eyes. "Jason likes you, you know."

It caught me a bit off guard. "I like him."

"Are you lovers?" He grinned.

The question made me laugh. "Now and then, I suppose."

"Good."

I wasn't certain why he had asked.

But he wasn't done with the subject. "I taught him a lot about lovemaking."

Involuntarily my eyes widened a bit.

"And, believe me, he was a worthy pupil. He masters everything he sets out to learn." He pried a splinter of wood from the hull, then bent it in two. "He first came to me wanting to know about shipbuilding. Then sailing; I taught him how to read the sea's moods. He's brilliant at everything. There are probably things he could teach you about sculpture."

It seemed unlikely, but I didn't say so.

"He seemed to think becoming my lover while he learned from me was a fair bargain. That was ten years ago. He was a beautiful boy then; now he's a man. But I would have taught him anyway. He was too good a student to ignore."

Why was he telling me all this? "I thought we came down here to inspect the hull."

"We did. Let him love you, Acastus." He smiled at me. "Love him in return. But don't expect it to last. Nothing ever does."

He was making me feel like a schoolboy. "Nothing?"

"Nothing at all. Believing in permanence is the root of tragedy. You're a beautiful young man," he said a second time, more pointedly. He got to his feet and brushed the dust off his clothes.

"Argus, there's something I have to ask you." I whispered, with a bit of emphasis, "In confidence."

He noticed something on one of the timbers. "What?"

"Is…is Jason really who he says he is?"

"He says that's who he is. It has never occurred to me to question it." He looked at me and shrugged. "I was living in Sparta when Jason found me. You should see them, you should see their army, all those beautiful men, all those pairs of lovers exercising together, rubbing each other down, oiling each other... When they're not out slaughtering people, they're having sex."

"Can we beat them, then?"

Unexpectedly, he laughed. "Of course we can. The Spartans are strong, but they're all soldiers, which is to say they're doggedly literal minded. That's a weakness to be exploited."

"Every soldier I've ever met has been literal minded."

"Of course. Knowing that—knowing how to use it—is one of the keys to being a good king, or rather, to staying one."

Argus was as cheerfully cynical as anyone I'd ever met. I decided I liked him. "Maybe you should give lessons to Pelias."

"Your father," he said in a confidential tone, "is a lost cause. I knew him when he was young. We were even lovers for a time—a short time. Pelias was quite an attractive young man."

"I don't believe it."

"No man believes his father was ever young and beautiful. And they all were—most of them, anyway." He shrugged. "He was drunk all the time, even back then."

Pelias had never given a hint they had known each other. "Are there any young men of promise in Greece you haven't taken to bed?"

"Not many, no." He seemed pleased with himself.

I decided to prod him. "And your wife...?"

"Oh, she had her revenge, all right. We never had any children. That was her doing. She knew I wanted daughters. I loved her, I genuinely did, and I did my marital duty whenever she would let me, but...but..." For a moment his mind seemed to drift somewhere else. Then he looked directly into my eyes. "It would have been nice to have daughters. Come on, let's see what the rest of this ship looks like."

We went through a hatch and down a corridor, heading sternward, inspecting each cabin and hold. They were all more or less like that first one, dark, dusty. It was so confusing, I couldn't even remember which one Jason and I had used, that first night.

At one point I started sneezing and couldn't stop; I must have sneezed a dozen times. Now and then Argus would rap on a wall or stomp on the floor or get down on his knees to inspect the wood and the seams. I gathered from his manner that things weren't quite as bad as he first suspected.

The cabin at the rear of the ship was the captain's. The door hung open. We went in. There was a heavy oak desk with a chair upholstered in brocade; Argus slapped it firmly, a cloud of dust filled the air, and I sneezed again. Dark red curtains covered the windows. There was a wooden rack full of charts; half of them were crumbling with age. In one corner, under a pair of windows, was the bed. I glanced at Argus awkwardly; he had sex on his mind a lot.

But he turned his attention to the maps, unrolling them one by one, scowling as bits of them flaked off, and reading them in the light from the windows. "These are years out of date."

I laughed. "We never go anywhere."

He took a particularly large chart and unrolled it on the bed. "This one's not so bad. Look. All of the Aegean, Asia Minor. Here's Troy and beyond it the Hellespont."

"Named for my ancestor." Phrixus and Helle had ridden their golden ram eastward, toward Asia. When they were crossing the water between the two continents, the girl fell off and drowned. The strait was named in her memory. Phrixus continued eastward, no one knew where.

Or at least that was the legend. Argus's eye twinkled. "The old sailors I knew when I was a boy used to say that passage was called the Hellespont generations before anyone had ever heard of the House of Athamas."

"Oh. But then, that makes sense, I suppose. Even if the people there had seen the girl drown—and even assuming there's any truth to the legend at all—how could they have known what her name was?"

He studied the map. Thinking about my unhappy ancestors made me fall silent. Phrixus. Ghosts. It was the last thing I needed on my mind. "Argus?"

"Hm?" He was preoccupied with his chart.

"I find it hard to believe in any of the myths."

"The gods are forces and ideas made poetry for our instruction. It wouldn't be wise to ignore them too completely."

"But are they real?"

For a brief moment I thought he was going to answer me. But he turned his attention pointedly back to the map. "This shows sirens, gorgons and harpies on half the islands in the Aegean."

"And are they really there?"

He lay back on the bed, sprawled himself across it, rested his head on a dusty pillow. "Ten years ago I would have tried to seduce you. Now I'm past it."

"I don't believe that for a moment."

"I told you, Acastus, nothing is permanent."

There must have been a sudden surge in the surf; the boat rolled sharply. I caught the edge of the desk to steady myself. Argus got up, brushed the dust off himself and took a quick look through the rest of the charts. Then we went back on deck.

Improbably, there was a crowd gathered on the pier. They were gaping up at the lighthouse.

Jason had climbed it. Not inside—not up the ladders Epiphanes used—but up the outside. He sat perched nonchalantly on the goddess's shoulder. Epiphanes was notoriously jealous of his charge; he never let anyone do that kind of thing. But it was not hard to imagine Jason charming him.

There were more waves; the deck rolled under our feet. I jumped down to the pier, then held out a hand to help Argus. Jason, 50 feet above us, called our names and waved. "Will they stay afloat?"

Argus cupped his hands around his mouth. "For a while, at least. But I won't vouch for how long."

"I don't want to come down."

"Stay there, then. I'll have Acastus show me the city."

"Have him show you where the whores hang out," he laughed.

Argus laughed too and put his hand on my shoulder, and we headed off toward the main square. For some reason I did not want to see the statue of Athamas and his children. I led Argus carefully to the far end of the marketplace, pointed out the various temples and statues. That one I dismissed with a few words, hoping he wouldn't ask any more about it. Thankfully, he didn't. It was plain enough that he didn't need to.

* * *

Jason, Argus, Pelias and I sat around the heavy oak table in the king's library. Pelias, as usual, had a cup of wine in his hand, but it was too early in the day for him to have drunk very much. Morning sunlight poured in through the windows. I had not had much sleep; Jason and I had spent the night making love. I had avoided the king's council meetings all my life; and I did not much want to be there now, either.

The king avoided looking at any of us and stared at the table top. "Perhaps they'll simply get tired and go home."

Jason, despite our vigorous night, seemed bright and rested. He glanced at Argus. "They're Spartans. They don't get tired."

"Of anything." Argus's cynicism was wonderful.

"Maybe Pagasae will beat them, then." Pelias looked hopefully at Jason.

"Be serious. Pelias, we have to do this."

After two days of thought and strategy, Jason and Argus had decided that the only hope for the city was to launch a united fleet against the Peloponnese, composed of ships from all the coastal cities, to strike at the Spartans' home ground. If that wouldn't get them to abandon their destructive progress, nothing else would.

But Pelias, for reasons he never made clear, disliked the idea. Perhaps it would have required him to act too much like a real king, too much a sober diplomat. "Why can't we just send our own fleet?"

"Are you serious?" Argus was appalled and he didn't try to hide it. "Ten rotting tubs, manned by out of practice crews? Do you expect the Spartans to die laughing?"

"Can't we refurbish them? Paint them, or something, to make them look more formidable?"

"Surely the Spartans have spies here."

He sighed. "Let's build new ships, then. And train new sailors."

"That could take a year or more. The Spartans will be on their way here as soon as Pagasae falls. No, we have to send to other cities. It's for their protection, too, after all, and it won't be hard for them to see that. People in Argos were talking about exactly this kind of alliance before I came here."

"Then they should take the lead." There was no clear reason why Pelias was being so stubborn. But he was beginning to be angry, too; his face reddened and his voice got a shrill edge to it.

"They're not next in the Spartan's path."

"We could—"

"Pelias." Jason spoke up loudly and firmly. The king looked startled. No one, not even his presumptive nephew, spoke to him that way. But Jason went right ahead. "We have to do this. It's our only hope. If you're not willing to take charge of the enterprise, then I will. We can't let Iolcus be laid waste."

There was more discussion. Glumly, reluctantly, Pelias agreed. I think he was a bit intimidated by Jason. At any rate, by the end of the meeting Jason was commander of our armed forces. He and Argus spent the rest of the day drafting a message to be sent to the kings of the other coastal cites. I went to my studio, to work on my sculpture of Jason. It was taking shape, slowly, steadily; it was becoming recognizable. Some nights I spent in his arms, in his bed, memorizing his body; others I spent reproducing it. I would not have him forever; I did not think I wanted to.

* * *

Late, near midnight. Jason stood before me, naked, on a block of marble. I walked around him, inspecting the lines of his body the way a buyer inspects a slave in the market; it annoyed him, as I wanted it to. The torches weren't positioned right. I adjusted them to highlight the lines I wanted.

"Do you have to be so persistent finding flaws in my body?"

"Everyone has flaws, Jason, even the gods. Hephaestus is lame."

"I have to go to the bathroom."

"Be still."

"But—"

I stood directly in front of him. His groin was near my face. But, still working with a clinical air, I ignored it. "You're a prince and a general now. We need a statue for the square. So stop fussing and let me get on with this."

He bristled.

I crossed the room to the marble and took up my chisel. It was the finest, purest, whitest piece of Parian marble I could find, smooth as butter, warm as flesh. I looked from it to him. Jason's face and body were emerging from it unmistakably. "Will you relax?"

"I can't help it. I have to piss."

49

"You're a soldier. You should have more self control."

"Acastus."

I had made him suffer long enough. "Oh, all right, go ahead then."

He jumped off the block and raced out of the room. Love is so complicated when it involves politics. But I was becoming more and more adept at the little games lovers play with each other, and I was enjoying them more and more.

I ran a hand along the torso of the statue. There was a place, on his right side, where he was particularly sensitive. When I kissed him there it drove him wild. I had made a slight hollow in the stone there, something only I would see or understand. I touched the place lightly with my fingertips, closed my eyes and remembered how he moaned. Love is power. Everyone in the palace knew we were involved with one another.

In a few moments he was back, looking a bit sheepish. "Sorry about that, but—"

"It's all right." I kissed him on the cheek. "I get caught up in my art, that's all." I wondered how good a liar I was being.

Jason kissed me back. And, as always, it excited me. We might have made love there, rolling around on the floor of my workshop, stone chips cutting our flesh.

But Pelias screamed.

And screamed.

It was worse than I had ever heard, and longer, and more wild. I stepped back from Jason. "I've been hearing that all my life, and I'm still not used to it. If there were no other reason for leaving Iolcus..."

"You can't leave. I need you."

"Need?"

"Want, then. I want you, Acastus. Call it love."

"What a romantic you are." I bit his earlobe.

"Ouch! Bastard!"

"There, there, Jason. What's love without a bit of pain?"

He laughed and slapped my backside. "Bitch."

Pelias screamed again, louder than before; then there were long, loud, low moans.

I put my arms around Jason's waist and rested my head on his shoulder. "God."

"We ought to go and see if he's all right."

"How would we know? He's always the same. I don't know if you could call it all right, exactly, but—"

"Acastus."

I sighed. "You're right. Let's go. If I'd thought you'd try to give me a conscience, I would have kept my distance from you."

He climbed quickly into his clothes, put an arm around me and we went out into the corridor. There were a great many people; the king's cries were worse than anyone could remember. Jason rushed me to the royal bedchamber.

There were dozens of people, servants, palace bureaucrats, all of them with torches and candles; I had never seen the room so bright. When they saw us enter, they parted to let us through. Pelias was sprawled on his bed, arms and legs spread as if he'd been tied down, but there was nothing holding him, at least nothing visible. His body was trembling and heaving, and his moans were unbearably loud. There was blood smearing his body, his clothes, the bed. Jason and I rushed across the room to him.

There were words cut into his chest: GIVE ME REST. Blood flowed.

Jason reached out and tried to touch him. But something, something unseen, pushed him back; he flew ten feet across the room. I ran to his side and helped him up. Without saying anything he glanced at me, then looked back at the king. Pelias cried out.

"Try and touch him, Acastus. See if you can touch him."

Not wanting to, really, I moved back across the room to the king's side. Reached out a finger, to touch his face. Something took hold of my hand and pushed it firmly away. A wave of cold came over me, and my arms broke out in gooseflesh; I started shivering. Blood from the cuts in the king's chest turned his bedclothes bright red.

Jason came to my side and soundlessly mouthed the word: *ghost*.

"No."

"What else can it be?"

"God knows. It can't be that."

"It wants rest."

"He did that to himself. He must have."

"And what caught your arm just now?"

I was still cold, freezing. I wanted to put my arms around Jason, if only for the warmth. The king's body heaved; there was a fresh spurt of blood.

Slowly, reluctantly, I turned to the people in the room. "All of you, put out your lights, will you please?"

They were obviously puzzled, but they did it. One by one the flames were extinguished. One large candle, at the far end of the chamber, gave the only light. And in the near darkness we could see it. The king was wrapped in a faint purple light. It covered him, enfolded him; it moved around and across his body like a living thing, something formless, some spectral jellyfish. He let out another moan. As we watched, something cut his flesh again, underscoring the words that were there: GIVE ME REST. Without quite realizing I was doing it, I reached out and took Jason's hand.

Slowly, very slowly, the purple glow faded from around Pelias. When I tried to touch him again, to blot up some of the blood with a cloth, I was able to. I left it to the servants to take care of him, clean him, quiet him.

Jason motioned to me to follow him out into the hall. Staring back at the kind's door, he said, "And so the city really is haunted."

"Or damned."

"Come on, Acastus. I think you can use some sleep."

"No."

"More work, then?"

"No."

"Then—?"

"I don't know. To see that happen… To see that happen to your father… Not that he's ever been much of a father, not that I've ever even cared about him, but…" I let Jason hold me for a moment, then pulled away. "Is it him, or is it the city, Jason? If you become king will that happen to you?"

He stared at me without answering.

"Or to me, Jason? Will it be me, because I'm his son?"

"How can anyone know that?"

"Where is Argus?"

"Asleep. He wakes up early in the morning, hours before dawn, full of energy. It isn't natural."

"He'll know what to do, maybe. Jason, I'm afraid. For him, for you, for all of us. I've tried to tell myself it wasn't real, but—"

"You've seen it before?"

"Once. There was no blood that time. I convinced myself it was a trick of the light. Everyone says this city was blessed by the gods."

He touched my cheek. He kissed me, very gently. "We can deal with it, whatever it is. You're right, we'll talk to Argus in the morning."

We slept in each other's arms, in Jason's bed not mine; for once there was no lovemaking.

Chapter Three
The Oracle

Argus gave us the obvious advice: We were dealing with a ghost, with something supernatural, or extra-natural, or preternatural. We should consult with the people who specialize in that sort of thing. And of the major shrines, Delphi was the closest to us. I asked him what was special about the place.

"The legend goes that Zeus sent two eagles from opposite ends of the world. He wanted to know the exact center. The eagles met at Delphi, and ever since it has been known as the navel of the earth. A special place, a mystical place."

"Why would he need eagles? He's god. Wouldn't he know?" I was always baffled by the stories about the gods needing mortal help. Why would they? After all, they're gods.

"Don't go asking too many impious questions, Acastus. I'm as skeptical as you are, but we'll be dealing with priests. They tend to be touchy."

We decided to travel by land. Argus argued for a sea trip. "We can dock in the Bay of Itea. Parnassus is a short way beyond it." But Jason and I outvoted him; we wanted to see the country—and the country boys. Argus grumbled about arthritis but finally agreed to a land journey.

Pelias, not wanting to make the journey, pretended to be too ill, too badly afflicted for a long journey. I don't suppose he could be blamed; he had suffered enough already at the hands of…whatever it was. Dealing with oracles might easily have overwhelmed him, particularly since they were apt to tell us his fratricide was at the root of the problem.

* * *

Winter turned severe; it was harsher than anyone could remember. Storms roiled the sea almost every day. Snowdrifts filled every corner of the city. Life came to a standstill.

It was a mixed blessing because, while it crippled Iolcus the Spartans were caught in it, too. Forced to abandon their aggression till spring, they turned back to their own city. On the forced march, hundreds of them died. It would be a long while before their army was at strength again. Greece—what I always thought of as the civilized part of Greece—was safe for the immediate future.

* * *

So it was not until springtime when we made the journey.

There were the three of us, Jason, Argus and myself, accompanied by a half dozen servants. Our journey took five days, but the terrain was friendly and we made good progress. Even the slopes of Mount Parnassus were easy to climb; generations of pilgrims had created good paths. Late on the afternoon of the fifth day our goal came into view. Delphi is reputed to be the most dramatic landscape on earth, a gorge torn violently out of the land between two peaks of Parnassus. And so it is. My first sight of it left me awestruck.

Then, spread out before us like a huge green bowl and lit by the sun's last rays, was the valley, or rather gorge, of Delphi. The mountains on either side, called the Phaedriades, dropped at such a steep angle it was perfectly thrilling; it wasn't hard to see why our ancestors had decided there must be something special about the place, perhaps even something a bit divine. Legend described the place as the navel of the world, a phrase totally meaningless but impressive sounding, inevitably the fabrication of priests. There were dark green pine trees by the thousand; and the olive trees for which the region was famous were beginning to leaf.

Below us, at the center of it all, was the town of Delphi and the sacred precinct. We were too far away to make out many details, but it was not as large as I would have expected. But the landscape... the landscape was overpowering.

* * *

We stopped at the top of a hill overlooking the gorge and put down our packs. The servants retreated a few yards and began to talk among themselves, or rather grumble; they naturally had the heaviest loads to carry, even though the three of us carried the gold and jewels that Pelias was sending as a bribe, or rather offering, to the god Apollo.

Argus rummaged through his pack and produced a skin of wine. "Here, drink. Have you been here before?"

I let him fill a cup for me. "No. My gods are too personal for this sort of thing."

"I know what you mean. But civic religion has its uses. Where would politicians be if they couldn't make a public show of their piety?"

"In prison?" Jason laughed and took a long drink from the skin, not bothering with a cup. "At least, *some* politicians are vigorous enough to make the journey here." I'm afraid my attitude toward Pelias was beginning to rub off on him.

But my father was the last thing I wanted to talk about. "It certainly is a magnificent landscape."

"Carved from the earth by Apollo himself." Argus didn't try to keep the sarcasm out of his voice.

But it bothered me. None of us seemed quite to believe in what we were doing. "Is there any serious chance something useful will happen here?"

"Of course." Argus sat down and took a long drink; he was all heartiness. "The Pythoness will prescribe some sort of public atonement for Pelias, he'll do it, and he'll feel better. Iolcus will have a functional king for the first time in a decade."

"Longer."

"Longer, then. Surely that's worth the offering of gold we're going to make here."

"And what if they simply tell us the king and the city are lost?"

"Oh, they never do that. There's too much at stake."

"Too much what?"

He seemed surprised at the question. "Too much money, Acastus. And too much power, which comes to the same thing."

Jason was staying, pointedly, out of our conversation. He climbed onto a high rock and surveyed the valley below. "The compound looks completely vulnerable. Anyone who wanted to could take it over and have the priests do his bidding.

"It's been tried. More than once." Argus took another drink, then tucked the skin carefully back into his pack. "Wars have been fought for control of the oracle. But the priests here are much too powerful for anyone else to take control."

I wanted more wine. "What kind of power could they have?"

"The only kind that matters: economic power. They can summon help from all over the Greek world."

This caught Jason's ear. He came and joined us. "How so?"

"The priesthood of Apollo goes back farther than anyone can remember. Hundreds of years, maybe a thousand. And every suppliant who comes here gives them gold or jewels or…" He spread his hands wide in the air, as if to say his meaning must be plain. "The first priests, back at the dawn of civilization, were Cretans. They claim that Zeus, or Apollo, or whichever god, promised them eternal wealth. So their great wealth is quite conveniently authorized by Olympus."

Great wealth. For the first time since we left Iolcus Jason actually seemed interested in Delphi. "And all that time they've been investing?"

"Exactly. They have holdings in every corner of Greece, most of the Aegean islands and half of Asia Minor. And they use their prophetic influence—and their numerous spies and agents—to steer things the way they want them to go. And that, my darlings, is organized religion at work."

It made perfect sense; but for some reason none of it had never occurred to me before. "But suppose they don't have interests in Iolcus? Suppose they've sold short?"

He shrugged. "Then our job will be to persuade them they have interests there none the less. That, plus a suitable offering of gold, is the only way to get a propitious oracle. We'll have to spend a few days talking with them, letting them pump us for information, before we consult with the Pythoness."

"It all seems fairly absurd." There was a touch of impatience in Jason's voice.

But Argus adopted a firm tone with him. "You want to be a king, don't you? This is what it's all about. I need another drink." He fished out the wineskin again and refilled his cup and mine. "Did you think it was all rubies and concubines?"

"No, of course not. But the world could stand some plain dealing."

"You're showing your youth." He laughed.

Jason bristled. "Give me a drink."

But it occurred to me that there was something missing from all this. "And what about the ghost?"

Argus frowned. "Oh. That."

"Surely the priests will have to deal with it, Argus. If they don't—I mean, if they ignore that kind of thing enough times—people will begin to realize—"

"The people never realize anything." Jason said it so emphatically I was startled. "All the priests have to do is make the oracle mouth some obscure nonsense. If the ghost vanishes, fine, they get the credit. If it doesn't, well, then that's our fault, because we somehow misunderstood the words of the god. Or weren't properly pious, or what have you. There are a thousand excuses that would sound plausible to true believers. I've never yet met a king who believed in the gods. They learn too much."

"And yet there is still the ghost. Or whatever it is." Its existence seemed to me the most significant thing about the whole business. And we were blithely ignoring it.

For once, neither of them could think of anything to say. Political cynicism only goes so far, especially in a situation like ours.

Jason hoisted his pack and motioned to the servants to take theirs up. "Let's get down there before it gets dark. There must be plenty of inns in the town, where we can spend the night."

Argus stretched and yawned. "Yes, all of them run by agents of the priests. Do we really want them eavesdropping on our conversations? Besides, I'm quite spent. I couldn't carry myself much further, let alone a sack of gold. Let's get a good night's sleep before we go down there." Sometimes it was easy for me to forget how old he was.

"If the priests are as canny as you seem to think, they must already know we're here. Or they will shortly."

"Indeed they do, or will. They've probably been keeping track of us since we left Iolcus. But let's not make it any easier for them than we need to. Besides—" He glanced at the servants, who plainly wanted him to win this little dispute. "—we really need to refresh ourselves before we confront the priests. It's always best to deal with them with a clear mind."

I was enjoying the hills and the view of the valley below us, and I wasn't at all anxious to get near the town and the oracle. I seconded Argus' opinion.

Jason grunted, set down his pack and found the wineskin again. The servants spread out of the ground, smiling. Apollo could wait.

* * *

That night was cool and very dark, darker than it ever was in the city. What seemed a million stars glistened above us. Now and then a meteor shot across the sky. I lay on the grass, wrapped in a blanket, and let myself get lost in it all. Perhaps the stars really are what the philosopher say: the souls of the gods and goddesses. It seemed unlikely anything less could be so beautiful.

I was roused from my reverie by someone lying down beside me. It was Jason. "Argus is asleep," he whispered. "I'm chilly." He pulled the edge of my blanket over himself, and I felt his warmth. Quickly he put an arm around me, then kissed me.

He snuggled up close to me, and we made love, softly, so as not to disturb Argus or rouse the servants. For once I let him take the top. If I could waken with some of Jason in me, Apollo would be simple to face. Then, our lovemaking done, I fell into that deep wonderful sleep that always follows it. In my sleep I felt Jason's body next to mine, his head on my shoulder.

There came a muffled sound, like the wings of a large bird. Stars glittered, the Milky Way glowed, and I felt soft feathers, soft as down, brush my face and enfold me. I knew it was a dream, but I wanted it to last. What could it be? I wondered in my sleep. Not Jason, surely not Jason; he was the least soft, downy and birdlike man I had ever known. But the feel of those feathers caressed me, and it was soft and wonderful. I closed my eyes tightly and luxuriated in it.

Sometime later I woke. And was happy Jason was still there,

nothing feathery about him. The stars above us had wheeled round, and the Milky Way arched high. A spray of milk from the breast of the Goddess, the priests called it. It seemed even less probable than most of their pronouncements.

"Jason." I whispered. "Jason, are you awake?"

I felt him nod. "You should be asleep, Acastus."

"You too." I put a hand on his chest. "But we're not."

"We should be. We'll need all our mental energy for tomorrow. Argus said so. No more lovemaking, not tonight."

"Mm-hmm." I fell silent for a moment. Then, "Jason."

"Hmm?"

"I dreamed. Something large, a huge bird enfolding me in its wings. What can it mean?"

"It means you had too much wine. Go to sleep, and let me do the same."

"I'm serious, Jason. What—"

"If you really need an explanation, tell yourself that the proximity to Delphi gave you a prophetic dream."

I fell silent, watching the sky, hoping for another meteor. None came. But I was quite awake now, and restless. "Jason?"

"Hm?"

"Are there… are there really centaurs?"

In the dark he chuckled softly. "Sometimes I forget how young you are."

It stung. "Argus said the same thing about you." I hesitated. "Are there?"

"The world is so wide, Acastus. If half the stories people tell are true, the wonders are so many they could never be catalogued. The centaurs are at least as real as the ghost of Phrixus."

"That isn't an answer."

"It is. You have seen the ghost. You know it is real."

"Yes, but I don't know what it is."

"Then you've answered your own question." He kissed me lightly. "Now stop being a pest and let me sleep. Good night, Acastus."

* * *

We woke before dawn, roused the servants and prepared for the trek down to the town of Delphi. There was something about the place that made us all keep quiet. Jason was his usual taciturn self, but even Argus stayed silent. Even our servants left off their usual grumbling. I wondered if it was the mystical nature of the place, at least its purported mystical nature, or whether we simply weren't quite awake yet. For whatever reason there was not much talk.

The two mountains, the Phaedriades, that flanked the gorge and reared up around us, were much more imposing than they had seemed before our descent into the gorge. Occasionally an eagle would soar off one or the other of them. I wanted to remark on them, but nothing I could think of seemed more than obvious. So I walked and watched the sky.

At one point one of them flew directly over our heads, so low it seemed as if it wanted to dive. I asked Argus if they were dangerous, or might be.

"No, Acastus, there are always visitors here, always plenty of people. The eagles must be used to human company, at least familiar enough to know we aren't fit food for them."

Jason moved beside me and whispered, "Maybe one of them was checking you out last night. Maybe that's what you felt."

"Don't be preposterous."

"Maybe it wanted to pose for you. Do you ever sculpt eagles?"

"Stop it."

"As you wish, little sculptor." He chuckled, and we kept moving.

* * *

We reached the outskirts quickly, still in relative silence. Delphi: the abode of Apollo. We were there.

A low wall surrounded the town. It couldn't have been much use for defense, but then Argus had explained Delphi's relative invulnerability. Over top of it, we could see the roofs of several temples. All of them were built of marble, and all seemed fairly new. But one, evidently older than the rest, towered above them; I knew it had to be the temple of Apollo. In a place reputed to be as old as the earth itself, the general newness struck me as odd, and I commented on it to Argus.

"Well, this hasn't always been the abode of Apollo, you know. He's a johnny-come-lately here."

"Really? I thought—"

"The first oracle here was devoted to Gaia, the earth goddess, back at the beginning of time, or at least the beginning of civilization. Times changed, the political climate changed, and Gaia yielded the oracle to her daughter Themis. Then Themis passed it on to the titaness Phoebe, and then goddesses went out of fashion and Apollo took the reins. But he took the additional name Phoebus in acknowledgment of the one he'd supplanted. And his supposed battle with the great monster Python became emblematic. I wouldn't mention any of this to the priests, though. Officially this has been the sanctuary of Phoebus Apollo since the dawn of humanity."

Jason laughed. "How can any thinking man take religion seriously?"

"Every religion is made of bits from earlier ones. It's just a matter of sorting out the pieces. But hush. We're here."

* * *

There were dozens of scattered buildings outside the town walls. A few peasants came and went on whatever business. Children played, dogs lazed in the sun and hens scratched the earth. And there were a score of shabbily dressed women and young men leaning provocatively against the town wall; they simply had to be prostitutes. To all appearances it was a town like hundreds of others in Greece, nothing special about it at all. But inside…

The gates were wide open. I wondered if it might be a market day, or if the priests were really that confident of their position. Ahead of us stretched the broad avenue called the Sacred Way, which curved through the town to the temple of Apollo, the proportions of which were quite beautiful. On either side of it were many smaller temples, so small we hadn't seen them over the wall, some of them evidently quite old, attesting to Delphi's antiquity. Over their entrances were inscriptions indicating which god or goddess they were sacred to. And of course there were also the newer temples. And there were other stone buildings, some of them large and quite elaborate, much more so than the temples. They had been erected by various cities to house their votive gifts to the Apollo. Inscriptions identified them as "Treasury of Athens," "Treasury of Thebes" and so on.

There were scores of people bustling about, maybe even hundreds. They crisscrossed the Sacred Way and headed into the side streets, where the town's day-to-day business took place. Fruit vendors pushed carts, souvenir vendors hawked their trinkets and, inevitably, children ran and played.

We stood just inside the gates for a few moments, taking it all in. Jason was quite rapt. "Look at all the treasuries. It's not hard to see what Delphi's real concern is."

From behind one of the gates, concealed from our view, a voice deep as thunder boomed. "Such impiety is not welcome here."

It was so unexpected we all fell silent. From behind the gate stepped a man, tall, impressive, apparently in late middle-age, dressed in priestly garb. He strode across the opening and planted himself imposingly in front of us. "I would suggest that you keep such frivolous notions to yourselves." He lowered his voice menacingly. "Or depart."

Argus was the first of us to recover his wits. "And may we know who is so instructing us?"

"I am," the man told us solemnly, "Theophanes. One of the Delphic prophets."

"Oh." Argus was amused at the man's pomposity, I could tell. But he suppressed it. "And we are—"

"You are Argus, Acastus and Jason of Iolcus, come here to expiate the sins of your city."

So they had indeed been keeping tabs on us. Argus shot me a quick glance, as if to say *I told you so*. Then he quickly turned back to Theophanes. "Not exactly, but close enough to correct. I congratulate you on your intelligence. But my understanding is that there are three Delphic prophets. Where are your colleagues?"

"In due time." The prophet tried to make his voice mysterious, but he merely sounded pretentious. I couldn't help giggling.

He glared at me. "This is Delphi. You must, as I said, adopt a more properly reverent attitude—" he lowered his voice again—"or leave without the god's counsel."

Argus turned hearty. "We have brought quite a sum of gold.

Carrying it is quite a burden. But if you wish us to go and take it with us—"

"Do not be hasty." The abruptness with which he turned friendly made me laugh again. But this time he ignored it. "You must be weary from your journey. Enter, and accept the hospitality of Apollo."

* * *

We spent three days there, seeing the sights and letting Theophanes— neither of his fellow prophets was in evidence—chat us up. We saw the famous Castalian spring, which flowed from a cleft in the mountainside, and which had inspired so many poets to rapture even though few of them could actually have seen it. Not far from it was another well-known place, the so-called Cave of the Nymphs; when we visited no nymphs were in residence, though.

Then there was the stadium where the Pythian Games were held every four years. Workmen were in the process of expanding it. Just beside it was the theater where the music and poetry contests, integral parts of the games, took place. And everywhere were bronze statues of gods, heroes, athletes, poets, musicians, scores of them, maybe even hundreds, all shimmering with that green, glassy glow that affects bronze nowhere else in the world. Theophanes, acting as our guide, smugly told us it was caused by the presence of the god in Delphi. I have never worked in bronze; I much prefer the feel of living stone beneath my chisel. But the workmanship of these monuments dazzled me.

Jason, being Jason, wanted to see all the assorted treasuries, but none of them were open to the public. They were guarded quite carefully by a mix of soldiers from the various cities plus agents of the Delphic priests.

Theophanes took us everywhere, telling us about all the ancient, mythic places and simultaneously prying into our reason for coming. Argus took the lead for us, dropping broad hints about our mission but being careful not to reveal too much about Iolcus' sad state. It was widely known that Iolcus had fallen on ill times, but the ghost and its curse had been kept quite carefully secret lest the alarming news should impact the city even more terribly. We had been careful not to mention it within earshot of our servants, even.

"Still," Argus had told us, "the priests make it their business to know everything that goes on in Greece. They may have spies within Pelias' palace itself." Glum thought.

By noon on the third day Theophanes seemed satisfied he had learned enough. "Tonight," he announced in tones he must have thought would impress us, "at the rise of the moon, the god will prophecy. You will come to the temple then, but first you must purify yourselves. Bathe three times, eat no food, drink no wine. You will partake of the god's banquet before being ushered into his presence. Wear only clean linen garments." He bowed deeply and with a huge flourish. "Until then, farewell."

We had installed ourselves at an inn run by a man with the improbable name Prophylaxis. He did not attempt to disguise the fact that he was watching our movements and eavesdropping on our conversations. If he was not, as Argus claimed, an agent of the priests, then he was the foulest busybody in Greece. Twice we caught him listening outside our door. We quickly got into the habit of whispering when we were in our room. We were especially careful not to mention the ghost. Our servants were quartered at a smaller inn outside the town gates.

The accommodations were spare but decent enough, I suppose. Still, Argus complained about the hardness of his bed. "This thing is killing my back. Who do they think we are, Spartans?"

Jason was indifferent to Argus' discomfort. "I'm hungry. Let's find a vendor and get some lunch."

"We're supposed to fast, remember?" Argus said it loudly enough for Prophylaxis to hear. Then in hushed tones he added, "We have to make a show of following instructions. We can't do anything to throw them off their game."

From his pack he got some salt beef and a skin of wine. That would have to hold us over till after the ceremony. We ate a good bit, then slept. "Best to be fresh for the god tonight. We'll need to have our wits about us."

I slept soundly thanks to the wine. And in my sleep I dreamed again. Soft, downy white feathers, like the feathers of a swan or an egret, enfolded me. Muscular arms held me and carried me into the sky.

I woke with a wild erection, and it took me a moment to orient myself. Jason was sound asleep in his bed across the room; they had not been his arms I had felt. For the longest time I lay there, trying to make sense of those dreams. I wanted more sleep but it would not come. The prospect of witnessing the oracle, plus the prospect of whatever my feathery dreams foretold, kept me awake.

I had never believed in the gods, not really, not quite, only in the Muses who guided my hand when I worked. But now…there were so many possibilities. I shouldn't have had wine with my meal. Can wine really make us prophets, can it give us a view of the divine?

* * *

And so it was time, time to confront the god, time to hear his wisdom—if that's what it was. Argus insisted we eat more before going to the temple; I had no idea why. But I wasn't very hungry. I only nibbled while the others ate their fill.

It was late twilight when we left our inn, carrying our sacks of gold, and there was a stiff spring breeze. Delphi was preparing for the night. Lights burned in windows; the sounds of music and laughter came from taverns and inns; the major streets were lit with torches. Here and there along the streets, even the Sacred Way, prostitutes both female and male loitered in darkened doorways. "Never mind these whores," Argus whispered to me. "We'll be dealing with priests—true professionals."

As always I was amused by his cynicism. "Is that the sort of reverence that will get us a favorable prophecy?"

He put down his sack to rest for a moment. "It's the kind you can expect from a cranky old man with a heavy load to carry and a sore back from that damned lumpy bed at the inn. Come on. Let's get this over with."

The sky above us was dark and flecked with clouds. Stars glittered among them, and in the east the moon, just past full, rose white and brilliant. And opposite it in the west the Evening Star shone brilliantly: Aphrodite, the embodiment of love. I half expected her to wink at me, to acknowledge the relative absurdity of our situation. We were on our way to ask a group of priests, who we believed to be frauds, for advice on dealing with a ghost we weren't even certain really was a ghost.

Jason had walked behind us, saying nothing. Then he moved beside me and took my hand. It surprised me and I started to pull away, then caught myself and squeezed his. Hand in hand we followed Argus in silence along the age-old Sacred Way. I wasn't at all certain what to expect when we reached our destination.

The temple of Apollo is, fittingly, the largest building in Delphi, the largest I had ever seen (though Argus said he had seen larger in Thebes and Athens). It sits imposingly on a rise at the end of the Sacred Way. It is made of fine white marble, the purest I had ever seen, so pure it was almost translucent, and scores of torches illuminated it. The fires danced and blazed in the breeze, and in their light the marble seemed almost to glow. Two dozen columns encircle the temple, giving it an air of harmony and rhythm which even the wild firelight could not disrupt.

Above the entrance, carved deeply into the marble, were the famous words, "KNOW THYSELF." Jason stood before the temple, staring up at the inscription. "Don't most men already know themselves?"

"You'd be surprised. Self-delusion is the hallmark of our race." Argus put down his sack and rubbed his back again. "But if I know priests, what they really mean is 'Know how much you can donate.'"

* * *

The temples of the gods in Iolcus are old, positively ancient, and not very big. The temple of Apollo seemed almost overwhelming by comparison, and the firelight gave it a magical appearance. As we climbed the steps to the entrance I felt small and insignificant. When I said as much to Argus he answered, "Do you think that's accidental? Good priests are masters of stagecraft."

Theophanes stood in the doorway, flanked by three temple servants. He was wearing a mask of the kind actors wear, this one midway between comedy and tragedy. I knew it had to be him, because he appeared unnaturally tall, imposing even; I suspected he was wearing lifts in his sandals. I recognized his voice, though it was muffled by the mask, as he intoned, "Welcome to the House of Apollo. The god bids you enter."

Argus handed his sack heavily to one of the servants. His relief at being rid of it was all too plain to see. "Greetings, Theophanes. We have brought these three bags filled with gold and jewels as offerings to the god. Have your servants see to them properly, will you?"

"Nothing material concerns the god." His voice boomed.

Argus snorted softly and stifled a laugh. "Oh. Well, we'll just take it back with us then, shall we?"

"Do not be irreverent, shipbuilder." He clapped his hands and the servants shouldered the sacks and hurried inside with them. Theophanes watched them, then turned back to us. "Come. Apollo awaits."

We followed him inside, first Argus, then myself, and finally Jason.

The interior of the temple was of that same pure white marble. There was a large anteroom, long and rectangular, with brightly polished walls. It was lit by scores of torches. Their light on the polished walls was almost blinding, especially after the nighttime city. Theophanes clapped his hands again, and more servants appeared, this time carrying trays of wine. The trays and cups were of gold; the show of wealth was not lost on me—or on Jason, who looked like a child on his birthday, greedily eyeing his toys.

Slowly my eyes adjusted to the bright light. The room was quite without ornamentation, the walls blank except for a large letter E carved above a second door, which I knew must be the entrance to the holy of holies. Theophanes announced, "You shall be summoned," and he strode through that second door. The inner room, in sharp contrast to the one we were in, was pitch dark.

The servants left their trays on a low table and departed. The three of us were quite alone. I looked around the chamber again. "E. Whatever can it mean—ectoplasm? Ether?"

Argus shrugged. "People have wondered for centuries. My guess would be 'expediency.'"

Jason drained his wine cup. "This tastes odd. Did either of you notice?"

"It is almost certainly drugged." Argus lowered his voice to a soft whisper. "To increase our susceptibility to whatever flummery they are preparing."

"That's why you had us eat first! To soften the effect of the drug!"

"Be quiet, Jason." He looked around anxiously. "We mustn't tip our hand."

But he was right about the wine.

The blank white of the walls had turned slowly to a rainbow of colors, all of them shimmering and dancing. Then the rainbows caught fire. And I watched, rapt. A spectrum of colors undulated on the blank white walls. The effect was perfectly hypnotic, and the knowledge that it was a product of the drugged wine did nothing to lessen it.

For what seemed an eternity but must have been a mere matter of moments I was lost in it. When a voice boomed, "Come!" it barely registered with me. Then I felt rough hands, Argus' hands, shaking me out of my trance.

"Sorry, Argus. The wine—I should have eaten more."

"Quiet!" he whispered. "We must make a properly reverent audience."

Theophanes, or perhaps one of the other masked priests, stood in the doorway to the Holy of Holies, one hand outstretched, beckoning us. He was impossibly tall, perhaps even divinely so, and he moved with unearthly slowness and fluidity. Drugged wine. As we approached him he stepped backward into the dark chamber, and we followed dutifully.

The interior of the chamber was black as ebony, lit only by a few candles whose light barely pierced the gloom. The room was so dark there was no way to judge how large it was, but I gathered from the echoes of our footsteps it must have been quite enormous; perhaps large enough to take up most of the temple's interior.

From out of the blackness two more temple servants appeared, carrying candles. Against the Stygian darkness the light from them seemed impossibly bright. By their flickering light the priest's mask made a monstrous appearance; he might have been a god himself, or a demon. He pointed to the floor, indicating we should remain standing where we were. Then he strode off into the blackness.

For a moment we stood there, not moving, staring into the divine night that enfolded us. The candlelight grew fainter; one by one they were extinguished completely. A bell, loud and discordant, clanged so loudly I had to clasp my hands over my ears. Out of the darkness a voiced thundered, "Prepare"

It was all so very dramatic. Argus had been quite correct: the priests were masters of stagecraft. No tragedy, however divinely inspired, had ever been so impressive. I was quite aware in part of my mind that each effect was heightened by whatever drug we had consumed in the wine, but that hardly made any of it less mesmerizing.

The bell clanged again, and suddenly torches were lit at the far end of the hall, which was farther away from us than seemed quite possible. Perhaps really were staring into divine infinity.

In that new light the golden tripod of the Pythoness became visible. It was three feet high; the three legs supported a seat, also of gold. It was quite without decoration or inscription. Its very plainness, oddly, made it seem very strange. I had been expecting the usual over-ornamentation, reliefs of the gods, holy words, but there were none.

Beneath the tripod, just visible to us, there was a cleft in the floor. I knew it had to be the famous chasm from which fumes emanated, coming from the very heart of the earth itself. They would enfold the Pythoness, induce in her a divine euphoria and inspire her to prophesy. The tripod's legs just barely straddled it. I wondered what kept it stable and prevented it from falling in. How deep was the chasm? Had there ever been accidents? Had some previous Pythoness fallen, ecstatic, into the bowels of the earth, never to be seen again?

More torches were lit behind the tripod, as if by magic. I realized that the temple servants must be clothed completely in black from head to toe. In the blackened room that made them quite effectively invisible. Stagecraft. There might have been dozens of them around us, doing…almost anything. The realization was unsettling, to say the least. I wondered if it was intentional, if we were supposed to be aware of the possibilities, to keep us off balance. And still more torches took fire out of the blackness; the tripod blazed brilliantly.

A curtain, so sheer as to be almost transparent, was drawn between us and the torches. It caught their light and became a shimmering wall of light between us and the sacred tripod. My drug-addled mind saw colors dancing on it.

Another bell sounded, this one less clangorous and more euphonious than the others. From the blackness emerged a woman, middle-aged, quite naked, her face perfectly blank. It was the face of someone possessed by the god, or at any rate by more of the priests' drugs. She walked as if hypnotized and took her place on the tripod.

Music began, soft, ethereal music, hypnotic music played on flutes and lyres. A drum kept the tempo. Where the musicians were, I could not tell. Like the other servants there were all in black.

Out of the darkness from which the Pythoness had come, the three priest-prophets appeared and took their place in a line at her right side. Their masks had grown larger, the countenances more fierce. In the light from the torches it was easy to believe they were demons sent by the god.

Mist, smoke, swirled up out of the chasm and enfolded the Pythoness. For long moments she inhaled it, and her face lit with ecstasy. Was it the god or a drug? She voiced a low moan, like someone in the throes of sexual pleasure. Louder and louder she groaned, moaned, cried, shrieked and her cries made a mesmerizing counterpoint to the lyres and flutes. The drumbeat continued steadily, insistently. Her body wrenched, twisted, and again she screamed. Once more I was reminded of someone in the throes of sexual madness. Apollo was possessing her. Apollo was making violent love to her, elevating her to the divine.

Gradually her cries and moans became more rhythmic, more controlled. Her voice lowered in pitch till it sounded like a man's. She wailed in time with the drumbeat. Her body twisted and contorted. "Ollu olla okkekkex!" she screamed. "Ollu olla okkekkex! Kokkalli modax merexnix olla kariadnes ollu!" Steadily, in time with the beat of the music, she intoned those mysterious syllables. She danced, she writhed, she chanted, the music played, the scrim between us and her shimmered and undulated, keeping time with her cries and contortions. We were hearing the voice of the god, the language of the gods.

There was a sudden flash of light, so bright it blinded me. I covered my eyes with my hands, and when I looked again the Pythoness had been transformed. In her place on the tripod was a beautiful young man, a naked young man in his mid-teens. He was slim, he was muscular, he had the body of a superb athlete. No, of a young god. His skin was as smooth and white as the purest alabaster, and his hair was radiant gold. So bright it seemed almost to be a halo around his head; so radiant it might almost have been woven from the

Golden Fleece. And his lips and eyelids were bright gold as well; in the dark room they seemed to catch what light there was and to flash in it. His penis was erect, and his pubic hair was shaved. Apollo. The young Apollo himself was there before us.

His body swayed and contorted in time with the music, as the Pythoness' had. Gradually, slowly but steadily, the beat quickened. Soon it was moving at a furious pace. It grew louder and louder in a wild, sensuous crescendo. He repeated the mystical words the Pythoness had voiced: "Ollu olla okkekkex! Ollu olla okkekkex! Kokkalli modax merexnix olla kariadnes ollu!" And then, without touching himself, the young god achieved climax. His seed erupted into the chasm below him. God was fertilizing the earth, at least symbolically for our benefit.

I realized that I had an erection myself. But before I could think or react, the music halted. Every light in the chamber was extinguished and we stood once again in total darkness.

Then after a long moment, slowly, one by one, the torches were relit. The tripod stood empty. The trio of priest-prophets stood immobile beside it. Soon a dozen torches blazed around them. And slowly, mournfully, they intoned their translation of the Pythoness' prophecy. "Thus saith Apollo:

"Savage land, Colchis. Savage people, Colchians.
"He hangs unburied in the serpent's lair.
"His soul cries out for sleep.
"His soul cries out for transport to the bright Elysian Fields.
"The ram of gold will give him rest.
"The ram of gold will heal his soul.
"The ram of gold will heal the city's woes for all eternity.
"Beware the ram of gold."

There was another blinding flash of light. When our eyes recovered lamps had been lit all around the sanctuary. The tripod stood empty before us, separated from us by its scrim, which shimmered slightly in the light from all the lamps; there was no sign of either the Pythoness or the young god who had taken her place. The priests and their servants had vanished as well.

We looked at one another. Argus was the first to speak. "Well, that's that. Does either of you feel different for having had a divine experience?"

Jason ignored the question and peered around the chamber. "Where did that boy disappear to? I'd like to have another divine experience with him."

"You mean you don't think that was really Apollo?"

"Don't be difficult, Argus. You don't believe in the gods any more than I do."

"Lower your voice if you're going to mouth such impiety." His whisper was urgent. "The priests can still make trouble for us if they suspect us of…well, of not taking them seriously."

His words surprised me. "What on earth can they do to us, cast an evil spell or something?"

"Don't be so naïve, Acastus. Lord, but you can be slow on the uptake. Let's get back to the inn and get a good night's sleep. We have a long journey ahead of us."

Well, we had what we came for, we had our prophecy—for all it might be worth. Somehow the priests knew that the fleece was in Colchis, and we had paid them enough for them to tell us so. Still groggy from whatever drug the priests had given us, we headed back to our inn, lighter by a load of gold, and slept long and deeply.

In the morning, knowing we had a long journey back to Iolcus facing us, we had a large breakfast and fortified ourselves with wine. Jason went off to fetch our servants; when they arrived they packed our things. We dressed for travel, settled our account with the innkeeper and headed outdoors.

The day was grey; the sky was as dark as I had ever seen it, threatening a rainstorm. There was a chilly north wind. Spring had not quite settled in yet, it seemed.

Across the lane from the inn there was someone sleeping on the ground, presumably a beggar. Our party made a lot of noise leaving the inn, and he woke. Still groggy, rubbing his eyes, he got to his feet. He was a boy, or rather a young man, fifteen years old or so, slender, muscular, with thick curly black hair and a deep olive complexion. Quite a beautiful young man, an almost archetypal Greek athlete. He was using a travel bag as his pillow. I wondered what could have led to his obviously reduced circumstances.

He picked up his bag, crossed the street and approached us. Or rather, he approached Argus. "You are the famous shipbuilder Argus, are you not?"

Argus did not want to be bothered; he kept walking. "Yes, I am. You must excuse us. We're leaving on a journey."

"I want to go with you."

He paused. "The begging here must be better than it could possibly be in Iolcus."

"I have been waiting for you all night. I am no beggar."

"Of course." Argus looked over his shoulder at me with an expression that asked *"Why me?"*

Jason was walking beside me. I saw him eye the boy with a speculative air. "Don't be disagreeable, Argus. We can always use an extra hand with our luggage."

Argus snorted at him. "Can't you wait till we get back to Iolcus to exercise your libido?"

"The boy looks quite fit. He can be of use."

"That's what I mean. Really, Jason, have you no self-control?" Argus lowered his voice to a whisper. "He is almost certainly in the employ of the priests."

Jason huddled with him. "If your suspicions are correct, Argus, everyone in this part of Greece is in their employ. We'll be spied on whether we take this boy or not."

But the boy had overheard this. "I promise you I am not one of their spies. In fact I'm anxious to get away from them." He smiled quite engagingly. "My name is Hylas. Please, take me with you."

Argus and Jason drew apart and signaled me to join them. "Don't you realize who he is?" Argus whispered. There was a note of urgency in his voice. "Taking him would quite certainly earn us the enmity of the priests—if not their actual wrath."

I was lost. "Who is he, then?" I looked back over my shoulder at him. He stood, tall and upright, watching us with an expression of concern or anticipation.

Jason was insistent. "Yes, I realize who he is. That is quite beside the point."

"It is precisely the point. We've come all this way to win the friendship of the priesthood here. Why destroy that over this boy?"

But Jason wanted him, and that was that. He made it quite clear he intended to have the boy and would not take no for an answer.

Hylas took up some of the luggage and we left Delphi as quickly as we could. Jason was happy, Argus was irritable, and I was quite bewildered. The servants, at least, were glad to have their loads lightened a bit.

* * *

The threatening storm held off, and we made good time despite the steepness of the roads. Going down, I had not appreciated, when we came down to the city, just how steep they were.

The boy Hylas shouldered more than his share of the luggage yet walked with a lightness and grace, even elegance. I could tell the other servants were glad to have him with us. But I was still quite puzzled by what Argus had said about him, by the concern he had voiced.

It was clear Jason wanted the boy. He kept walking beside him, chatting him up, more and more overtly. But Hylas, also quite clearly, had no interest in him. His attentions were on Argus. I confess that Jason's growing frustration gave me a good bit of amusement.

Argus, to his credit I suppose, did not want Hylas. Whether that was because of his concern that the boy was a priestly spy or a simple lack of sexual interest, I couldn't tell. I prodded him. "Half the men in Greece would be delighted to have a young man like that show interest in them."

He grumped. "I'm an old man on a long journey. Leave me alone to ache on peace."

So both of my companions were frustrated by Hylas' presence in our party. I enjoyed it, probably more than I should have.

On one of our rest stops I approached Hylas. "You're causing quite a bit of drama among us. Is it usual for you?"

He blushed. "I'm afraid I've never felt as attractive as men keep telling me I am."

"You are." I smiled.

"Please, Prince Acastus. You are not much older than I am. I prefer older men."

"So do I. You are too young for my taste. Don't worry, I'm not propositioning you."

"I wish Prince Jason felt that way."

"Jason propositions every man he meets. He is a politician." I smiled. "I'm only a sculptor."

"The priests say he is the real power in Iolcus, or will be soon enough."

"The priests confide in you?" I couldn't have been more surprised to hear him say it.

"Well, they did." He returned my smile shyly.

Then I noticed that his bag was partly open, and a golden gleam showed from inside, a mass of fiber like a, well, like a golden fleece. It took me a moment to realize what it was. "Do they know you've taken that?"

He shrugged. "It's only gilt, not real gold. There are no more pilgrims at Delphi now, and none are due for weeks. The priests have so much gold it practically oozes out of their pores. They'll never miss it until they miss me myself, or if they do they can have a wigmaker fabricate a new one easily enough."

Now that I understood who he was, or rather who he had been, I could see traces of powdered alabaster in his hair and in the wrinkles around his eyes. God was with us, quite literally.

"Tell me the truth, Hylas, why have you come with us?"

"Let's just say I find being a god boring, especially when that god is really just a servant. I want adventure. I want to go with you when you sail to find the Golden Fleece."

Young men as beautiful as Hylas usually get everything they want. I looked him up and down and I knew that, for better or worse, I was seeing an Argonaut. And who knew, having someone who can wrap men around his finger might well prove an asset. Of course, sooner or later he'd meet someone who could dominate him; that was inevitable. But…

Chapter Four
The First of the Argonauts Arrive

"Well, we knew that Phrixus had fled east on the ram. And Colchis is farther east than any land we know of." Argus was explaining to Pelias our best guess as to the meaning of the prophecy. "Or at least that has always been the story."

Pelias had had too much wine, as usual. And he bore the marks of the ghost, or whatever it was, which had kept up its relentless assault on him during our absence . He wore long, heavy robes despite the spring weather, but the robes could not cover his face, hands and arms. There were cuts, bruises, scratches; even his beard was matted with dried blood. It was plain enough to see why he was eager to believe the oracle, or at any rate to believe the most convenient interpretation of it. "Colchis, you say. Everyone has heard of that place. Everyone has. But where the devil is it?" He looked from Argus to me. "Is it even real?"

I shrugged. "The oracle seems to think so."

"We tried to get the priests to give us more specific information, but you know how these things are." Jason wanted to be helpful, if only in the interest of calming Pelias so we could get him to make a decision and perhaps actually to do something. "They talk in riddles. And they limit themselves to one riddle per customer."

"But you saw the god." Pelias was anxious for positive news. "You received his word that the city will be healed."

"For all eternity." Argus, as usual, did not try to hide his skepticism. And he was careful not to tell Pelias that the "god" had come back to Iolcus with us and was now one of the palace servants.

"Then go. Take our best ship and sail to Colchis, wherever it is. Find it. Find the Golden Fleece and find the body of Phrixus. Bring them home. Iolcus must be released from this curse. There must be no more deformed children born here, no more premature deaths, no more women dead in childbirth." He hardly needed to add, *And I myself must suffer no more.* His battered body said it more eloquently than his tongue could.

We turned to go, but before we reached the door, Pelias let out a shriek. We looked back. His face had been slashed. Blood flowed. He held up his hands, trying to stanch it, but the cuts were too deep and the flow too copious.

Argus rushed to his side and pressed a linen cloth to his face. "Call servants. Have them run and fetch a painkilling salve."

"Yes, Argus. At once!" Jason rushed out. I heard him calling the servants.

Pelias cried out again. The blood streaming down his face was mixed with tears. I thought, *Yes, he is a fit king for a city like Iolcus.* He was my father, but we had never been close and I had no love for him. But seeing him there, bent and tortured, I could not help feeling pity. Pity mixed with fear.

* * *

Argus, Jason and I sat around the table in the royal council chambers. With us were three of Pelias's councilors, two priests and a magistrate named Gereontes. With Pelias crippled by his wounds and his abject fright, it had fallen to us to govern the city. As the male members of the ruling house, the heaviest responsibility naturally fell on Jason and me. It was not a role I relished, but there was no one else.

In our absence Pelias had turned to his priests for advice on dealing with the ghost but, not surprisingly, they hadn't been of much use. All they gave him was the usual priestly gibberish: pray, sacrifice to this god or that one—nothing that had helped him deal with the situation in the least. To be fair, no one else had come up with anything helpful either. So finding the Golden Fleece and giving Phrixus his rest seemed the only available course of action or at least the most plausible one.

Argus was as unhappy as I was assuming a leadership role. He grumbled repeatedly that he was a naval architect, a shipbuilder, not a policy maker—and what's more, he was not even an Iolcan. But there was Jason. Jason would happily have assumed the throne on his own, but I suspected that Argus trusted him as little as I did, and he was a decent enough man to work with me and not let it happen. If Jason sensed that Argus and I were conspiring to keep his ambition in check, he never let it show.

Pelias, before his incapacity, had been a jealous king; he had never chosen strong men to be his advisers. And he never let even them assume much authority, with the result that none of them had the experience to govern properly. So the burden of rule fell to our little triumvirate, with not much more than token participation of the councilors.

"So, how do we proceed?" Jason asked.

"How do you mean?" I confess I was a bit out of my depth. "Are you asking what we do about Pelias? Or how do we decide what to do about the ghost?"

"Either. Both."

"And then," Argus added, with clear distaste, "there is the oracle. And the question of Colchis. Would it be wise to mount an expedition to a place we can't even be certain exists? Can the city afford such an undertaking, even if we decide we want to do it?"

"What else can we do? Nothing else seems to have much chance of working." Jason clapped his hands, signaling that we wanted wine.

Hylas was waiting on us. He got a skin and poured for us.

Since our arrival back in Colchis he had charmed everyone he met, from Pelias all the way down to the kitchen help. I strongly suspected Jason had taken him to bed already. At any rate he had been privy to our councils. Since he already knew about our planned expedition, there was no reason to exclude him. And of course there was always the chance he might recall something of use he had heard the priests say.

"Perhaps," Jason mused, "we can persuade Pelias to abdicate."

"In favor of you, Jason?" I couldn't help laughing at the frankness of his ambition.

He shrugged. "You've told us often enough you have no desire to succeed him. Who does that leave but me?"

"Who indeed?" Argus was amused as I was. "What a noble man you are, Jason, offering to rule a haunted city. What would you do as king that you aren't able to do now?"

"Iolcus is not haunted. There is no such thing as a curse. Any sensible man will tell you so."

Kallikrates, the priest of Hecate, spoke up. "There is most certainly such a thing. How else to account for the city's sorry state?"

"How indeed?" asked the priest of Athena, Melicanthus.

Argus ignored them and went on with the discussion. "And yes, Jason, there *is* the ghost. Whether it is Phrixus or not, whether it is cursing the city or not, it is real. We've seen it, and we've seen what it does to Pelias. You are so brave to want to take his place and suffer as he does." He smiled a benign smile.

It seemed to come as a new thought to Jason, one he didn't like at all. "Then…then…we must do as the oracle advised. We must find a way to give this specter its rest. We must go to Colchis, wherever it may be, find the Golden Fleece and bring the body of Phrixus back to its native city for burial."

"And end the curse." I was more and more amused. "Which you just told us does not exist."

"Stop baiting me, Acastus."

Kallikrates assumed a more confident tone. Talk of the oracle was right in his line. "The words of the Pythoness cannot be disregarded lightly except at grave peril to the city."

I could see the twinkle in Argus' eye. He had been itching for a chance to goad the priests. "The words of the Pythoness, Kallikrates: 'Ollu olla okkekkex.' Pure gibberish. It was the priests, not the Pythoness, who told us to go to Colchis."

"Even so." Kallikrates was serene.

"So we have your word, the word of a priest, that the words of priests must be obeyed. Splendid."

Gereontes spoke up. "You really should restrain your impiety, Argus. Kallikrates is here in his capacity of councilor and priest. He speaks for the goddess. Mocking him."

"Or at least he claims to. Toying with priests is harmless fun, Gereontes." Argus was plainly enjoying himself. "So little fun is left to me, at my age. Don't deny me this, too."

"I deny no one anything," said Kallikrates solemnly. "I merely serve the city. And the gods, of course."

"Of course."

"At any rate," Gereontes went on, "we have no definite

intelligence concerning Colchis. I have always heard it is at the far end of the Black Sea. And I understand that there is a great deal of amber there. Troy, it is said, has opened up trade routes to the place. An expedition—" He looked from one of us to the other. And just like that he dropped his pious tone and became the practical-minded councilor. "If we could establish good relations with the Colchians, the amber trade would make Iolcus the wealthiest city in Greece, hence the most powerful. Dispelling the curse would be an added benefit."

"If what you've heard can be relied on."

Jason had not appeared to be much interested in our discussion once Argus and I scotched his ambitions. He clapped his hands for more wine, and Hylas took an amphora from a sideboard and refilled our cups.

But this talk of wealth and power made Jason perk up. "Amber, you say. We must indeed mount an expedition, then. If what you know of Colchis is accurate, we can hardly afford not to go there. We must at least go to Troy and see what we can learn there."

It seemed to me we were getting nowhere, just piling one bit of speculation on top of another. "I agree. But if the Trojans aren't helpful, how on earth do we verify anything?"

Melicanthus drew himself up importantly and said, slowly and gravely, "We need an oracle to guide us—to guide our expedition."

Argus rolled his eyes and snorted. "Another oracle!"

"What would you suggest, then? Human knowledge fails us. We need solid information about the unknown. Where should we turn but to the gods?"

"Where, indeed?" For once Argus did not sound too ironic.

* * *

On that inconclusive note our meeting ended. As we were leaving the council chamber, Hylas picked up another amphora of wine and headed toward the kitchen. I caught him by the shoulder. "Hylas, you've made yourself so completely at home here. The Delphic priests were fools not to make you happier."

"They seemed to think I should be happy merely to be in service there."

81

"You're such a sweet young man. Everyone says so."

He blushed. "Not Argus."

"Argus doesn't think anyone or anything in the world is sweet. You shouldn't let him bother you."

He looked away shyly. "It does bother me. I told you once, my taste is for older men, your highness. I'd give anything to have him love me. I thought, or hoped, that by entering your service I might—I might—"

His shyness was so very fetching. "Please, Hylas, just call me Acastus. Everyone does. Royal privilege is not a thing I wear well."

"Yes, your highness." He looked quickly away, embarrassed. "I mean, Acastus."

"Who are your parents? They must have been proud to see you in service at Delphi."

"My parents died not long after I was born. They were killed by a bear in the forest. I was raised by an aunt and uncle, but I was always a burden to them. They never missed a chance to let me know it. So as soon as I could, I left. And the priests at Delphi…they used me any way they wanted to." His meaning was only too clear.

"And so here you are." I smiled at him and put a hand on his shoulder. "You're like a poor orphan in a fairy tale, suddenly fining himself in the king's house."

Finally he looked me in the eye and smiled at me. "I guess that's what I am. Living here in the palace and attending beautiful men like Prince Jason." He looked away again. "And you."

I was embarrassed to hear him say it. I had to shift the conversation to a more neutral topic. "Tell me, Hylas, do you know anything about sculpture?"

"Statues? No. I mean, I've seen plenty of them, of course, and I know that's what you do, but—"

"No one has ever asked you to pose? You are such an attractive young man."

"Me? Pose for a statue?"

"Yes, you, pose for a statue. You know that I'm a sculptor."

"Well, yes, but—"

"I have been thinking of doing a study of Zeus and Ganymede. You would be a perfect model for it. Any god would be a fool not to be enchanted by you."

He blushed. "But I—I—"

"I've been pestering Argus to be my Zeus. The two of you together... It might give you a chance to get close to him. Please, agree to pose for me."

Hylas was wide-eyed; he seemed to have no idea what to make of the situation. "You could order me to, you know."

"Yes, I know. But that isn't my way, not at all."

Again he blushed, even more deeply. "If it would please your hi—I mean, if it would please you."

"It would. Very much. You know where my rooms are?"

"Yes, Acastus."

"Come to my workshop this evening after dinner, then."

"Yes, your hi—I don't know how long it will take me to get used to calling you by your name instead of your title." He blushed.

"Just keep reminding yourself that I'm no one special. Sooner or later, everyone realizes it."

"You are too modest."

"I'm not the one blushing."

* * *

Things in Iolcus could not continue as they were. Every night Pelias' screams filled the castle. Some nights they were so loud people could hear them echoing down in the city and even in the near countryside. They came to the place alarmed, thinking they had heard murder, or assassination.

The city's slow decline continued. Women expired giving birth to malformed children. Monstrously deformed animals were born, calves with five eyes, sheep with three sets of teeth. People left, or they died mysteriously. Nighttime screams filled the streets. Phrixus, it seemed, was no longer content to torment only the king. An air of melancholy gloom settled over everything and everyone. Something had to be done. But what? What would really work?

* * *

The six members of our council met again. By this time it was clear, inescapable, that we had to act. And the action that was needed was quite clearly an expedition to Colchis. It would, we all hoped, restore the city's prosperity by giving us a corner in the amber trade. And, who knew, it might actually rid us of the ghost. If nothing else it would give the people faith that something was being done.

Amber: the stone that seemed divine in its golden luster, divine in its airy lightness and transparency, unlike any other gem. It was believed quite literally to be divine—fragments of the sun, broken off and fallen to earth. Amber: gift of the sun god. Amber: our city's future.

Kallikrates brought a piece of that marvelous stone that had been given to the sanctuary of Artemis by a devout traveling merchant from Argos. He produced it and passed it around the council table. "Look at it, all of you. Feel its ethereal lightness. How is it possible for a stone to be so light, so airy, so golden and yet so transparent? How could it be anything but godly?"

"Equally to the point," Jason added solemnly, "how could it not make Iolcus wealthy?"

Melicanthus fingered it when it came around to him. "I agree that we must do everything we can to revitalize Iolcus' economy. But I daresay all the amber in the world will not help us till we have found a way to exorcize the ghost of Phrixus and dispel his curse. That makes an expedition to Colchis doubly urgent."

"Yes, of course. We must assemble the best crew possible." Jason was suddenly the practical leader, not the dreamer after wealth. Or perhaps he was both. "We must send heralds to every corner of Greece, inviting any athlete or soldier who thinks himself worthy. And our heralds must mention, or at least hint at, amber. That will ensure they all come. The Trojans can be daunting; we'll need a crew of at least 40 of the ablest men. No, 50. And we must arm them as formidably as we are able. Oh, and they must proclaim a country-wide truce to take effect at once and last till we return from our voyage. Let us hope everyone will agree to it.

"Argus, we will need a ship. Go to the harbor tomorrow and inspect our fleet. Find the ship that is best suited to our needs, and make plans to restore it and fit it for our journey. If none will do, we'll have to build a new one. Prepare the plans for it as quickly as possible.

"Meanwhile, Acastus and I will make the journey to Dodona to consult the oracle for directions. *Specific* directions. We must make it clear to the priests that our largesse depends on them giving us, clear, unambiguous guidance, not the usual vague prophecies."

Melicanthus bristled at this. "Vague? The words of the prophets, vague?"

Argus snorted and laughed.

"Yes, Melicanthus." Jason was resolute. "We will not leave without the intelligence we need. The priests will understand. If there's one thing they understand it's a donation."

"I protest this blasphemous talk! My cousin Philetaxis is chief priest at Dodona."

"Excellent. Then you too will come with me, to make certain he understands what we require of the god."

"But—"

I spoke up and told Jason that I had no desire for another trip to another oracle. "I should stay here to make whatever decisions need to be made to keep the city functioning."

I half expected Kallikrates and Geriontes to protest that they could assume the reins of government. Thankfully neither of them did.

We debated for a time whether to send out our heralds at once or wait till the word from Dodona had been secured. But the situation in Iolcus was worsening by the week, and we decided to lose no more time.

* * *

That night Jason came to my bedroom. I had grown not to trust him, and I didn't want him there... but then he was such a beautiful man. The light from my candles caught his hair and made it glow like a halo. Lust got the better of me.

In bed he whispered to me, "Acastus, I wish you would come with me to Dodona. We could bring that young serving boy you are so smitten with. Think of the fun we could have with him."

I was abashed to realize my interest in Hylas had been so obvious. "He is modeling for me, that's all."

"Of course."

"It is the truth, Jason."

"If that's your story... Never mind, kiss me."

We started to make love. Through it I thought of Hylas. I was not in love with the boy—he was far too young for my taste—but I admit I was infatuated by his beauty, and I couldn't help but wonder what kind of lover he'd make when he matured.

Jason's cynicism irked me. When he first came to Iolcus I told myself Aphrodite must have sent him for me. But now... Not Aphrodite but some more capricious god. And his visit that night was not out of love or even simple friendship and affection; he wanted to persuade me to travel with him to Dodona, that was all. I pushed Jason away, told him I was too tired for sex and sent him away. He was not, after all, what I wanted, not at all.

In all our deliberations Jason had never once expressed anything like piety for the dead, for the memory of my poor ancestor Phrixus. But Phrixus occupied my own thoughts. I knew all too well what it was like to have an unloving father. But to have your father actually try to murder you... It was much too horrible to contemplate. If there really was an afterlife, and if our ghost really was the ghost of Phrixus, I owed it to him to do everything I could to give his soul rest. Jason, it seemed clear to me, was much more interested in amber than in the spirit of the poor boy whose father tried to kill him.

When I finally got to sleep that night I had that same dream again—the one I'd had at Delphi. Feathers, soft, radiant white feathers enfolding me. But this time I could see they were the wings of a beautiful man. He rose into the air on his wide, magnificent wings and beckoned me, earthbound me, to join him, to love him among the clouds. When I woke, the sheets were wet. The winged man of my dreams had been more loving than Jason, who I had once wanted to love.

* * *

"It seems to me," I told Argus the next afternoon, "that we are overlooking something."

We were at the harbor, inspecting the fleet. We checked out one ship after another, and each time Argus had frowned and pronounced it unfit for the kind of long expedition we were planning. Timbers creaked ominously; in some cases wood had swelled and split; two of the ships were even infested with termites, which seemed wildly improbable to me. Not to Argus. "In Iolcus? Everything here is improbable. But what are we overlooking?"

"Athamas tried to murder both his children, remember? He was polluted with the blood of both. How can we be certain our ghost is the ghost of Phrixus and not his sister Helle?"

"Ah, the ghost again."

"Yes, the ghost again. It is at the root of all this, after all."

"And do you think a female ghost, the spirit of a small girl, could really be inflicting such violence on your father?"

"Women can be abominably violent. My sister Creusa, for instance. The old myths are filled with bloodstained, murderous women. If Phrixus made it to Colchis, whether it was on a flying ram or not, Helle may have as well."

"You have never been to Asia Minor, Acastus, to Troy and its environs. The people there tell the story that as the golden ram was soaring over that water separating the two continents, Helle slipped and fell off its back. She plunged into the water and drowned. They call the waters where it happened after her—the Hellespont."

"Yes, you've told me so before, remember? But even so. Whether she reached Colchis or not, Athamas was ultimately responsible for her death. It may be she who is haunting Iolcus now, seeking rest, or vengeance."

Argus fell uncharacteristically silent.

"The ghost we have seen is a vague apparition, Argus. It could be Helle, couldn't it?"

"It could be anyone at all. Or for all we know it could be no one at all. But try and convince Jason that we should sail no farther than the Hellespont. Try and persuade him to forget the amber trade. Good luck to you."

He was right. There was the prospect of amber in Colchis; there was none in the waters where Helle drowned. "But if the ghost—"

"Raise it in council, Acastus. If nothing else we should bless those waters and sacrifice to Helle as we pass through, out of piety for your tragic ancestress if nothing else."

"Let us hope that will be enough to propitiate her. If she is the ghost."

"Let us hope more than that. Let us hope she will bless us in return."

"Bless us?"

"Bless our expedition, Acastus. Who knows, maybe her blessing will extend to Iolcus itself."

We ended our inspection of the ships with that glum exchange hanging in the air between us.

Argus resolved to build a new ship for the venture. "We must find the best fir wood in Greece for her. She will be fitted with 50 oars, for Jason's 50 athletes. And she will be the soundest, strongest ship I have ever built. Let's get back to the palace so I can work on her design."

As we walked back though the city to the palace I decided to voice the thought that had gone unexpressed between us. "Argus?"

"Hm?"

"What if Helle doesn't bless us? Suppose our journey suffers under the same curse as Iolcus?"

We stopped walking just in front of the temple of Hecate. Argus turned to face me, put and hand on my shoulder and leaned forward to kiss my forehead. "In that case, Acastus, it may fall to you to assume the kingship, like it or no. And I know you well enough to know that would be a curse indeed."

* * *

We recruited a cadre of heralds. It was not hard to assemble a corps of willing young men; many had been conscripted as soldiers against the threat posed by the Spartan army the previous winter and were no longer needed for that service. And the prospect of getting away from Iolcus for a time was more than enough to make them willing serve as heralds. Jason and I prepared the announcement they were to make in the cities they visited. It hinted at the possibility of the amber trade quite heavily; the ghost and the curse were soft-pedaled—hardly mentioned at all, in fact.

I felt a bit guilty disguising our problem that way, but Jason kept reminding me that amber really would solve many of our difficulties. Why make a point of something that might scare men away?

Argus got to work designing the ship for the voyage. His drawings for her were beautiful, graceful, even elegant. I insisted we name it after him: the *Argo*. He protested, but I got Jason and the rest of the council to go along with me. So the *Argo* it would be. It was decided I would remain in Iolcus to oversee the preparations for quartering our legion of 50 "Argonauts," as we came to call them.

I wanted Argus to pose for my Zeus and Ganymede. But he kept insisting he was too busy, designing the ship, planning a trip to search for wood good enough to go into it, preparing for its construction. I managed to get him to sit still for me long enough to make a few sketches with Hylas, that was all. Hylas, on the other hand, was only too happy to pose.

"I told you, I love older men," he told me shyly. "Boys my age bore me. Do you think Argus would—I mean, does he want a lover?"

"You'll have to find that out for yourself, Hylas."

"How? I mean, I've never tried to, er, to attract a lover before."

"You'll learn."

"But does Argus—"

"You'll learn, Hylas. Give it time."

Argus, for his part, finally confessed to me that he was a bit smitten with Hylas—and that was why he was so reluctant to pose with him. "You know, Acastus—you must certainly realize—how incredibly beautiful the boy is. Standing there with my arms around him for long stretches of time, both of us naked… I don't know how I could restrain myself."

"Why should you? Zeus loved Ganymede. That is the whole point of this sculpture. And you're certainly aware that Hylas idolizes you. It shows when he's in your arms."

"So you want to sculpt us both with erections, is that it?"

"Leave the sculpture to me, Argus."

I must confess their mutual attraction came as a surprise to me. It is natural enough for boys to love men and vice versa, I suppose, though I never did when I was younger. And for that matter, I confess that Argus' discomfiture amused me. I only hoped he'd let Hylas down gently, if it came to that.

* * *

A few days later, Jason and Melicanthus left on their trip to Dodona, in the far northwest corner of Greece. Jason had wanted to take one of the ships, to sail south, round the Peloponnese and then northward to

89

Dodona. But Argus insisted the ships weren't even fit for a voyage that short, and so Jason and his company prepared for an overland trek.

They had quite a distance to travel; we were not expecting them back for weeks, perhaps even months. They took a good-sized train of servants, all the supplies they were likely to need and, of course, a sizable store of gold for the priests. Their trip would take them through the territory of the Dolopians, who were not always friendly, so Jason took a cadre of armed soldiers. We all hoped Iolcus would not see any trouble from Sparta while they were gone.

I had never been to Dodona and I knew it only by its reputation. "An oak. They get their prophecies from an oak." I asked Argus to explain it.

"Yes. The prophetic oak at Dodona is huge, perfectly titanic. You should see it someday. The priests claim it is the oldest living thing on earth."

"And it talks." My native skepticism was unshakeable.

"Well, no, not exactly. The priests do the talking for it."

"How convenient."

He laughed. "My cynic's nature is rubbing off on you. Good."

"Is being a cynic such a good thing, then?"

"A good cynic, Acastus, questions everything. But he does it not out of caprice or frivolity but in order to learn what is true."

"So questioning whether an oak tree can really be prophetic isn't simply a matter of common sense?"

"It comes to the same thing. But at any rate, the oak does not literally talk. The wind stirs its leaves and murmurs in them, and the priests hear the voice of the god in the whispers."

"As I said, how convenient. They don't even have to feed, clothe and house a Pythoness."

Again Argus chuckled. "You are a young man after my own heart."

"Good. Let's find Hylas and you can pose some more."

* * *

The following weeks were largely uneventful. We waited for word of Jason's progress, but none came. Argus and Hylas posed for me when I could get them both to stand still at the same time. The one unhappy bit of news was that old Epiphanes, the lighthouse keeper, died. It was a peaceful passing, unlike so many in Iolcus; he died quietly in his sleep. His son Cleobis took his place in charge of the lighthouse.

Argus worked feverishly on the design for the *Argo*. Things in Iolcus might almost have passed for normal but for the birth of an occasional litter of deformed puppies. Once a brace of blind deer wandered into the market square. A group of young boys had no trouble at all capturing and slaughtering them; their families would have liked to dine on the venison, but it was foul.

At night... Pelias' torment continued. Every midnight he cried out in agony and in terror; every morning he bore fresh bruises and cuts.

Finally Argus announced that he wanted to journey to the forest of Arcadia, where the finest, strongest, tallest fir trees in Greece were found. He mounted an expedition and took several dozen slaves with him to cut and dress the timbers for the ship.

Hylas wanted to go with him. Argus steadfastly refused. "I'll have enough on my mind without that distraction."

"Someday you'll come to your senses, Argus. Half the men in Greece would kill to have a boy that beautiful infatuated with them."

"They can have him. I'm an old man and I have a ship to build."

It was cloudy, threatening rain the day they left. Half a dozen emotions crossed Hylas' face as he watched them go; none of them were pleasant. "When will they be back, Acastus?"

"As soon as they can. Who knows how long it will take? Argus is the best shipbuilder in the country. He'll know what he's looking for. And then of course they'll have to transport it back here."

"He's going on this great expedition with you and Jason, isn't he?"

"The *Argo* is his ship. He'll have every right to come along."

He looked away shyly. "I can come, too, can't I?"

"We'll have to see. Are you strong enough to pull an oar? To hold your own against the best athletes in Greece?"

"I can try."

He wanted it very badly. It seemed unlikely there would be room for him. I put him off as best I could, but he knew I was stalling for time.

91

* * *

Late one night Pelias' shrieks woke me. There was a particular note of terror in his voice. It was too disturbing; I knew I could not get back to sleep. The servants would tend to Pelias at least as well as I could. I needed fresh air and decided to take a walk. Outside there was a chill breeze and light rain. I wrapped my cloak tightly around myself.

The fire in the lighthouse burned brilliantly. Young Cleobis had learned his job from his father all too well. In the mouth of the harbor I could see a pair of dolphins playing.

Not far from the palace was the royal graveyard. The ashes of generations of Iolcan rulers had been interred there. I don't know what impulse took me there, but I soon found myself wandering among the crypts, grave markers and cenotaphs. The lintel above the door of the largest mausoleum, and one of the oldest, was inscribed with the name of Athamas, my forebear. A stiff wind arose, and I pressed myself against the door for shelter.

"Athamas," I whispered, "my forefather, tell me what I need to know to rule well and decide wisely. Is the legend of your crime really true? Is it your son Phrixus who haunts my father, your descendent, and who curses the city?"

There was a sudden rain squall, which subsided quickly. Overhead the clouds parted, revealing a gibbous moon. I realized suddenly that I was not alone. Pelias was there, staring at me, wild-eyed. The clouds parted and a shaft of moonlight hit him. He cried out, and a broad cut opened diagonally across his chest. "Acastus? Acastus, is that you?"

"Yes, Pelias."

Blood trickled down his stomach; he made no move to stop the flow. Softly, sadly he said, "Oh. Oh. I thought you were my son Acastus." He turned and went, heading back to the palace.

If Athamas had heard me, if he tried to answer my supplication, there was no sign of it. Unless my father's presence was an answer. But then, the gods themselves never acknowledge our entreaties. Why should I have expected it of an ancestor? The rain began again and, feeling both foolish and a bit lost, I went back to the palace and my bed.

Early the next morning Hylas woke me.

"Acastus! Acastus, get up?"

"Hm?" I was groggy. I had not had enough sleep, and morning was never my time of day under the best of circumstances.

"Something is happening."

"Yes. You're disturbing my sleep."

He shook me. "There are wrestlers. Come and see."

I sat up in my bed and yawned. "Wrestlers? What the devil are you on about?"

"Well, one wrestler. And his brother is with him. Down in the city, in the very heart of everything. They are naked."

"Wrestlers always wrestle naked. You know that perfectly well, Hylas. What on earth is so urgent that I—"

"These men are beautiful. Like gods. Everyone says so. And they say they'll wrestle all comers. Come and see." He took hold of my hand and pulled.

"I can dream about beautiful men without leaving my bed."

"They are sons of Zeus, and they say they are here for the expedition of the *Argo*."

"The—?" Finally he had caught my attention. "All right, Hylas. Let me wake up, will you?" Wearily I clambered out of bed. "Hand me my tunic. Wrestlers."

A few minutes later we were in the square. Quite a crowd had gathered; evidently this wrestler was putting on quite a show. I pushed through the throng, dragging Hylas behind me.

And there they were. Two men, close enough in appearance to be twins. They were tall, beautifully muscled, with wavy black hair worn shoulder-length, piercing green eyes and rich olive complexions. One of them had another man pinned to the ground with his knees. I recognized the loser as one of our soldiers. He was a good athlete, but it appeared he had been bested by this stranger without much trouble. The other stranger—his brother?—stood by and watched, grinning. He wore only a slender support strap, evidently for modesty.

I took a step forward, and the wrestling match stopped. Our soldier got to his feet, dusted himself off and saluted. "Prince Acastus, these men—"

Before he could finish one of the strangers, the one who had been watching, cut him off. "You are Acastus, Prince of Iolcus? Greetings, sir. We have come to join your expedition."

So the message our heralds were spreading was getting results already. "Yes, I am Acastus. Welcome to Iolcus. And who might you be?"

"We are the Dioscuri, the Twins, sons of Zeus and Leda. I am Castor. This is my brother Polydeuces."

The second man, the wrestler, stepped toward me, hand outstretched. "Please sir, call me Pollux. Everyone does."

"Sons of Zeus." I hoped my tone wasn't too ironic. Every royal family in Greece claims to be descended from some divinity or other, and so does anyone with the least shred of ambition. Our own family claims descent from Poseidon, something I had never been able to take seriously. "Let me invite you to the palace."

"We are at your service, sir."

They had with them a pair of servants, to carry their luggage and equipment. There would be more than enough room for them in the palace's servant's quarters. Hylas took up some of their burden, for which they were clearly quite grateful.

As we walked we made conversation. Pollux asked me how many others had gathered for the expedition. "You are the first. But our heralds have only been abroad a very short time."

"They will come. I am sure of it." Castor exuded confidence. "Your heralds are proclaiming the greatest adventure in Greek history. How could any man of quality fail to come?"

"How indeed?" I should have expected our Argonauts to have healthy egos, but the thought had never occurred to me. And Castor, as it turned out, was the worst. "Of course, not all of our company will be the sons of gods. We could hardly expect that." Taunting athletes was, I'm afraid, a guilty pleasure.

But the Twins were impervious to my irony. Castor rambled on. "And not all will be such superb athletes. My brother is widely acknowledged to be the best wrestler in Greece. But...you said 'our company.' "

"Yes."

"Do I take it you mean Iolcus' company?"

I nodded. "I will be coming on the voyage myself."

"But...but..." The idea seemed to have left him flabbergasted. "But you are merely a scul—"

"Merely a sculptor? I'm the best swimmer in eastern Greece. No one has bested me yet." It was petulant of me, I suppose, but I couldn't resist the boast.

"Then you've never swum against my old friend Euphemus."

"No, he has never had the nerve to come here."

"He will. And he is certainly your better."

"We'll have to see about that, won't we? If he actually has the fortitude to come here." Castor's arrogance was already beginning to annoy me. I added, in the most offhand tone I could manage, "Besides, the company of *Argo* will need brains as well as brawn. If only to conduct diplomatic negotiations with the Trojans and Colchians."

It was plain to see that neither of them liked the sound of this. Athletes, especially athletes who think they're the sons of a god, always think their muscle can untie any knot. Castor said glumly, "Well…this is a Iolcan enterprise, after all. I suppose it makes sense in a way that a member of their royal house should come along, even if he has nothing much to contribute."

I of course didn't want to tell them about Argus' and my growing distrust of Jason which was more than reason enough for me to go on the expedition. And I knew this bickering was not exactly a promising way to welcome the first of the Argonauts to Iolcus. Fortunately Hylas spoke up, dispelling the tension. He introduced himself as my friend, not as a servant, which by this point he was. "You are from Sparta, are you not?"

"We are indeed of the Spartan royal house. Our sister Clytemnestra is married to King Agamemnon, and our other sister Helen is wed to his brother Menelaus."

It occurred to me they might be spying for their city's army. It was to be hoped the truce would forestall any more aggression on their part.

Hylas pressed them for news. Castor shrugged in a way that suggested no news could be more important than their presence. I was liking him less and less. But Pollux offered, "The big news is from Argos. You have heard by now that Hercules went mad, killed his family and tore down half the city walls. He is busily performing various labors for King Eurystheus as atonement."

"Oh, we were hoping he'd join *Argo*'s crew. I'd love to meet

95

him." Hylas' tone made it clear his interest in Hercules was more than idle curiosity. Are all adolescent boys so forward? I wondered. Was I, when I was as young as Hylas?

We were at the palace. "Let me have the servants make rooms ready for you. We are preparing housing for all the Argonauts, but I'm afraid it isn't quite ready yet. In the meantime, are you hungry?"

Castor barked, "Not ready? That does not sound very hospitable, Acastus. Or very promising."

"As I said, you are the first to come."

"Even so. We—"

Pollux cut him off. "Castor, stop being so rude. We were already traveling abroad from Sparta when we got word of the expedition, and we got here so quickly. I'm sure palace quarters will be fine for the time being."

I decided I liked Pollux. His brother, though... I got them installed in their rooms, left Hylas to tend to them and headed for my workshop. Sculpting always relaxed me.

I had finished all my preliminary sketches for Zeus and Ganymede. If I could shape the marble like the best of the sketches, it would be a fine piece of work indeed, one I could be proud of. I had dispatched a team of servants to Paros to secure a slab of good marble for it. It was a sea voyage, and I hoped they could find the marble quickly and get back before the *Argo* sailed. Meantime I began work on a smaller piece, a discus thrower, to fill the time.

* * *

Two days later word came from Argus that he had found a stand of firs that would yield perfect timber for the *Argo*. He requested that I send more laborers, so he could get them cut and trimmed, then brought back to Iolcus; he was, it seemed, most anxious to get started on the actual construction of the ship.

Meanwhile, a message came from Jason. "Do not finish work on the prow of the *Argo*." That was all. None of us had any idea what to make of it. But I forwarded it to Argus with one of the new laborers, since he was the one it most concerned.

Just after that, another candidate for the expedition arrived. His name was Echion, and he was the most famous herald in Greece, as renowned for his clear, loud speaking voice as for his diplomatic skill. He would make a welcome member of our company—and, happily, another one who was not an athlete.

Then two more came, another pair of twins. They were Idas and Lynceus, and they were so close to being identical they actually spoke in unison most of the time. Lynceus was famous for his extraordinarily keen eyesight. He quickly learned to amuse us by standing atop the palace, at the very pinnacle of the high city, and telling us in minute detail what was happening in the harbor, at the other end of town. He could describe the people there, their clothing, even what kind of fish a given woman had purchased in the market.

Castor obviously resented the attention Lynceus received. He kept making snide comments to the effect that he could not possibly see such and such an object Castor had deposited somewhere far away. Every time, to Castor's great annoyance, Lynceus described it perfectly.

Work was proceeding apace on the Argonauts' quarters. I hoped everything would be in place before many more arrived. We were running out of room in the palace. The dining hall was getting more and more crowded as more Argonauts arrived. Every night we held a symposium, where the conversation ranged from love to politics to religion, and they were seeming more and more like minor mob scenes.

At the same time we began receiving messages from other cities, agreeing to our proposed truce. I could not remember a time when one Greek city was not at war with another. As often as not, multiple wars had raged simultaneously, and there had even been instances of a group of cities forming a league to make war on another group. If nothing else came of our expedition to Colchis, at least the country would know a brief spell of peace on our account.

* * *

Every afternoon Castor and Pollux would exercise with our soldiers. Pollux was by far the better athlete of the two, but you would never know that from Castor's constant boasting. Echion, in addition to his talents as a herald, was an excellent archer. Most days he joined the workout.

One afternoon as he was aiming at a target at the far end of the Field of Ares, a voice behind me said, "He will miss. Wait and see."

"Really, Castor, you have to curb your jealousy of the others." I turned to face him, and to my surprise, it was not Castor at all. I quickly glanced down at Echion again. And, indeed, he missed the target.

"You are Prince Acastus? The boy Hylas told me I could find you here." The man was of middle height, with straight black hair worn below his shoulders. He smiled at me. "I am Amphiaraus, the Seer. Your expedition will need someone with my abilities."

I had heard of him. "Amphiaraus. Welcome. But...er...I'm afraid we were planning a company of athletes."

"Even so. Look down there." He pointed. "Castor is about to trip and twist his ankle."

And so Castor did.

"Now watch Echion. He will miss the target on his next shot, then make bull's-eyes on the next two, then miss again."

I watched, and it happened exactly as he said it would. I had heard of men with the gift of second sight, as it was called, but I had never met one. My experience with mystics had been limited to the priestly flummery at Delphi. With Amphiaraus, prophecy, at least in small matters, appeared to be real. And he was perfectly correct. We would be sailing uncharted waters to an unknown part of the world. A seer, a *real* seer, could easily prove to be the difference between success and failure. I welcomed him and took him down to the field to meet the others.

Our venture was beginning to look even more interesting than I had expected.

* * *

One by one our company grew. We quartered them in the palace, presented them to Pelias, did everything we could to make them happy and content to wait for the *Argo's* construction and launch. And they were in fact happy enough as our guests, enjoying the hospitality of the palace, exercising on the Field of Ares with our soldiers and each other. Predictably, courtesans both male and female from the city came and plied their trade, and the Argonauts were only too happy to, er, patronize them.

Our band was joined by Atalanta, the famous virgin huntress, the fastest runner in Greece. She had dedicated her virginity to Artemis, who in turn rewarded her with her great speed. Every afternoon, exercising with the others, she would run laps around the Field of Ares, with such amazing swiftness it seemed miraculous. And so, thanks to the goddess, it was. Castor expressed, shall we say, amatory interest in her, but she had no trouble leaving him in the dust every time he got too forward. And she would laugh at him, quite pointedly, which piqued him even more.

"Women are supposed to submit to men," he told her irritably. "Learn your place."

Atalanta laughed at him as usual. "I have already learned *your* place, Castor, which is far behind me." I took an instant liking to Atalanta.

Another newcomer was the famous warrior from the Lapith tribe, Caeneus by name. Caeneus was quite extraordinary: He had once been a woman and had been transformed into a man by Aphrodite. He formed a quick bond with Atalanta, who said he was the only man among us who could understand her. Castor and a few of the others taunted him as "man-woman," but when he defeated all comers in various athletic games—the discus, the javelin, the high jump—they stopped laughing.

Whether it was the woman in him showing through or just natural beauty, I found Caeneus quite uncommonly attractive, and I asked him to pose for my discus thrower. He was happy to oblige me. Yet he made it clear he had no erotic interest in me. "Do you proposition all your models?" he asked.

"Not all, certainly, but most." I couldn't help grinning at the question; no one else had ever asked. "I only choose the most beautiful men."

"Good. Then you don't need me for a sex partner. Work your marble, and let me tend to my own flesh."

Over the following weeks we became good friends. His candor, and his refusal to defer to my princely whims, was so refreshing. And he was so astonishingly handsome, even among our company of athletes, heroes and demigods, that I took pleasure merely being near him.

* * *

A week later the building for the Argonauts was finally complete. It was meant to be temporary, lasting only long enough to quarter them till we sailed, so construction went quickly. It was located next to the palace, so the move was not at all burdensome and most of the company were only too happy to move there. Hylas had taken charge of staffing it with a full compliment of servants; the boy was proving resourceful and invaluable as an assistant to me.

But Castor, predictably, found the move an insult to his dignity as a demigod. "So we are not deemed fit to live in the palace."

"You were told your first day here that the Argonauts would have their own quarters, their own building, Castor. And you complained then about being quartered in the palace, if I recall."

He grumped and groused, but he went to the new building with everyone else, and within a few days he was acting as if he were its sole proprietor.

Pelias had been as gracious to the visitors as he could manage, I suppose, but what with his nightly torment and his heavy consumption of wine he was half mad, no more a fit host than he was a fit king. But having the first of the Argonauts stay in the palace temporarily and hear the screams in the night and witness the purple haze that was the ghost did serve one purpose: It made quite irrevocably clear to them why Iolcus needed their help and why this expedition was necessary at all. I even heard Amphiaraus explain to the others that if the crew of the *Argo* could not manage to dispel the curse it might well spread to other cities, perhaps even to the whole of Greece.

* * *

The ghost… the prophetic ability of Amphiaraus… the preternatural strength of Pollux in the wrestling games and the speed of Atalanta…the uncanny vision of Lynceus… It was all beginning to erode my skeptic's nature, my conviction that there was nothing in the world that could not be explained simply and rationally. I had, I suppose, experienced something like the presence of the gods, or at least something not easily explainable, a few times—the overpowering lust I felt the first time I saw Jason, for instance; and those dreams, those feathery dreams that seemed so inescapably real—but lust was lust and dreams were merely dreams. There had never been anything to shake my confidence in mind and reason.

And then...

* * *

I could not remember the night any more vividly. It had been a week since the completion of the Argonauts' house. Several more volunteers had come to Iolcus. There was Idmon, another seer. And Mopsus the Lapith, an old companion of Caeneus. More were coming every day; soon enough our company would be complete.

Then, late one night, as I lay in my bed waiting for sleep, I heard Hylas' voice in the corridor outside my room. "Acastus! Acastus! The most wonderful thing is happening. Come and see!"

"Come in, Hylas."

The door opened. He was out of breath. Whatever was happening had excited him. He was so agitated I couldn't help laughing. "What is it? More wrestlers?"

"Gods!" He rushed to the bedside and tugged at my arm. "Or demigods, or daemons, or... I don't know. Something marvelous. Some*one* miraculous!"

I yawned and got out of bed. Whatever had excited him had to be mostly a matter of a boy's fantasy. There was, I knew—or thought I knew—nothing in the world really miraculous. "All right, I'm coming. Let me get dressed, will you?"

"Hurry. I'll wait in the hallway."

I yawned again and muttered, "Why can't miracles happen in broad daylight?"

When I joined Hylas in the hall a few moments later, I was still feeling grumpy. "All right, take me to your miracle."

"This way." He started to lead me toward the ascending staircase that led to the palace roof.

It surprised me. "We're not going down to the city?"

"You'll see."

"Don't be so smug. What is happening?"

"You'll see."

101

I rolled my eyes. "Fine. I'll see. This better be worth getting out of bed for, that's all."

The corridor was dark. "Shouldn't we take a torch or some candles?"

"You'll want your eyes to be adjusted to the darkness."

"Stop being so mysterious, Hylas. What are we—"

"Look."

The doorway onto the roof faced east. It was one of those nights when, quite by accident, the moon happened to be rising directly opposite the door, framed by it. It was so large and white as it topped the horizon it dazzled my eyes for a moment. By the time they adjusted we were out on the roof.

Iolcus was calm that night; I don't think I had ever seen it so peaceful. The lighthouse fire blazed and bathed the city in its bronze light. Aphrodite gazed out over the Aegean with that timeless look the old sculptors did so well but that I myself could never seem to master. The sea rolled gently, and tender waves lapped the shore. Boats bobbed like toys in the harbor below us; even our decrepit fleet looked majestic in the glow from Aphrodite's torch. There was only the gentlest breeze. I looked down on it and thought for the thousandth time how much I loved it all.

On a similar night, with the city bathed in moonlight and torchlight, Jason had once stood side by side with me, looking out over our city. "Look at how still it is, Acastus. Still like the sepulcher. Iolcus is a city crying out for tragedy."

But I could not let myself think such things about my city, not that night. I chose to focus on its beauty, its serenity.

Normally the moon's light washes out the fainter stars. But they blazed, thousands of them, despite the moon's brightness that night. Even the Milky Way, faint as it was, showed improbably clear and bright, arching across the night sky. It was all so very beautiful. I found myself thinking that, yes, Aphrodite must love us all, must love Iolcus.

I sighed and yawned; he had gotten me out of bed to see the stars, which I had seen a thousand times before. Iolcus and the sky above it were especially beautiful that night, but... "Fine, Hylas, I've seen it. Now let me get back to bed. I need my sleep."

He caught my arm. "You haven't seen anything yet. Wait."

"Do I have to?"

"Look! Look up!"

There were meteors. Suddenly a dozen or even more of them shot across the heavens. Then even more of them appeared, streaked and died. They radiated from a place near the Milky Way. "I've seen meteors before, Hylas. I want to go to sleep."

"No, look!" He pointed east, toward the rising moon.

I followed his gesture. There was something crossing the moon's face. A bird? Then another one followed the first. They circled one another playfully. More meteors, birds? I was more and more annoyed. "Fine. I've seen them. Now I'm going back to bed."

"Stop being so impatient, Acastus. Watch and wait."

I resigned myself to remaining on the roof and watching the sky and the city, at least till Hylas was satisfied or too tired to be so insistent.

Those birds crossed the face of the moon again. They were larger now; they were flying toward us. There was something...not right...about their outlines. They were...I wasn't certain...larger than they ought to be, or not properly formed, or... I watched as they approached us. More and more rapidly they flew, swifter than the swiftest birds I had ever seen, swifter than the speediest falcons.

Closer and closer they came. And finally I was able to make out their forms quite definitely. They were not birds at all. They were men, winged men, soaring through the moonlit sky to Iolcus. In only moments they were above us, and in the bright moonlight and the fire from the lighthouse I could see them clearly. Two men, lean, muscular; they had the bodies of young athletes. And their wings, their marvelous wings spread impossibly wide. One of them had wings of purest white; his companion's wings were white tinged with black around the edges. But the light of the moon made their wings glisten like polished silver. They swooped and dived in the air over us, then flew off back toward the moon.

More meteors filled the sky, and more. A rain of them lit the night sky, and the winged men were outlined against them.

I was dumbstruck. Men like birds, men with wings, men able to fly above the earth where the rest of us were bound. Men arriving like gods, amid a shower of stars. In only an instant I remembered my dreams, the feathered man embracing me, enfolding me in his wings, carrying me into the sky. It could not be; those dreams could not have been foreshadowings. Argus had taught me only too well what frauds prophecies were.

I blinked stupidly as I watched them fly away into the night. Winged men. Such a thing was not possible, yet there they were. Creatures from dreams were not real, yet these men were there before me. They circled the lighthouse and their wings caught its light and blazed bright and golden.

They rounded it three times and flew toward us again. When they were over the palace they swooped, pinwheeled, soared upward then down again. One of them, the one with the pure white wings, flew just a few feet above my head, and I heard him laugh as he passed. "Watch out for falling stars!" His voice was sweet, musical. The tip of his wings nearly brushed my face, and for an instant I was frozen, lost momentarily, impossibly, in my dreams.

Hylas squeezed my hand. "You see? They've been flying over the palace for nearly 20 minutes now."

I couldn't take my eyes off them. "Yes, but...but who are they? *What* are they? And what on earth are they doing here?"

More laughter came from the sky. They flew nearer to us, ever lower. Then gradually, with the lightness and gentleness of a falling feather, they landed on the roof and stood side by side not ten feet from us.

For the first time I could make out their features. Tall, lean men with pale complexions and thick, curly blond hair. Their eyes were so astonishingly blue that they seemed to glow in the moonlight like a cat's. Their jaws were square and resolute, and when they smiled at us their smiles were perfectly dazzling. Their skin was pale white, quite unlike the usual complexions of Greeks. They were as beautiful as any men I had ever seen...and they had wings, like young gods.

One of them, the one whose wings were tipped with black, reached out a hand toward us. "Greetings. I am Zetes, and this is my brother Kalais. We are the sons of the North Wind, and we seek Acastus, prince of this city."

"I... I am Acastus." I stepped forward and took his hand. "Welcome to Iolcus."

Suddenly from behind me came a deep voice. Pelias was there. "Demons! Winged demons, come to carry me off to hell!"

I turned and looked. He was standing there trembling, hand outstretched, pointing at Kalais and Zetes. There were fresh wounds; a large cut extended up his left cheek across the bridge of his nose, and his tunic was stained with blood. Several feet away, it was possible to smell the wine.

It was so unusual for Pelias to leave his chamber anymore for any reason at all. His presence there, indeed the entire situation, was so completely unexpected I froze, quite uncertain how to react. But Kalais stepped forward and bowed to Pelias, slowly and gracefully. "No, sir. Most certainly not. You are King Pelias, are you not?" He glanced at me from a corner of his eye, and I nodded. "We are here, sir, to join the expedition to free you and your city from this curse."

"No!" Pelias bellowed. "Demons from the pit of Hades!"

Zetes joined his brother, and they both bowed deeply. "No, sir. Honestly, we are here for your benefit. We will use all our abilities in your aid."

"Fiends!" he screamed. "Agents of hell!" His body began to tremble violently, and he fell. The ghost, the purple fog, appeared and enveloped him. Lying there, his body writhed and contorted. Blood gushed from that fresh cut on his face. I tore a strip of cloth from my nightclothes and used it to stanch the flow. The only thought in my mind, that instant, was a recollection of Jason's words: a city crying out for tragedy.

But kneeling over him, I whispered in the most reassuring tone I could manage, "Sh. No, Pelias, they are friends. They are here to help you, to help all of us." I glanced up at them. They stood there, side by side, watching, not moving. For all I knew, Pelias was right, and they really were demons from the underworld. But they were so beautiful. Could agents of hell be so lovely, so graceful? My mind told me that, yes, they might be what Pelias suspected. But my every instinct told me the reverse.

Kalais stepped forward and got down on one knee beside me. And he did, the tip of his wing brushed my face. And I felt the same thrill I had felt all those nights in my dreams. My dreams were made real, at least for that instant. Gently he stroked Pelias' brow with the tips of his fingers. In the sweetest, most reassuring voice I had ever heard he told Pelias, "Sleep, sad king. All will be well in time. You'll see. Sleep now."

105

His words and his calming voice worked. Pelias closed his eyes and, for the first time in months, smiled.

Hylas and I managed to walk him back down to his bedchamber, and a pair of servants got him into his bed. Soon enough he would be asleep. I hoped the ghost would leave him to his rest, for once. The winged men followed.

Kalais and Zetes were twins, perfectly identical except for the black tipping on Zetes' wings. They were such astonishingly beautiful men I could hardly take my eyes off them. I led them to the dining hall, where Hylas waited for us with an amphora of wine.

We made conversation, the kind of small talk strangers make on meeting. They had come from Corinth, where our herald had spread word of the *Argo*'s expedition. They'd have been at Iolcus sooner, but they had encountered numerous storms on the way. I told them about the new quarters for the Argonauts and asked if they needed any special accommodations. "I mean, can you sleep in ordinary beds, or..?"

"We'll be fine." Zetes smiled a sly smile.

Kalais added, "You'd be amazed at what we can do in a bed." He reached across the table and stroked my forearm, and he lowered his voice. "You *will* be amazed."

I pulled back reflexively. But Kalais fixed me in his gaze and smiled the same mischievous smile as his brother. I stammered, uncertain how to react. It was not that I didn't find him attractive; I was in fact quite dazzled by him. And it wasn't that I wasn't flattered by his flirting, not at all. But my brief, disappointing infatuation with Jason had made me skeptical of romance, maybe more than I should have been.

"Relax, Acastus." Zetes was more than slightly amused. "My brother flirts with everyone." He shrugged and grinned again. "So do I, for that matter. I can't wait to meet the other Argonauts."

Hylas offered to show them to their quarters, we said good night, and they left.

* * *

Twins. Beautiful men. I had never, er, disported myself with a pair of twins, and I found myself wondering what it would be like. Did they play together? Would they?

Then suddenly another thought struck me: Kalais and Zetes. Castor and Polydeuces. Idas and Lynceus. So many royal houses in Greece had produced twins. Hercules, son of Zeus, had a mortal twin, Iphicles. And there were so many more. Alone in my bedchamber it struck me: was I born a twin? Did I have a brother, and was he exposed at birth at the shrine of Hecate? Was it really he whose ghost haunted us and cursed the city? It seemed only too plausible, or at least possible. It would explain why the city's decline began around the time of my birth.

My old nurse Anticleia lived in a tiny room at the far end of the palace. I rushed there; if anyone knew the truth, it would be she. I knocked at her door agitatedly and went in without waiting to be invited.

Anticleia was older, tinier and frailer than seemed possible. Her back was bent with age, her hands deformed by arthritis. She was in her nightclothes, black homespun like every garment she owned. She went wide-eyed when she heard my voice in her room. "Acastus. I thought you had forgotten all about me, forgotten that I'm alive, even."

I was too anxious to make small talk. I asked her what I wanted to know. She shook her head sadly and turned away from me. "I don't remember a thing, not a thing about your birth."

"Look me in my eye and say that."

Still gazing at the wall she repeated, "Can you not see? Age has made me blind. Nothing. I remember nothing of it. Nothing at all."

I took her by the shoulder. "You are lying, Anticleia. Tell me."

"Nothing. There is nothing I can say."

I narrowed my eyes. "You were sworn to secrecy. Is that it?" Another thought struck me. "You! You were the one who exposed the child!"

She would not look me in the eye. I knew I had found the truth.

"Why, Anticleaia? Was he deformed? Limbless? Eyeless? Or was he simply one prince too many?"

She began crying. "It was all so long ago. It was my duty. How many times…" She sobbed. "How many times has your father cried that we killed the wrong son?"

The words cut me, and cut me more deeply than anything my father had ever said or done to me. Without saying another word I left Anticleia to her tears and blindness and went back to my room.

107

In the night I heard my father's cries as the ghost tormented him once more. And in my bed in the darkened room I whispered, "I don't know who you are, whether Phrixus or Helle or my unnamed brother. But torture him, make his soul cry as mine does tonight. Make him hurt, make him bleed."

I prayed. For the first time since childhood, I prayed. For the rest of the Argonauts to come, for the ship to be built, for all of us to embark on our expedition, to leave Iolcus and its ghost and its malformed children and its countless other sorrows.

A city crying out for tragedy, Jason had called it. How much more tragedy could a city bear? Alas, I was to find out.

Chapter Five
Kalais; Orpheus; Love

"So, who is it, Pelias?"

I had promised myself I would not confront him about my twin brother. But I had been silent about his behavior—and about his treatment of me—for far too long. I had had a brother, and thanks to Pelias he was no more, and he had lived only the briefest moment. I had gone to the king's bedchamber by the first light of dawn. I wanted him sober and therefore accountable.

He roused himself from sleep slowly. His face, arms, torso were covered with cuts and bruises. He seemed to have trouble opening his eyes and focusing them. "Wh—who—?"

"Wake up, Pelias, and talk to me."

Finally he came to his senses. "Oh. It's you."

"Yes, it's me. You remember, the son who has to run your kingdom for you. I want an answer."

"An answer." His face was blank.

"Who is the ghost, Pelias? Is it really Phrixus or even Helle? Or is it someone else, like your brother Aeson or my own nameless brother?"

"It is too early in the morning for this, Acastus. Leave me in peace."

"I am here now precisely because it is early. If I wait two hours, you'll be drunk again. Who is the ghost? Does it talk to you? Does it have a name?"

He sat on the edge of his bed. "You know its name. You know it perfectly well, as well as I do. It is Phrixus."

"Not my brother? Not the infant you had slaughtered?"

For a long moment he fell silent. He wanted to ask me how I

109

knew, how I had learned. He looked at me with a trace of terror in his eyes. Finally he said, "It is Phrixus." His voice was soft and sad. "Now go away. Have one of the servants bring me a flask of wine."

He lay back down in his bed and closed his eyes. Sober or drunk he was much the same man. That was that.

* * *

I went to the roof of the palace to be alone and think. Iolcus' decline had to be related to Pelias' dissolution, but how? There had been other wine-mad, irresponsible kings, yet somehow their cities had survived them. All I could think was that the ghost really was a ghost and really was Phrixus, and he really had cursed the city. But that went against my every rational instinct.

From out of the sky, from out of the sun, there came a voice. "Acastus, do you want to be alone? May I join you?" It took me a moment to realize it was Kalais. I looked up and shielded my eyes from the sun. Before they could adjust to the brilliant light, he landed gently on the roof beside me.

"You'll have to forgive me, Kalais. I'm not exactly used to having company swoop down upon me from the sky."

He laughed. "If you knew how many times I've heard that…"

"You're… you…" I looked him up and down. It was the first time I had seen him in broad daylight. His hair was fine and golden, like the sun itself. His eyes were as blue as the sky—bluer, even. His body was perfect, simply perfect, wings and all. "I'm not usually tongue-tied. But you and your brother…"

"What about us?" He was clearly amused by me.

"Well, I mean, you have wings. You can fly." Even as I said it I knew how stupid it sounded.

"Yes, we can. Is that so unusual?" His voice was deadpan.

"Well, I mean, yes. You can… you have…"

Again he laughed. "I'm playing with you. Sorry. I wish you'd learn to relax with me. People always react to us the way you do. It makes it so hard to form friendships." He looked straight into my eyes. "Much less anything more. Being the son of a god can be so lonely."

"That isn't the kind of thing one expects the son of a god to say."

"Even so, it is true. Look at Hercules and the madness Hera has visited on him. For that matter, look at yourself. You are descended from Poseidon, they say. But do you feel different than anyone else?"

"Of course not. But Poseidon is—"

"A myth? It wouldn't do to say so too loudly or too often, not when you're planning a naval expedition. Our fathers and forefathers can be so horribly jealous. Besides, many people think my father Boreas is a myth, too. That hardly explains this." He spread his wings wide and flapped them once. A rush of air brushed my face. His wings were gloriously pure, silvery white, like new snow on a mountaintop untouched by mankind.

"Good god, you are a beautiful man!"

"And you," he took a step toward me, "are the same. They say you are a champion swimmer. And it shows." He abruptly threw his arms around me and kissed me. His wings, still spread wide, enfolded me. And it was—it was—it was my dreams made real. It could not be, it was not possible, but when Kalais kissed me my dreams were made all too real, concrete and tangible.

I lost myself in his arms, in his wings, and I kissed him back as hard and as deep as I could. Our cheeks touched and he whispered, "Beautiful Acastus, we share divine blood. Do not let me be alone."

I rested my head on his shoulder and held him as tightly as I could. "Lovely man, divine man from the sky, I will not. But... but..."

"Yes, Acastus?"

"If there are gods, and if we are descended from them, why has my life been so sad? Why has everyone I've ever loved died?"

Before I could realize what was happening he put his arms around me in a tight grip, a wrestler's grip, and lifted me. There was the sound of his wings. And faster than my eyes could blink we were in the air, soaring over Iolcus. I saw the palace complex retreat far below us. The morning sun, reflected off the Aegean, was dazzling. And sunlight reflected off the great Aphrodite guarding the harbor. Looking down on it I felt—there was no way to avoid the thought— like a god. Air rushed past us and it was refreshing, exhilarating. Birds—seagulls, sparrows, a redtailed hawk—scattered and flew away in terror.

"Kalais, this is wonderful!"

"*You* are the wonder, Acastus."

"No, I mean it. You—"

"I mean what I said every bit as much as you did."

He kissed my cheek. I turned my head to see him and he was smiling like a schoolboy up to mischief.

"Kiss me again, Kalais."

He did. There in the air far over Iolcus we kissed like lovers, like divine lovers.

We circled the lighthouse. I reached out and touched the tip of its torch. Through the window that was the goddess' eye I saw Cleobis watching us with a look of alarm on his face. Then he recognized me and his expression turned to one of frank puzzlement. Uncertainly he waved. Laughing I waved back and shouted "Good morning!"

Below us there were people on the docks. They looked up. A few of them waved and shouted my name. We flew low over their heads, and they scattered.

"Kalais, I'm slipping. Please, let's land."

He tightened his grip on me and flew out over the water.

"Kalais, I'm losing my grip."

"Don't worry. I have a firm hold on you."

"What will people think?"

"Why should we care? We have divine blood, remember?"

He wheeled around and headed back toward the palace. In a moment we had landed back on the roof.

I had to catch my breath. "That was thrilling, Kalais. And exhausting."

"What do you have to be exhausted about?" He laughed. "I did all the work. Flying, carrying you."

"Are you joking? I was holding on for dear life."

"You have to learn to trust me."

"Will we be doing that often?"

"If I have my way, we will."

We embraced. His arms around me felt wonderful. Softly I whispered, "You'll have to bear with me. Trust, I'm afraid, has never come easily to me. After a lifetime with my father... Can I ask you something?"

"Certainly." His wings enfolded me.

"Are you real? Are you really who you say you are?"

He kissed my cheek but didn't answer.

"I've never... the gods have never seemed real to me, none but the Muses. Yet here you are."

"I'm no god." Kalais let go of me and stepped back. "I've seen your work in other cities. You are a good artist, perhaps even a great one. Who guides your hand when you sculpt? Who gives you the divine ability to make what you make?"

"My mother dedicated me to the Muses when I was born."

"Then you know the gods too. Not in the same way I do, not in that immediate manner, but—"

"Teach me. Guide me through your world, Kalais. I want to know the gods as you do. A week ago, a day ago I wouldn't have believed you exist, wouldn't have believed you are even possible. Now you seem the only real thing in the world to me."

We embraced and kissed again. Softly Kalais said, "We live in the same world, Acastus. We have experienced it differently, that's all. We have known different parts of it, like any two men."

And still again we kissed. His wings wrapped around me. I laughed softly.

"And what, little Prince Sculptor, is funny?"

"Nothing. It's just that—"

"Yes?"

"Argus will be back soon. I can't wait till he meets you. I want to be there, to see his reaction."

* * *

As it happened, Jason returned before Argus. On the day of his return we convened an impromptu council meeting. Hylas poured wine for us all then took a seat beside me at the table. There was not much to be discussed but a report on the journey to Dodona. Melicanthus had traveled with Jason but was content to let him do most of the talking. Jason, clearly pleased with himself, placed a long, linen-wrapped bundle on the table before him.

"What is that?" Kallikrates asked.

"In time. Be patient. It is something that will make us all."

"But—"

"In due time, Kallikrates."

Melicanthus added glumly, "That parcel has been a deep, dark secret for Jason since we left Dodona. Even I haven't seen what's in it."

Their journey, Jason told us, had been a success. "The oracle confirmed what we had already heard, that Colchis lies at the far end of the Black Sea, farther than any Greeks have ever sailed before. And that the Fleece is there. And that..." He paused dramatically.

"Yes?" I prodded him.

"And that Colchis is rich in amber. If anyone would know about that, it would be the priesthood. Let us hope our expedition is as successful as this journey was. We will be made men and the future of Iolcus will be secure." He looked around the council table, beaming.

It seemed to me he was not mentioning the thing we most needed to hear. "But Jason, you went there for explicit directions. Did they give them? Do you have a map, or—?"

"No, no map, Acastus. They advised that we simply to stick to the southern shore of the Black Sea. We will reach Colchis eventually."

"But how long a voyage will it be?"

He shrugged. "Not long enough to take us over the edge of the world, Acastus. But there is no need to worry. We will have something no other mariners have ever had, an infallible guide. We will," he told us, sounding impossibly happy with himself, and gesturing to the bundle he had brought, "have this."

With a flourish he unwrapped the parcel. There were three layers of linen, and he opened each layer carefully. Then finally the contents lay on the table before us. And it was...

I couldn't believe my eyes. It was a log, a small log, nothing more than that. Its ends were sawed off neatly, but it was otherwise an ordinary log or large tree branch. We all stared at it, *gaped* at it. A log; all Jason's dramaturgy had been for a chunk of wood. No one seemed certain how to react.

Finally I recovered myself. "That is it? A tree limb?!"

"Yes, that is it." He was smug. "With this, our expedition cannot fail."

"How? Is it going to draw termites away from the rest of the ship?"

"No." Melicanthus seemed numb. "If that is what I think it is…I hope it is not, that's all."

Jason paused again for dramatic effect. He looked around the table, gauging our reactions to what we were seeing. Finally he told us, "This is a branch from the oracular oak, the oak of Zeus at Dodona."

Melicanthus was aghast. "No! You can't have done this! You can't have committed this sacrilege!"

"Calm down, Melicanthus. The priests offered us guidance. All I've done is take their guidance one step further."

"But how can you have done this? *When* did you do it?"

"Our last night there. You were off partying with the priests and some local whores."

Kallicrates was equally astonished. "But…but you have stolen a piece of the oak. You have purloined a piece of the god's property. This will bring down his wrath on all of us."

"Will the two of you please relax?"

Gereontes spoke up. "How can you expect us to relax, Jason? What you seem to think a harmless bit of thievery may well bring down the wrath of Zeus on the whole city."

"Hogwash. It is a tree limb, a sacred one but a tree limb, nothing more. It is not as if it were a consecrated object taken from the Holy of Holies. But when Argus incorporates it into the prow of our ship—how can we fail to reach our destination?"

"If it is 'a tree limb, nothing more' how can you expect it to help and guide us?" I seemed to be the only one at the table not shocked by Jason's act of impiety. In fact it struck me as being perfectly in character for him. I knew him well enough to know his skepticism concerning the gods and the oracles. And his talent for manipulation was hardly lost on me. This branch, this scrap of the oracular oak, would if nothing else inspires confidence in the crew, confidence in our mission. And of course it might well not be what he said it was; it could easily be an ordinary tree branch after all. But believing that a thing can be done is always the first big part of doing it. Jason must have known that as well as I did. Stealing a piece of the oak, or pretending he had, was a masterful piece of psychology.

I was left feeling conflicted. A week earlier I would have scoffed at the suggestion that a god could communicate through the branches of a tree. But that was before I met Kalais, my beautiful Kalais, son of the god of the north wind. There could be no other explanation for him and his brother, at least not one I could think of. Years earlier my friend Brygus, the fisherman, had told me there was more to the world than I knew or imagined. Kalais and Zetes were the first incontrovertible proof I had ever had that that was indeed the case.

But of course that raised another problem: If there really were gods, and if one of them really did speak to humanity through that oak, then Jason's act of theft was indeed gross impiety, and it could indeed bring down divine wrath on our heads. And the gods…for the first time I was forced to consider that they might be real. Kalais was real. I knew that as well as I knew anything in the world. He had carried me above the earth and kissed me there in the sky. And he was—he had to be—the son of a god.

But despite the objections we raised, Jason remained firm in his insistence that he had done nothing wrong and that his theft would be the making of us all, not our undoing.

There was one other piece of business to discuss. There had been a series of reports that a large wolf had been sighted in the outskirts of the city. It had not done any harm yet, but people were concerned that it might attack, perhaps even carry off a child. Melicanthus claimed it was the first sign of the god's displeasure, and Jason, predictably, scoffed. Gereontes offered to lead a detachment of soldiers to hunt down the beast.

Our meeting ended with Jason the only one who felt good about our prospects. I had a growing sense of foreboding. We were committed to the voyage. It could well spell the end of everything.

* * *

I took Jason to the Argonauts' building, which everyone had come to call Argo House, to meet them. They were exercising in the yard, naked and sweaty, when we got there, and I introduced everyone. The moment we arrived he became his usual gregarious self, jovial and warm with everyone; and he joined in their exercise. It was obvious to me he was sizing them up for their sexual possibilities, but none of them seemed to notice or to care. Jason had that effect on people.

Idmon stood apart and watched. "So that is Jason in the flesh," he said, sounding dubious.

His tone puzzled me. "Yes. Who else would it be?

"Oh, don't get me wrong. I'm not voicing disapproval. Not exactly. He is quite a beautiful man. But you see, Jason and I are going to become lovers."

"You are going to— Excuse my skepticism, Idmon, but how could you possibly know that?"

He smiled a rueful smile. "I am a seer, remember?"

"Oh. Of course. It's so easy for me to forget. I am so unused to—to—"

"To what, Acastus? I've seen your work. You of all people must know what it is like to be touched by the gods."

"Yes, I suppose I must. I'm not accustomed to think of it in those terms, that's all."

"With the company you are assembling here, you must get used to it. And I would say fairly soon." He pointed to the sky above us.

"Yes, yes, of course."

Kalais and Zetes were not working out with the others. Any of the usual forms of exercise might damage their wings, Kalais had explained to me.

As we stood watching them soar and dive, Idmon finished what he had been saying. "Jason will love me then forsake me." He lowered his voice to a whisper. "For a woman."

"You must be mistaken, Idmon, or misunderstanding what the gods have shown you. I've never known Jason to be attracted to anyone but men. He has never even mentioned marriage."

"It will happen!" He said it with such force and emphasis it startled me. "Kings need wives, if for nothing else to give them heirs for the continuation of their dynasties." Then abruptly he turned rueful. "And I will not survive the voyage." He whispered, "I will not want to."

I wasn't certain how to react. "Should you perhaps not come with us, then?"

He shook his head sadly.

Finally, lamely, I said, "We have another seer among us. Perhaps Amphiaraus can see something you do not. Something happier."

"There is no changing what the Fates have decreed. But look!"

117

He pointed to a place off in the hills. The twins had flown there and were hovering, to all appearances excitedly, above a certain spot. "They have seen the wolf!"

They left the place where they had been hovering and flew back. In a matter of moments they lit beside Idmon and myself. "The largest wolf I have ever seen is in the woods," Zetes told us breathlessly.

Kalais embraced me and kissed me lightly on the cheek. "It is enormous. I've never seen a creature like it. And it seems to be coming this way."

Amphiaraus left off his exercise and joined us. Mopping the sweat from his face, he smiled and told us, "You are all quite mistaken. There is no wolf."

"How can you say that?" Zetes was plainly annoyed at having his word doubted. "We have seen it. You haven't."

"I have seen it indeed," Amphiaraus insisted.

"In your mind? With your mind's eye?" Idmon was likewise rankled. "I have seen it too, Amphiaraus."

"You have seen what you thought was a wolf. You are quite mistaken, all of you."

I wasn't sure what to make of the situation. What is one to think when two seers have two conflicting visions?

From the field Jason announced, "It must be time for our midday meal. Let us go to the refectory."

We went inside. The dining hall in Argo House was set up with rows of tables, not all of which were in use yet, of course. The servants set out our meal, overseen by Hylas, and we all tucked in.

But just as we were finishing a slave rushed in with a message from Gereontes. "A great wolf has been seen in the forest outside the city. Gereontes' men have it at bay. He urges you all to arm yourselves with spears and nets and come join him to slay the beast."

I looked around, and all the Argonauts—all but Amphiaraus—nodded their assent. We got to our feet and went to the armory to get the weapons and shields we would need. Hylas followed happily, like a boy on his first adventure, which he was.

Amphiaraus lagged behind. When I looked back at him questioningly he simply told me, "Do not let them be too hasty with their weapons. I have told you: there is no wolf."

"Are you coming or not?"

He got slowly to his feet and sighed. "I suppose so."

I hesitated, not certain what to make of his pronouncement and his manner, then found my resolve and joined the others.

It was decided that Kalais and Zetes would fly on ahead and hover over the spot so that we could find it easily. We armed ourselves and rushed through the forest; fortunately the paths were well worn. Our goal was not far outside the city walls; the wolf did indeed seem to be heading for Iolcus. In only moments we reached the clearing amid the trees where Gereontes and the soldiers were awaiting us.

There was indeed a wolf, the largest I had ever seen, as large as a young bull. Gereontes' men had encircled it and were closing in on it, spears at the ready. It growled and snarled and looked from one man to the next, as if gauging which one to attack, its eyes blazing red. Our party quickly joined them to tighten the circle. All except Amphiaraus, that is, who stood apart, a smug, ironic smile on his face, and Jason, who all too plainly did not want to get too near the wolf.

Mopsus advanced on the beast, dragging a net behind him. A few of the others closed in. Just as he was about to toss his net over the animal a voice bellowed from among the trees. "Stop! Do not strike! Not unless you wish to reduce your number by one!"

It was Argus, back from his mission. He was accompanied by two slaves, who he left among the trees; he strode into the clearing and approached the wolf. To everyone's astonishment he walked right up to the animal, patted its head and shook it by the scruff of its neck, as one would a favorite dog. In a calm voice he said to the animal, "You know better than this. How many times has this kind of behavior gotten you into trouble?"

The wolf, apparently cowed by this, sat back on its haunches and whimpered like a scolded puppy. Argus looked around the group till he spotted me. "Acastus, how could you let this happen?"

I was completely lost. "What on earth do you mean?"

"And you, Amphiaraus. Surely you know better than to risk what might have happened here."

Amphiaraus shrugged and made a vague gesture. "I tried. No one would listen. You know how pig-headed athletes can be."

Argus was still petting the wolf. He scanned the company again. "And you, Hercules. You surely know better than this. Where are you?"

We all looked at each other, puzzled. But Hylas spoke up. "Hercules is coming here?!" He could not keep the excitement out of his voice.

"He's not here yet? I thought for sure he would be. Yes, Hylas, he's coming to Iolcus to join the company of *Argo*. We heard several days ago that he had finished his labors for King Eurystheus and was coming to join the Argonauts."

"Hercules, coming here!" Hylas looked from one of us to the next. "We will meet him, actually meet and get to know him!" I had seen boys and young men who adulated older men before, but Hylas was so eager it was almost comical.

"Calm down, boy." Argus was amused by him and made no secret of it. "There is someone else you must all meet first." He turned to face the wolf. "Well? What on earth are you waiting for?"

The wolf took a step backwards. It reared up on its hind legs and...and...in the briefest instant it was no longer a wolf! It transformed into a man, a tall, rugged man with piercing black eyes and a magnificent muscular build.

Amphiaraus crossed the clearing to him and shook his hand. "Greetings, Autolycus. You must apologize to everyone for causing such alarm" He then introduced us all one by one. Kalais and Zetes when they saw the episode had ended, lit among us. Jason stayed back, as if he was unsure what to make of the situation or what to expect.

I had heard of Autolycus before and a few other men like him. But, typically, I had dismissed them as myths. But, quite unarguably, this wolf-man, this werewolf, was real.

"Stop gaping, Acastus, and come meet the newest member of our company."

I walked up to the man and shook his hand, or paw, or whatever the correct term would be. I introduced myself and welcomed him to Iolcus in the name of Pelias and all the Argonauts.

Autolycus grinned and took my hand. "I am indeed sorry for this furor. I'm afraid my playful side got the better of me."

"You might have been hurt. Or worse yet killed. Or even worse than that you might have killed one of us."

"There was no danger of that, Acastus." He took a knife from a sheath at his waist and quickly drew it cross his forearm. Blood flowed, a great deal of it. Then in an instant the wound healed and the flow stopped. "You see. I can be hurt, but never for very long. And as for the rest of you, I only kill in self-defense."

Everyone had relaxed but Castor, who was still visibly tense and appeared angry. "We were coming at you with swords and spears. It would have been self-defense. We could have been—"

"There was never any chance of it, Castor. I would have transformed before it came to that."

"Still. Anything might have happened."

Argus got between them. "Stop being so disagreeable, Castor. Let's all get back to the city for a rest and a good meal."

"And a bone or two for Autolycus," Castor muttered.

Jason finally approached the center of the clearing and introduced himself to Autolycus as the captain of our expedition. Then he approached Idmon, took him aside and whispered something to him. Idmon smiled and nodded; they kissed each other lightly on the cheek, took each other by the hand and led us back to Iolcus. Idmon's abilities as a seer were at least that accurate. I wondered—hoped—that the rest of what he had seen for himself would prove less accurate. He was a good man and he deserved better than what he had seen for himself.

Kalais took me in his arms and flew me on ahead of the others. I looked down on the great Aphrodite that guarded the harbor and thought, yes, the Argonauts are indeed forming onto a company of lovers. It was too early to know what would develop between Kalais and me ultimately, but for the moment his arms and his wings felt, well, heavenly.

The rush of air as we flew tore the tunic from my shoulder. I had to struggle to keep it up. When we alit at the palace we stood and waited for the others. Kalais reached under his tunic and handed me an ornate brass pin with a cleverly worked lead clasp. "Here. So you can preserve your modesty from the seagulls next time we fly."

"You're making fun of me." I was abashed.

"Affectionate fun, Acastus."

I asked him if he had ever encountered Autolycus before.

"Only briefly. He is a son of Hermes, and like his father he is a notorious thief."

"Being a werewolf isn't enough?"

"Evidently not. His divine father, in addition to giving him the power to transform into a wolf, also gave him the ability to change the color of anything he steals. If he steals a herd of black cattle he can turn them white, so he cannot be suspected in the disappearance of the black ones." He paused then went on ruefully, "I suppose he may come in handy on our expedition…if we need a thief…or if we all become thieves ourselves."

Seers, winged men, a virgin nuntress, a wolf-man… Our company was getting more interesting by the day.

* * *

Over dinner Argus told us he had found the finest timber he had ever worked with. His servants were transporting it back to the city and should arrive in a day or two. "We can get to work building the ship at once. There are some good old shipbuilders here in the city, though I daresay they're out of practice. If all the Argonauts will help with the construction, we can have the *Argo* ready to sail in no time at all."

Jason mentioned the prophetic timber he had brought. "It will guide the ship infallibly."

"Or maybe we could just roll dice to determine our course." Argus was true to form. It wasn't hard for me to see why Hylas had fallen in love with the man. Perhaps Aphrodite would smile on the two of them; I hoped so.

"Really, Argus, have a little piety."

He laughed. "So you have begun respecting the gods, have you, Jason?"

I decided to get between them and change the subject. "So what is the news about Hercules? When and how did you hear it?"

"It's being rumored everywhere I passed. Our heralds have spread word of our expedition very effectively. And all Greece seems excited by it. I'm sure we'll be getting more than enough volunteers to man the ship."

"Man? Man?!" Atalanta's voice came from behind me. From her tone she was quite peeved. "How typical of men to use that term."

Castor got to his feet and glared at her. "Atalanta, the virgin huntress. Your reputation has preceded you. And you are reputed not just for your speed but for your disdain for us men. You really should get better in touch with the natural order of things."

Across the refectory Caeneus jumped to his feet and shouted, "Don't let up, Atalanta! There are far too many egos here, and the worst of them need pricking."

"I don't know Caeneus, my old friend. Castor here seems to want only men."

He laughed. "Whatever shall we do with the women folk, eh? Especially when they're better than the men. I used to get that all the time when I was a woman, even though I was the best fighter among the Lapiths—except my friend Mopsus, over there."

Castor looked as if he wanted to continue bickering, but Argus shot him a warning glance, and he fell glumly silent.

And so, it seemed, we had another Argonaut, a most unexpected one. What could be more unexpected than a man who turns himself into a wolf?

* * *

That night Hylas came to my studio and offered to do more posing for my Ganymede. I told him there would be no point till the marble arrived from Paros. But he seemed to be reluctant to leave.

"Acastus?"

"Hm?" I looked up from the sketch I was working on.

"Have you ever been in love?"

I fingered the pin Kalais had given me. "I don't know. How do you know a thing like that?"

"Well...I mean..." He looked away shyly. "Why doesn't anyone love me?"

"Love takes time, Hylas."

"I could love Argus. He ignores me."

"Argus is intimidated by you, I think. And he has his mind on the construction of the ship. You know how important that is."

"And before Argus came to Iolcus, I offered my love to Jason. He didn't want me either."

I laughed softly. "I can't imagine Jason wanting anyone who isn't the wealthy son of a king—at least."

"And you—"

"You're only a few years younger than I am myself, Hylas. And like you, I like older men."

"They—all of them, Jason, Castor, all of them—they take me to bed, and when the morning comes they make it clear they're through with me."

I took him by the shoulders. "Now listen to me, Hylas. You are as beautiful a young man as any of us have ever seen. Take their attentions as a compliment. Love will come."

He rested his head against my chest, and I had the feeling he was fighting back tears. "I hope so. I hope so."

* * *

And then the next day a young shepherd named Hermas, who I had met once before, came running to the palace to tell us that Hercules was on the outskirts of the city. We were in the midst of a council meeting, planning to marshal the city's resources to get the *Argo* built as quickly as possible. Jason had spent a long night drinking and having sex; he was hung over and all but useless. It fell to me to take charge.

"You're certain it's him?"

"I've seen him: tall, muscular, magnificent, with a body like a god come to earth. And he's wearing the lion skin they say he always clothes himself in."

Hercules. His inclusion in the expedition could easily insure our success. But...rumor had it that he had torn down half the walls of Thebes in his madness. If those rumors were accurate, his madness could also spell our ruin. Or the ruin of Iolcus, if he went off his mind again.

Hylas was sitting at my side. "Is he as handsome as they say?"

"Even more so. You should see him. You should see how strong his profile is, how luxurious his hair and beard."

Hylas retreated into silent reverie. He didn't need to speak; the look on his face told me what fantasies he was having. I thanked Hermas for bringing us the news and dismissed him.

Hercules. I had to make certain nothing happened that might set him off. A meeting of the Argonauts was summoned hastily and I cautioned them all to handle him as gently as possible. "We want him with us. We have all heard stories of his violent madness, and we must do our best to keep him calm and happy."

If I had had to predict which of the Argonauts would find this objectionable, I'd have guessed Castor, and he did not disappoint me. "So one of us is to receive special treatment."

"For heaven's sake, Castor, if his madness begins again it could be the end of us all. Do you want that? For once, be tactful. You are a son of Zeus like him. Surely you can find it in yourself to be considerate to a half-brother."

He grumped. "Would even Hercules kill his brother?"

Pollux saved me the trouble of responding. "He killed his wife and children, Castor. Why would the fact that we're his brothers stop him? Besides, you know how difficult you can be, how petulant. There are times I want to kill you myself." He made it sound like a joke, and everyone in the room laughed uneasily. But we all knew he was in earnest.

Castor started to say something, but I cut him off. "Good, then family unity is our watchword. Let us go and meet our brother."

* * *

Hercules arrived at the palace a short time later. He was everything I had ever heard, tall, muscular, perfectly magnificent; thee was no way to mistake him for anything but a god or the son of a god. And there was not a trace of his madness. He was brimful of good humor and gentleness; given his overpowering physical presence his personality seemed quite incongruous. But everything about him, absolutely everything, made me want to welcome him to Iolcus and the company of Argonauts.

Protocol demanded that he present himself to Pelias or to me, as rulers of the city. But before I had a chance to talk with him and get to know him, Jason stole him away from me. They went off together and became lost in...I don't know, in conversation, in thought, in each other's company...

Hylas looked at Hercules as if he were gazing into the face of Zeus himself. When Jason monopolized him, the disappointment in Hylas' face was plain to see.

Kalais and I went up to the palace roof again to spend time together.

"I think my brother is a bit jealous of you, Acastus. You and I

125

have been spending so much time together. Zetes and I have always been inseparable."

"How inseparable, exactly?"

"Don't be morbid. Everyone thinks twins are also lovers. Zetes and I...well, I'll be honest with you, we did play a bit when we were boys. But we've never been what you'd call lovers. And now that I've found you..." He spread his hands wide apart in a gesture that asked, *What can I do?* "There's no chance anyone will ever mistake Zetes and I for lovers again."

"I still can't quite believe we really have found each other." I squeezed his hand lightly. "I've always been a skeptic about the gods and demons and oracles and all the rest. Yet here you are, a man with wings, and absolutely beautiful in the bargain."

"I've never really felt beautiful, Acastus. Never till I met you, at least. I've always known what a freak I am. *We* are—Zetes feels it even more acutely than I do." He put his arms around me. "When I'm with you I don't feel a freak at all. Is that what love is?"

I gestured at the lighthouse far below us. "Perhaps it is simply her power you're feeling. If there's one god I want deeply to believe in..."

"I talked with Argus about you. He told me you're cynical beyond your years."

I laughed. "What's the saying? 'The cynic questions everything in order to learn what is true.'"

Kalais kissed me lightly on the cheek. "I've known other sons of other gods. None of them have ever made much of it. We all just get on with our lives as normally as we can. Even Hercules, till Hera made him mad. Zetes and I...we've never been able to do that, never had the chance to pretend we're normal. We fly, we have wings, there is no way to hide them. I remember trying once when I was a boy. But they showed even under the loosest cloak. Wherever we go people make much of us. "Fly into the heavens for us! Do loop-the-loops!'" He held me tightly. "Be a cynic about me, Acastus. Believe I'm only human."

"Human is good enough for me. More than good enough. Besides..." I kissed him. "I find your wings more beautiful than I can say."

We kissed for what seemed like eternity. It may really have been eternity. At least, I would gladly have been lost in time in his arms, in his kiss.

I finally managed to pull Hercules away from Jason. Close-to, it was easy to see the man's incredible power. Muscles never stopped rippling beneath his skin. It would be easy to think they had lives of their own. Even when he blinked or scratched his nose he radiated strength. They say he once brought down the walls of a town merely by shouting at them, and I could believe it.

"We couldn't be more happy to have you with us, Hercules. Everyone knows you are your father Zeus' favorite."

"Yet even he couldn't preserve me from the jealous wrath of his wife." His voice was strong and powerful but the tone was half-sad, half-bewildered. I had the impression he was restraining himself lest insanity take him in its grip once again. I also suspected that the god's gifts to him were purely physical, not intellectual.

Yet he did not try to hide his well-known ego. "Besides," he added, "I am the greatest hero in Greece, and your expedition will be the ultimate challenge for Greek glory."

"Oh." I made myself smile. "Of course."

Hylas, inevitably, was with me, at my side. He looked up at Hercules the way I used to look up at the lighthouse when I was a boy, with wonder, admiration and even a bit of religious awe. "They say you like boys, Hercules. Do you?"

I laughed. "Hylas, don't be so forward."

"I can't help it." He reached up and touched the edge of Hercules' lion skin. "Do you need a squire? I'd love to be your squire."

Hercules ran his fingers through the boy's hair. "I don't actually need one, no."

"Oh." You could have read the disappointment in his face from the other side of Greece.

"But that isn't to say I wouldn't like one."

Hylas' face lit up like a child on his birthday. "Really?"

"My spear weighs a lot. Do you think you can manage it?"

"I can try my best, sir!"

"Hercules, call me Hercules."

That was that. The great man had found himself an adoring acolyte. I was happy for Hylas, but… If the goddess deranged Hercules' mind again, he would be the first one in his path. There were so many possibilities, not all of them happy. I had grown quite terribly fond of Hylas; in many ways he had become like a little brother to me. The thought that his adolescent hormones might be placing him in harm's way was not at all a happy one. Was that, I wondered, the kind of thing I'd be feeling if Pelias had not had my own brother killed?

Still, I wanted Hylas to be happy while he could. Human happiness is such a fleeting thing; the gods always saw to that.

* * *

The spring weather turned dark and rainy. Every day for a week we had storms, some of them quite violent. Ships moored in the harbor slammed into each other and into the pier and were damaged. No one said so, but we were all happy the *Argo* hadn't been constructed yet.

I told Kalais he should ask his father to ease off for a while, so we could get our ship built and launched.

"Boreas is the north wind. You know that, Acastus. But these winds, savage as they are, are blowing from the west."

"I didn't mean it seriously. Do the gods ever really concern themselves with what we need?"

"I want these storms to cease as much as you do, perhaps more. When the winds turn this beastly it's impossible to fly. A stiff blast of air could damage my wings. Even the rain is a problem. It soaks them, weighs them down, so flight becomes out of the question."

"They're not water-repellent, like a bird's wings?"

"Feel them."

I did; I stroked them and, yes, they were soft, warm and light, not at all like the wings of a bird.

Yet Kalais cooed like a dove. I noticed that he was becoming excited. Who could have thought that wings might be an erogenous zone?

"Stop," he whispered, "you're making me self-conscious."

"Self-conscious? Is that what you call it? Let's go to my room and make love."

Despite the wind and the rain, new Argonauts kept arriving. Among them were Phalerus, the famous Athenian archer; Butes the beekeeper, who was said to understand the language of insects; and most interestingly to me, Orpheus, the divine singer, the son and devotee of Apollo.

Orpheus was a man of middle height, with hair that was quite blond and eyes that were so dark they seemed to pierce everything and everyone they looked at. He had no servants with him, and the only thing he brought with him was his lyre. I welcomed him, but I couldn't help remarking that a singer and harpist was not exactly the kind of man we wanted for our expedition.

"You will need brains as well as brawn, creative thought as well as brute force. Art produces heroes too, Acastus."

"So it does, but—"

"I've seen your sculptures in cities all around Greece. What they do to men's eyes, my music does to their ears. And I daresay we both touch their hearts."

"I'm flattered, Orpheus. But—"

"If nothing else, you will need someone to provide a beat for the oarsmen."

"Yes." There didn't seem any point arguing. I repeated that he was welcome, introduced him to the others—those that didn't already know him—found him quarters in Argo House and provisioned him with clothing and other necessities. He strummed his lyre and sang me a brief paean of thanks.

* * *

That night, a storm raged over Iolcus. As we all sat around the refectory for our after-dinner symposium, servants extinguished the torches and all but a few candles. When I asked one of them who had instructed them to do that, he merely pointed to Orpheus. "That gentleman there, sir."

"Did he say why?"

"Not specifically, sir. He merely said that he wanted to demonstrate that he belonged here, that's all."

They cleared away the dinner plates in hushed silence, as if they knew something…out of the ordinary was about to happen. Then, their chore finished, they quietly disappeared. I saw a few of them peeking in from the next room, the kitchen. No one of us seemed willing to speak and break the unaccustomed silence.

129

Then Orpheus took up his lyre. He took his place between two candles; his was the most fully-lit face in that large room. We all waited with, as they say, hushed breath. Something was about to happen. We knew it involved Orpheus and his storied music, but…what could it be? What song could prove he deserved a place among the Argonauts?

He stroked the strings lightly, lightly with the plectrum, and the sound that filled the air was unspeakably sweet. And he began to serenade us with sad, gentle songs of love, love that was all too fleeting, love that vanished even at its height. The beat was slow and hypnotic, and the variations in the tune, which often ran counterpoint to the beat, were downright sensual. Even the least emotional, the least artistic, the most energetically athletic among us, left off our accustomed fussing and fidgeting and listened—and slowly, inexorably got caught up in it.

Orpheus strummed his lyre and cooed his songs. The music was low and seductive, even erotic. He sang a hymn on the love of Zeus for Ganymede. The melody he played were odd and sweet and even at times discordant, yet it was possible to hear in them the pulse of love, the rhythm of sex, the throbbing warmth of bodies entwined. It was possible (or so it seemed) to feel the very thing the boy Ganymede had felt in the Zeus' arms, the very thing the god had felt when he embraced him. Another hymn followed, this one of Aphrodite and the beautiful young man Adonis. The pulse and throb of the lyre strings grew. We became more and more enraptured by the lyrics, the melody, the amorous hum of the music. One by one each man in the room, even the most argumentative, became rapt as he listened to the love songs of Orpheus.

I saw Jason fondle Idmon's thigh and kiss it gently. Phalerus and Mopsus embraced and kissed. And Castor and Zetes, and Idas and Echion, Pollux and Amphiaraus, and on and on. Hylas buried his face in the breast of Hercules, and Hercules kissed the top of his head and fondled him. Even the servants came slowly back into the room and got caught up in the song of Orpheus, embraced one another, kissed one another, fell to the floor and began to make love. Only Atalanta, who had pledged her virginity to Artemis, was unmoved; she quietly left the room.

Kalais' wings enfolded me, caressed me, aroused me. The tip of his wing stroked my chest, my stomach, moved even lower down my torso, all in time to the hymn Orpheus sang. I could easily have believed that the lovely god Eros himself was in the room, instilling us all with the divine spark, the godly energy of love.

I touched Kalais' wing and he moaned softly. I caressed it gently and his moaning became more rhythmic. He breathed in time with the music, and so did I as I caressed his snow-white wing, as I loved the beautiful purity of it. Slowly he wrapped me in his other wing as well, and I kissed and fondled it, too. He let out the sweetest moan. I buried my face in his chest and nibbled his nipples, and his moaning became ever so slightly louder.

I had had men's arms around me before, had relished their embrace. But never had I known the exquisite feeling of being so completely enfolded inside another man, so completely surrounded, engulfed by him. I kissed Kalais, kissed his wings, his arms, his mouth. Even there in a corner of the refectory I knew the divine feeling of having him carry me among the clouds and make love to me there. When I closed my eyes we were among the clouds, we were touching heaven itself.

"Acastus," he whispered, "look!"

We were among the stars; it seemed I could reach out and touch the Milky Way. The beat of Kalais' wings echoed the rhythm of Orpheus' harp. I felt him penetrate me and I knew that momentary spark of the divine, that fleeting rush of Olympian pleasure men call orgasm.

When I opened my eyes again we were in the refectory, exactly where we had begun. Orpheus had fallen silent. Kalais' chest was moist with the juice of my love, and I was covered with his. I tasted it, and it was the sweetest thing ever. All the other Argonauts were there; some of them were still making love, some had fallen apart in sweet exhaustion, some slept in each other's arms.

Orpheus climbed softly onto a table. When he saw that we had finished he stepped down and crossed slowly to us. "Acastus, you see the gift of the gods to me. I can bring men the very touch of divinity itself. This night I have made the Argonauts one, united them with my art."

Kalais rose to his feet. "You have indeed, Orpheus. We must have you with us. We must feel again what we have felt tonight.

Other promises of divine favor are not tangible, cannot be touched. Yours, on the other hand…"

Both of them looked to me. I took Kalais' hand and said, "Yes. You have done more with your art than I could ever hope to do with mine. You are more than welcome here, Orpheus. You have made us a company of lovers. With the divinity you have imparted, how can we possibly fail?"

Chapter Six
The *Argo* Embarks

Over the next two months Argo House became more and more the center of activity in Iolcus. Increasing numbers of Argonauts arrived, most of them with squires or other servants. Shipwrights, carpenters and other skilled workmen from all over Greece came to Iolcus, seeking employment on the construction of the *Argo*. And a group of weavers were put to work making the canvas sail for the vessel. Beyond them, there were dyers, preparing to give the sail its crimson color. It was to sport the royal arms of Iolcus side by side with a representation of the golden ram; a crew of expert women prepared to do the intricate needlework. Housing and feeding them all became a bit of a problem, but Argus reminded us that the more of them we employed, the faster the ship would be built and the expedition launched.

Melicanthus wondered aloud how many of them had come merely for the free lodging and board, not to mention the salaries they were earning. Argus was only too happy to spar with him. "It always bothers priests when anyone else receives any form of public largesse. Public money should go to support the temples, nothing more. Isn't that right?"

"They are draining the treasury," Melicanthus grumped.

Jason got between them and reminded Melicanthus of the potential economic benefits to the city from our expedition. "Do you think the temples won't get their share of the proceeds from the amber trade?"

Melicanthus grumbled on. Priests.

In addition to all the recent arrivals, workmen from the city were engaged in the actual construction of the *Argo*. At the same time, the

Argonauts themselves and their various servants and retainers explored the city, which helped the local economy quite considerably. And that in turn served to increase public support for our expedition. I had never thought of the voyage as a kind of public works project, but that is certainly what it became.

In time, quartering all the Argonauts' servants and slaves became a bit of a problem. The fact that they would be unable to bring their various attendants along on the voyage came as a glum but inescapable realization to a few of them. Castor, typically, complained loudly about it. Thankfully most of them were sensible enough to realize that the facts of an ocean journey with a crew of 50 heroes, and the limited space available on a ship, would render it impossible to bring servants along.

The one exception was Hercules. He insisted he bring Hylas with him, much to Hylas' delight. And, well, he was Hercules; no one had the gumption to tell him no. I confess that I myself didn't have the nerve. I was all too sensitive to the unhappy fact that Hercules, magnificent as he was physically, was psychologically unstable. Hera had made him mad; he had killed his family and destroyed, or half-destroyed, whole cities; and that was that.

But I must say that his love for Hylas had a remarkable calming effect on him. He was clearly smitten with the boy, and so was Hylas with him. I don't think I had ever seen two people so completely mad for each other. They were inseparable. Wherever Hercules went, Hylas followed; and Hercules, it was quite apparent, wouldn't have had it any other way.

It wasn't unusual to see Hylas riding on Hercules' shoulder as he moved around the palace compound or the city. I began to think Hercules might make a better Zeus for my sculpture than Argo would. Alas, Hercules proved even more energetic and harder to pin down. He refused, and refused emphatically, to pose. Not even Hylas could persuade him to stay still long enough to do it. If Hercules didn't want to pose, then, well, he didn't want to pose. I had to warn Hylas not to goad him too much on the subject. The operative fact was—and had to be—that bringing Hylas on our voyage would help keep Hercules calm and happy, and we needed him to remain that way. No one could have proposed a better reason for bringing the boy.

At least I hoped so. There was always the possibility that his infatuation with Hylas was one more manifestation of his madness. I decided to keep careful watch on them.

* * *

Needless to say, theirs was not the only love among the Argonauts. With all those beautiful athletes living and working in close proximity, desire was all but certain. We had men of every type and description, blondes, brunettes, redheads, short men, tall men, slender men, burly men, young athletes, mature athletes... all of them in superb physical condition. More than once I found myself wishing I had time to sculpt them all. No sculptor had ever had better models for sculptures—discus throwers, wrestlers and every other kind of athlete. I contented myself with sketching as many of them as I could, when my administrative duties gave me the time. The marble could always come later.

When two of them began making love, their lust quite inevitably spread among the others like fire in a dry forest. Jason, in particular, was happy to seduce or be seduced by one Argonaut after another. In addition to Idmon, he flirted with Zetes, Phalerus, Butes and any number of the others. It almost seemed as if he were using the residents of Argo House as his personal harem. Not that any of them minded; Jason was indeed a beautiful man. And the erotic activity was hardly limited to just him.

And of course it wasn't only among themselves that desire flourished. They bedded slaves and servants, both male and female, and once more the servants complied happily. What's more, whores from the city, again of both sexes, were only too pleased to ply their trade among these magnificent (and wealthy) athletes. Argo House was a beehive of sex, lust and love. But no—in a beehive only the queen gets sex; Argo House was much more democratic than that.

Even Argus received his share of amorous attention. Pollux, Butes and several of the others had courted him, but he remained focused on the work at hand, so they turned their attentions elsewhere. Argus was the one rock of stoicism in our company; if a boy as beautiful as Hylas could make no headway with him, there wasn't much hope for any of the others. I have to say I admired him for it—in theory. In practice, every moment I spent loving Kalais made Argus seem a bit of a fool. He was happy, and I knew that in his long life he had know his share of lovemaking, perhaps even more than his share. Yet seeing him remain celibate among all the athletic lust was a bit baffling, even unsettling to me. Old age is its own mystery, I suppose.

Sex aside, we were a company of men with a purpose, and none of us lost sight of it for long. Work on the *Argo* continued, fussily overseen by Argus. It early became clear how carefully he had planned, and that all his planning would pay off. A special area of the harbor was cleared and a boat slip constructed according to his specifications. Each morning Argus, Jason and I, accompanied by the band of Argonauts and as many servants as could be spared from Argo House and palace work, plus all the city workmen, would make our way down to the harbor for the day's work.

Timber was being cut, tempered, waterproofed. Crews of workers labored at each task. Argus had selected his woods quite deliberately; each had its place in the ship. There was oak for the keel, ash for the beams and oars, cedar and pine for the hull. Each piece had to be shaped precisely for its place in the ship; even a small gap could prove disastrous. It was the most elaborate puzzle imaginable, yet Argus remained quite firmly in control of it.

The carpenters worked with assiduous care. Other crews prepared pitch, according to Argus' private recipe, for treating, waterproofing the wood and sealing whatever cracks we might find in the hull. Sail makers labored in a separate part of the city. And a special detail of guards was created to keep all the camp followers from distracting the workmen.

* * *

But above and beyond all this activity, for me at least, there was my growing love for Kalais and his for me. We slept together, dined together, exercised together. And of course we made love. Daily, almost hourly it seemed. I had never dreamed passion could be so intense, never dreamed the touch of a man, the caress of a man, his taste and his feel could be so wonderfully all-consuming.

When I was with him I forgot everything else, forgot Iolcus, forgot the Argonauts, forgot Hylas and Hercules, forgot Jason and the Golden Fleece…

Each day I grew more and more comfortable in his arms. The first few times he carried me into the clouds I was awkward and even a bit frightened. But soon enough I was quite at home there, almost as much so as he was. How could I ever have dreamed that making love in the sky could feel so natural? It was like being on Olympus, like being a god. When Kalais and I weren't together I came to my senses—a bit—and realized how foolish such thoughts were. Then I would see him again, hear his voice, smell him, taste him, and there I would be among the gods again, performing aerial acrobatics undreamed-of before I met him.

Would it last? *Could* it last? The thought struck me one night as we snuggled in bed. "Kalais, are you mortal? Will you age like me, or…?"

"I don't know. How can I know? Zetes and I have aged—we have grown from annoyingly cherubic little boys into men. How much more we will age…how can we know? We can be injured; that is clear. We've suffered all the mishaps that all boys and young men do. More, even. If you could have seen how clumsy we were when our wings first developed and we had to learn to use them… Just look at the scars on my knees."

I laughed, bent down and kissed his knees, then fell back into his arms again.

"What I do know, Acastus, is that I love you. I will be with you as long as the gods permit."

For what seemed the thousandth time we kissed and made love.

* * *

Hylas confided in me during one of his posing sessions. "So this is love, Acastus. This is what it's like. This is the rapture the poets sing about."

"Well, some of them, anyway." I was wry. "Our poets seem to be inspired by war and slaughter as much as by love."

"Don't waste your phony cynicism on me. I've seen you and Kalais. You know what love is as well as I do."

He had a point, of course. But somehow, something made me, I don't know, hesitant to encourage him to become any more infatuated with Hercules than he already was. "Kalais lets me be myself."

"As does Hercules. I'm here with you now, posing for your statue, not with him."

"Yet when you ask him to pose with you…" I let the thought hang in the air between us.

There was something, well, a bit manic about the way Hercules doted on him. It seemed vaguely…I don't know, unhealthy. I hoped it wouldn't ultimately trigger more madness in the man.

During another posing session, Hylas voiced something that alarmed me. "Acastus, have you ever been with a woman?"

"No. I can't say I've ever wanted to. Why do you ask?"

"I… I've seen some girls and women in town who, well, who excited me. Even some of the whores."

"Do they excite you more than Hercules does?" I tried not to sound too concerned.

"No, of course not. That wouldn't be possible. But still…"

"Be quiet, Hylas. I want to get the line of your shoulder right."

I did not want to find out how Hercules would react if he found Hylas making love to anyone but him, least of all a woman. In time, my worst fears were to be realized.

* * *

None of this is to suggest that erotic adventures were all that happened among us. The Argonauts exercised daily, most often in the morning. And all their assorted attendants, servants, slaves were kept busy tending to their every wish. There were times when the palace compound resembled nothing so much as an anthill, animated by constant comings and goings. It was, in its way, rather wonderful to watch. The acropolis of Iolcus hadn't seen so much energy, so much activity, in as long as I could remember.

And of course the focus of all this activity, the essential center of our lives, was the construction of the *Argo*. Argus had planned it so carefully, so thoroughly, so meticulously, and everyone was only too happy to submit to his supervision. All of us, from the lowliest slave to Hercules himself, pulled his weight. The carpenters and shipwrights alone made an impressive cadre.

The first big step in construction was the laying of the keel. Argus had found a perfect oak in Arcadia, magnificently tall and strong, and the woodworkers had shaped it into a fine, beautifully curved keel for us. It was one hundred 50 feet long, and its lines were as graceful as any statue.

Normally it would have taken a large crew of men to set such a timber in place and hold it steady while the beams were fastened to it. But Hercules undertook the job himself. Massive as it was, he held it rock-steady, positioned it perfectly. And he raised it and held it steady again when it was time to fasten the ship's ribs to it. One man, doing all that exhaustive work, labor that would easily have drained a large crew of workmen. Hercules didn't even break a sweat.

I knew his reputation, of course. Everyone in Greece did, and I daresay everyone in the civilized world. But this was the first time I had seen him in action, seen a display of his Olympian strength. Not for the first time I found myself thinking that, yes, there must be gods. Hercules must be the son of a god. There was no other plausible explanation for what I was witnessing.

Rather than tiring Hercules, the work seemed to exhilarate him, At the end of a day's work he turned his attentions to Hylas and to no one else. Hylas undressed him, prepared his bath, sponged him clean, dried and clothed him. Hercules luxuriated in the boy's attention and lavished affection on him in return. The rest of us might have been wraiths in his world, mere shadows cast by the blazing light that was Hylas. It was wonderful to watch their love. Wonderful and troubling.

* * *

"Kalais, you are the son of a god." We were in bed, cuddling, snuggling against a cool night.

He laughed at me. "That again? Are you ever going to stop harping on that?"

"You mistake my intention. I want—no, I need to know how that works. I mean, if you are divine, or half-divine, what can ever constrain you? What gives you the discipline to refrain from doing anything you want?"

"What keeps you from making ugly sculptures?"

"That's not the same thing at all."

"It is, Acastus. Morality and art spring from the same impulse."

It was a new thought, one it would take me time to digest. I fell silent, turning it over in my mind.

But Kalais narrowed his eyes. "You mean Hercules, don't you?"

"Am I that transparent?"

"Hercules seems content. And productive. How much longer would the ship's construction take without him? He's being perfectly compliant. He takes direction from you and from Argus, if only because he wants to please the boy he loves."

"That's what troubles me. If Hylas' affections should wane—or shift to someone else—how would Hercules react?"

"Is that likely? The boy seems quite smitten."

"You know what boys are like. There's a new love story every week. If that happens, how will Hercules react?"

He was silent for a long moment. "I see why you're concerned. Iolcus—or the *Argo*, for that matter—would not be safe."

"Do the gods who father men retain any influence over them? If we pray to Zeus would he restrain his demigod son?"

"I don't know. I wish I knew. The gods make distant fathers. Boreas has barely been present in our lives. You have Poseidon's blood in your veins, at least a bit. Has he ever visited you?"

"No. And he let my brother be killed."

"You had a brother? I didn't know."

I told him the story. "Having Poseidon's blood didn't save him, did it?"

He fell silent again.

But I couldn't let it go. "Of course, you are assuming our family really is descended from Poseidon. It may just be convenient propaganda."

After another long silence Kalais whispered, "Wouldn't the god have taken revenge on a family telling such a lie about him?"

"Hasn't he?"

"And…Zeus... I don't know, Acastus, I simply don't know." He fell silent for another long moment and snuggled in my arms. Then he whispered, "I'd give anything to know my own father." He laid his head on my shoulder. "The mad have their own morality. Perhaps we are all mad, even the gods."

I fell asleep with that thought on my mind.

* * *

And so the *Argo* took shape. I had never seen a ship being built before—as I've said, the Iolcan fleet had been built long before I was born. The construction was quite wonderful to see. The small army of workers, including the Argonauts and Hercules himself of course, worked with as much discipline and purpose as any real army, as much as even the Spartans.

She was to be a three-leveled vessel. The main deck would have posts for Jason, Argus and the helmsman, plus room for a bank of eighteen rowers. The first lower deck was for eighteen more rowers, meaning that at any given time 12 Argonauts would be free to rest, sleep, exercise, make love or whatever. (Of course when we had a good wind, the sail would do the work, leaving us all free.) And the lowest deck held our sleeping and eating quarters. I had seen Argus' designs, of course, and they were sleek and beautiful as any sculpture or painting. But the actual ship, as it took form, was even more astonishingly lovely. The ship had curves as graceful and sensuous as any gymnast.

Jason had made a point of seeing that his limb from the oracular oak was incorporated into the prow. Argus argued that it might weaken the vessel, perhaps disastrously so, but Jason wasn't about to give in. "It will guide us. We shall need it." And so it was inserted into the keel, just before the figurehead. Argus insisted that sculpture was to be my work. He wanted an image of Aphrodite. "She is not usual for seagoing vessels, but our mission is not usual either."

I knew by then that there was no point arguing with him. Fortunately the wood for the figurehead was pine, soft and easy to work. I produced a lovely rendering of the goddess in under a week. If anyone noticed she had the features of Kalais, they were discreet enough not to say so.

* * *

The night before the launch the three of us, Jason, Argus and I, stood on the deck. I couldn't resist needling Argus. "So this is why you've been oblivious to Hylas, and to every other lover who's courted you. This ship is your lover."

"You've been inhaling the fumes from the pitch."

"I'm serious. Butes wants you. He's cultivated a hive of bees and coaxed them to make the sweetest honey I've ever tasted. He did it for you, but you remain—."

"Since when are bugs a token of love?"

"Not bugs, Argus, *honey*. The sweetest honey in the world."

"Don't bother me with this romantic nonsense, Acastus. We launch in a few days. I have to go over everything twice—three times, if need be. We don't want any accidents."

* * *

Argus could deny it as much as he liked, but it was ever more apparent that he loved the ship that was coming into being in our harbor. As it took shape more and more completely, he doted on it more and more. He worried over every detail like a fussy old maid over a young suitor. As the ship came nearer to completion more and more of us noticed his devotion to it.

"Of course I'm being obsessive," he grumped. "Someone has to be, and I'm the only one qualified. Do you really want to take a chance on slipshod workmanship in an unknown part of the world?"

He had a point and we all knew it. Still, it was fun poking at him and hearing him bark at us in return.

Under his fussy old maid's eye, the *Argo* took magnificent form. Its lines were perfect; they were the lines every ship should have had from the time of the first sailor. Occasional visitors from other coastal cities sketched its least detail. Future ships would resemble the *Argo* everywhere in Greece and, I was certain, everywhere in the civilized world. The *Argo* was the ship of ships.

* * *

Through all of this time I was never able to forget Pelias and the ghost, and Iolcus' curse. Deformed animals, misbegotten children were born with more and more alarming frequency. Misborn beggars sat starving in the streets or, if they were strong enough, went from door to door begging scraps of food. It was not possible to walk through the streets and not encounter the armless, the legless, the

142

eyeless. And these were young people, people who should have been the hope of Iolcus, not its shame.

Kalais got into he habit of flying me to the harbor each day, I did my share of work on the *Argo*, same as everyone else. Flying meant I would not see the cancer spreading in my city.

But still, I knew it was there. I took the initiative to open a small hospital for them, staffed with two physicians. Six of Iolcus' ubiquitous black-clad old women served as nurses; inevitably they were rumored to be witches, and I hoped they were. Witches could only help. Kalais joked that he hoped all that black cloth would not depress the patients even more.

"It isn't amusing, Kalais. All my life I've watched Iolcus deteriorate. The voyage of *Argo* is our hope and our meaning. If we can't believe in the Golden Fleece—if it is not real—we are lost."

He held me more and more tightly each night.

As for Pelias, his ailments continued, as did his nightly cries and screams. If the Golden Fleece proved unreal, at least we knew the ghost had real form. Its vengeance was too horrible for me to watch. Pelias, realizing it, closeted himself in his rooms ever more thoroughly.

To help palliate his anguish he took two young women from the city, Gorgias and Angoritha, as concubines. They were in their early twenties, and they both dressed in the same black robes as the old women. I was grateful he hadn't taken younger girls, as so many Greek kings did; to subject children to the horror he lived with would have been unthinkable.

He made love to them in the daytime. After dark they fled his quarters in horror, only to return the next day when the cries and the haunting let up. The old women, the crones who claimed to know magic, took care of them, gave them charms against the ghost and taught them prayers to protect themselves. For what it was worth, the ghost never harmed them, only Pelias.

* * *

Through all of this the *Argo* neared completion. The final steps were painting her hull and installing the sail. Argus had decided on bright yellow paint, the brightest I had ever seen, to represent our goal of the

Golden Fleece. All of the details—the rails, oars, mast—were painted vivid crimson to match the sail. Once it was hung, the sail caught the least breeze and billowed in it. It was made of cloth dyed a deep sunset red, and it was blazoned with a representation of the golden ram and the royal arms of Iolcus in vibrant golden thread. Argus kept it carefully reefed, awaiting our departure, but even with its sail furled *Argo* was the most remarkable vessel anyone had ever seen.

* * *

Members of our expedition had been arriving in Iolcus steadily. The last of them, an old friend of Argus, who he had invited specially, arrived on that same day the ship was completed. He came directly to the harbor, where the final details were being painted.

At first sight he was not terribly prepossessing; he scarcely seemed like a man who'd be at home in a company of great athletes. He was of average height, and while his arms and chest were quite muscular, nothing else about him suggested any particular prowess. He moved slowly and steadily, not at all like an athlete—or an Argonaut.

Argus shook his hand heartily and introduced him to Jason and me. "This is my old friend Tiphys."

I had never heard of him, but Jason had. "Tiphys the helmsman?"

He blushed. "Well, yes. I'm a bit embarrassed that you know my name."

"Everyone says you're the most skilled helmsman in the world. Welcome! There's certainly a place for you on the *Argo*."

My ignorance must have been apparent. Argus clapped him on the shoulder and told me, "You must surely have heard of his adventures steering ships past the monsters Scylla and Charybdis."

"Exaggerations, I assure you." Tiphys shook my hand. "We Greeks have never heard a story we can't make better with a little imagination."

"It sounds as if we'll get along just fine, Tiphys," I laughed. "Welcome to Iolcus."

And so our company was complete. 50 superb athletes, plus Tiphys, Argus, Jason, Hylas and myself. I'm afraid I'd been spending so much time with Kalais I hadn't gotten to know the others very well. The one exception was Euphemus of Taenarum, the famous swimmer. He had I had formed a friendly rivalry and had held a number of swimming contests. I usually managed to best him thanks to my knowledge of the harbor's currents.

And there was Periclymenus, the famous shape-shifter; "Great" Ancaeus, a son of Poseidon; "Little" Ancaeus, from Phocis, who had traveled the world as far as Egypt and Palestine; Meleager of Calydon; Polyphemus of Arcadia, who understood the language of birds; Nauplius of Argos, another son of Poseidon and a noted navigator…and…and… All athletes, all heroes, all excellent at what they did. If our band could not retrieve the Golden Fleece, the such a thing was not possible.

* * *

A ramp of heavy, free-rolling logs was assembled so that the ship could roll down into the sea. That afternoon Argus fussily saw to it that she was lowered to the harbor. We boarded her for a trial cruise a mile or so from the harbor and back. Argus had to inspect each detail of the ship while she was actually under sail, to make certain no last-minute adjustments were needed. And Tiphys was glad of the chance to get the feel for her helm.

We took our oars randomly. That night at the farewell banquet we would draw lots for our permanent places. And so for the first time the *Argo* went under sail.

One big problem became apparent at once. And the problem was Hercules. He pulled his oar with such strength the ship turned in circles. Argus confronted him. "Hercules, ease off. Pull a bit less energetically."

Hercules grunted at him and kept rowing.

"Hercules please. Take it easy. There's no emergency."

"I *am* taking it easy."

It was obvious that, whether he was showing his strength intentionally or not, we would need two men to pull opposite him, to compensate.

Other than that, there were no problems. When we reached the mouth of the harbor and were heading back to the dock, Euphemus and I caught each other's eye. It was clear we had the same thought. In unison we dove into the water and began swimming ahead of the *Argo*. We raced, heading back to her moorings. For once I wasn't able to outstrip him. We reached the pier simultaneously, well ahead of the ship.

We climbed out of the water and embraced each other, laughing.

"It's a pity you're already spoken for, Acastus."

"Look on the bright side. You've got 50 more opportunities for love."

"Love? Who said anything about love?"

I sighed. "Athletes."

A moment later the *Argo* reached the dock. They moored her and, led by Hercules, the company stepped back onto the dock, Argus poured a libation to Poseidon, with a prayer that no problems would develop. "May our journey be peaceful, happy and successful."

After the ceremony, walking back up to the palace and Argo House, I ribbed him. "An atheist like you offering a libation to the sea god." I couldn't help laughing. "We really do live in an age of wonders."

"Be quiet, Acastus. You might want to spend some time hoping that is the greatest wonder we'll encounter."

Kalais swooped up behind me, lifted me into the air, and we sped ahead of all the others. When he set me down on the palace roof I told him softly, "I only hope your wings can protect me from…from…"

"From what, little prince?"

"Don't patronize me, Kalais. So much depends on the outcome of this voyage. My family, my city, my life…"

He kissed me. "Whatever else happens, our love will survive. But there's a favor you can do me."

"Hm?"

"Try and stay dry. I don't want you wetting my wings down."

"Yes, sir."

He slapped me playfully on the backside. "Why did I have to fall in love with a smartass?"

"You know the old saying—we get the love we deserve. Let's go and get ready for the feast."

* * *

That night we feasted—the word is inescapable—royally. The refectory in Argo House saw a whole troop of servants, all our usual ones plus a cadre of extra help from the city. The palace kitchen had been busy all day long preparing a banquet worthy of a company of heroes. Inns and bakeries across Iolcus had been commissioned to provide still more food and wine. There was beef, venison, poultry of all kinds, fish fresh from the harbor. And cakes and pies of every description. Jason had planned it all. "We must have a feast that will leave no doubt in the Argonauts' minds how deeply we value them."

"It would be nice if Pelias were here to tell them so."

"His absence speaks volumes more about the reason for this voyage than his presence possibly could."

There were speeches by Jason and Argus. I myself reiterated the generous welcome all our guests had already received. Everyone who merited anything like a position of leadership or deference was called upon to speak, and the free-flowing wine gave us all eloquence (or at least it dulled the wits of everyone in the hall to the point where we all *seemed* eloquent). Only Pelias, as noted, failed to appear, something for which I was more and more grateful the more I thought about it. Hercules, with Hylas at his side, challenged us all to make our journey one the world would still celebrate a hundred generations from now. Tiphys, who had known Atalanta for several years, joked that he felt sorry for any man who got on her wrong side. "And that means probably all of us. Gentlemen, let us all watch our asses."

From the back of the room Mopsus shouted, "Hylas won't have to watch his ass. Hercules has been taking good care of that."

We all paused and fell quiet, unsure how Hercules would respond to this. But after a drunken moment he tossed back his head and roared with laughter. He leapt to his feet hoisted Hylas up to his shoulder, turned his head and kissed the boy's thigh. Hylas himself was laughing so hard he almost fell down, but Hercules caught and kissed him.

When the dinner plates had been cleared, there was still more wine. We drew lots for our positions on the ship. Happily, Kalais drew the oar directly behind mine; we would have plenty of chances to whisper to each other.

Then the Argonauts formed small groups of friends, lovers, men who had known each other in the past, new rivals or nodding acquaintances. Perhaps inevitably, arguments broke out, and a few of them were so heated they threatened to turn into all-out fights. I was most happy to see Atalanta best Castor; the ribbing he took went on for hours. But before any of the men could lose control completely, Orpheus took up his lyre and sang a song that soothed everyone's mood. While he sang Periclymenus entertained us shifting his shape from one creature to another. He and Autolycus had a contest to see who could change into the more convincing wolf.

In time we all became quiet, lulled by Orpheus' lyre. And then, perhaps inevitably, we heard Pelias crying out, from his quarters in the palace. It served to sober us, every bit as much as Orpheus' song had. There was a ghost. There was horror in Iolcus. None of us must ever lose sight of that.

* * *

Next morning we awoke before dawn—every one of us; not one was slug-a-bed. We dressed quickly and quietly. Then we and our servants, carrying our gear, made a silent procession from the palace hill down to the harbor in the grey morning light. Shadows were still dark; wisps of fog threaded among the buildings. No one seemed inclined to talk, even to whisper; the contrast with the previous night's boisterousness couldn't have been more marked. It was as if we were all wishing for the world to remain as peaceful as it was at that moment. No one wanted to disturb the mood. We reached the harbor quickly.

And there, like it or not, our sober mood was dashed. A crowd had assembled on the dock, come to see us off. They did not share our hushed mood but talked, played music, laughed. As we approached, more and more of them assembled. They cried out my name and the names of all the others. "*Argo*!" "The Golden Fleece!" "You will be our salvation!" "Hurrah for the Argonauts!"

Several of us tried to protest that we didn't deserve such accolades, but the people weren't about to be put off. I waved in acknowledgment of their enthusiasm and shouted, "You do us too much honor. We are only men."

"Yes," someone yelled, "but what men!" and there was more cheering and general laughter.

They produced crowns of laurel leaves and put them on our heads amidst more cheering. Finally we managed to break free of them and embark.

Argus was first on board the ship. He directed a small group of servants, who had gotten everything arranged to his satisfaction. Our own attendants took our personal things down to the lower hold, where beds had been assigned. Small cards had been set about the hold, indicating whose things went where.

Tiphys took his place at the helm, and Jason and Argus stationed themselves on either side of him. I eagerly sat at my assigned oar, as did all the others. We were ready to cast off.

Suddenly a curtained litter, borne by four footmen, broke through the cheering throng. The curtains bore royal insignia; I recognized it as Pelias'. When the footmen set their burden down, the curtain parted and the king climbed unsteadily out onto the dock.

"Argonauts," he bellowed, moving to the pier's edge, "I hail you! May your journey bring long life and prosperity to us all!" An attendant handed him a ewer of wine, and he solemnly poured it into the sea. "May Zeus, Poseidon, Apollo and all the gods who protect sailors grant you success and a speedy return!"

The crowd roared its approval.

At that instant Pelias tottered, lost his footing and nearly fell off the pier. One of his footmen caught him by the sleeve at the last possible moment. Kalais, who was standing at the rail behind me, leaned close and whispered, "Evidently pouring the wine out instead of drinking it was too much for him to bear."

"Quiet, Kalais."

Just precisely then the top of the sun climbed above the eastern horizon. Its rays, reflected and redoubled by the sea. made the crimson sail seem to blaze. Jason, ever the politician, pretended not to notice the king's misstep. "Cast off!" he called, and the crowd cried out its acclaim. I knew that every last one of them must be thinking the same thing I was: hoping the king's unsteadiness was not an ill omen.

In only a moment that *Argo* was underway. We sailed directly into the rising sun. The sail billowed in a gentle breeze. It was gentle, but it was more than enough to propel us forward. We shipped our oars. The sea ahead of us was as calm and serene as any traveler could wish; only the merest ripples broke the surface.

I stepped once more to the rail. As I looked back at the harbor, back at the one city I had known and loved, I felt Kalais come up behind me. He put his fingers on my shoulders; his wings enfolded me.

"You must know what I'm thinking, Kalais."

"Sad thoughts? Troubled ones?"

I nodded.

He kissed the back of my neck. "Then think of this. Think of our love. It can weather any tragedy the gods might visit upon us. Think of us, together."

"I wish I could believe you. There are too many other..." I kissed him. "I should be excited, Kalais. We are embarking on a great adventure. But all I can feel is apprehension"

"You worry too much. Do you want to become an old woman?"

"Be quiet. Hold me tighter."

And so we sailed on into the trackless waters of the Aegean.

Chapter Seven
The Women of Lemnos

The *Argo* was as cunningly designed as any ship I'd ever sailed on. Argus had constructed her so wonderfully there was almost no sensation of forward movement. We skimmed the surface of the sea as lightly it was as if we were weightless. It was the most astonishing sensation. With the wind pushing us forward, we were able to ship our oars and enjoy the ride.

Just outside the mouth of the harbor a pod of dolphins greeted us. I had the impression they had been waiting there. They were beaked like birds, a kind I had never seen before. Men pointed, laughed, called out to our aquatic brothers.

I couldn't resist the temptation. I stripped off my tunic, dove in and swam among them. A moment later Euphemus followed. The dolphins clicked and whistled a welcome to us, and we all kept pace with the ship quite effortlessly. Several of them rubbed their bodies playfully against me. I'm afraid it had an erotic effect. I looked up, hoping Kalais wasn't able to see my excited state. But he was there, watching and grinning. "Come back aboard! Your playmates are making me jealous!"

Jason moved next to him. "Yes, come on back aboard, Acastus. You'll need your energy when the wind dies and we have to row."

Euphemus ignored him. "Come on, Acastus. Let's try our stamina. I'll bet you tire before me."

"You have a bet."

Euphemus was a good swimmer, perhaps even better than me. But I had been swimming with dolphins since my earliest years. I knew them, their habits, and they knew mine. I coaxed a pair of them to bear me up and carry me along. The look on Euphemus'

151

face as we sped past him was quite something. "All right," he shouted, "you win. I should know better than to challenge someone in his home waters."

A few minutes later we climbed back on board. Kalais was waiting to towel me off. "You conquer the sea as readily as I conquer the sky."

"A pair of demiurges, that's us."

He slapped my backside. "Why are you always so damned sardonic?"

I toweled my hair. "It's the way I register despair. Let's see if anyone has opened a cask of wine."

Everyone was on the top deck, enjoying the wonderful transport Argus had made for us. There was bread, olive oil and wine.

Zetes pulled his brother aside and whispered something to him. I found myself standing next to Atalanta. Close-to, she was quite a beautiful woman, tall, with dark, seductive eyes and billowing black hair. She always wore a silver armlet with the image of the full moon. I wanted to ask her to pose for me. But with our voyage all ahead of us, there seemed no point.

"You're quite the swimmer, Acastus. And—do you actually know the speech of dolphins?"

I felt myself blushing. "Not really. It's just that I've swum among them so often, I know their... Did you see me? I mean, my erec—" The thought she had seen my excitement in the water had me feeling abashed.

She laughed. "Everyone did. And I have seen naked athletes before, you know. Every woman in Greece has. You men aren't exactly modest about your bodies." Her eyes twinkled with mischief. "Besides, I liked what I saw. I find you reassuring."

"Reassuring? Is that really the word you mean?"

"Yes, reassuring. I've seen you with Kalais. There are at least two men on this journey I know won't bother me."

As if to make her point Great Ancaeus, who had already had too much wine, planted himself beside her and tried to kiss her. She pushed him away. "See what I mean? He's been making a nuisance of himself since he arrived in Iolcus. And he's not alone. Even that boy, Hylas, has come on to me. At least I think he did. He's so awkward it was hard to tell for certain."

I laughed. "Don't ever tell him you thought so. He'd die of embarrassment."

"Don't worry. Knowing how to handle men is the essential part of preserving virginity."

I decided I liked Atalanta and wanted to get to know her better.

Kalais came over to me. "Come and watch me. Zetes and I are going to race. I want you to see me beat him."

Atalanta kissed me on the cheek. "Go watch your lover."

And that is how our voyage began.

* * *

The wind was fair. It picked up especially briskly in the morning and late afternoon. It died off in mid-afternoon; that was the only time we had to row. But even rowing was a pleasure, since Orpheus' lyre gave us our rhythm. His music seemed to propel us as surely as our oars did.

We quickly got into a routine, quite invariable from day to day. During slack periods I got into the habit of sketching various members of the crew. I planned ultimately to make sculptures of as many of them as possible. Ours was likely to be a historic journey; a memorial to it and its crew would be more than appropriate. Of course, I was assuming we would be successful, but then how could I not?

* * *

We headed northeast, in the general direction of Troy. There were no maps of the Aegean, or rather there were too many of them, all contradictory, none really reliable. Knowing precisely where to head was more a matter of having an experienced helmsman and navigator, which, in Tiphys and Nauplius we were quite fortunate to have. Their instincts—their "noses," as they always said—pointed us infallibly in the right direction.

And then there was Jason's branch from the Dodonian oak, which Argus had incorporated into the *Argo*'s prow per instructions. Several times a day, when the breeze was blowing, Jason would make a show of listening to it. Then he would consult with Tiphys and

Nauplius, and they would make whatever corrections in our course he deemed advisable.

Late on our second day out I caught him by the sleeve. "Jason, there's something puzzling me."

"Hmm?"

"Well, I've understood that the priests of Dodona hear the voice of Zeus when the wind rustles the oak's leaves."

"So they do."

"Well, the prow of the *Argo* has no leaves. What are you hearing?"

He stared at me fixedly, disapprovingly. "You are too much a skeptic, Acastus. You ask too many frivolous questions."

"I'm asking seriously. Is this all a sham to make us think we have divine guidance?"

He looked around and lowered his voice conspiratorially. "I hear the voice of the god. Not every time, not infallibly, but I hear it. You aren't trying to set any limits to his power, are you?"

"No, but—"

"Then stop asking impertinent questions."

And that was that, at least in Jason's mind.

* * *

The Aegean is dotted with islands, some so small as to barely be mounds of rock in the water, some large enough to be formidable city-states in their own right. We had brought enough food and wine to last a week; there seemed no point to bringing more, since we could always be certain of finding an island friendly enough—or commercial enough—to provide us with more than enough to replenish our stocks.

We passed one after another, scores of them. Some were no more than stones protruding from the water, but some were quite substantial, covered with vegetation and, in the case of the larger ones, clear signs of habitation. Sometimes there were cities clearly visible; sometimes there were no more than a few huts and fishing boats on the strand. We tended to avoid the inhabited ones, never knowing what kind of reception we might get.

Out principal lookout was Lynceus, the twin brother of Idas. His nickname, a play on his name, was "Lynx-eyed," and he more than lived up to it. While many of the islands we passed were close or in the middle distance, many others were no more than dots on the horizon. Lynceus never failed to tell us accurately what they were like: whether inhabited or not, barren or not, fertile or not, how populous... When another lookout was on duty and spotted an island, Lynceus was called. We were as safe in his hands as we were with Argus, Tiphys and Nauplius. We had every prospect of a prosperous voyage.

* * *

The first place we planned to stop was Lemnos, an island with ancient ties to Iolcus. If the old annals were right, Lemnos had originally been colonized by Iolcans, and for their first several centuries—until they were strong and productive enough to become their own state— the Lemnians had been our colony. Relations between the two had always been cordial, and we were sure of a friendly reception there. Lemnos had a walled, fortified capital, Myrine, that was the envy of the Aegean. Not even the Trojans, always acquisitive, had been able to breach its defenses.

Iolcus had had no communications with Lemnos for over a year. That was not exactly unusual in the Aegean world, but calling there would be doubly useful. It would afford us the chance to restock the *Argo*, and it would shed light on that minor mystery.

Late in the afternoon of our fourth day at sea, Jason consulted with his oak again and the "noses" of Tiphys and Nauplius. He announced that we could expect to drop anchor in Myrine's harbor sometime that evening.

I for one was glad of the news. I hadn't quite got my sea legs yet. Setting foot on land would be a pleasure.

* * *

It was after dark when Lemnos loomed on the horizon. Lynceus called to Jason, Argus and me to join him at the prow. "There's something wrong. I can't see any movement."

A look of concern crossed Argus' face. "Are you certain? Watch for a moment."

He did. "There's nothing. I can see a few lights in the high city, but there's nothing in the harbor. If it weren't for those few lights in Myrine's acropolis, the island would only be a darker blackness against the night sea."

Argus shaded his eyes. "In the whole long history of seafaring, there has never been a harbor without waterfront cafes, and they always stay open late into the night."

"Well," Jason said, "we appear to have found one."

No one seemed to know whether to be suspicious or puzzled—or both. All I could think to say was, "Watch for a few more moments, Lynceus." Argus signaled to Orpheus to leave off his music.

We waited silently as Lynceus peered into the distance. Finally he told us, "No, there is nothing. No one walking through the streets, no deeper shadows moving against the darkness, no lights being turned on or off. Everything is perfectly static." He lowered his voice. "Perfectly dead."

Jason called the order to row slowly, very slowly toward the island. He whispered to us, "This isn't right."

"You've been here before?" I asked.

"Yes, several years ago. Thoas, the king, had quite a lively court, and the people were full of fun and merriment. The harbor bustled all night long."

Argus had been thinking. "Perhaps they've adopted more austere habits than when you were here. Or when I was myself, a good 20 years ago. Their economy is a fishing economy, no? Fishermen go to bed early so they can rise before dawn."

"And the high city?" Jason's voice was barely as whisper. "Why is there no movement at the palace or in the temples? Why so few lights?"

"I'm merely thinking out loud," Argus added. "I was here once also, well before Thoas succeeded to the throne. But I remember it well as Jason does. It's the last island I'd expect to be so still. Even at night it was a merry place."

We drew steadily closer. Lynceus told us, "I can see people now. A row of them: soldiers. They are in full armor, with shields and crested helmets, standing with spears at the ready."

I squinted and tried to see, but the night was too dark. I could make out the lights in the acropolis, nothing more.

156

Jason gave the order to light torches. "We don't want them to think we're being anything but open and friendly. Echion?" he called.

"He's below, sleeping. He just finished his shift on the oars."

"Someone go and fetch him." Jason peered at the blackness that was Lemnos. "Acastus, give the order for everyone to arm himself and put on armor. Let us hope Echion can be as persuasive as his reputation has it. I don't want the first stop on our voyage to open with hostilities."

A moment later Echion joined us at the prow, still yawning and rubbing his eyes. "What's wrong?"

Jason quickly explained the situation. "When we're close enough, we'll need you to hail them and get us a good welcome."

"Here, Echion, have a cup of wine." I poured for him. We'd need him to be awake, keen and alert. "They say you can charm honey from bees. It's looks like we may need just that."

Argus muttered, "If it isn't too late for it."

From behind us came the laughing voice of Butes. "Not my bees, you can't"

Zetes came forward. "Kalais and I can fly ahead and see what's happening. The night will cover us."

"No." Jason clapped him on the shoulder. "Your white wings would stand out like beacons and give you away.

"Wait!" Lynceus' voice took on a note of alarm. "They're moving. And lighting lights."

We watched. Lights appeared; armor glinted off them. Then the lights descended to the water. The Lemnians were launching boats.

None of us moved. They could be up to anything—preparing a friendly welcome, a hostile one, a peaceable greeting or a warlike one.

"They are small boats, not warships," Lynceus told us.

"Thank the gods," Jason said softly. Every one of us must have been thinking it too.

We watched and waited. But none of the boats moved. Except for the soft sounds our oars made in the water and our slow, steady, forward movement, the world was still.

At length Echion told us we were close enough for his voice to carry clearly to the harbor. He stood boldly in the prow. "Citizens of Lemnos!" he called. His voice was, as a herald's voice should be, quite stentorian. No trumpet we could have blown would have sounded as loudly. But despite its volume it was as warm and inviting as a human voice could be. "The Princes Acastus and Jason of Iolcus greet you. We come in brotherhood and peace!"

We waited. Nothing on the island moved; even the boats were still. Echion continued. "King Pelias of Iolcus sends his warmest regards and bids you welcome us, his envoys, in the spirit of amity that has always existed between our two cities." His voice echoed faintly through the night. A dolphin, or perhaps merely a fish, leaped playfully out of the water beside us.

Finally there was movement. One of the boats left the harbor and made to meet us. We all knew it was a good sign. A number of boats coming at us might mean hostilities—might mean anything at all; one was merely coming to greet our ship. It was probably coming to check us out, too, but that was to be expected.

Echion went on. "We are the company of the ship *Argo*, on a mission for our city—the motherland of Lemnos."

The boat continued its advance. As it neared, by the light of its torches we began to make out its passengers. Besides the two boatmen who rowed, there were six soldiers, all in armor, all carrying spears. The boatmen were in armor as well. One of them hailed us. "We bid you welcome to Lemnos. Queen Hypsipyle sends her greetings." The oddness of it struck us all immediately: it was not the voice of a herald, not a male voice at all. It was the voice of a woman.

A female herald? Queen Hypsipyle? Surely it was King Thoas who ruled the island. We conferred among ourselves as the boat continued to approach. Lynceus surveyed the boat and told us, "Everyone on board is a soldier. I can see no women on board."

"But we just heard…"

He shrugged.

We had to return their greeting; courtesy demanded it. The protocol was clear. Fortunately, there were standard formulas of greeting. Echion shouted one while we tried to make sense of the situation.

Lynceus surveyed the boat again. "Wait—something is not right."

"Something else?" Argus was his usual wry self.

Jason muttered, "Be quiet, Argus. Echion, what can you see?"

"If the riders on that boat are soldiers, they must be the smallest soldiers on record. I think they must all be women."

"Women?" It was easy to hear Jason's bafflement. "Lemnos is one of the best-protected islands in the Aegean. Why would they send women masquerading as soldiers to meet us?"

"Why indeed?" Despite his gruff skepticism, it was easy to hear that Argus was as concerned as the rest of us.

"Atalanta!" I called softly. "Get up here. I think we may need you."

She rushed to join us.

Kalais whispered, "Let me fly ahead and see what I can."

"No!" I didn't even attempt to keep the urgency out of my voice. "Your wings would catch the light from their torches. You'd be far too easy a target."

"I can fly high enough to be out of range of any spears they might throw."

"I said no, Kalais. Anyway, from that height you couldn't see anything Lynceus can't see from right here."

The boat was closer. It would be even with us in a matter of moments. Jason gave the order for us to heave to, to greet them, and for all of us to make doubly certain our arms were at the ready. He spoke in hushed tones and added, "Just in case. Let us hope their intentions really are cordial, and all this oddness will be explained."

"To the captain and crew of *Argo*, we bid you the most generous welcome to Lemnos." There was no mistaking it now: it was definitely a woman's voice. But close as they were, we still couldn't see anyone identifiable as a woman. The speaker was standing at the prow of their boat. He—*she* removed her helmet and shook her hair down about her shoulders. We looked at one another, baffled. "Please accompany us into the harbor. We will see that you are properly moored."

They hove about and began rowing back to shore. Jason ordered our oarsmen to follow. "Doff your armor. We don't want to present anything but a friendly face."

"What's going on?" I asked. "Argus, do the Lemnians draft women into their army?"

"Not that I recall. Nothing like." He was staring after the boat and looking as bewildered as the rest of us.

In a few minutes we were at the dock. We tossed a line to the soldiers there and they made us fast. Jason ordered half our crew to remain about; I, Argus and the rest followed him down the gangplank.

The woman who had greeted us approached. She was a bit tall for a woman but still shorter than an effective soldier ought to be. Yet she was wearing a complete kit of armor, and she moved with the bearing of a seasoned soldier. Torchlight glistened off her black hair. "I am Clytophana. Queen Hypsipyle will receive you in the morning. For the time being we ask that you all remain aboard your ship."

Jason put on his politician's smile. "And how is her majesty? And how fares my friend King Thoas?" He leaned heavily on "my friend," just in case memories needed to be jogged.

"Her majesty will, I am certain, be pleased to see you again. You will be summoned in the morning."

"May we not seek shelter in Myrine? Hospitality would seem to require—"

"Till morning, then." She saluted smartly, like a good soldier, turned and left us. That was that, it appeared. Unhappy and bewildered we re-boarded the *Argo*.

Several of the Lemnians removed their helmets. Unsurprisingly they were women. Clytophana issued some orders we couldn't quite manage to overhear, but she was evidently instructing her troops to keep us on the *Argo*. Then she and the rest of them headed up to the high city, whose lights shone far above us.

Argus looked as if he'd just eaten something bad. "Somebody get me some wine."

The Argonauts had been watching and listening to all this. None of them seemed to know what to make of the situation. Some of them reached for wineskins; others talked among themselves, trying to make sense of it all.

Idmon stepped forward. He moved quickly to Jason's side. They had been enamored of one another, as passionate as Kalais and I, to the point where everyone took it for granted they were committed lovers. Whether they really were, whether Jason was quite capable of real love or even real affection, I had no idea. He may simply have thought it advisable to keep one of our seers near him. Idmon, for his part...well, I had never been able to forget his sad prophecy for

160

himself. And despite his evident infatuation, I had the feeling that neither had he.

"Jason," he said to his lover or would-be lover, "something is not right. We should move on, and quickly."

"You know we have to stop here. We need water and other supplies." Jason meant it for all of us, not just Idmon.

"There will be other islands with plenty of water."

"Now, don't argue, Idmon. Lemnos and Iolcus have strong bonds of friendship. We will be fine."

Amphiaraus stepped forward. "If we will be fine, and if Lemnos is so friendly to us, why are they confining us to the ship? What kind of hospitality is that?" He lowered his voice and added slowly, "This is not a healthy place for us."

We had two seers in our company, and both were warning that we shouldn't stay at Lemnos. It had to matter. But Jason turned pensive. "Relax." He raised his voice. "All of you, relax. If there really is something wrong here, isn't it our duty to find out what, and to correct it?"

From the stern Hercules bellowed, "We are the Argonauts. We are the bravest company of heroes Greece has ever produced. If there is something amiss in Lemnos, who better to put it right?"

Hylas was beside him. "Hercules is right. We must all trust Jason to lead us through whatever comes."

"Thank you, Hylas, and thank you, Hercules." Jason grinned like a schoolboy. "Now hear me, all of you. We must stay on board here tonight, but I am certain that will change come morning. Tomorrow we will stow our new supplies and leave."

Softly, in tones so low only Jason, Argus and I could hear, Idmon said, "No, we shall be delayed here. This island is a place of death."

Jason ignored this. Argus and I exchanged glances, but there was nothing we could do.

More wineskins were passed around, and we went below to our bunks. Little Ancaeus and Atalanta remained above, to keep watch. The night was dark; there were meteors.

* * *

The lower hold, where most of the bunks were, was so crowded Argus had found room to move a few bunks up to the first sub-deck. Eight beds were there, moved close together in pairs. Two were for Hylas and Hercules, two were for Kalais and me, two for Zetes and Polyphemus—who had become quite as enamored as Kalais and I—and the fourth pair were for Jason and Idmon. Lynceus and Autolycus had also become quite close but there was no more room for a double bunk; they would simply have to make do on the bottom deck.

"You still won't have any privacy," Argus told us. "No one does, on a ship. But there's room near the prow for six beds, and there's no point breaking up couples who belong together."

Kalais and I snuggled. As always he enfolded me in his wings; it was a feeling I never got tired of. When the others were asleep he whispered to me, "Let's fly, and see what we can see."

"The Lemnians ordered us to stay aboard."

"Aren't you the least bit curious what's going on? They'll never see us in the night sky. Come on."

We slipped up to the main deck. Atalanta noticed us; Kalais held up a finger to keep her quiet. Her eyes twinkled. We made certain no Lemnians were watching lifted into the air.

It was late spring but the night was chilly. I held Kalais tightly, as I was used to doing. We soared straight up, flew over the harbor from a height. A dozen Lemnian soldiers were picketing the dock; they obviously didn't trust us to remain aboard. Happily there was no sign they had seen us go aloft.

The acropolis, the high city, loomed ahead of us. There were more lights there now; evidently they believed us when we said we were friends. We flew higher to remain unseen. Below us, flames in cauldrons roared around the palace, lighting it brilliantly. The temples to the various gods were likewise well lit. People came and went, some of them in an obvious hurry.

"Do you see it?" Kalais asked me.

"What do you mean?"

"The people."

"What about them, Kalais?"

"Look closely. They—it is quite incredible, but they are all women."

"No! That can't be!"

I peered down. He was right. There was not one man in sight. Not one.

* * *

Next morning we were all up at dawn. It was a blindingly bright spring day. The sun was as brilliant as I had ever seen it, and cumulus clouds flecked the sky. Argus had told me about the beauty of the Aegean sky, the intense, dazzling blueness, but he hadn't really prepared me.

Kalais and I conferred with Jason and Argus, telling them what we had seen. Jason was puzzled by it, perhaps even troubled. But when we urged him to hoist anchor, cast off and continue to a more cordial island for provisions, he dug in his heels. "We are welcome here. We have ties to this place. Nothing bad can happen." And that was that, at least as far as he was concerned.

Other members of our crew had also noticed the oddity of it. Idmon and Amphiaraus formed a united front to warn Jason once again. Nauplius told us he had charted a course for more friendly waters. Even Hercules seemed troubled, which was quite uncharacteristic. But Jason was not about to be shaken in his resolve; he evidently thought that the sign of strong leadership. "If there really is something wrong here, and I doubt there is, we owe it to the world to learn precisely what it is, and to right it if we can and to spread the warning if we can't."

We had a good, hearty breakfast. Just as we were finishing, Clytophana, accompanied by a detachment of female soldiers, arrived at our mooring. "Her majesty will be pleased to greet you all at the palace. All of you. There is no need to leave guards on board your ship. Our troops will be more than pleased to look after it." She paused, then added, "and you will have no need of armor or weapons. Hospitality requires it."

We conferred quickly. Jason wanted to follow their wishes. But when Hercules said he wanted to remain on board with Hylas, there was no room for argument. Not from the rest of us, at any rate. But Hylas, impetuous boy that he was, insisted he wanted to come along and see the acropolis and the palace. Hercules, the indulgent older lover, acquiesced.

Kalais and Zetes said they wanted to remain on board as well. "We never quite know how people are going to respond to us," Zetes explained. "We won't be stopping here long enough for it to be worth the bother of making an issue of your winged crewmen."

Echion turned back to Clytophana. "We appreciate your offer to see to our ship." I smiled and lied as smoothly as I could. "But several members of our crew are nursing injuries. It would be much better for them to remain here."

She frowned at this. But to insist we all come nonetheless would have seemed quite suspicious. It was clear she was unhappy but we left her no choice. Some Argonauts would stay behind to mind the ship.

Argus interjected before she could respond. "'Her majesty'? Will King Thoas not be present to welcome us?"

"His Majesty, King Thoas is not in residence at present." I don't think she meant to sound mysterious, but that was the inevitable effect.

Hercules, Kalais and Zetes, Great Ancaeus and a half dozen others stayed on board. The rest of us, carrying only the kind of light weapons that we could conceal effectively, our knives, trooped up the path to the acropolis. Clytophana led us at a brisk pace.

The path was steep, much more so than the path to the palace in Iolcus. But it was broad; we were able to walk six abreast. Our escort accompanied us, six of them on either side. We were ordinarily a talkative lot, but there was not much conversation as we climbed the path. At the top were more armed, armored soldiers.

The temples in the high city were smaller than the ones at home. They were all made of fine white Parian marble but gave the appearance of not being well maintained. The one exception was of marble so bright, so highly polished that when the morning sunlight struck it. it was almost blinding. Oddly, it was the only temple with no inscription identifying the god to whom it was dedicated. The temples surrounded a broad central court, 12 of them, one for each of the Olympians, or so I assumed.

At the far end of the court was the palace. It seemed to be the oldest building on the acropolis by a considerable measure. It was of some grey stone and was fronted by an order of Doric columns bearing a frieze of some battle scene that was not immediately identifiable. Armed guards were posted on either side of the entrance and at the corners of the building. It was not hard to see that like the soldiers the previous evening, they were women not men.

We were ushered into a small anteroom; with all of us there it was quite crowded. Clytophana disappeared into the palace interior. We were left to our own devices. No one offered us food or wine. There was not the least trace of hospitality.

The walls were adorned with murals of mythic scenes—Arachne spinning her web, Aphrodite committing her adultery with Ares, and so on. Most of them seemed to be spanking new, unlike the palace itself. We all looked around, gawking like tourists, taking it all in.

There were servants in evidence, coming and going as palace servants will. Most of them were boys, quite young ones, no more than five of six years of age. There were also a few old men, not many; they were quite aged, 80 years old or more. Some of them had to support themselves on canes. At Iolcus servants that aged would be sent into a peaceful retirement; I wondered how much use these could be. At any rate, they were far outnumbered by their female counterparts.

Very young boys and very old men. They were the first men we had seen, Everyone else—soldiers, servants, waterfront habitués— were women. The oddness was driven home to me: We had not seen any men anywhere, not men in the prime of life. Idmon and Amphiaraus had warned us. There was something not right in Lemnos.

I whispered about it to Argus. He shushed me. "Do not assume we aren't being watched and listened to."

Jason likewise warned me to keep my voice down. "I'm sure it will all be explained in due course. There's no need to find anything ominous in it all. Besides, a bit of feminine company is most welcome."

Hylas had been listening to us. He chimed in, "Yes, some of the women we've seen are quite charming."

"Don't get carried away, Hylas," I cautioned him. "You have the lover you've told us for months you've always wanted. Remember?"

"I only said—"

Atalanta laughed. "He's right. Having the company of women makes a most welcome change after all of you men. At least I know

165

the women will not covet my virginity." She wrinkled her nose. "Not most of them, anyway."

Argus snorted at her. "We're in the Aegean islands, Atalanta. The women hereabouts are famous for…well, for being content without male companionship."

Clytophana reappeared and told us we were expected in the throne room. "Please follow me."

Argus couldn't help himself. "We were just telling Atalanta, here, that she may find Lemnos quite a warm island."

Atalanta elbowed him in the ribs. Clytophana, her puzzlement easy to see, led us through the palace to the throne room.

It was small, not much larger than the anteroom where we'd waited; it was quite crowded with all of us. Clerestory windows set high in the walls admitted light but not much of it. Bright fires set in huge braziers blazed around the room's perimeter. On a dais at the far end were two thrones, one covered in dark grey cloth. The other was golden, or at any rate gilded, and was a bit smaller than its companion. The gold caught the firelight and glistened.

On the gold throne sat, in regal majesty, Queen Hypsiplye. I had been expecting a rather older woman, but she appeared to be in her mid-thirties. Even though she was seated it was clear how tall and— the word is inescapable—queenly she was. All in all, she was a most striking woman, with deep blue eyes and lush golden curls. I noticed Hylas staring at her; his eyes were almost popping out of his head. I quickly stepped in front of him.

Clytophana gestured, and we stepped forward to approach the throne. She announced us. "Prince Acastus, Prince Jason, Argus the Shipwright and their company, from our sister city Iolcus."

I noticed Jason bristle when my name was mentioned first. He was not about to let me steal whatever thunder there was to be stolen. Before anyone else had a chance to speak, he stepped quickly ahead of the group and made a slight bow to the queen. "Your majesty, King Pelias of Iolcus sends warm regards. I am your humble servant Prince Jason."

Hypsipyle nodded in acknowledgment. "We are gratified by the goodwill of Pelias, and we bid you all welcome to our island of Lemnos."

It seemed to me that Jason was eyeing her with more than

diplomatic interest. And unless I was badly mistaken she was returning his scrutiny. For the moment I made nothing of it; that kind of mutual interest on their part could only help us.

But I decided I had to keep our formal reception moving. I stepped to Jason's side and decided to voice the obvious. "Your majesty, I am Prince Acastus. We were hoping to meet with King Thoas. I hope his majesty is not unwell?" It was perhaps a bit impolitic of me, but I thought that if none of us mentioned the blaringly obvious it might seem suspicious.

"My husband and most of the men of the island are off on a hunting expedition. I fear we have had a rather disastrous year. A series of storms struck us and destroyed our crops. There is famine." She put on an artificial, political smile. "We are expecting them to return any time now."

"I see. How unfortunate—for ourselves as well as for Lemnos. We were hoping to replenish our supplies here."

"We will of course accommodate you as best we can. But I fear in our reduced circumstances…"

"Please do not concern yourself overmuch, your majesty." Jason was all unction. "There are plenty of other islands on our route."

It was not the most convenient situation, and it only added to my discomfort. Amphiaraus caught my eye; his expressions said, "I told you so." But Hypsipyle positively beamed at Jason.

There was more—a great deal more—of the kind of formulaic palaver expected of every host everywhere who welcomes guests. That thread of flirtation between Jason and Hypsipyle ran through it. It was only too obvious what was happening between them.

At length the queen announced that we would be quartered in the palace. "But your majesty, how can you possibly have room for all of us?" I asked. "Surely we must leave and find an island where Fortune has been more kind."

"Do not concern yourself, Acastus." She positively beamed not at me but at Jason. "Our men and their expedition have drained many of our resources, but we are hardly destitute. If nothing else, their absence has left a great many vacant rooms in the palace."

Our situation—and the state of affairs on Lemnos—was troubling me more and more. The absence of the men seemed less and less plausible the more I thought about it. If they really were off hunting, it must have been the largest hunting expedition in history. Why would a hunting trip have required all the men on the island? Why would Thoas have entrusted the defense of Lemnos entirely to women?

I decided to err on the side of caution, to the extent it wouldn't make her suspicious. "We are most happy to accept your hospitality, Hypsipyle. But please understand that a few of our men are unwell. They have remained on the *Argo*, and it would perhaps be best for them to remain there lest they spread contagion." No need to tell her Hercules was among our "unwell" shipmates.

She paused for a fraction of a moment, as if considering this. I was afraid she would insist on bringing them ashore, to have them treated by some female physician. But she put on a politician's smile and told us, "Very well, if you think that best. The rest of you, please follow Clytophana. She will see you to your quarters and arrange for all your needs. Gentlemen."

The queen rose to go. She took a few steps away from the throne, then stopped. "Oh, and I should like to confer with Captain Jason. If you would come with me, we can work out the logistics of your stay."

Argus nudged me. He had seen what was happening between them as well as I had. "Your majesty," I spoke up, "our mission demands that we not tarry here more than another day or so. Very little planning should be necessary."

Another artificial smile. The queen was not used to being contradicted. "Even so, Prince Acastus. Jason, as leader of your crew, and I have things to talk over. Please do make yourselves at home in our palace."

She left. That was that.

Jason, looking like a cat who'd found a dish of cream, followed her.

I caught Idmon's eye. He did not have to say "I told you so." The words seemed to ooze from his every pore.

* * *

We were made comfortable in palace quarters. Attendants—all female—saw to our needs. Each of us was given food and a good measure of wine. I presumed the latter was to put us into sound sleep.

Idmon had the room next to mine. Once the attendants were gone he joined me. "This place is not right. I told you before. Do not count on the *Argo* leaving tomorrow—or anytime soon."

"Your second sight has made you too much a fatalist, Idmon."

"You saw Jason and Hypsipyle, you saw their, er, mutual interest."

"Yes."

"Amphiaraus and I do not always see the same future. This time our prophecies are in complete accord. Ask yourself, Acastus, why would the king have taken all the men on the island with him? Why wouldn't the army be enough, or even just a part of it?"

I ran out of ways to bluff him. "You're right," I sighed. "Something is wrong. Even if Thoas led an expedition to find food, there would be a few men left here. Not every man is suited for military service. My father never stops telling me that I'm not."

Neither of us said much more. Nothing would have helped. Idmon left me and went back to his room to spend the night—alone.

Alone. I needed to see Kalais. When everything in the palace had gone still, I retraced my way back to the entrance. Outside, no one was in sight. The temples were all lit with torchlight, but there was no sign of any priests or priestesses, temple functionaries or anyone else.

I stole my way back down to the harbor. There were a few women coming and going from inns and cantinas, but none of them paid much attention to me. It was not hard to steal back to the *Argo*.

"Acastus!" Kalais beamed like a schoolboy with a fresh piece of candy when he saw me. We kissed. The caress of his wings seemed the sweetest thing I had ever felt.

A moment later Zetes and Hercules joined us. "What are you doing here?" Zetes asked in hushed tones. Before I could answer Hercules roared, "Where is my Hylas? Is he all right? If they've done anything to him, I'll—"

"He's fine, Hercules. Why wouldn't he be?"

"I miss him," he grumped.

"He's only been gone a matter of hours. Calm down."

"If they hurt my boy—"

"Will you stop it? No one has hurt anyone. No one will."

"You came to see your bird-man. Why didn't Hylas come to see me?"

169

I sighed. "Go to bed, Hercules. Hylas has had a long day. He's probably asleep by now."

Muttering vague threats under his breath, Hercules went below.

"That man scares me." Kalais kissed me again and rubbed his cheek against mine.

I looked at Zetes out of the corner of my eye. "You go below, too. I want to be alone with the man I love."

He laughed and went. Kalais waited till he was gone, then told me, "I meant what I said about Hercules. He's been taunting us, baiting us all day. 'Why doesn't Hylas so this? Why doesn't Hylas do that? When will Hylas—as if it's our fault the boy wanted to see the acropolis."

"He'll be fine. We all will." I hoped I sounded more sincere than I felt.

We made love, once, twice, three times. Then, half-exhausted, I made my way back up the path to the acropolis. A pair of young girls were playing behind one of the temples. I wasn't sure if they saw me.

* * *

Next morning we were all given breakfast, a fairly meager one. Several of us commented that Lemnos might really be experiencing a famine, if only a minor one. The need to find food would certainly explain the absence of the men.

Most of our crew seemed to have slept well; they looked quite awake and alert. Well, *most* of us. Little Ancaeus and Nauplius had paired off and spent the night drinking and making love. They both looked quite drained. As for myself, even though I'd gotten less sleep than most, I felt fine—perfectly exhilarated, in fact. Except for the absence of the Lemnian men, everything seemed in order. Hypsipyle would tell us what supplies we could have, arrange to have them loaded on the *Argo*, and we'd be on our way.

Then we were summoned to the throne room. None of the palace servants attended us there, which I found a bit puzzling. Our experience on the island had been the oddest mix of the commonplace and the baffling. I scanned our crew and found Hylas. He looked as if he were still half-asleep. "I hope you've been faithful to your lover, young man." I tried to sound stern, but he laughed at me.

"A couple of the servant girls spent the night with me."

"Sh, keep your voice down. We don't want anyone repeating that to Hercules."

"Relax, Acastus. My room is a distance from the others. I'm sure nobody saw."

"Good. I hope you realize what a lion you have by the tail."

"Relax, will you?" He brushed it off. Was he really so confidant he had Hercules in thrall?

There was no point drilling him. "Where is Jason?"

He shrugged. "Nobody's seen him."

I moved off to ask a few of the others. Jason's whereabouts were a mystery. I forced myself not to think of the obvious solution to it. Idmon and I were becoming friends.

Then without warning Clytophana appeared and announced the queen. Hypsipyle swept into the room. Not at all to my surprise she was accompanied by Jason. They walked holding hands, like young lovers. Jason was smiling in a self-satisfied way, like a cat that had found spilt cream. I caught Argus' eye; he had clearly been expecting this, too.

"Good morning to all of you," the queen announced. She was the very picture of the gracious hostess. "I hope you all slept pleasantly."

No one answered, and she went on. "I am afraid I must deliver some unfortunate news. You are all aware of our diminished circumstances here on Lemnos. The famine plus the lack of able-bodied men means that…well, I fear we will not be able to provide you with the supplies you require. At least not immediately. We are sending to the more far-flung parts of the island to see if we shall be able to meet your needs."

Argus and I exchanged glances again, and he took a step forward. "Does your majesty have any idea how long we will be delayed?"

"Not long, I hope. But I fear it is impossible to say precisely."

I spoke up. "I am certain Prince Jason must have explained to you that we are on a most important mission. Let us hope we will not burden you any longer than absolutely necessary."

Hypsipyle did not like my impertinence, and she smiled to show it. "Of course not, Acastus. In the meanwhile, there is another matter he has brought to my attention. He tells me that some half dozen of

171

your men are still aboard your ship. All of you were quite explicitly invited to join us here in the palace."

"I am sure your majesty will understand that Hercules and the others are not feeling well. They—"

"Hercules?!" She raised her voice, glanced at Jason then back at me. "I did not understand that Hercules is among your crew."

I was pleased at her discomfiture—if nothing else. "Oh, yes indeed. I'm surprised Jason didn't tell you."

Jason glared at me. But to have shown anger would have stolen our focus away from Hypsipyle. He was too much the politician for that. But I was pleased to have sewn a bit of discord between the lovebirds.

"He did not." She recovered herself. "Perhaps he assumed that you or Argus would. At any rate I must insist you bring your remaining men to the palace."

"Surely your majesty must understand," Argus said softly, "that we must have at least a skeleton crew to protect the *Argo*."

"And surely you in your turn must understand that we must take no chances with the security of Lemnos." Touché. She turned to Jason. "You will see to it that they are brought up at once."

He bowed slightly. "Your majesty."

Without another word she left the throne room. Jason was still standing beside the throne looking half-foolish, half-angry. He strode down from the dais and passed me very pointedly to confer with Argus and Nauplius. It appeared that all the Argonauts would be Hypsipyle's guests shortly.

The men were filtering out of the throne room by twos and threes, chatting or walking in silence. Things on Lemnos were not what any of us had expected. I caught up to Hylas just as he was leaving.

"You heard. Hercules will be here soon. Don't do anything to anger him." My voice was stern, and he looked a bit startled. In all the time we'd known each other I had never given him an order.

"Don't worry. I can handle Hercules."

"For goodness sake, Hylas, stop and think with your brain not your cock. Hercules enraged is capable of tearing down cities. He killed his own children. Do you think he'd stick at slaughtering a lover who's betrayed him?"

He froze; it was obviously a new thought. "Oh." His voice was very small.

"You wanted him, and you got him. Now in the name of all the gods keep your wits about you. And keep those girls at arm's length."

"I... I... they're so... I... I guess I'll have to."

"Yes, I guess you will. He's more than capable of killing all of us and tumbling half this island into the sea."

* * *

And so, accompanied by a detachment of Lemnian guards, Argus and I went to the harbor and told Kalais, Zetes, Hercules and their companions aboard the *Argo* they would have to join us at the palace. We had a hasty conference way from Hypsipyle's soldiers.

"We are certain not all is right here," I whispered. "We don't know quite what, yet, but—"

"Leave it to me," Hercules thundered. "I'll find out soon enough. If they've harmed my sweet Hylas—"

"Your Hylas is just fine, Hercules. For heaven's sake, keep your voice down."

Kalais touched my shoulder. "Are you all right? Amphiaraus and Idmon seem so certain there is trouble here, I was concerned about you. All of you."

"No, we're all fine, Kalais." Argus looked around and lowered his voice a bit more. "But there are no men on the island. None."

"None?! How is that possible?"

"Shh. Our guards." I gestured at the armed soldiers who'd escorted us.

The Lemnians prodded us to get the last of our belongings and proceed up to the acropolis. There was no time to fill our men in on everything that had transpired.

Back at the palace a woman named Polyxena, who we hadn't seen before, met us and introduced herself as the chief housekeeper. "It will be tight, but we have found quarters for all of you."

"Kalais and I will be happy to share a room," I told her, smiling.

"That would not be proper." She brushed aside any objections and led us to the additional guest quarters. They were located in a far wing of the palace. Kalais and I exchanged glances; we would find each other soon enough again, and we hardly had to say the words.

Hercules, on the other hand, was determined not to go along with Polyxena's arrangements. "There is a young man here, one of the earlier arrivals, named Hylas. I prefer that he and I share quarters."

"I am terribly sorry, but as I explained—"

He grabbed her by the shoulder and squeezed. Polyxena let out a cry.

I took Hercules' hand and removed it from her. "I believe I neglected to introduce my friend, here. This is Hercules of Tiryns. You will perhaps know him by reputation. He is the son of Zeus, the destroyer of Argos."

She paled; a look of abject fear crossed her face. "I see. I—I didn't realize." Working to regain her composure, she fell silent and brushed off her peplum. "Of course the Son of Zeus may have whatever accommodations he chooses."

"Good." He laughed. "Take me to Hylas, or bring him here. At once."

"Of course."

I couldn't resist. "And as I told you, Kalais and I will be most happy to share a room, thus relieving you of the problem of housing us separately."

"Of course." She went to fetch Hylas.

Once she was out of earshot we all broke out laughing. "I always knew you'd be invaluable, Hercules."

* * *

We were served a spare dinner than night. Argus, Kalais, Zetes and I shared a table. Jason and Hypsipyle did not join us. Just as we all sat down to eat, Polyxena announced that Hypsipyle would be most pleased if we would confine our movements to the acropolis. "This is for your own safety," she told us in concerned tones. "There have been rumors of plague on the far side of the island. Until we have had the opportunity to investigate, you would all be well advised to remain up here and take no chances."

"I see." I put on a tight smile. "Why do you suppose it might be that none of us have heard these rumors, not even the men who were stationed at the harbor?"

She brushed the question aside. "Her majesty has already discussed the matter with Prince Jason, and he agrees that would be the wisest course."

I asked Polyxena where her queen and our captain were.

"They are dining in private. Their relationship has become most cordial." She looked around the room from one of us to the next, daring anyone to make a comment. "It would behoove you all to follow their suit and not say or do anything disagreeable."

With that she left us, rather imperiously I thought. Except for a few serving girls we were left to our own devices.

Castor approached me. "Is there some reason why you're being such an ungracious guest, Acastus?"

Argus got between us before I could take the bait. "The question is, are we really guests at all, or are we…something else?"

But of course I could never resist baiting him. "Why are you concerned, Castor? Are you getting friendly with the serving girls?"

He looked around our table, obviously hoping to find someone to speak up for him. No one did, so he went on. "The Lemnians are being most hospitable to us, as much so as their circumstances permit. It ill becomes us to—"

"Your supper is getting cold, Castor." Argus was in no mood for him. Unhappily, barely concealing his anger, Castor went back to the table he shared with Pollux and the two Ancaeuses.

Kalais put a hand on my shoulder. "Calm down. He really is getting matey with some of the palace servants, by the way. You have heard, haven't you?"

It caught me off guard. "No, I haven't. But I suppose it doesn't surprise me."

Zetes wiped his chin with his napkin and drained a cup of wine. "Some of the others are, too. I suppose with all the men away, the women here are easily, er, approachable."

I didn't like the sound of it. I certainly respect everyone's right to make love where he may, but this seemed… well, ungracious on the part of guests. And possibly dangerous. Taking advantage of the Lemnian men's absence. Jason, Castor, Hylas and…how many others? I wondered, was it just the young serving girls, or… I made a mental note to keep my eyes and ears open.

After dinner Kalais and I took a stroll around the temple

courtyard. Torches blazed brilliantly all around us. And Kalais' wings provoked comment everywhere.

Just beside the temple of Poseidon we spotted Tiphys and a woman in her twenties kissing and fondling one another. When he saw us, he took her by the hand and rushed her off into the shadows behind the temple.

I was feeling more and more disquiet. When we went back to our quarters in the palace, Kalais wanted to make love. But I was too distracted. I kissed him lightly and apologized for disappointing him.

"You have other things on your mind, Acastus."

"Yes."

* * *

Days passed, more and more of them. When we entered the second week on Lemnos it was clear to all but the most obtuse of us that something was badly out of joint. Jason and Hypsipyle were clearly enamored of each other. Mopsus and Clytophana were likewise. And Pollux and Polyxena. And any number of our other men were, er, dallying with various servants, slaves, female soldiers and whatnot. I had the distinct impression the women were deliberately being as alluring and seductive as they could be—most peculiar behavior for wives who purported to expect their husbands home at any time.

Worse yet, it couldn't have been any more obvious we were prisoners on the acropolis. Argus and I had tried to leave once, to go down and check on the ship. Soldiers stopped us at spear point. "Her majesty requests that you remain in the high city." That was as far as we got.

I asked Argus to come to my room; there I conferred with him about our situation. "We have to be off on our mission. The city we left behind is dying a slow death, and it is up to us to reverse its fortunes. Argus, what can we do?"

He shrugged. "What *can* we do? Our leader, our captain is besotted with the queen. You know Jason as well as I do. Once he sets his mind to something, that's that. His mind or in this case his cock."

"We have to do something. More and more of our men are being, what, hypnotized or something."

Kalais had been sitting quietly on the bed, listening to us. At last he spoke up. "Hypnotized? Is that the word? More like bewitched."

Argus snorted. "So we're on an entire island full of witches? No, that couldn't be possible."

"Why would it have to be magic? Sorcerers use potions to besot their victims."

"Then why aren't you besotted as well? Why aren't I?"

I interrupted their debate. "Kalais and I are so deeply in love Hecate herself couldn't get between us. And as for you—" I found myself laughing. "Look at yourself. You're the oldest man I've ever known. I doubt if Aphrodite herself could get a rise out of you."

"Don't be rude, Acastus."

Kalais got to his feet. "Look, we need more information. We've had no way of knowing if there really is a famine on Lemnos. As bad as things seem, it may all be perfectly reasonable. If the crops really have failed, it's understandable that we haven't been given the supplies we need. And women without their husbands might easily be tempted to…well, you know."

"There doesn't seem to be much we can do, Kalais, not with guards keeping us on the acropolis."

"Yes, none of us have been able to use the main path down to the harbor. And the other paths seem to be blocked to us as well."

"So?"

"Think, Acastus. Your lover has wings, and so does his brother. Tomorrow morning, before first light, Zetes and I can fly out of here and check out the rest of the island. We should be able to see what crops there might be, then get back here before dawn."

I felt a fool being reminded that we had two winged men among us. It was such an obvious idea I started to slap myself in the head. Kalais caught my hand and kissed my temple instead.

But my brain was working now. "It seems to me we have something else these women may not be counting on."

"Hm?" Argus was watching us, amused.

"We have a woman of our own. Argus, you are closer to Atalanta than I am. You are old friends. See if you can't persuade her to—"

"Of course! She won't need much persuading. She confided to me two nights ago how unhappy she is at being delayed here."

* * *

The next morning we met on the roof of the palace, seven of us, myself, Argus, Kalais, Zetes, Polyphemus, Idmon and Atalanta. The roof was large and rectangular, 30 yards by, perhaps, 50. It was a brilliant, clear morning; the sun was quite blinding. Despite that the air was chilly. We wore cloaks, which was just as well, since they provided plausible cover for the twins' wings. The Lemnians certainly knew about them; it's not that we thought we could keep them secret. But they were quite determined to keep us on the acropolis. It seemed advisable not to give away our plan any earlier than we needed to.

There were four guards posted at the four corners of the roof. Soldiers, woman soldiers, dressed in full armor, complete with shields, swords and spears. "What can they be guarding against?" I whispered. "Up here, I mean. Are they expecting a flock of belligerent magpies?"

"Keep your voice down," Argus cautioned. "We must give the appearance of good, dutiful guests."

Of course there was no way we could keep that up for long. There were things to be done. Zetes, looking around but trying not to seem furtive about it, began to undo the cord of his cloak. "Let's get on with it."

"Be careful, Zetes." Polyphemus put a hand on his shoulder.

"Don't worry." Zetes grinned. "I'll be anxious to get back here to you."

I started to unfasten Kalais' cloak when, quite abruptly, Idmon appeared on the roof and rushed across to us. "I know what you are planning." He was out of breath, and his voice was hushed. "I beg you to reconsider. This will not end well."

"More of your doomsaying, Idmon?" Atalanta was wry.

"I mean it. There is death in the air."

She made a show of sniffing. "Really? I don't smell anything."

One of the guards, an expression of stern concern on her face, crossed to us. "What is going on here? You should all be preparing for breakfast."

Argus answered her. "You can see how clean we are. We've already washed." He held up an arm. "Here, smell. As clean as the proverbial whistle."

She scowled. "Don't dawdle up here. The queen wouldn't like it."

"Oh, we simply wouldn't dream of dawdling."

She snorted and stomped back to her post at the corner of the building.

We turned back to Idmon. I asked him to tell us what vision he had seen for us.

"We are Greeks. Death and tragedy are our birthright. They are in our very veins, in our nerves. They flow through us as surely as our blood does."

Argus laughed. "You should be a playwright or a martician, Idmon. Better yet, a priest."

I could tell Atalanta was trying to think of something impertinent. But before she could speak, Kalais stepped forward and cast his cloak off. "Come on, brother." Then to Argus and me he said, "We'll be back in no more than an hour. Lemnos is not a very large island; it will not take us long to survey it."

Without another word Zetes doffed his cloak and they lifted into the sky. For the hundredth time I found myself realizing how graceful they were, as graceful as swans, as herons, as beautiful as comets or meteors. And one of them loved me. The goddess must favor me, I told myself, indeed she must.

My reverie was interrupted by someone grabbing me by the shoulder. I turned and saw that it was one of the soldier-guards. She screamed. "You should not have let them do that. Your men are not permitted to leave the acropolis, and you know it." It seemed to me that she emphasized the word *men* ever so slightly, giving it a faint air of distaste.

I put on my best political smile. "What should I have done? How could I have stopped them?"

"Do not be facetious, Iolcan."

"Believe me, that is the last thing I would ever want to be."

She ignored me, raised her spear and hurled it upward, after our winged men. It fell pathetically short of them; they were already disappearing into the distance.

A second soldier came and joined her. "Your bird-men are flouting the queen's orders. Her *specific* orders."

"They are scouting the island for food that your people may have overlooked. In the midst of a famine how could that be a bad thing?"

The first one scowled. "Her majesty—"

Argus got between us. "Surely her majesty would be pleased if our people can find new supplies of food."

Neither of the soldiers knew how to respond to this reasonable statement. The fact that it concealed our real purpose was lost on them. Finally, the second one, frowning deeply, told us, "Well... we'll have to report this."

Argus put on a hearty smile. "Please do, by all means. I am certain the queen will be pleased that we are doing our best to help alleviate the food shortage."

Muttering vaguely, they went back to their posts. Our party looked at each other, grinning. We had gotten away with it, at least so far.

But Kalais and Zetes were hardly the only weapon we could deploy. I put a hand on Atalanta's arm. "Now, what have you been hearing?"

"Nothing particularly informative." She shrugged, then stooped to pick up the brothers' cloaks. "These women are being singularly tight-lipped. The official story is the official story, and that's that."

"There must be at least one or two women here who like to gossip. Gossips are everywhere—old women, irreverent young girls...even Argonauts."

She laughed at this last. "There is one young priestess in the temple of Aphrodite, named Marsilia. She likes me, and she seems to like talking even more. I think I may be able to get her to open up."

"Ply her with the best wine you can find."

"She is a priestess, Acastus. She is chaste, and her lips never touch wine."

Argus snorted. "You can't possibly be that naïve."

"Argus, you—"

"Stop it, both of you." I tried to sound firm and princely and leader-like; it did not come at all naturally to me. "You can bicker all you like once we're off this island and back at sea. For now..."

Atalanta blushed slightly. "You're right. We all know what an unnatural situation this is. Unnatural and ominous." We all looked at each other; it was so obviously true. "I'll do my best to pump Marsilia for what I can learn."

"Good. Do it. As quickly as you can manage—without making

her suspicious, of course." I looked up into the sky where Zetes and Kalais were mere spots in the distance. "Let us hope all will be well, then."

"I'll do it."

With that we all went back down into the palace proper. Atalanta went off to change her clothes and then to meet the priestess. The rest of us headed for the refectory to have a late breakfast.

The room was nearly empty. A few pairs of men sat around the room, talking intimately; they were obviously lovers among us. Off in the far corner Hercules sat alone, brooding. There was no sign of Hylas.

I watched him. "Argus," I whispered, "I'm getting more and more nervous. Look at him."

"You're right; I've been noticing too."

"What might he do when it dawns on him the situation we're in here?"

"Let us hope that dawn never comes."

I took a place at a table and he and Polyphemus sat next to me. "Is that a reasonable hope?" Polyphemus was forcing himself to stare down at the table, not at Hercules. "I mean, he's not the brightest man in the world. Perhaps he—"

"Keep your voice down." Like him I avoided staring at our great hero. "Hercules is a marvel in his way. He is all the power and passion of Greece rolled into one man. But deep thought, I'm afraid...well...."

"No," Argus said wryly, "the gods left that out." He glanced quickly in Hercules' direction. "When he realizes fully that we're prisoners here, or what Hylas has been getting up to with the serving girls..."

"I don't think we have to worry about Hylas. I had a good talk with him and he realizes his, or rather *our* situation"

"Good. Let us hope he is the first teenage boy on record to use common sense."

We looked at each other, and our faces reflected our glum concern. After a moment a serving girl came to us and we asked her to bring us food and a measure of wine.

* * *

An hour later the three of us, warmed and fortified by our wine, went back up to the roof to await the return of our flying scouts. There was nothing that could happen to them, yet we were nervous. Polyphemus in particular was on edge. "I wish they'd get back." He paced back and forth a short way. "I won't be able to relax till I can hold Zetes in my arms again."

"You know I feel the same about Kalais."

Argus watched us both and said nothing.

The same four guards or lookouts or whatever they were still stationed at the corners of the roof. They glowered at us when they saw us. One of them took a step toward us and raised her spear in a menacing way. The one who had confronted us earlier, and who I took to be the commander, gestured to her to back off.

We took our places at the center of the roof. Polyphemus was quite noticeably on edge. I was too, but I hoped it didn't show so obviously. I was grateful at least that Idmon wasn't with us, mouthing more prophecies of doom. That was the last thing our mood needed.

The day was still bright and filled with sunshine. Under other circumstances it would have been quite refreshing. I scanned the horizon for Zetes and Kalais.

Lemnos was like most every other island in the Aegean. A tall central peak, Mt. Vigla, rose at the center, dominating the landscape and the sea around it for miles. Around it were low, rolling hills; then beyond them the land was flat or nearly so, except for the acropolis. That flat land was where the people lived, worked, farmed.

In all of it, there was not a thing moving. There was no wind, and even the sea had gone flat. No birds flew; I could not remember ever seeing a day when there weren't gulls and terns swooping and diving over the water. Everyplace I had ever been, every city, every island, had had eagles, signs of Zeus's omnipresent protection. Today...nothing. I moved to the edge of the roof, which was surrounded by a low wall, to look down at the harbor. The guard's commander pointed her spear at me and barked, "Get back!" That was the end of that.

Polyphemus called out, "Acastus, look!" He pointed to a place in the sky to our north.

I could just make them out—two figures like huge birds in the distance. They moved quickly toward us, and it rapidly became apparent they were Kalais and Zetes. I rushed to rejoin Polyphemus and Argus. "Sh! We don't want to do anything to alarm the guards."

Argus shaded his eyes to see our winged companions better. "Our guards are already tense enough. I hope our friends—your lovers—have sense enough to approach slowly."

"If they saw the spear that was thrown at them when they left, they will certainly be cautious."

I glanced quickly around. The four guards were at stiff attention. They had seen the flying men too. The commander shouted, "Be at the ready!"

Ready for what? I wondered.

Zetes and Kalais drew closer. And still closer. When they were 50 yards away they waved to us. Polyphemus and I waved back. Argus looked around, I had never seen him on edge before; he always took everything in his stride.

Closer and closer the brothers flew, slowly, slowly. When finally they were at the palace they circled it, again slowly. I was as always moved by their grace, their elegance, so much so that for a moment I clean forgot about the guards.

They flew just above our heads, then began to lower themselves to join us on the roof. One of the guards shouted something incomprehensible. A second one did the same. What happened then happened so quickly none of us had time to react.

A spear shot into the air, narrowly missing Kalais. A second one followed. It struck Zetes in the top edge of his right wing, piercing it, breaking it. He plummeted down as we watched in horror. There was a quick instant when his left wing flailed wildly, trying desperately to keep him aloft. Blood spurted from him, spraying us. Kalais made a mad attempt to reach him and break his fall, to no avail.

He fell heavily, struck the edge of the roof, then fell to the ground below. We rushed to see if he was all right. Kalais landed beside me, crying, "My brother! My brother!"

Below us he lay, crumpled, the wounded wing hemorrhaging blood. His arms and legs moved, his left wing flapped feebly, then he was still.

"Zetes! My brother!"

He rushed down through the palace, and the rest of us followed. When we reached Zetes several Lemnian women were already there with him, both soldiers and random bystanders. They were staring at Zetes in a detached way, as if they were looking at a package someone had dropped. None of them raised a finger to help him or even to examine him to see what help night avail.

We pushed through them, led by Kalais of course. Zetes was quite still, quite pale and growing paler by the second. His left wing was broken, snapped nearly in half, and blood was gushing from the large artery that ran along the top of it. Even as we watched in those first moments, the flow became more and more weak. It was clear that in a moment it would stop.

Kalais got down on one knee and bent over him. "My brother, my brother. Please don't go, please don't leave."

Zetes' lips moved; he was trying to talk but didn't have the strength to do it. The earth all around was bright red with his blood.

Kalais looked around at the crowd of women and screamed, "What on earth is wrong with you people? Someone get a physician. Someone do something to help this man!"

The women stood impassive, watching, as if they were seeing a tragedy in the theater. Not one of them moved.

The run of blood from Zetes' wing slowed to the merest trickle. Then it stopped. Kalais lifted him gently into his arms and kissed him. "My brother, my brother, no, no!" He began to weep, more violently than I had ever seen a human being cry before.

He lay Zetes' body gently on the ground again. Then he buried his face in Zetes' chest. Crying uncontrollably, his words smothered by his brother's body, he muttered, "What kind of fiends are you that can watch a man die and do nothing for him? What kind of place is this?"

I put a hand on his shoulder as lightly as I could. "Come, Kalais, there is nothing we can do. I will see to his body and some of our men will arrange for the funeral pyre. It is done."

"No, no, my brother, half of me!"

I tried to raise him to his feet, but he resisted me. His weeping was getting louder, more uncontrolled. He pushed me violently away. "My brother! Leave me alone with my brother!"

"Kalais, please. Come with me." I whispered it. "This is not healthy. There is nothing any of us can do now."

He looked up at me, his face was as wet with tears as if he had just been bathing or swimming. "Nothing? How can there be nothing?"

I took him by the shoulder and tried to raise him again.

"Nothing? We are the sons of the North Wind, the sons of a god. How can there be nothing? Our father, who is in heaven—"

I bent and kissed his cheek. "You know that can't happen. Not even the gods have that power. Come with me now. Let us go inside. You need rest, you need sleep."

Slowly he got to his feet; then he threw himself into my arms, still crying. "I need my brother. I need the other half of myself. Acastus, I need *you*. Hold me."

"I am holding you, Kalais." I made my voice as gentle as I could.

"Hold me tighter."

Through all of this Argus had said nothing. Now he put a hand on my shoulder. "Take him inside," he told me softly. "I will see to Zetes. I will begin the funeral arrangements."

Kalais' tears had not stopped, not even slowed. He held me as tightly as a newborn child clutches its mother. I led him into the palace and to our room, then I lay him in his bed.

"Acastus, you are all I have now, all I have in the world. Be with me."

I lay down beside him and held him. We kissed. In a few moments his sobbing became softer and he was asleep. Even in his sleep tears streaked his face.

I had never had a brother except my infant twin who was slaughtered, who I never knew. I had never been at all close to my sisters, had never wanted to. Seeing the love between these Olympian brothers, seeing its depth and intensity, its unbridled and never-spoken power unbroken even by death, was like peering through a door into a new world.

I loved this man. I knew it, and I knew my love for him could never be broken.

* * *

Once I was certain Kalais was deep asleep I went to off to find Clytophana. She was in the administrative chambers. "I want to see the queen. Now."

"You are a guest here." Her smugness positively oozed. "You are in no position to make demands."

I caught her by the arm and squeezed. "I want to see the queen now!"

My ferocity astonished her. "I—I will notify her."

"Tell her to come to the throne room. And tell her to bring Jason." I let go her arm, and she rubbed it.

"Very well. You may await her there."

"Tell her in fifteen minutes."

"Very well, Prince Acastus."

I rushed back outside to where Zetes had fallen. Argus was there, on one knee, bending over the body, wiping the blood off it. He looked up at me as I approached. "These women are appalling, Acastus, barbarians. How can they even make a pretense of being civilized Greeks?"

"What on earth have they done now?"

"It's not what they've done, it's what they haven't. None of them has offered me the least assistance here. When I asked them for cloths to soak up the blood they stared at me blankly. When I said I'd need materials for building the pyre they gaped as if I'd suddenly grown a second head. Then they all just…walked away without saying a word. They were less concerned about this—" he gestured at Zetes' corpse "—than they would be about a spilled wineskin or a soiled apron."

"They murdered him. He was murdered. There is no other way to think of it. But—"

"Help me move him. We can at least put him somewhere a bit more dignified and in a more decent position. If we leave him here in the sun…" He did not have to finish the thought.

We carried him into the shade of a nearby olive tree. I noticed several women, including four soldiers, watching us from a distance. None of them made a move to help.

Just then Great Ancaeus, Nauplius and several of our other men came out of the palace and rushed to help us. Nauplius was carrying a bedsheet. Word about what had happened was spreading quickly among all of our company. "Kalais came to us in the dining hall. He told us about…this."

"I thought he was asleep."

186

"No."

When we had placed his body safely under the tree and covered it with the sheet, Great Ancaeus offered to lead the group of them to find firewood for the pyre. I told Argus we were to have an audience with Hypsipyle, and we headed quickly back into the palace.

When we reached the throne room she was just entering and taking her seat. Jason stood beside her. Their faces were set into royal impassivity. If it was intended to impress or intimidate, it failed. Clytophana took a position to one side of the dais and stood there at attention.

Ten other soldiers took up positions at the sides of the hall and at both entrances. Watching them from the corner of my eye, I bowed slightly to the queen. "You have heard what has happened?"

"I have."

"You will of course instruct your people to assist us with the preparation of the body and the building of the pyre." I did not need to add that laws of hospitality demanded that.

Hypsipyle looked slowly from me to Argus, then back again. Measuring her words carefully, she intoned, "Your winged men left the acropolis, against our express wishes."

I started to respond, but Argus cut me off. "He and his brother were scouting the island for food. Surely in the midst of this famine you could have no objection to that."

She raised her head imperiously. "Your men are not to leave the acropolis again. Is that understood?"

'Yes, Hypsipyle. But surely—"

"Not again!" She shouted it, then seemed to remember she was trying to be calm and in control of the situation. "I shall double the guard to ensure you obey."

Her manner was so pompous and aloof, given the tragic situation, I was appalled. I glanced at Argus from the corner of my eye and, typically for him, he was suppressing laughter. "Your majesty," he said, "you cannot possibly with to leave Zetes' body unattended and polluting the acropolis. The gods would condemn any city that could countenance such a thing. Our request for assistance is hardly out of line."

She fell silent for a moment, gestured to Jason and they had a quick, whispered exchange. For an instant she gaped at him as if he'd said the most appalling thing in the world. Then she recovered her composure and reassumed her royal manner.

"Very well, then. You may send six of your men to gather wood for the funeral pyre from the adjoining forest. They will be under heavy guard. If any of them attempts to leave the area, the guards will enforce our orders any way necessary.

"Jason informs me that you do not have a priest in your company. We shall provide a priestess to officiate, so that everything will be done properly, in a way that is pleasing to the gods. That is all." She rose to go.

I decided not to leave things there. "Excuse me, Hypsipyle, but I'm afraid that is *not* all. There is the matter of the soldier who slaughtered our man."

She stopped, taken aback, obviously not used to being addressed that way even by visitors who are also of royal blood. She glared at Jason, then turned to face me. "The soldier will be dealt with appropriately. And *that* is all."

She swept from the room grandly, as if she were queen of something larger and more important than an Aegean island. Jason moved to follow her, like the obedient lapdog he had evidently become. I jumped onto the dais and caught him by the arm. "Jason, how can you remain silent? Can you not see what is happening here?"

"What is happening here, then?" It was clear he didn't want to be talking to me. "What has happened except your flagrant violation of Hypsipyle's orders? She has every right to—"

"One of your men is dead. In the name of all the gods, how can you be so composed and compliant?"

"I have things under control. I am your commander. You must trust me." He said it loudly enough for Clytophana and the other soldiers to hear.

To trust Jason was something I had already learned not to do. I was not at all certain what, other than sex, was going on between him and the queen, but I was quite convinced it was not good. Until I had more information it seemed wise to make a show of diplomacy—with our own captain as well as the Lemnians. I tried—I could not be sure how successfully—to cover my suspicions and deep misgivings. "Very well, then."

Argus stepped forward. "You are coming to the funeral rites, are you not, Jason? The funeral rites, such as they will be."

He smiled a tight smile. "Of course. Zetes was a good man, a beautiful man. How could I not want to see his spirit sent to heaven?" He made a slight bow and left without another word. No one knew better than I that Jason had nothing resembling piety, that the gods and heaven were nothing more than convenient fictions for him. What he was up to, I could not guess. But…trust him?

Clytophana stepped forward from her post and announced that the audience was over and we were to leave the throne room. We had no further business there. That was that.

* * *

Word of Zetes' death spread quickly through all our company. Responses varied from pure sorrow to anger to calls for rebellion. We decided to hold an informal council in the palace dining hall so that all views could be aired. Everyone attended but Jason, who was off with Hypsipyle; Atalanta, who was plying that priestess for information; and Kalais, who was much too grief-stricken to leave our room.

Ten of Hypsipyle's soldiers stationed themselves around the perimeter of the hall. They were clearly there to eavesdrop and to intimidate us. But we were too sad and too angry to be intimidated so easily.

As leader (in Jason's absence) I spoke first. I reminded everyone of Zetes' astonishing beauty. "We still have Kalais, yes, but the time may well come when more than one winged man may be necessary. You all know Kalais, and you all know of my love for him. He lies in our bed, weeping desperately and saying that with his twin brother's death he is now only half a man. We are Argonauts. We cannot let this happen to one of our crew—two of our crew—and do nothing."

Tiphys suggested we make a show of force. "We have let these people bully us. But this, this is too much. They have obeyed the conventions of hospitality, but not the spirit… We cannot let Zetes' death do unavenged."

Castor, on the other hand—and to no one's surprise—pointed out that Zetes was, after all, flouting the queen's restrictions, which she had every right to impose on us. "Perhaps the soldier didn't mean to kill him at all, only to intimidate him. It would have served as a reminder to all of us that we are guests here."

"And what," Tiphys countered, "has Zetes actually been reminded of? Will he go to the Elysian Fields more compliant?"

Then Hercules spoke up. Everyone listened. "Tiphys is right. We cannot let one of our number be slaughtered this way and not, I don't know, do something about it." He pounded a table with his fist, and there were cheers.

Argus counseled caution. We were isolated on the acropolis, without weapons. Time would make the correct course of action clear to us. We concurred, some of us unhappily, and our council ended.

The rest of the day I spent overseeing preparations for the funeral and, when I could, spending time with Kalais. To their credit, the Lemnians did permit us to gather the firewood we needed for the pyre, and they provided the animals for sacrifice. But none of them ever conceded in the least that their soldier had committed a horrible crime against hospitality.

We sent another legation to Hypsipyle, demanding her consent to hold funeral games in Zetes' honor. She refused.

Late that afternoon, just at sunset, were held the funeral rites. The priestess of Hecate, Marsilia, presided, sacrificing the appropriate animals, intoning the prayers, lighting the pyre. There was no wind; the smoke rose straight up to heaven, which is always a propitious sign.

Atalanta moved close to me.

"Is that the priestess you know?" I asked her. "The one you've been chatting up?"

She nodded, then whispered, "I haven't learned too much from her yet. But it's clear there's something wrong on this island, and she is troubled by it."

"You have no idea what?"

"No. Give me another day or two. I'm sure I can learn something." She moved quickly off through the crowd. I thought I saw Marsilia make quick eye contact with her then go back to the prayer she was intoning.

Through the entire ceremony Kalais stood beside me, holding my hand tightly and weeping quite openly again. Polyphemus stood on my other side and held my other hand. He was not crying as Kalais was, but it was easy to see the grief in his features. When the flames died down and the ashes cooled, we gathered them up. By that time a brisk, cool breeze had arisen out of the north. Kalais said it was their father, come to gather his son's ashes to his bosom. We scattered them on the wind and in a few very short moments they were gone. The first of the Argonauts had departed.

* * *

That night everything on Lemnos was hushed, expectant. There were no clouds in the sky; a gibbous moon sailed among a thousand stars. The north wind had not abated. It gusted and howled among the temples on the acropolis; it shook the trees and made the stars shimmer and twinkle. Ships moored in the harbor rocked violently. No one walked abroad in the high city; no one seemed to want to talk, not us, not the Lemnians.

I managed to calm Kalais, to comfort him and put him to bed. Then I went to the dining hall for a late meal. There was not much on offer, only some porridge and a cup of cold, vinegary red wine. I hailed one of the serving women. "You must have something better to drink than this."

"I'm sorry, sir. The famine..." She shrugged and moved quickly away from me.

The famine. I had not pressed Kalais too hard for what he and his brother had seen; there would be time enough for that. But he did tell me that there was no sign of the much-touted famine. "The fields are green. Women work in them. Orchards on the mountain slopes are heavy with grapes already—this early in the year. If there is a shortage of food, it is because with the men gone there are not enough people to tend the fields properly." But there was no point arguing with the servant; I was to be given nothing better than what I had, and that was that. I finished eating and went back to our room.

All of us had been housed in the same wing of the palace. Our room was at the center of them all, with Argus in the chamber to our right. Oddly or ominously none of our rooms had doors. Most all of our men were already in their quarters; the last few were in the halls, talking, playing quietly at dice. I said goodnight to them and went into our room.

One candle burned on a table across the room from the bed; it was quite low and would go out soon enough. Kalais was fast asleep. He was muttering something in his sleep, something quite unintelligible; and even in the dim candlelight I could see that his face was wet with tears. I bent down and kissed them away, as lightly and gently as I could. Then I undressed and crawled into bed beside him, doing my best not to disturb him. In only a very few moments I was asleep.

And was awakened, I had no idea how much later, by a scream in the dark. The candle had burned out; faint light came in from the corridor. It took me only a moment to come to my senses, and I realized that the voice I had heard was Kalais'. He was up, out of bed, and he was struggling with someone. I leaped to my feet and groped my way to his side. As soon as the assailant realized Kalais was not alone, he—she?—most likely she—bolted from the room.

"Acastus," Kalais cried hoarsely, "I am wounded. She had a knife."

I rushed from our room into the hall. 20 feet from our door a torch burned. I took it from its sconce and rushed back to Kalais.

He was standing by the side of the bed, quite naked. There was a huge gash along his right arm; blood flowed freely and copiously. He had pulled up the bed sheet and was using it to stanch the bleeding. "Here," I cried, "Let me do that. Hold the torch."

As I daubed the wound I could see it wasn't deep. Once the flow of blood slowed, a bandage would be sufficient to bind it. He would not need further medical treatment. Given our increasingly alarming situation and the fact that the only physicians we might use were Lemnian, I found it reassuring.

But just that quickly I heard voices out in the hallway. After making doubly certain Kalais was all right, I rushed out to see what was wrong.

The corridor was dark; I had taken the nearest torch, and the next nearest ones were 40 feet away. By the light that reached us I saw that Idas was standing in the doorway of the room he shared with his brother Lynceus, calling the alarm. "Help! Oh, Acastus, someone attacked us! Lynceus is wounded on his leg."

"We were attacked, too. Kalais is cut. Did you see who it was?"

He shook his head. "Our light had burned too low."

From the far end of the hall there came the sound of another scuffle followed by a roar, or bellow. We could just see a figure dressed all in black run out of another of our rooms and dash around the corner. There were armored soldiers on guard. None of them moved to catch the attacker.

"Quick," I cried, "run and follow her. Catch her if you have the chance."

"Her?"

"You've seen this place. There are nothing but women. Run!"

I thought the room the attacker had run from was the room occupied by Hercules and Hylas. It didn't seem possible; who would be mad enough to attack Hercules? I moved quickly down the hall to their room.

As I approached, Hercules came out and took another torch from the wall. Seeing me, he cried, "They've assaulted my Hylas." It seemed to me he was in distress and on the verge of tears—angry tears. "My Hylas." He slammed his fist into the wall, and the wall trembled. The guards, startled, alarmed, scattered in terror.

"Is he hurt?"

"No. I reached out in the dark and pounded whoever it was. Acastus, it was a woman. She screamed when I hit her."

"Let's check on Hylas."

By now others had awakened and come out into the hall. Argus was among them and I quickly filled him in on what had happened. "Take a torch and check all the rooms. Make sure everyone is aliv— is all right."

In only a few moments we were certain everyone was okay. Hylas, thankfully, was all right. The wound on Lynceus' leg was not deep. Argus bandaged it; he told us he thought Lynceus would be fine in a few days at most.

The cut on Kalais' arm was deeper but not too deep; Argus said he would have to keep it in a sling for a few days. "Unless his divine blood can make it heal faster. He's lucky the knife missed the large artery in his wing. He might easily have gone the way of his brother."

"Don't say that, Argus, not even in jest."

"What makes you think I'm joking? It is a serious enough gash."

There was considerable anger among our men, quite understandably. There was a lot of sentiment for storming our way off the acropolis and down to the *Argo*. Argus urged restraint. "We stopped here for supplies, remember? If we sail away now, without getting them, what will we have accomplished?"

"We'll have saved our skins, that's what." Castor's reply met with cheers and applause. "This is an outrage, an hideous breach of hospitality."

"And how," Argus asked calmly, "would you suggest we accomplish this storming? The Lemnians have heavy arms; we have none but what we carried with us on our persons from the ship. A few knives, Hercules' club…" It was all too clear why the Lemnians had wanted us unarmed.

This quieted our men down. I took advantage of the lull. "There is a mystery here. We must unravel it."

Suddenly Hercules bellowed, "Unravel, hogwash. They attacked my Hylas in his sleep. If they had killed him they'd likely have killed me next. Every moment we remain here we are in danger. *Mortal* danger." He pounded a fist against the wall again, and the building shook. "I could bring this palace down on their heads and break the skulls of the ones who survive."

"And on our heads as well." Argus made a show of keeping calm. "Is that what you want?"

"Let Argus and me go and confront Hypsipyle, Hercules." I did my best to sound conciliatory. "Once we've heard her response to what has happened here, we will know better what course to take." Then I whispered in his ear, "There are almost certainly women listening to us. We must be guarded in what we say in their hearing till we understand our situation fully."

He glared at me. "You understand. I will act."

"Hercules," I whispered urgently, "we can't take on their entire army while we are unarmed ourselves. By all the gods, keep your wits about you. Hylas is all right. Go to him. Make love to him. And let us do our job."

He glared at me. Fortunately, just at that moment Hylas came out of his room and joined us. He had heard our exchange. He took Hercules by the hand and calmed him. "Hercules, you know Acastus is right. Let him and Argus do what they must. They are our leaders, and we must trust them. Please."

It was easy to see Hercules, that unbridled force of nature, melting under the boy's influence. That, I thought, is the power of love in action.

But it wasn't merely Hercules whose anger was soothed by his presence. The grumbling in the ranks eased off as well. Seeing it was almost magical. But the anger of the Argonauts could not be contained much longer. We knew we had to remedy our situation or worse would come to worst, and soon. "Hylas, you have been exploring the palace. Do you know where the armory is?"

He nodded.

"Good. We may find ourselves having to storm it. Atalanta?"

She stepped forward.

"Go to your priestess. Do what you must to learn what you must."

She saluted me, turned and went.

Very quickly the two of us rushed off to confront the queen. By the clerestory windows along the hallway we could see that it was almost dawn. The day ahead would be long and difficult. If we could not persuade Hypsipyle to begin treating us decently, as guests not prisoners, things would become even uglier, and soon.

We stormed past one rank of guards, then another. Clytophana and three heavily armed guards had been stationed outside the queen's chambers. "What do you want here?"

"You know perfectly well what we want and why we are here. Stand aside."

"Her majesty—"

"Her majesty will see us whether she wants to or not."

"You must—"

We pushed past her. It occurred to me that bringing Hercules along might not have been a bad idea after all. But fortunately the Lemnian soldiers were all women, small, not likely to put up a formidable resistance.

Hypsipyle was still in bed, sitting up, reading a scroll of some kind. Two servants, female of course, were giving her breakfast. Beside her, lying on his side, evidently still asleep, was Jason. The covers were pulled back off him, and I remembered at once why I had been so attracted to him when we'd first met. Naked, and with an erection in his sleep, he was as magnificently beautiful as any man I

195

had ever seen. But I could not let that distract me from the business at hand.

"What is the meaning of this unconscionable intrusion into my living quarters?" Hypsipyle smiled; she knew perfectly well why we were there. "The laws of hospitality demand—"

"The laws of hospitality demand that a host not serve her guests a knife in the dark." I was not about to put up with any of her nonsense.

"Why, Acastus, whatever can you mean?"

So she was going to play with us. "We want to know what is happening on this island. It is time you began to deal with us forthrightly."

"Why, I have no idea what you mean, Acastus." She was the portrait of innocence.

I looked at Argus, in frustration. He adopted a milder tone than I had been using. "We have been kept here against our will long enough. We demand that you remove your guards and permit us to return to our ship and leave this island. If there is indeed a famine—and our scout Kalais tells us otherwise—you should be anxious for us to leave and unburden you of the necessity of housing and feeding us."

"Why, good gracious, Argus, I'm afraid I don't recall you requesting permission to leave before now—before this remarkably unappealing behavior on your part."

"Do not play games, Hypsipyle. One of our men has been slain. There was just an attempt made on three more of us."

"Dear me, what can you mean?" She tossed her scroll aside and one of her servants picked it up. Jason stirred in his sleep but did not waken.

I was not about to be toyed with, not any more. "This has gone on long enough. We have lost one of our men, and as Argus said there have just been attacks on others of us. If we suffer any further outrages, and if our departure is delayed any further, we shall have no choice but to permit Hercules to—"

"What Prince Acastus means," Argus took a step forward and planted himself in front of me, "is that our noble companion Hercules is exhibiting signs of the madness that took him on the mainland. You will certainly have heard what he did to Argos, and to his own wife and children."

For the first time a look of concern crept into the queen's

features. Had she bitten off more than she could chew or digest? She worked to disguise it. "I understand your concern, Argus, and it will of course be taken under advisement." She quickly resumed her composure and her queenly manner. "But of course you cannot leave until your captain, here, has awakened and regained his senses. I am afraid he had a little too much wine last night."

"In the midst of a famine." I assumed a tone of mock-pity. "How inconsiderate of him. Is he drugged as well as drunk?"

"Hm?" Jason opened his eyes and looked up at us groggily, then scanned the room. "What's happening, Hyp?"

"We have just been asking her the same question." I put on a tight smile. "Good morning, Jason. Has anyone tried to assassinate you today?"

He sat up and looked around again. "What in Hades are you talking about? What are you doing in the queen's bedchamber?"

"We were about to ask you the same question." I told him what had happened. Before he could respond a dozen servants appeared, overpowered us and led us out of the room. Our little audience ended as inconclusively as it began.

* * *

There was no resolution possible, not with Jason, not while he was where he was. But the situation was bad and growing more dire by the day. I could not forget the sight of Zetes, lying so uncharacteristically on the ground, blood pouring from his severed wing. Jason would not act; that much was clear. It fell to me to be the captain of our band, like it or not, ready or not.

I asked Amphiaraus and Idmon to advise me. We went to the roof of the palace. The guards would keep a close eye on us there, but at least we could move to the center of the roof, far enough from them that they could not hear us if we spoke in low voices. Argus came too. I would have been quite lost without his counsel.

"So, what do the two of you see? You must be able to make more sense of our situation here than anyone else."

Amphiaraus shrugged. "I'm afraid not. You know that prophetic visions cannot be turned on at will. I know this island is black with death. More than that…"

"I know likewise," Idmon concurred. "When I ask the gods to let me see more clearly, I get a vision of Lemnos enshrouded in a cloud black as night. Each time I see it, it gets darker, less penetrable."

"Clouds, night," Argus snorted. "We need concrete information. How can we act if we don't understand our situation? We know it is serious, perhaps even dire. But the details… Not that I blame the two of you—far from it. I blame the gods, who tantalize us only to torment us."

"So now you believe in the gods?" I was wry.

Before he could respond, Idmon urged him, "You must have a little more respect for the order of things, Argus. Even if you do not accept the physical existence of the gods, respect them as forces and ideas made poetry for our instruction."

"Then why on earth don't they instruct us? Idmon, I—"

"Stop it, both of you. We are here for strategy, not controversy. It is clear for now that the gods, real or not, will not help us. We are quite on our own. More than one philosopher had taught that that is the human condition. Let us hope that Atalanta—"

"What could Atalanta possibly tell us that we don't already know? We are trapped here—prisoners."

"But why, Argus? There is some awful secret here. We all have our suspicions. We must. But—."

It was clear Argus was impatient with our situation, not with Idmon—or me—personally. "We are prisoners here, not in name but in fact. We must act soon."

"Be patient just a bit longer, Argus. Atalanta will learn what's what soon enough."

* * *

And so she did. Late in the afternoon she found me exercising in a small field beside the palace, with Kalais watching. And I was watched too, inevitably, by a group of Hypsipyle's soldiers who were pretending to work out as well. Atalanta looked pale, quite drained of her usual color. Kalais commented that she looked quite deathly.

"I have just come from the temple of Hecate, from Marsilia."

My ears pricked up. "And?"

"Not here. We must talk someplace private." Her air was part mysterious, part cautious. I wasn't at all sure what to expect.

She led us across the temple square to a place behind the temple of Hecate. There was a small grassy quad surrounded by low shrubbery. "The temple of the goddess of death." I tried to sound sardonic, hoping it might lighten the atmosphere and lighten whatever news she had for us.

But her manner remained grave. Looking around to make certain we were quite alone, she lowered her voice and told us, "Thoas and his men are not off on a hunting expedition."

"That is hardly a surprise. Where have they—"

"They are dead." She paused to let this register. "All of them. Every last man and boy. All of them killed in a single night."

It was the last thing I expected to hear. Words failed me. I looked at Kalais then back at Atalanta. Kalais found his voice before I did. "What happened? A raid by some rival island, or—"

"The women killed them. Murdered them all in their sleep. Lovers, husbands, fathers, all of them slaughtered."

When I finally found my voice I exclaimed, "Wh—how? Why?"

"Sh, keep your voice low." She looked around again. We were quite alone. "The men... well, they were men. They loved one another and ignored their wives. The women bore it as long as they could and then—" She spread her hands as if to indicate there were no more words for describing the slaughter.

"Hypsipyle did this, orchestrated this?"

She nodded. "Marsilia and the other priestesses argued against it, but the sentiment among the women was too fierce. And so one midnight..."

Kalais and I looked at one another, each waiting for the other to speak, neither of us quite knowing what to say to this. I'll admit I was quite lost. Nothing in my experience prepared me for what I had just heard. "But... but even if this is true, why on earth are they holding us here? What can they hope to accomplish?"

"And why did they kill my brother?" Kalais' voice was trembling, I couldn't tell whether from anger, sorrow or horror. And why the attempt to kill more of us?"

"I need to sit." Atalanta almost literally collapsed onto the grass. It was so unlike her; she was always so vigorous. We sat facing her, and she continued. "Well...the women realized that without men there would be no more children. They needed...for lack of a better term…breeding stock. A new generation would come of age not believing the love of man for was more than the love of man for woman. Once a sufficient number of the women were with child, the knives would fall again. They planned to dispose of the loving couples among us first. Hence the attacks. The rest would be disposed of soon enough."

Someone was approaching. We looked around and saw Argus. "He slapped his chest heartily. "Here you are. I've been looking everywhere. Someone said he'd seen you coming in this direction, so I—good grief, this looks like a funeral."

"You are closer to the mark than you realize, Argus." I motioned to him to lower his voice. "Sit down. Brace yourself."

Atalanta repeated for him what she'd just told me and Kalais. Argus listened with growing alarm. When she finished, he looked at each of us in turn. "What on earth do we do? How do we get out of here?"

"Well," I said, "Hylas can guide us to the palace armory. Once we've located it, with Hercules in the van it shouldn't be too difficult to storm it, arm ourselves and fight our way back to the harbor. We have out knives for the initial assault on the armory."

"Yes, but…" Again he looked at each of us.

"But what?"

"Can we do much at all without Jason? He is the leader of the expedition, after all. Without him, the other men might—well, who knows what they might decide to do, without him. They could easily decide to abandon the expedition."

Atalanta responded, "Acastus can lead us."

"Thank you for the vote of confidence, Atalanta." The suggestion had thrown me off balance, I'm afraid. "But I'm a sculptor, not a ship's captain and certainly not a military leader. I can take my turn commanding the *Argo*. But…no, we need Jason."

"That could be a problem."

Kalais had been quite silent through all this. But now, "Why, Atalanta? What do you mean?"

"Well," she took a deep breath, "Hypsipyle has promised to make him her king."

I was aghast. "You mean he knows what happened to the men?"

"That, I don't know. She may have made her promise contingent on Thoas and the others not returning. It's hard to believe he might be as cold-blooded as she is."

"I'm not so sure." Even Argus was sounding shaken. "He wouldn't be the first man to be blinded by ambition." He looked at me. "And we've seen Jason's ambition."

"We'll have to find some way of convincing him his ambition is misplaced here. Argus, you and Atalanta go to him and tell him what we've learned. For now, we'll have to trust his judgment."

"And if worse comes to worst and he doesn't believe us? Or worse still, if he already knows what has happened here and he wants to capitalize on it?"

"As I said, for now... We must begin spreading word among our men of what you've learned, Atalanta. Tell them quietly, on the sly, by ones and twos. Let us just hope for the best."

* * *

They found him taking a constitutional around the acropolis. He scoffed at what they'd told him. He knew Hypsipyle to be a good woman, he said. That was that.

The four of us met again, and I had sent word to Amphiaraus asking him to join us. Atalanta and Argus filled him in. I knew Jason well enough to know that nothing short of a drastic event would shake him, now.

"Amphiaraus, what does your prophetic sight tell you will happen here? Will there be blood?"

"I see blackness, not blood, Acastus. You know prophetic sight is not always clear."

"And your colleague Idmon—will he leave Lemnos with us— alive?"

He seemed baffled that I'd ask about Idmon so specifically.

"Wh—"

"Idmon told me once of a vision he'd had, that he would not survive our expedition. Is that so? Is Lemnos where he will meet his end?"

"I don't know, Acastus. I wish I knew." He turned pensive. "I've had many premonitions about this journey, but not so specific, none about Idmon."

201

"We must find him and send him to Jason. We must tell him to be as seductive as he can. He must take Jason to his bed tonight. And we must make certain Hypsipyle hears about their liaison."

"And then," Amphiaraus added glumly, "we must hope that neither of them falls to the queen's vengeance."

* * *

Argus undertook to find Idmon and explain the situation to him. And he made certain to tell him we'd be watching his room vigilantly all night. Nothing terrible could happen. I myself went off to find Hypsipyle. I would talk to her on the pretext of wanting to send a few men to check on the *Argo*, then mention casually that Jason and Idmon were, er, renewing their friendship.

Atalanta was to collar Marsilia and keep her occupied lest it dawn on her how thoroughly she had given away the game.

Most importantly of all Kalais was to find Hylas and learn for certain he had found the armory, and if not to help him search it out. They were to organize our men as discreetly as possible for a midnight raid on it. We would be armed by dawn's first light.

None of our group was to have any further contact with the others, except by subtle signals. That way we could know that everything was proceeding smoothly yet not arouse suspicion. The only exception was for Kalais and myself; if we slept apart it might look odd.

Our plan was in place. One way or another, with or without blood, we would be leaving Lemnos with the morning tide.

* * *

Late at night. Well past midnight. Kalais and I took a stroll. The night air was cool and crisp, and a first-quarter moon scudded through banks of clouds. Only the brightest stars rivaled its white brilliance. But in the west a mountain of heavy black clouds was building. We would have rain before morning. Brisk wind was picking up.

Kalais wanted to go aloft. "Let me make one more flight, to see if perhaps Hypsipyle has amassed her soldiers."

"No, Kalais, in the air you are too much of a target."

"I'll take care. They will never—"

"I said no. I don't want to lose you. I love you far too much." We embraced, kissed. It occurred to me that we were making targets of ourselves as fully as if we were in the night sky. But our love was too strong to be resisted. In that moment I wanted to escape from Lemnos more than ever. "Let's go inside. Hylas and the others must be ready to arm by now."

"Let us hope."

The hall was dark, as usual, lit by widely spaced torches. Idmon's room was at the end of the corridor, well past the last of them. Just across the hallway from it was Tiphys' room; he would help us in what we had to do. We stationed ourselves there. Soldiers, spaced even more widely than the torches, were stationed as usual along the corridor. As we walked past them, quite ostentatiously hand in hand, they stared impassively straight ahead. We hoped none of them would notice or think it odd that we weren't going to our own room.

Everything around us was in shadow, or near-shadow. And everything was quite still. Our footsteps and even our breathing seemed to echo. I help my finger to my lips, signaling Tiphys to remain silent.

Footsteps. Someone approaching. We braced ourselves. In the dim half-light we were finally able to make out Hylas, sauntering casually, as if the darkened passage was the most natural place in the world for an evening walk. He passed the door where we watched and waited. In the most offhand way he gave us a thumbs-up sign. Yes, they had found the armory. Our men were at the ready.

Hylas turned and walked back the way he had come. He would be waiting in his room. For long minutes there was absolute silence. Nothing moved; even the torches' flames seemed frozen in time.

Footsteps again. Voices, talking low. It was just possible to make them out: Idmon and Jason. Idmon's seduction had worked. In the near darkness we saw them walk hand in hand down the hallway. At the door of his room they paused and kissed, a long, deep kiss. Then, arms around one another, they went inside.

More minutes passed. The sounds of their passion came to us faintly but distinctly. Everything now depended on the Lemnians.

And they did not disappoint. A figure, cloaked, all in black, crept carefully along the hallway, keeping close to the wall opposite us. There was the glint of light reflecting off something: a knife, a long knife or a short-sword. Jason was to be assassinated like Zetes, like Thoas, like all the men of Lemnos.

The black figure reached the door, paused, raised her knife and slipped rapidly inside. As quietly as we could, so as not to alarm her or alarm the guards, we inched across the corridor.

"Now, Acastus!" Idmon screamed out, almost in terror.

We rushed in, wrestled the soldier to the ground and took her knife. Tiphys held the knife to her throat; the look of fear in her eyes was most satisfying.

"Are you both all right?"

Idmon nodded. Jason held out an arm to show me he had been cut. In the shadowy room his blood looked black. Kalais tore a strip of cloth from his tunic and bound the wound.

"Now, Jason, do you see where we are? Do you see the death that haunts this island?"

He nodded.

When his wound was bound I whispered, "Come! To the armory! Let us take Hypsipyle, join the other Argonauts and leave this hellish place."

We gathered our men and rushed along the corridors. The soldiers who saw us were alarmed but outnumbered; they let us pass without making a fight. We reached the armory without incident and took shields, swords, spears.

Only moments later we were at the queen's bedchamber. There were four guards; we caught them unawares, overcame them easily and took their swords.

Jason said in urgent tones, "Let me do this."

"You are wounded. Tiphys or I can—"

"I have to be the one." He rushed inside and we followed.

In the instant it took us to reach him he had dragged the queen from her bed and held his sword to her throat. "Lover!" he sneered. "Be my husband! Be my king! Rule side by side with me!" He spit the words in her face, laughed derisively and pricked her skin with his sword.

"Jason, stop!" she shrieked.

"I'll stop when my men and I are quit of you altogether. Come on." He pulled her to her feet by her hair. To her credit, Hypsipyle did not whimper anymore but took it, well, like a man. We rushed from her chamber. When the guards saw her position they made no effort to interfere.

Hylas led us through the halls to the armory. Our men had overcome the guards there and armed themselves. Three dozen of them awaited us. The others were outside already.

We soon joined them. Along the way one soldier after another saw the queen our captive and made way for us. Soon all of our company was assembled. Hercules rushed to Hylas' side. "You are safe. Thank the gods."

"Hylas has been of immeasurable help to us, Hercules." I tried to sound as reassuring as I could manage, given our still dangerous position.

He grunted and hoisted the boy to his shoulder. I took an instant to give thanks that he had never realized that "his boy" had been sleeping with women.

We crossed the temple square. Jason, his sword still at Hypsipyle's throat, led the way. Small bands of soldiers and civilians made way for us. In only moments we were at the top of the path leading down from the acropolis. A dozen guards were stationed there. Like their comrades, they yielded to us when they saw their queen our captive.

In moments more we were at the harbor, boarding the *Argo*. The wind was blowing stiffly, and the first spray of rain soaked us. Waves were swelling and crashing, and the ship tossed in them. Crossing the gangplank was tricky. Only two of us fell into the sea; we quickly fished them out.

Hypsipyle demanded we release her.

"No, not till we're ready to leave your accursed island." Jason's face by torchlight was granite. "We won't be able to cast off in this weather. You will remain with us till we can. Nothing else could guarantee our safety."

That was that. We posted guards, and the rest of us settled into our bunks to try and sleep. Tiphys calculated that there would not be a favorable tide till mid-afternoon. Tomorrow we would be gone.

Chapter Eight
Hylas

The storm kept growing. Winds were ferocious, waves were worse. The *Argo* rocked wildly. We stayed below for safety; several of us were thrown into the bulkheads and injured badly in the ship's mad rocking. The few guards we left on deck had trouble keeping their footing; fortunately no one fell into the water. Few of us were experienced sailors; for the first time since we left Iolcus there was seasickness among the crew, which didn't make our confinement below deck any more pleasant. As desperate as we were to leave Lemnos, we had no choice but to wait out the storm.

"The North Wind is raging, furious at the death of his son," Idmon told us.

"Then why on earth does he want to kill his other son?" Kalais, still in mourning for his brother, was weathering the storm less well, even, than the rest of us. I sat near him and tried to put my arm around him, but he pushed me away. "No, Acastus. The way I feel, not even your arms can comfort me."

Finally around nightfall of the second day the storm began to abate. The rain and wind continued but less fiercely. There would be a favorable tide just after dark, and we would finally be away from that mad island.

Castor and Pollux took a dozen men ashore and led an impromptu raid for provisions. They got us water and food enough to last several days, no more than a week if we stretched. We would certainly find more as we traveled. Happily they got what we needed with a minimum of blood being shed; we were more forgiving of the women of Lemnos than they had planned to be of us.

There had been some brief discussion among us, led by Orpheus,

Atalanta and Pollux, or taking the remaining Lemnian old men and small boys with us. But Argus pointed out that the *Argo* was not large enough to hold them; it had been designed for a company of 50, no more. And besides, we still needed supplies. What food and, especially, water we had—even with what we could take from Lemnos—would barely be sufficient for our present company for any considerable time. We could hardly accommodate anyone more. And so, unhappily, we had no choice but to leave the male children and grandfathers of Lemnos to their fate. My faith in the gods was growing. I prayed silently to Apollo that our stay on the island, forced though it was, might have made the women more humane, brought them to their senses, and that the boys would have long, healthy lives.

Jason took to his cot and nursed his wounds. He assured everyone that he would be all right in a few days, but in the meantime command of the ship fell to me. He did not exactly sulk in bed, but neither did he take part in our planning and our discussions. He didn't have to tell us what he had on his mind, really; it was possible to see in his eyes his regret over his vanished kingship.

I consulted with Nauplius and Tiphys. "Where do we head once we're away from here?"

"Northeast to Asia Minor, toward Troy and the Hellespont. I think." Nauplius was trying to make sense of several conflicting charts. "One of these maps, believe it or not, places Troy on the coast of Macedonia."

Tiphys was even less certain of our future. "If the weather doesn't return to normal—if this damned wind doesn't abate to its usual state—we won't have much choice where we go. Or where we stop."

I looked from one of them to the other and put on what I hoped was a convincing smile. "You're both far more experienced sailors than I. But I hope you're wrong. Our situation can't be quite that bad, can it?"

Neither of them returned my smile, so I went on hopefully. "After all, we have the divine oak to guide us."

Their faces were stone. There wasn't much point trying to fool them with false optimism.

At any we made several quick forays ashore for more food and for our meals. We kept expecting the Lemnians to try and fight us, but evidently they had learned not to trifle with us. Then with the night tide on the second day we were finally able to leave Lemnos. Needless to say, no one was sad to see the last of it.

That is not to say the storm let up entirely, just enough for us to leave the harbor and sail out into the sea to continue our journey. Clouds remained darker and heavier than I had ever seen them. The wind was still so strong Tiphys had trouble keeping us on course. We had to reef our sail or the wind would have snapped the mast. Waves occasionally threatened to swamp us. Rain was blinding. Several times Hercules had to help Tiphys with the tiller or we would have been dashed on the shore of some small barren island. Every few hours the storm would abate, the wind and rain die down, only to pick up again with the same ferocity.

Still, we made progress. Progress to where, precisely, we could not be at all certain. We would have to rely on the gods to preserve us, our ship and our mission. I often found myself remembering what some philosopher said about hope being cruel but essential, because it prolongs human suffering yet there is no life without it.

After two nights and days of sailing in the ferocious wind and waves, the storm finally ended. The clouds broke and we could see the sky. The evening star, which the faithful believe to be the fiery soul of Aphrodite, blazed brilliant white in the west, behind us. As the clouds thinned, more and more stars became visible. Nauplius used them to put us on course for Troy and the Hellespont.

* * *

We passed one small island after another. None of them was large enough or green enough to offer any promise of provisions. At least a few of them had springs or small streams; we put ashore, filled our casks and left.

Finally, on the fourth day, a large island, lush and green, came into view on the far horizon. Lynceus spotted it first, of course, and described what he saw for the rest of us. Nauplius hastily checked his maps. "As near as I can determine, that must be Samothrace. It looks to be about the right size, and the geography is right." He pointed to the highest peak on the island. "The central peak must be Mt. Phengari, still capped with the last of the winter snows. Let us hope I'm right. It means we're still on something like the course we want."

Samothrace: the abode of the Great Gods, the center of their cult and their mysteries. One of the holiest places in the Greek world, and one of the oldest. The gods are known there not by their modern Greek names but by ancient, mysterious names, names perhaps as old as time. As word spread among the crew, we could barely contain our excitement.

Atalanta in particular was thrilled. "I made a pledge when I was still a girl that one day I would make a pilgrimage to Samothrace, to do homage to the goddess in her most ancient aspect. And now, here I am."

"Don't get too excited yet," I told her. "Nauplius is only guessing that's where we are. With all this bloody wind blowing us around like a dry leaf, we could be anywhere. Egypt, Cyprus, anywhere."

"Do you always have to be such a stick-in-the-mud, Acastus?"

"If you had grown up in the house of Pelias, you'd be stuck in a lot of mud yourself."

The island came closer and closer. Lynceus shaded his eyes and told us, "I can see a city. Beyond it, on the slopes of the mountain, there is a complex—a temple complex, I think, built of white marble."

It sounded more and more as if Nauplius had been correct. The gods or the wind or mere chance were bringing us to Samothrace.

We were approaching the island from the northeast. Since we had sailed from Iolcus, then left Lemnos, heading northeast, we should have been approaching it from the southwest. Nauplius fussed over his charts, trying to make sense of it. Finally he gave up in frustration. "All I can think is that the bloody wind must have turned us around and around, probably more than once."

"Or perhaps," said Amphiaraus, who had been eavesdropping on us, "the gods have somehow brought us here for reasons on their own."

"You trust the gods, Amphiaraus." My dogged skepticism kicked in. "I'll trust the wind. Even when it sends us spiraling."

Jason had come on deck and had been listening too. "Then perhaps, little cousin, your trust is misplaced."

I bristled at this. "Do I take it you're resuming command, Jason?"

"It appears that someone has to." He shrugged. "Someone with proper piety."

A hundred wisecracks streamed through my mind, but I kept silent.

Finally a small flotilla of boats—mostly fishing vessels—came to meet us and escort us into port. They hailed us as if we were returning heroes. The man in charge, who was the only one of them wearing armor and a helmet, hailed us. "I welcome you to Samothrace in the name of the Great Gods, whose home this is. I am Lephistos, mayor of the city of Palaeopolis."

Echion returned his salutation. "We are the Argonauts, the crew of the ship *Argo*, voyaging to Asia Minor on a mission for King Pelias of Iolcus. We happily return your goodwill, and we look forward to enjoying your fair island."

"We are well aware of you and your mission. Word has spread far and wide throughout the Greek world, and even beyond."

"You do us honor, sir. We shall be most pleased to enjoy your hospitality."

* * *

Palaeopolis was a small city, a good bit smaller than Iolcus, but it was crowded and full of life. Men, women, children in great numbers teemed through the streets. The marketplace was as busy as any on the mainland. The activity in the fishing fleet at the waterfront was as lively as our own at Iolcus. As many ancient buildings attested, the city was as old as recorded time, perhaps even older.

"After Lemnos, I feel as if we are alive again," I told Argus as a pair of boys ran past us in the street, nearly knocking him over.

"I could do with a bit less life," he grumped. "Anyway, after Lemnos, Hades itself would seem lively."

As was always the case, the people were astonished by Kalais' wings. Several of them pressed him to give a demonstration of his flying, but I explained that he was still in mourning and that would not be appropriate. Hercules also, when people learned who he was, became the center of considerable fuss. Hylas beamed with pride at his lover's celebrity.

We were made comfortable at the mayor's palace. Lephistos

proved a most companionable host, plying us with food and wine, telling us expansive tales of the island's history. We settled in on luxurious stuffed cushions—rich red ones—and savored our wine as he grew expansive. "It is told this is the first place the gods ever set foot on earth. There is, as I am certain you must have noticed, very kittle agriculture here. Samothrace is much too hilly and rocky for it. But the gods, may their names be revered always, have blessed us, and we have never known want. Trade is robust; the sea yields up its wealth; abundant springs refresh our thirst. Even the worst Aegean storms tend to bypass us.

"The gods here are not worshiped under the names you know. Demeter, in her aspect as the great goddess of forest and mountain, manifested herself to the people here as Axierus. The god you know as Hermes, here known as Cadmilus, is her consort. Their sons are the fertility gods Dardanus and Aetion, gods of the stars and serpents. Here on Samothrace they are invoked by no other names."

Jason in turn told him about our adventure on Lemnos—being certain to give the impression he himself had discovered the women's villainy and planned our escape. Argus kept shifting impatiently and clearing his throat at Jason's more blatant exaggerations. Jason was annoyed by did his best to ignore him and keep talking.

Lephistos listened attentively. "We shall certainly spread your story as widely as we can. The world must know of their perfidy. But you"—he wrinkled his brow in obvious concern—"you have polluted yourselves with Lemnian blood, the blood of your fellow Greeks. You must permit us to purify you by initiation into the mysteries of the Great Gods."

"We appreciate your hospitality, your offer and your concern." Jason played the diplomat. "But surely initiation must take place in stages, as it does with the divine mysteries on the mainland. A matter of weeks, perhaps, or months? I am afraid we cannot spare the time. Our mission—"

"Pray do not concern yourselves on that account, Prince Jason. The gods have long since given us leave to compress the preparation time. Both stages of initiation may be done in a single day."

That settled the matter quite neatly. We were to become initiates—all of us save Atalanta; the mysteries were for men exclusively. Jason disliked having his will overridden—he must have

211

been feeling less and less in charge of the expedition—and Argus grumped to me privately about superstition and needless delay. But most of us were only too happy for the chance to be cleansed and sanctified—whatever that might have meant to each of us particularly.

Atalanta bristled at her exclusion. "Am I not part of this company?"

There was nothing to be said. It was hardly our idea. I suggested she apply to Lephistos for an exception to be made in her case; and I promised to support her if the opportunity arose. She did, and I did; Lephistos prayed to the goddess, and the exception was granted.

"If you were not among the Argonauts…" he told her.

But she was, and so the matter was settled.

Next morning we were dressed in ceremonial white garments and led in procession by a band of naked youths—athletes by the look of them—up the road to the temple known as the Anaktoron, on the side of the mountain. The temple, as Lynceus had first told us, was made of gleaming white marble, the purest and whitest I had ever seen. A quintet of priests greeted us—likewise robed in white, and crowned with wreaths of laurel—and instructed us in the rites to come.

No initiate may reveal the exact nature of the mysteries. But I may say that in the Holy of Holies in the Anaktoron I experienced the presence of the Great Gods. It moved me unutterably and transformed my life. When we emerged we were *all* transformed. Even Argus, garrulous old skeptic, was uncharacteristically quiet.

That night we were feted as new devotees of the Great Gods. There was wine, music. Naked youths, the same ones who had led us up the mountain, served us and danced for us. The priests blessed us all, even blessed the *Argo*. Next morning we would continue on to Troy and Colchis.

We were up at dawn, refreshed and made new by our experience on Samothrace. Nauplius spent time with some of the local fisherman, gathering reliable navigation instructions against the possibility that another storm might blow us off course. He assembled a detailed map that would serve to guide us safely to the coast of Asia Minor.

While he was thus occupied, I spent time chatting up various islanders for what they might know about Colchis. Did it really exist, as the prophecies we'd gotten seemed to tell us? If it did, what kind of reception could we expect there? Did they really have the Golden Fleece, and was Phrixus really buried there?

"Buried?" An old Samothracian man smiled cryptically. "Not buried, no. Not what you would call buried at all."

"What on earth do you mean?"

"You will see," he said in his best baffling manner, "when and if you get there. Colchis is a strange land."

Jason, typically had drunk too much the night before, and was no use at all in gathering intelligence. (He would make a fit successor to Pelias.) He climbed blearily onto the *Argo* and promptly fell asleep. The rest of us boarded soon after.

And so, with a fair south wind, we set off once again on our voyage to the end of the earth.

* * *

The wind carried us till mid-morning, when it died down. We could wait till it picked up again, or we could row. Jason chose the latter. He had gotten sufficiently over his hangover to assume command again.

All of us but those whose wounds hadn't healed yet took to the oars, and before long we were making good time, almost as good as we had on the wind. Orpheus and Lynceus were the only hale men who no one expected to row. Lynceus took his place at the prow, to watch the sea ahead of us. Orpheus took up his lyre and gave us the rhythm. Soon we all fell into the seductive beat of his music and rowed as if we were hypnotized.

Hercules and Hylas shared an oar. It was clear to everyone but Hylas himself that Hercules could have done just as well without him. In fact Hercules was so strong the ship once again tended to pull in circles on his side; I had to ask him, carefully, tactfully, to take it a bit easier so we could maintain a steady course. Castor and Pollux had the oar on the opposite side from him; they stroked frantically, unwilling to let any of us see they were incapable of keeping up with him. Despite their best efforts, it was all too apparent. When they heard me ask him to ease off, they glared indignantly. I pretended not to notice and resumed my own oar. Ultimately Jason had to move some oarsmen to the opposite side of the ship from Hercules. Others were given a respite from rowing, for which they were most thankful.

No islands passed our view. No dolphins swam with us. There was nothing in sight on every side of us but the blank sea. Soon even Orpheus' lyre began to seem monotonous. I could see any number of our men growing restless. Hercules in particular was looking itchy and impatient. Every few moments he would goad Castor and Pollux to try and keep up with him, then he would row even harder and more energetically leaving them, so to speak, in the dust.

After an hour or two he stopped, got to his feet and yelled, "All of you, what kind of men are you? What kind of Greeks? Row! See if any of you can outlast me! Who among you has the most stamina? We have a mission, by all the gods. Let us see if we can make Asia Minor by nightfall."

He took his seat again and began to pull his oar even more fiercely than he had before. The rest of us, spurred on by his challenge, did likewise. Orpheus played a livelier, more intensely rhythmic song, and the *Argo* lurched forward.

Everyone rowed at the peak of his strength—almost madly. The ship sped along, skimming the sea, seeming almost to leave the water and fly. Hercules pulled like a man possessed. Hylas tried to keep pace with him, but soon he had to let go the oar, sit back and watch his semi-divine lover with an adoring grin. One by one, the rest of us also gave up the contest, till only Hercules was still rowing. With the oarsmen redistributed we had stayed on a steady, straight-ahead course.

The suddenly a loud crack! rent the air. Hercules' oar had split quite in two under the strain; the bottom half splashed into the sea and fell rapidly behind us. Hercules leaped to his feet, laughing, and cried out, "Not even Poseidon himself can outlast me!"

"Be quiet, Hercules!" Idmon looked around in alarm, as if he thought the great god might rear up out of the water and revenge himself for this impiety.

Hercules let the upper half of his oar fall into the water.

Before any of us could say another word, Lynceus cried out, "Land ho!"

Ahead of us, on the far distant horizon, was a thin line of green. Vegetation, perhaps a forest. We had reached Asia Minor.

Nauplius consulted his charts and announced, "It these are accurate, and I think they are, that is the territory known as Mysia. Several of the fisherman told me about it, and they had nothing but good things to say. The people are friendly and the land is rich and prosperous. We should have no trouble at all replenishing our supplies. There are forests and streams in great numbers, all of them guarded by nymphs."

Argus stared at him, not trying to hide his skepticism. "Nymphs."

"Yes, nymphs, Argus. That is what they told me."

Before they could take to bickering I stepped between them. "Let's wait till we make land and see for ourselves."

"See the nymphs." Argus was not to be shaken.

"Are nymphs so much less probable than winged men, Argus? Let's just wait and see."

Soon we were near enough for all of us to see the lay of the land. There did not seem to be a natural harbor, but there were several coves and the mouth of a small river where we could put in. Tiphys steered a steady course into the largest of them, which was the river mouth. We drew close, dropped anchor, then ran the gangway down to the shore. Jason assigned a few men to remain on board an guard the ship then led the rest of us ashore.

Almost at once a throng of people came out of the woods, singing a song of greeting. They carried large skins of wine, and they crowned us with wreaths of roses. Jason, beaming at the warm welcome, exchanged greetings with their leader, who introduced himself as Phelaxes. Jason in turn introduced us and explained our mission.

Phelaxes made a long and rather windy speech, regaling us with compliments, praising our valor (of which he could have known nothing, but of course knowledge is beside the point in diplomacy), offering us the hospitality of his people, and on and on. We were to be guests of honor at a welcoming feast that night. In the meantime everything Mysian was at our disposal.

Jason told him our first priority would be to replenish our water supply with water from their river.

"The river Chius is not really fit for drinking," Phelaxes told him. "But nearby are many springs whose water is as sweet as any on earth. And through the forest to the west and over those hills you can see is the famous spring called Pegae. Its water is sweet and fresh, and it pours into a deep pool inhabited by beautiful water nymphs."

Argus couldn't resist himself. "Water nymphs. And are they big water nymphs?"

The sarcasm was lost on Phelaxes. "Big? I didn't know nymphs come in different sizes. But they are as beautiful as any nymphs anywhere."

"Please excuse my cynical friend," Jason told him, his voice dripping with disdain. "There has never been a gift horse whose mouth he did not want to examine."

After all our days at sea, and after the horrible experience on Lemnos, we were anxious to explore the pine forest of Mysia. The trees were tall and luxuriant, of the richest, darkest green. Choruses of birds sang in them. The landscape was irresistibly beautiful, and not quite like any I had known.

Mysia was a land of wood. Everyone lived in small wooden houses, and even the temples were built of lumber, with statues of the gods made of wood. I found the workmanship quite good. There was a natural amphitheater whose seats were wooden benches. And there was not a piece of marble in sight. Argus told me he found it distressingly primitive. "Cities should be made of stone. Forests should be left to grow and prosper."

I couldn't resist. "The nymphs would agree with you."

He scowled. "Sometimes, Acastus, I worry about you."

Hercules announced he wanted to find a tree tall and stout enough to provide him with timber for a new oar. Butes the beekeeper said he wanted to find some good hives, so he could lay in a large enough store of honey to last the rest of our voyage. "My nose tells me the honey here will be especially sweet." Phelaxes assured him it was. Several of the men stripped and dove into the Chius, splashing and playing like children.

Kalais and I decided to take a walk in the forest. Hylas attached himself to us and tagged along. "Hercules is off looking for his oar. I can occupy myself in your company, if you don't mind my coming with you. If you don't mind, that is."

"No, not at all." Kalais smiled at him like a protective older brother. "But I'm not quite over my wounds yet. I'm not sure how far our walk will take us."

"That's all right. I just want a bit of exercise, and your company."

We decided to walk the path to the spring Pegae. It was late afternoon. The forest was bathed in sunset colors. There were wildflowers everywhere, violets, primroses, buttercups and dozens of other kinds. Birds sang exuberantly. Mysia was quite a little paradise, really.

"Do you regret growing up in a city?" Kalais took my hand.

"Iolcus has its pleasures too, you know. If nothing else, there are opportunities for a sculptor like me. Here…what would I sculpt? Wood nymphs?"

"Argus has been a bad influence on you, Acastus."

We crossed a string of low hills. There before us in a small dale was the spring. It was a large one. Water flowed out of a cleft in a rock ledge quite abundantly. It cascaded down a series of little terraces, then over a waterfall where it plunged into a large pool, large enough for a man to swim in. Even at a distance we could hear its water rushing and falling.

When we reached it, the depth, clarity and blueness of the pool astonished us. It was so deep the water in its bottom was a deep midnight blue; we could not even see the bottom clearly, it was so deep.

And there was something even more astonishing. Nymphs, there were nymphs, real water nymphs, swimming in the depths of the pool. Beautiful young women, quite nude and with lovely, supple bodies, circling and playing in the water. Their bodies were almost translucent, like the finest, purest alabaster. And a faint, shimmering glow surrounded them.

I told myself they couldn't really be water nymphs. Wood nymphs and water nymphs were imaginary, something nurses told children about to lull them to sleep. Yet there they were. They had to come to the surface. They had to breathe. Didn't they?

"Yes, Acastus nymphs are real." Kalais knew me well enough to know what I was thinking. "As real as winged sons of gods, as real as the gods themselves. You simply don't see them often, that's all."

Despite my skeptical expectation, they did not surface to breathe. They were under the water for an impossibly long time, and finally even I had to concede there was something, well, extra-natural about them. They circled, swam, played like young birds in the air, and we stood and watched like country bumpkins gaping at a great temple.

So spellbound was I by the sight of them, I quite forgot that Hylas was there at my side. But he jarred me out of my little trance. He nudged me with his elbow then stepped into the pool, up to his ankles. "They're beautiful. Kalais, Acastus, they are more lovely than anything I've ever seen."

The nymphs, for the first time, noticed us. They looked up through the water, and their gaze fixed on the boy. I could see them mouthing words and, incredibly, their voices came to us, a chorus of sweet women's voices speaking in unison. "Hylas! Hylas!" they whispered. "Beautiful Hylas!"

I looked at Kalais. "How can they possibly know his name? How can they know anything but dampness?"

"Curb your cynic's mind, Acastus. They are divine creatures, or at least semi-divine. You have felt the presence of the Great Gods. What are a few nymphs?"

Hylas looked back over his shoulder at us. It was hard to read the expression on his face. He seemed to be lost between bafflement, delight and...something else. Lust, perhaps?

One of the nymphs swan close to him and began stroking his feet, his ankles, his calves, then swam swiftly, playfully away. "Hylas," their voices intoned. "Beautiful Hylas, come swim with us."

A second nymph, then a third, did the same as that first one. Their hands reached up and fondled Hylas' legs, his thighs. They almost reached up and touched his cock beneath his tunic. "Beautiful boy, most beautiful of all mortals, come swim in our pool," they intoned. We have never seen a boy so beautiful. Come see what pleasure we can give you."

Hylas' expression changed to one of pure delight. His smile was so broad, his teeth so white and even. The nymphs stroked his legs, fondled them, caressed them. His erection showed through his clothing. He seemed lost for words but finally whispered coarsely, "They want me." I had never seen the boy so completely rapt. He took another step into the pool of Pegae. The water came up his calves nearly to his knees.

"Hylas, come share your ethereal beauty, your youthful beauty with us. Leave your friends. Come swim in our spring and we will give you pleasure like no man has ever known." Their hands once again reached out of the water, up his thighs, up to his groin. They fondled him, and his growing erection showed through his clothing more and more clearly.

I looked at Kalais, frowning, as if to say I found it all rather disturbing—which I did. Embarrassing and disturbing.

Then their manner changed. They began tugging at his tunic, tearing at it, pulling it and him. Startled, Hylas resisted. They tugged harder and harder, and he struggled against them. Finally he lost his footing and fell into the water with a splash. The nymphs kept pulling him further and deeper.

His expression changed at once from one of intense boyish pleasure to terror. "Acastus, Kalais, help!"

We rushed into the water and caught hold of him. More and more nymphs swam toward us; they would pull him under the water if we let them. The nymphs kept pulling, but we were stronger and managed to free him from their grasp and pull him onto dry land. His tunic tore in the struggle, and he was half naked.

He was coughing and breathing heavily. "By all the gods, that was horrible!"

I decided to be wry, hoping it might have a sobering effect. "You see what happens when you decide to be unfaithful to your lover?"

"I wasn't being unfaithful. I was…they were…I wanted to…"

"We know what you wanted to do." Kalais helped him to his feet. "It was all too visible. It still is."

Hylas looked at his erection which was still throbbing like, well, like a teenage boy's erection, and covered it with his hands, embarrassed. "I…I…"

"Relax, Hylas." We had toyed with him long enough. I put an arm around his shoulder. "We know what boys your age are like. If a snake slithers across your foot you get an erection."

But he was still shaken. "They wanted…they wanted to… Acastus, what would they have done to me?"

"They told you, didn't they? They are not the first to tell you how beautiful you are, Young Apollo."

He blushed.

"Come on. Let's get back to the *Argo* and get you a new tunic before Hercules gets back. I'd hate for you to have to explain this to him."

* * *

That night the Mysians honored us with a welcoming feast. An enormous bonfire was banked in a clearing by the riverside in the midst of the pines; it must have reached 30 feet into the air. Musicians played for us, and Orpheus cheerfully joined in. Folk dancers in colorful costumes performed quite a lively presentation. A troupe of clowns entertained us, performed a burlesque of Aphrodite's infidelity to Hephaestus. Wine flowed copiously and thee was food in abundance. And the Mysians laced our wine with powdered mushrooms. "They will expand the horizons of your perception," they told us. All the Argonauts watched, laughed, clapped in time with the music, even Argus. It was quite wonderful, especially given the fact that none of the Mysians knew us. Even Castor seemed to be relaxed and enjoying himself for once.

Autolycus entertained a group of Mysians by turning into a wolf and back again repeatedly. Periclymenus, not to be outdone, changed into a bear, a lion and a dozen other creatures, to the Mysians' delight. Orpheus sang hymns to various gods.

Jason drank heavily. I saw Idmon, standing apart, watching him with something like concern. When Jason fastened onto a young Mysian man, Idmon's expression turned completely glum. He turned away and walked back to the *Argo*. I had been tempted more than once to tell him his concern, his love, was wasted on Jason, but of course love is quite blind and cannot be coaxed into vision. Besides, Idmon was a seer; his own second sight could tell him what he needed to know, if he would only look.

Hercules, in typical Herculean fashion, got drunk early and passed out. Hylas nudged him a few times, trying to wake him. "Hercules, you're missing all the fun."

"Fun?" he growled. "You go and have fun. You're the boy. I am a god." He rolled over and struck the earth with his fist. Everyone felt the tremor. Hercules went back to sleep.

Argus was enjoying himself quite outrageously. At one point I saw him with a young girl and a young boy, one on each arm. He kissed each in turn. Then, noticing me watching him, he left them and crossed the clearing to me. "This is wonderful. I was beginning to fear our reception everywhere would be as evil as Lemnos or as solemn as Samothrace."

"I'm glad you're pleased. I honestly think this is the first time I've ever seen you smile."

"There's no use trying to annoy me tonight, Acastus. I'm having too much fun. Come and goad me tomorrow."

"I'm not trying to annoy you, Argus. I merely—"

"Don't try and snow me, either. I know you far too well. Why don't you go find your little friend Hylas? He seems to have vanished."

I looked around, slightly alarmed. If we let anything happen to the boy... Hercules was still deep asleep, which was probably just as well. I scanned the clearing, and Argus was right. There was no sign of Hylas anywhere.

I quickly asked around. No one knew where he was. Butes said he saw Hylas disappear among the trees. "Over there," he pointed.

I had to go and look. As wonderful as the feast was, I liked Hylas too much to let anything happen to him.

There was a path, and I followed it, moving as stealthily and quietly as I could. Some 50 feet into the woods I found him. He was sitting on the ground, leaning against a hemlock tree. He had stripped. There was just enough light from the bonfire to outline his body. He was...what is the phrase?...pleasuring himself. The image came into my head of him sitting on the tripod at Delphi, masturbating, ejaculating in service of the god. At least this time he was doing it for himself.

"Hylas." I made my voice a whisper, as soft and gentle as I could manage. "Come back to the feast, Hylas."

He looked up at me. "By all the gods on Olympus, you startled me. What do you want?"

I smiled. "You. I want you. To make certain you're safe and all is well with you."

"Sit down with me."

I did. His voice sounded...not troubled, but not exactly calm either. "What's wrong?"

"I'm...Acastus, I'm so confused."

I pointed at his erect cock. "Confused? Is that what you call that?"

Abashed, he covered it with his hands and reached for his cloak. "I love Hercules. You know that."

"Then...?"

"Those women today, those nymphs... They wanted me."

"Everyone wants you, Hylas. Enough people have called you beautiful by now for you to believe it."

"No, that's not what I mean. They really wanted me. They said so. They wanted me."

"Like those girls on Lemnos, right?"

"No! They were girls, and they were plain. That was just play, nothing more. I wanted to see what it was like to make love that way. But these! These were beautiful women, magically beautiful. And they wanted me. Me!"

"They tried to pull you under, Hylas. You would have drowned. You can't be desperate enough for sex to—"

"No, you don't understand! I panicked. They didn't want to pull me under the water. They can't have meant anything bad. They wanted me." He lowered his voice and looked away from me. "And I wanted them." Then he looked back at me. There was a bit of anxiousness in his eyes. "I can't stop thinking about them, Acastus. Their touch, their beautiful voices, their lithe bodies... You should have felt how incredibly sensual their touch is."

"And they wanted you." I tried not to sound too stern or disapproving. I wasn't that much older than Hylas myself, after all. And as strange as my life had been, his had been even stranger. But I had to try and make him see sense. "Have you already forgotten how terrified you were? Hylas, they wanted you in their world, under the water. Is that what you want?"

He only repeated, "They wanted me. Those divinely beautiful women wanted me." He seemed to be almost spellbound by the thought. Seeing him, hearing him was more than mildly unnerving.

"Hylas, come back to the feast. Promise me you won't do anything foolish. Promise."

Glumly, with obvious reluctance, he made the promise. He dressed, and we went back to the others. I kept a careful eye on him for the rest of the night, and he seemed to be the only one there not enjoying himself. Finally, he curled up next to Hercules and fell asleep.

* * *

I awoke early the next morning. There was still mist obscuring the sun. The last embers of the bonfire were still glowing. Everyone, Argonauts and Mysians alike, had passed out from all the wine. Hercules had drunk more than a gallon, more than anyone else could have; he was sleeping soundly and snoring loudly. Everyone else had paired off to make love, it seemed. All the usual couples, and Lynceus and Autolycus, and various Argonauts with various Mysians... Jason had finally gone back to the ship and lured Idmon ashore; they were curled up in each other's arms, smiling blissfully. All the others were likewise sleeping the sleep of heroes.

I wandered among them all, trying to wake up fully and clear my head. No one was stirring in the least. There were not even any birds chirping their morning songs. The only sound punctuating the silence was the occasional hooting of a solitary owl somewhere off in the forest.

I decided to check on the *Argo*. We had left a few men stationed there, but even they had found some skins of wine. They were, singly and in pairs, sleeping as deeply as the people on land. They had obviously been, er, cavorting together. Wine has the power to unleash lust in even the most stoic human being; perhaps that is what makes us human. I had the fleeting thought that if all the power of all our lust could somehow be harnessed it could drive the *Argo* all the way to Colchis and back again.

Back on land, I stood for a moment over the slumbering figure of Kalais. Even deep in sleep he was more beautiful than anyone I had ever known—or, I told myself naively, ever would know.

I couldn't resist touching him. I never could. Lightly, so as not to wake him, I bent and stroked his wings. He moaned softly and smiled a broad smile. "Kalais," I whispered, "I love you."

"Mm-hmm." He stirred, rolled over and went back to sleep.

Then it suddenly hit me: Hercules was sleeping alone. The last thing I remembered of him, he had Hylas in his arms. Where was the boy? A sense of alarm overtook me, wild, irrational alarm. This was not right. This could not be right.

I shook him and asked him softly, "Hercules, where is Hylas?"

He opened his eyes a slit. "Hm?"

"Hylas. Where has he gone?" I tried not to make my voice sound too urgent.

His eyes opened wider. He groped the ground beside him and felt the nothing that was there. "Why, he's right here. I—" Groggily he sat up. "Hylas! Where is he?"

"That's what I was asking you."

He closed his eyes and tried to focus. "He—he woke me up a while ago and said he was thirsty."

I glanced over my shoulder at the path to the spring. "Yes? And?"

Hercules' head was still numb from the wine. "He—he—then he said he was going to find a pitcher and go somewhere, to some brook or stream or something."

"To a spring? Did he say 'spring'?"

He lay back, yawning widely. "What difference does it make? He was thirsty."

"For the love of the gods why didn't you stop him?"

"Why should I? He was thirsty. Go away and let me sleep."

He had to have gone to the Pegae spring. Hoping it had been merely for water and not for the nymphs, I rushed along the path, a sense of foreboding overtaking me more and more with each step. Reaching the spring seemed to take an eternity. Then finally I heard the waterfall and the splashing of the rivulet.

Everything but the water was still, as still as a grave, and there was no one in sight. On the ground beside the pool lay a clay pitcher on its side. No. It could not be. They could not have taken him. He could not have let them.

"Hylas!" I screamed. "Hylas, where are you!" My voice echoed through the woods,

There was no sound but the gentle splashing of the water.

"Hylas!!" I shouted even louder.

The depths of the pool, not lit by sunlight, seemed darker than ever, almost black. I knew it was foolish, but I splashed into the water, screaming, crying, "Hylas, Hylas!"

There was nothing. No sign of him, no sign of the nymphs. I stood there, splashing the water, and found myself crying. "Hylas, Hylas, please come back."

From behind me came a voice. "He is gone, Acastus. Calling him will do no good." It took me a moment to realize it was Kalais.

I turned. "You startled me."

He moved closer and put his hand on my shoulder. "Come out of the water, They'll take you, too."

"They don't want me. I am not as beautiful as Hylas."

"You are, to me. But that isn't the issue. If you anger them and are foolhardy enough to step into their pool, they could do anything." He grasped my hand and led me onto dry land.

"We don't know for certain they took him. If there are wild beasts in these woods—"

He pointed at the pitcher and said nothing.

"Kalais, we can't simply do nothing. We have to organize a search."

"Look into the water, Acastus. See its black heart."

He was right, and I knew it; my heart told me so. I fell silent for a long moment, still crying. I had formed such a close bond with Hylas. To lose him like this... Then another thought struck me. "Hercules! Let us get back to the others. When Hercules learns Hylas is missing, he could do anything. Destroy the ship. Tear down half of Mysia. Kill all of us. There's no telling what he could do."

"Hercules' madness has passed."

"But this—this could bring it back. Kalais, we have to organize a search. If there is a chance of finding the boy, however remote—"

"Hercules is still asleep. As drunk as he was last night he could sleep half the day." He gazed down into the waters of Pegae. "But you're right. Let us get the others and search. If Hercules reacts the way you think he might, your mourning will soon enough be replaced by terror."

Chapter Nine
Phineus and the Harpies

Hercules did not go mad in the way we feared. He did not fly into a rage and attack us, demolish our ship, tear down Mysia. We lost him in another way, a way that was quite understandable, perhaps, yet equally mad.

When we got back to the clearing we found him still sleeping deeply, as deeply as only a demigod could. The other Argonauts were waking, yawning, rubbing their eyes; some of them were already up and about. Kalais and I took Jason aside and explained to him what had happened. "We must organize teams of searchers, against the possibility that we are wrong and Hylas has merely become lost in the woods."

"Yes." Jason was, still again, hung over rather badly. We could see that he was struggling to think clearly. "And even if you are right, making a show of searching for Hylas may perhaps help to keep Hercules calm. You are quite right to be worried about his reaction to the news."

"Where is Argus?"

"He's inspecting the ship, making certain no maintenance is needed before we set sail again."

"Go and get him, Jason. We need his counsel."

* * *

And so we searched. Argus quickly confirmed our conviction it was necessary. Parties of four combed the forest. The Mysians helped; they didn't want Hercules on a rampage any more than we did. But hours of searching produced nothing. There was no sign of Hylas but that pitcher at the spring, nothing to guide our thoughts but our knowledge of what had happened before.

It was mid-afternoon when Hercules finally began to stir. Still half-asleep he groped the ground beside him, clearly expecting to find Hylas there. When he didn't, he opened his eyes and sat up. "Hylas!" he boomed. "Where are you?"

Jason and I were standing together at the other side of the clearing. Jason looked at me. "Go and tell him."

"You are the captain, Jason. It's your job."

"Hylas was your boy, your special case. Without you pleading for him we'd have left him in Delphi."

My contempt for Jason had never been higher. He was not going to act like a leader except when it suited him, which is to say when it was to his advantage; that couldn't have been plainer. And so timidly, terrified of what to expect but trying bravely to hide it, I approached Hercules. "Good morning, Hercules."

He yawned like the lion he was. "Morning? The sun is already high."

"Well, good afternoon, I mean."

He yawned again and looked around. "Where is Hylas?"

I got up my resolve and said it. "Hercules, no one knows. He has disappeared."

"What?!" His voice thundered.

"He went into the forest to get some water. We found his pitcher beside the Pegae spring. But there is no sign of him." I did not have to feign my unhappiness.

Slowly, almost ponderously he got to his feet. "Where? Show me."

"There is nothing to see, Hercules, only water."

"Show me!"

I knew we must not upset him any more than we could avoid. I led him into the woods, to the spring. For a long moment he stood gazing down into the water. "He has fallen in and drowned. But where is his body? He should be floating there."

Suddenly he turned and uprooted a small tree, then threw it into the pool. He roared with something between anguish and rage as he tore up more trees, boulders and hurled them into the pool. Its once-clear water became roiled and muddy. I caught him by the arms and tried to stop him; he lifted me and tossed me 20 feet. Terrified I got to my feet again.

Then, not content with that one tree, he began to tear up the stream bed, ripping rocks from the wet earth, scooping great handfuls of mud from the streambed. He pounded the rocks that formed the waterfall till they were pulverized. Water coursed into the woods in a vast sheet. The Pegae spring and its pool were no more. What became of the nymphs I could not imagine. Hercules, all unknowing, had had his revenge.

I had to try and calm him down, bring him to his senses. "We don't know what happened. Hercules, anything could have happened. There are wild animals in these woods, bears, lions, panthers. One of them could easily have…" He glared at me; I didn't know if he could tell I wasn't being honest. "Or he might simply have wandered off and gotten lost. There was mist this morning—thick fog, the thickest I've ever seen."

He struck a fist into his palm. "We have to search more!"

"We are searching. Parties are combing the forest even now. Even the Mysians are helping. If he's alive, we'll find him."

"Acastus, I…" Suddenly he sat down on the forest floor. "You know how I love him."

"Yes."

"I… I can't lose him. I can't. I've…you know I've done some terrible things in my life." Much to my astonishment I saw a tear come to his eye. Then another. In a moment his face was streaked with them.

"Hercules, we'll do everything we can to find him."

I might just as well not spoken. Hercules was lost in his grief. Hercules the demigod, the legendary hero, the son of Zeus himself, was crying like a lost child. "I've done terrible things. And knowing I've done them has tormented me. I killed my own children, slaughtered them. My sleep, my dreams…" He looked at me. "Loving Hylas, knowing that he loves me is the only thing that has brought calm and sanity back to me."

There wasn't much I could say. I took him by the land and led him back to the *Argo*.

* * *

We searched three days. The first day Hercules helped. After that he stayed in his cot on the ship, weeping madly. Seeing the great man so reduced was terrible, but there was nothing to be done.

I knew—Kalais and I knew—what had happened, knew that Hylas had been drawn into the waters of Pegae and vanished. We took turns watching the place where the spring had been, hoping to see some trace of the nymphs once again. They never appeared. With their pool gone there was hardly a way they could have. Had they somehow gone somewhere else? If so, had they taken Hylas? Or were they simply, like him, gone? I did not want to know.

The conviction was growing among everyone in our crew that further searching was pointless. It was time to resume our voyage. Hercules would, in time, move past his grief. Or so we hoped.

* * *

"Hercules, we're leaving now, on the next tide."

He stared up at me from his cot. "No."

"Yes. We have to. We're on an important mission. We've looked everywhere; you know that. We simply can't find him, and we can't delay any longer."

"No." He got to his feet. There was anger in his face, anger mixed with something else. "You can go if you want to. All of you, you can go to hell for all I care. I have to find Hylas."

Jason tried to make him see reason. So did Argus. But he would not be moved.

The Mysians gave us what supplies they could. Phelaxes approached Jason and me. "You are making for Colchis, isn't that right?"

"Yes."

"That can only mean you are after amber."

Jason made a noncommittal reply. It didn't fool Phelaxes for a moment. "Let me give you some advice. You will be sailing past Troy, a few score miles north of here. Do not stop there. They guard the amber trade quite jealously."

Jason, typically, tried to brush this aside. "We have nothing to fear. Our men are the best warriors in Greece."

"Perhaps so, Prince Jason. But no matter how good your men

are, the Trojans have an army. They can muster a force to outnumber you without even stretching their resources."

It was clear that Jason didn't like the sound of this. He fell silent. I thanked Lephistos for his counsel and bade him farewell.

Hercules stood on deck and watched us load the last of our supplies on board. aboard. But mostly he stood quite still and stared blankly into the woods. The boy he had loved was there, somewhere, somehow. Jason had a final word with him, tried to sound consoling. It had no effect. Argus and I tried again; he would not be persuaded to come with us. "You go. I wish you godspeed. But I will stay and find Hylas. He is lost. He needs me. I know it."

The tide was at its full. We had to leave. Hercules leaped into the water and gave the *Argo* a mighty shove, to send us on our way. Then he ran into the forest shouting, "Hylas, I'm coming. Your Hercules is coming."

That was the last any of us saw of him. From a distance we could see trees being toppled. Grief, bitter grief, grief beyond words but not beyond deeds, it seemed, no matter how futile those deeds were.

Years later I heard that Hercules had taken a new wife and fathered children, and that he had founded a city in Asia Minor. I never knew if those rumors were true. History would be kind to him, or kind to his legend, at least. When I thought of him from time to time I always found myself hoping it would also be kind when it talked of his great love for the boy Hylas.

* * *

Following Phelaxes' advice we hugged the coast and made good time. The Mysians had given Nauplius still further directions to speed us on our journey. He now had good, reliable charts and, better still, good visual cues to guide us.

But a dispute arose among us whether we should heed his counsel and avoid Troy. If Hercules had still been with us there would have been no debate; he could easily have torn down the walls of the city, Trojan army or no Trojan army. But without him... to many of us caution seemed advisable.

As we neared the plain of Ilium we pulled farther from the

shoreline. Lynceus scanned the horizon for us. Even without his preternatural eyesight we could see that Troy was a great city, as great as any on the Greek mainland. Its walls towered above the landscape, plainly visible to even the weakest eyes.

Lynceus, of course, could see much more than any of the rest of us. He announced that there was a great army exercising on the plain. "Their numbers are greater, even, than the most dedicated band of heroes could defeat. Phelaxes' advice was indeed sound."

"Fine, so we simply sail on past and hope they don't spot us." Jason announced it as if it were the result of long, difficult thought, but for once his native...what shall I call it? *Caution* proved quite wise.

The Trojans did indeed spot us. They sent a small flotilla of ships to pursue us. But Argus had built our ship well. We moved so fleetly they had no chance of catching us.

* * *

In fairly short order we reached the mouth of the Hellespont. This is the body of water purportedly named for my ancestor Helle, the sister of Phrixus. Legend had it that it is where she fell off the back of the Golden Ram as it carried her and her brother away from Iolcus to Colchis; she fell and downed, and the Hellespont has been called that in her honor ever since. As with all our family history, I had no idea how much of this story to believe. Aside from the fantastic tale of a flying Golden Ram (which is no less believable than my divine winged lover, I suppose), how likely is it that people in Asia Minor would have known who Helle was, much less named a major body of water after her?

One way or another, the Hellespont stretched before us, and we had to navigate it if we were to reach our goal. I made my way to the prow and whispered a silent prayer to the spirit of Helle, asking her to guide and protect us—just in case.

It is a narrow strait leading north-northeast from the Aegean. There are swift, treacherous currents with many eddies and backwaters, and a great many rocks, some small and some larger, some visible and some hidden just below the surface. They are known widely as "the Clashing Rocks" from the enormous number of ships

231

that have been dashed to pieces on them. There were also reputed to be whole islands that floated, twisted, gyrated in the waters. We had what we hoped were reliable charts, thanks to the Mysians and Samothracians, to get us past the rocks; those islands, if they existed, were another matter.

The Hellespont leads into a small, calm sea called the Propontis, which in turn leads to another strait called the Bosporus which is quite as perilous as the Hellespont. That in turn would take us to the Black Sea and, we hoped, tranquility.

But there is always danger before peace. We anchored at the entrance to the Hellespont, and Jason, Nauplius, Argus and Tiphys surveyed the waters ahead of us. Lynceus joined them and scanned the way ahead of us.

The waters were indeed swift and were running opposite the direction we had to steer. Everyone would have to row, and row vigorously; even the Argonauts still nursing wounds would have to help. We would have to hope our oars—and the *Argo* itself—were strong enough to survive. Tiphys told Jason and Argus they would have to help him man the tiller.

When I was a boy I would go out with some of my fisherman friends as they sailed the Aegean. And occasionally we would get caught in storms, some of them quite violent. The currents of the Hellespont made them seem calm by comparison. The *Argo* rocked, reeled, twisted, bolted in every direction. At moments I thought we would capsize but she always managed to right herself. Sometimes the current would pull us backward, till Tiphys managed to steer us into a relatively calm backwater. We would recover ourselves quickly and get back to rowing Nauplius and his maps managed to keep us away from all but a few small rocks; we scraped them but the hull was never breached. Of the floating islands we saw never a sign.

Then at last we reached the Propontis. The water still flowed southward but was less turbulent. Tiphys steered us into a small cove to one side. We had the chance to rest before tackling the Bosporus.

* * *

Jason decided we should have a council before continuing. "The Bosporus still lies before us. Once we have braved it we will be in the

Euxine, commonly known as the Black Sea. None of us has ever been there before, so we have no way of knowing whether its blackness is physical or of the spirit."

"Everyone we talked to on Samothrace and in Mysia," Nauplius interjected, "told us that the sea's name comes from its being a darker shade of blue than the Aegean. And they all said it was fairly tranquil."

"Let us hope that was correct." Jason was smug. "At all odds, no one has been able to give us anything but sketchy directions to Colchis once we're through the Bosporus. Even Amphiaraus and Idmon can see nothing of use to us. We know we'll have to head east, along the sea's southern shore. All we can do is go that way and pray to the gods for safety."

"Those would be the gods that placed these turbulent waters in our path?" Argus was his skeptical self.

But at that point Kalais came forward. His wounds had finally healed, and he was something like his old self. "Listen, we do have another option."

"Yes?" Jason was impatient. Still another of his leadership decisions might be called into question.

"Don't be so testy, Jason." Kalais smiled an expansive smile. "I have relatives in this region. They can be counted on to help us."

"Relatives." Jason was deadpan.

"Yes, relatives. Our—my—sister Cleopatra is married to King Phineus of Salmydessus, a short way up the west coast after the Bosporus. She has given him twin sons, and I haven't seen them since they were infants. They must be well into adolescence now. If we land there, Phineus will be certain to help us with instructions for steering our course to Colchis."

This struck me as eminently wise counsel but Jason, typically, disliked it. "We are not on a mission to reunite you with your sister, Kalais. We should press forward."

Amphiaraus spoke up. "I met Phineus once when he was on a diplomatic journey to Argos. He is a good man, and not only that but he has prophetic gifts, very sharp ones. His counsel could be quite valuable to us."

"Prophetic gifts!" Jason was in a testy mood. "Prophetic gifts, prophetic gifts! Am I the captain of this expedition, or am I not?"

233

"I thought this was a council." I was wry, quite amused at his attitude. "Do you want advice from the rest of us or not?"

"And I thought," Idmon offered, "that you valued prophesy. Else why that oak branch in the prow?"

Jason glared at him. It was becoming more and more clear that more and more lines of stress were appearing in their little love affair.

Argus spoke up to back Kalais' suggestion. Jason argued. Then both Tiphys and Nauplius likewise backed Kalais. "If I have to steer us through unknown, possibly treacherous waters, I want all the foreknowledge I can get," asserted Tiphys.

There seemed no logical argument against that, so westward to Salmydessus it would be. Part of me was pleased that Jason was no longer the autocratic captain he plainly thought he should be. His judgment was not to be trusted; self-interest motivated him, and we all knew it. On the other hand, we were without a firm leader. I didn't know whether to find that alarming. Our joint, collective wisdom seemed sound enough, and the arguments for Kalais' proposal seemed beyond reproach. Yet...

"Fine." He acquiesced but with ill grace. "We'll go to Salmydessus so Kalais can play with his nephews. In the meantime, let us rest for an hour before we broach the Bosporus."

I suggested that before we set sail again we erect an altar to Helle, to pray and bless her and thank her for our safe passage through the waters named for her. Once again Jason disliked anyone but himself suggesting action for us. but everyone else agreed. Even Argus went a long with it, I suspected more to annoy Jason than out of any sense of reverence. But we build the altar and sacrificed a young doe we caught wandering nearby. There were prayers. Jason stood apart from it all, sulking.

* * *

"Why have you never mentioned your sister before?"

Kalais and I found ourselves alone, below deck, for the first time since leaving Mysia. Between kisses and embraces we talked.

"Cleopatra is our mortal sister. No wings, nothing even slightly godlike about her. Boreas acknowledged her as his child when she was born, so there is not much doubt, and she must have divine blood flowing in her veins. But when we were growing up there was no sign of it."

"What a fascinating family I've married into."

"Don't be smug, Acastus. At least we don't have any infanticide in our history. Or any ghosts."

"Touché."

We kissed. We couldn't stop kissing. Quickly, briefly, we made love. Then we lay in my cot, nuzzling and talking.

"Do you miss Hylas, Acastus?"

"Very much. He was such a sweet boy. I keep wondering what he might have accomplished if he had grown to adulthood…if those nymphs hadn't… And how he must have suffered when they… He wanted love, that's all. And even the love of Hercules wasn't enough for him."

"Perhaps his spirit is still with us on this voyage."

"His spirit? His spirit was drowned with his body, Kalais. I can't spend any time wishing for such a thing."

"If our spirits do not outlast our bodies, what is this expedition about? And why did we bother with an altar to Helle?"

I felt myself choking back tears. I had loved the boy; he had been the brother I'd never had in reality, or rather he was exactly what I'd imagined my brother would be. Perhaps my slaughtered brother's soul inhabited Hylas when he was born. How could I know? But one way or the other, our family was a family of death.

The tears finally came, not many but I couldn't hold them back. This was the first opportunity I had had of grieving, really grieving for Hylas. I buried my face in Kalais' chest and he enfolded me in his wings.

* * *

The Bosporus was every bit as violent as the Hellespont but thankfully shorter. Water rushed out of the Black Sea on its way down to the Aegean. At places it spun us around so wildly it left some of us dizzy and disoriented. Jason, for once acting like a true captain, shouted order after order to keep us focused and in or near the center of the channel, away from the most jagged, threatening boulders.

At one point I called out to Orpheus, who was struggling at his oar, "Why don't you get out your lyre and sing a lullaby to these waters?"

He laughed. "Show me its ears and I'll happily coo a warm melody into them." The strain was showing on him; he was a musician not a sailor, and he was unused to such strenuous demands on his physical resources. It was not at all characteristic of me, but I prayed a silent prayer to his father Apollo to keep him alive and fit. I started another prayer, this one to all the gods of Olympus, to keep us all safe; but we became trapped in a particularly violent whirlpool and I had to leave off praying and work, like the whole crew, to stay alive.

Then we were through the channel and into the Black Sea. To my surprise the morning sun was not much higher in the sky; our ordeal had seemed much longer than it really was. Once again we had managed to navigate a dangerous passage with no serious damage to the *Argo*. We had scraped some rocks but none of them had actually punctured the hull.

There was still a strong current as the water flowed into the Hellespont. Tiphys steered us into a cove and we settled in for another rest period. Then it would be on to Salmydessus and King Phineus.

Everyone in our crew needed a rest break and needed it badly. Kalais and I snuggled again. Jason called Idmon and they, likewise cuddled together. I caught sight of Polyphemus, and it was easy to see that resting without Zetes in his arms was painful for him. The sight of Hercules' empty cot spoke eloquently about what had happened to him and Hylas. I tried to close my eyes and sleep, but there was too much sadness on the *Argo*. Instead of sleeping I merely closed my eyes and held Kalais tightly. Whether he was able to sleep I did not know; but I knew that he too was still grieving. I could feel his chest heave as he mourned his brother in silence.

* * *

Once we were rested we moved on. Salmydessus was two hours up the west coast. There was a mild south wind, but we rowed briskly and made good time.

It turned out to be a city-state on the edge of the sea. It was middle-sized, not particularly impressive as cities go. There was a harbor, a fishing fleet and what looked like a small navy. Dominating the city, on a hill above it, was a typical acropolis, several temples and a palace. It all gave the appearance of age.

As we drew near, Lynceus became concerned. "I'm not seeing many people or much activity."

Ominous words. Could it be another Lemnos, another place where death awaited us?

A boat left the harbor and made straight for us. It was rowed by four sailors; two men, obviously officials, stood in the prow. One of them was the herald; he called out a standard, formulaic greeting to us, assuring us the Salmydessans welcomed us as friends. "King Phineus has seen your coming in a vision." Echion responded in kind, explaining who we were and why we had come to Salmydessus and informing them that the brother of their queen was in our company.

They conferred hastily. "We were not aware that the queen has a brother. The news is most surprising to us." Once more they put their heads together and whispered. Their herald then introduced his companion; he was Polypraxis, major domo to the king. He and his herald had still another hasty conference

"You are most welcome," announced the herald. He and Echion exchanged more of the formulaic greetings, and even though these were rubrics they had voiced a hundred times before, they made them sound fresh and spontaneous. That was their training as members of the Guild of Heralds, whose membership transcends nations and encompasses all of the known world. They are the grease that keeps relations between cities and between whole nations running smoothly.

We followed their boat and rowed into the harbor, and once we had moored the *Argo* Jason led a party ashore. Argus and I went, as usual, along with Kalais, Pollux, Atalanta and several others. Kalais, as was his habit whenever he in a strange place, wrapped himself in a cloak to hide his wings.

Polypraxis was waiting there for us, looking vaguely troubled. He mouthed more diplomatic formulas, the kind of thing every traveler to every city hears time and time over. Echion answered him in kind. I noticed, oddly, that Polypraxis was wearing a red scarf around his neck despite the warm day.

Then he turned to Kalais. "Do I have the honor of addressing the brother of queen Idaea?"

Kalais did not try to hide his bafflement. "Idaea?! I am the brother of Queen Cleopatra, daughter of the god Boreas. She reigns as queen here. I attended her wedding to King Phineus myself."

"Oh, that explains…" He seemed for a moment not to know what to say, then he recovered himself. "I regret to inform you, sir, that your sister died two years ago."

For a long moment Kalais fell silent. Then, softly, he asked, "And what of my nephews?"

Polypraxis seemed uncertain what to say. He hemmed and hawed in a way quite unlike the professional diplomat. Finally he dropped any pretense of a diplomatic manner and told Kalais softly, "They are imprisoned, sir, in the king's dungeon. Accused of treason by the new queen."

"New queen." Kalais had gone numb with the news; his voice was flat and was completely without tone or character.

"Yes, sir. King Phineus has married Idaea, high priestess of the goddess Dicte. She has given him an infant son."

My mind raced to remember, and it finally came to me. Dicte was the death goddess on Crete. How—*why?*—could an Asian king have married one of her priestesses? Is it possible he wanted to import her cult to Salmydessus? Crete had been a civilized island yet vestiges of barbarism flourished there, and the cult of Dicte was one of the worst. There had even been rumors of human sacrifice.

I looked around the harbor. As Lynceus had said, there were nowhere near as many people as there ought to have been. Some fishermen spread their nets to dry; a few women and children worked at maintaining them; some other children, not many, ran and played. The city seemed to be dying every bit as much as Iolcus was.

Jason stepped forward, and Echion introduced him as our captain. "Where," he asked, "is King Phineus? Why has he permitted this?"

"To which 'this' are you referring, Captain Jason?"

"Take your choice."

"You may ask him yourself, sir. My instructions are to take you to the palace at your earliest convenience. The king will be pleased to greet you there."

"Let us go to meet him now, then."

"As you wish." He hesitated for a moment then added, "Might I suggest you bring scarves and wrap your faces in them?"

"Why? Is the king giving a costume ball?"

"Very droll, sir. The reason will become quite clear when we reach the palace."

Four of us—Jason, Argus, Kalais and myself—followed him up the narrow causeway to the acropolis. Again and again I was struck by the relative sparseness of the population and the lack of activity. Even a smallish city should have been busier than this. We passed through the central square and it was all but deserted.

There were six temples on the acropolis, one each for six pairs of husband-wife Olympians. It was an odd arrangement but not quite unorthodox. Then I noticed that the farthest of them, the one that should have been dedicated to Ares and Aphrodite, was damaged. The deities' names had been chiseled off the pediment and the name of Dicte had been painted over the place where they had been. I exchanged glances with Argus and Kalais; they had noticed it too.

Midway along the central path was the palace. It was evidently quite old, built in a very crude Doric style. As we approached, a foul odor met our nostrils, an odor of decay or waste matter. Was the garbage dump nearby? Before any of us could say anything about it, Polypraxis pulled his red scarf up about his face, covering his nose. The gesture was smooth, offhand; it was evidently common practice.

Seven broad steps led up to the palace. By that point the rank smell was terribly strong, almost overpowering. Polypraxis turned to face us. "Your scarves, gentlemen."

He did not have to repeat himself. We quickly wrapped our scarves tightly around our faces. Even through the layers of linen the stench penetrated.

"Please wait here, gentlemen, while I announce you." He glanced quickly up at the sun, which was well past its zenith and beginning to sink in the western sky. "It is nearly time for his majesty's evening meal. Might I suggest that you would do better to go back to your ship and return here in the morning?"

None of us quite knew how to react to this. We looked at one another; the others were clearly as puzzled as I was. Before any of us could answer him Polypraxis made a quick bow and moved toward the palace door.

"Wait." Kalais caught him by the elbow. "I asked you about my nephews."

"In good time, sir. Please believe me, I don't mean to be mysterious, but conditions herein Salmydessus are not...are not..."

"Usual?" Argus helped find the word he wanted.

He made a slight bow, tightened the scarf around his face and went into the palace.

We were left standing at the doorway. It was clear none of us knew what to make of the situation; it was far removed not only from our expectations but from anything in our experience. Kalais in particular seemed troubled. To have lost not only Zetes but his sister Cleopatra as well came as a terrible blow to him, and it showed. I took his hand and squeezed it.

I whispered to Argus, "What on earth is happening here? Argus, I have no idea how to respond to—"

Jason was tightening his scarf around his face. "Let us just play for time until we know better what is happening in this city."

Suddenly a line of three servants—slaves, by the look of them—appeared, each carrying two trays heaped with food for what would most certainly be a sumptuous meal for the king. Like us, and like Polypraxis, they had covered their faces. They moved quickly, each of them scanning the sky overhead. One of them was gazing upward so intently he stumbled on the top step, but he recovered himself quickly. In an instant they had disappeared into the palace. They had not even taken notice of us; their movements were that purposeful.

Still again we looked at one another, our bafflement plain to see. Kalais was the one who broke our silence. "Has this place gone mad, or have we?"

"It is certainly an unusual city." Argus was sanguine. "Let us hope we do not find something here as awful as what we found on Lemnos."

"Shh." Jason hushed us.

Polypraxis was back, his face still wrapped in red linen. "I regret to inform you, gentlemen, that his majesty will be unable to receive you. It is the hour for his evening meal."

"So we saw. But he must certainly—"

"If you will return at first light, gentlemen, and before the hour for his morning repast, he will be most pleased to welcome you. I urge you to leave now and quickly."

That was all. We tried asking him a few questions, but he was so

240

impassive it became quickly apparent we were wasting our time. More bewildered than ever, we returned to the *Argo*. At least we got away from the awful stench.

As we were going down the causeway to the city proper we heard something unearthly, something between a screech and a hiss. One more piece of the mystery we were facing.

* * *

We had our own dinner, a quick one, then Kalais suggested he and I take a walk in the city. Lynceus and Atalanta came with us. At worst it would give us some good exercise; at best we might learn something of what had happened in Salmydessus. Various other Argonauts also decided to take strolls and headed off to explore Salmydessus as well. In a short time, we would cover the city, and at least some of us might gather some useful news.

It was late afternoon, nearly sunset. Shadows were lengthening; the narrowest streets were already dark. The marketplace at the central square is always the busiest part of a city, so we decided to head there. Sunset was happening and shadows were long. Just as we were a few hundred yards from the ship Lynceus called out, "Look, up in the sky!"

Two large flying things were approaching the acropolis. At first glance we thought they were birds. But the closer they came the more details we could make out. Great bat-like wings, slender bodies like women, skin green and scaled like reptiles, huge talons that looked like they could easily disembowel a horse. They soared overhead and seemed to be heading for the palace. What on earth were we seeing?

Kalais grabbed me by the shoulder and took Atalanta by the hand. "Quick, let us get under cover."

"Why? Kalais, what on earth are those things?"

"Come quickly. I don't want them to see me."

We ducked into the nearest shop. It turned out to be a baker's. Kalais' face was pale. He still had a tight grip on my shoulder. I gently removed it. "You can relax now. There's no chance they'll see us in here."

Every muscle in his body was tense; I could see that. "Kalais, will you tell me what those things are? What on earth did we see?"

Atalanta echoed the question. Kalais took a careful step back into the street and looked skyward. Seeing nothing, he rejoined us in the shop.

"Well, Kalais, are you going to enlighten us?"

"I've only half believed in them. If I hadn't seen them with my own eyes…"

"Will you please tell us what we saw?" Atalanta was as lost as I was.

"But…*Crete*. They should be in Crete." He seemed more than a bit numb. I was beginning to fear for him. "Crete is their abode, or so I've always heard."

I was growing more and more impatient. "Will you please stop being so cryptic and explain yourself? What on earth—"

"Harpies." Kalais said the word as if it was self-explanatory.

But it wasn't, at least not to Atalanta and me. She prodded him to go on.

The shopkeeper interrupted, telling us he was about to close for the night and we would have to leave his premises.

Back in the street Kalais went on. "The harpies," he explained in a somber tone, "are the daughters of the Cretan death goddess and thus, horrible as it is, they are distant cousins of mine. They are foul creatures; they bring destruction wherever they go. But I've never heard of them going anyplace outside Crete and its neighboring islands. Part woman, but also part bat, part snake…they are an amalgamation of all the ugliest nocturnal things wrapped into female bodies."

He wore a numb expression. I repeated the word. "*Harpies*. I remember hearing of them when I was a boy, but I always thought they were imaginary, something mothers use to frighten their children into behaving." Crete had famously sunk into semi-barbarism after the death of King Minos and the fall of the civilization he had built. Hideous gods had taken root there. But those were legends—as the things we had seen were most certainly not.

"So did I," Atalanta said. Like Kalais and Lynceus she was scanning the sky for signs of the evil creatures. "But evidently they are all too real. But as you said, they belong in Crete. This is the shore of the Black Sea. How on earth—"

He shrugged. "It is one more mystery in a journey filled with them."

It hit me. "You heard what Polypraxis told us. This new queen, this Idaea, is a priestess of Dicte. That would explain—"

"Yes. It explains how they came here." Lynceus had not stopped looking skyward. "But why?"

I couldn't stop watching Kalais. A dozen different emotions crossed his face, fear, bafflement, resolve…

Finally he said, "There are two people who can explain all this, if we can get to them. My nephews. They must be 12 or 13 years old now, perhaps even a bit older, more than old enough to tell us what we need to know. The three of you get back to the ship. Stay there, and make sure all the others do. The harpies are murderous creatures."

"Atalanta and Lynceus can go back, Kalais. I'm going with you."

They left us, praying that we'd be careful and keep our wits about us.

The sky was darkening when we climbed the path to the acropolis. There were a few clouds drifting across the sky, obscuring stars and planets. When we were at the top of the path we saw a meteor streaking to the east. I wondered aloud if it was a good omen or a bad one. That horrible odor, that scent of death and decay, came to us almost at once. We covered our faces. It helped, but the air was positively sickening.

"Shh. The guards will hear."

I looked around. "What guards?"

Kalais scanned the scene as well. "You're right. This place is abandoned. We might as well be in a desert."

"Perhaps they think that overpowering stench is defense enough."

The awful reek emanating from the palace made us cover our faces again. With no one to see us, we made straight for the palace, not bothering to hide our movements. Once there, we walked around the building, looking for windows at the base that might open from the dungeon. A line of low shrubs surrounded the palace; they must have been decorative originally, but most of them were dead or dying and the rest were growing wild. At the rear we found a window, low to the ground, fronted with iron bars. We bent down to try and see inside. The blackness was Stygian.

"Hello," Kalais whispered. "Is anyone there?"

From inside came the sounds of someone moving. We could not see who it was.

But instantly a voice answered in a normal tone, not bothering to hush. "Who is it?" It was the voice of a boy.

"My name is Kalais, son of Boreas."

"Kalais! That is the name of our uncle. Who are you, to have stolen it?"

"I am no thief. I am Kalais, as I said, the brother of Queen Cleopatra. With me is Prince Acastus of Iolcus. I am your uncle. And you—what are your names?"

"We are Urion and Podarge." There was a long interval. The two boys whispered inside. It was possible to detect desperation in their voices. Finally one of them said, "If you are our mother's brother, let us feel your wings." A small hand reached out through the bars, followed by another.

Kalais removed his cloak and turned his back to the window. The boys' hands stroked his wings, but they could only reach the bottom of them, no more.

"Are you fooling us? Are those really wings on your back, or—?"

"Yes, they are real. I give you my word."

"The word of a stranger to prisoners. How much is that worth?"

"Ask me something about your mother, something only her brother could know."

Their exchange went on for several minutes. Finally the boys were convinced.

"Idaea has had us imprisoned here. She wants our father to disinherit us and make her infant son his only heir. Something is happening to our father, something neither he nor anyone else can resist. We don't know what, but we can hear him screaming in terror many times each day. And we hear the shrieks of some wild beasts, like nothing we have ever heard before. Smell the air. It is air only fit for loathsome creatures to breathe. You can tell something is horribly wrong here."

"We will find a way to set you free and end…whatever is happening. You have my word."

He took their hands. They seemed not to want to let go; they grasped him as if it meant their lives. But finally they released him.

Kalais bent and kissed their hands, repeating his promise. We went back to the *Argo* and told Jason and Argus what we had learned.

* * *

At first light Jason, Argus, Kalais and I went back up to the acropolis. We found Polypraxis waiting for us at the foot of the palace steps. His face, as usual, was wrapped in a scarf. We followed suit and covered our own.

Polypraxis greeted us. "The king is awaiting you. Please follow me."

"You expect us to go into that building? With that overpowering stink emanating from it? What kind of hospitality is that?"

"You will see. Come."

"What on earth can be causing that appalling stench? Why does the king tolerate it?"

He glanced quickly up at the sky. "Please, gentlemen, we must hurry. Soon it will be time for the morning meal."

"We do not expect to be fed," Argus grumped.

"That is not the problem, good sirs. Please, the king is awaiting you." He turned and began to ascend the palace steps.

Before Polypraxis could take a second step I caught him by the shoulder. "And the queen, this Idaea? Will we meet her as well?"

"I fear not, Prince Acastus. Her Majesty has taken up residence in the temple of Dicte. This way, please."

We entered the palace. The interior, unlike the façade, was quite beautiful. Room after room was freshly painted and well-kept, though there were occasional piles of litter here and there. But there was no one in sight, no servants, no slaves, no retainers. The palace was quite empty. It was as if we were walking through a huge mausoleum.

Worse yet, as we walked deeper and deeper into the palace the stench of decay, of filth, grew stronger and stronger. Kalais had a fit of coughing, and we waited for it to pass.

We entered a large room, evidently a banquet hall. And at once it was as if we had entered another place entirely. Rows of tables, many of them on their sides, filled the place. Dishes and tableware were scattered everywhere. Rotting fruit, bread and meat covered large stretches of the floor. And there were piles of what looked—and smelled—like excrement and pools of what appeared to be urine. The rank odor of the place was overpowering.

"What is this?" Argus demanded. "Why have you brought us to this pigsty?"

Instead of answering, Polypraxis merely gestured to a far corner of the room. Sitting on the floor, partially concealed by a fallen table, sat an old man. He was thin, emaciated, almost a living corpse, and he was rooting through a pile of garbage like an animal. His clothes were covered in filth; his beard was matted with it. If the palace was a stone tomb, he was a fit inhabitant.

"Who is there?" he asked feebly.

"Your majesty," Polypraxis said, "these are the travelers I told you about. Princes Acastus and Jason, the famous shipwright Argus and Kalais, brother of your late wife."

"That is King Phineus?!" Jason could not hide his incredulity.

"Yes, sir. Please excuse me, now. I have other business to see to." He bowed, further covered his nose and mouth with a hand, turned and departed quickly.

We were left gaping at the empty room and the pathetic old man at the far end of it. Slowly, feebly he got to his feet. "Yes, Prince Jason, I am Phineus." The voice was weak.

Now that we could see him clearly, his pathetic state was clear. Phineus was more thin than any living being I had ever seen, almost completely emaciated, like a man dying of starvation which, we soon learned, he was. He might have been any age from 30 to 70.

Jason approached him slowly, not trying to hide his bafflement. "You know me?"

"I know all of you. The gods have given me the gift of second sight. I know why you are here, and I know what you want. I even know what Kalais and Acastus did at the back of the palace last night."

Argus stepped forward and joined Jason. "King Phineus, I have traveled widely, yet I have never seen a king living in conditions like these. Tell us what is happening here."

There was something…odd about Phineus' demeanor. He had not once looked at any of us. It struck me. "You are blind."

"Yes."

"Who has done this to you?" Jason's tone was indignant and growing more so.

"The gods." Phineus actually laughed. "Zeus, Apollo, Hera... They gave me my preternatural second sight to reward me for service to them. Then, when my prophecies proved too accurate and made them uncomfortable, they stole my natural vision from me."

"Your majesty, I am Prince Acastus of Iolcus."

"I know it."

"You said you know why we are here."

"I do. You want to know how to reach Colchis and purloin the Golden Fleece. And I will tell you. But there is a price."

Jason was suddenly resolute. "Name it."

Phineus fell silent for a moment. A weak smile crossed his lips. "You will see."

We should have brought Idmon or Amphiaraus with us. One or both of them might have been able to cut through his silence and explain what he wanted, if only in general terms. Phineus repeated softly, "You will see."

We had no idea what he meant, what he wanted of us, and we looked at each other, our bafflement showing clearly in our faces.

Then he went on. "In a few moments the slaves will be here with my breakfast. It will be quite clear to you then."

There was not much we could do but wait. Why his breakfast would make anything clearer, none of us could fathom. Why he would try to eat in those surroundings, amid that awful stench was a mystery none of us could penetrate. Why was he living like this?

Kalais took a step forward. "Phineus, I am Kalais, brother your late wife Cleopatra. I was here at your wedding."

"I know. I remember your voice."

"Cleopatra gave you two sons, my nephews Urion and Podarge. I—"

"There are two others you must concern yourself with first. Ocypete and Aellopus. They will be here before long."

Almost as soon as he finished saying it, a line of three slaves appeared, each carrying three trays of food. Fruits, breads, soups, meats of all kinds, more food than one man could possibly consume. They kept looking back over their shoulders as if they were afraid they were being followed.

An abundance of food—and for just one meal. There was such plenty. How was it possible that Phineus was so thin, so very like a living corpse? How could a man with such a variety of good food look like he was starving?

The slaves spread their trays not on table but on the floor in front of Phineus. Then they turned and ran from the hall as if they were feeding a wild beast, not a king. One of them paused, very briefly, at the door and looked at us, quite perplexed, as if he thought we might be mad.

Phineus wasted no time. He quite literally dived at his food, scrambling for as much of it as he could take at once, stuffing it into his clothing like a rabid beggar.

And then…

Like a flash of lightning two…two *things* flew into the hall and descended on him. I realized at once that they were the harpies. Five feet tall with wings like bats, scales likes lizards, long writhing tails like snakes, venom dripping from their mouths, every inch of them covered with slime. And they were female; their breasts were plain to see. As foul as the room smelled, they reeked even more. They grabbed at Phineus' clothes, pulled at his beard, scratched his face with their claws. He flailed at them wildly, unable of course to see them, trying futilely to strike them, but they would fly a few feet away, then fall on him again when his guard was lowered. All the food he had gathered to himself tumbled to the floor, and the harpies gathered it up and ate it. When they were sated they hovered above the rest of it, urinating and defecating on it, making it quite uneatable.

Phineus cried, "Stop! Stop tormenting me! What have I ever done to harm you or to show disrespect to your mother Dicte?"

The harpies chortled madly and went on with their disgusting task. Then when their "work" was done they hovered in the air directly above Phineus, defecated on him, and then soared out of the hall again. Phineus was left sitting amid befouled food and waste, covered in filth himself. He groped blindly, trying to find something that might be fit to eat. Kalais stepped forward and found a few bits of fruit that were still edible and handed them to him. He devoured them greedily.

The entire episode cannot have lasted more than three minutes; it was over so quickly, and it was so shocking, we had no time to react. It was quite unlike anything any of us had ever witnessed, and we were frozen into immobility by the sight. And the sad state of the King of Salmydessus became all too understandable to us.

Phineus ate the food in his hands, salivating over it like a rabid animal; his sad condition lowered him to that pathetic state. Almost choking, he was eating so fast, he croaked, "And there, gentlemen, is my price. Rid me of these fiends who torment me at every meal I try to eat, and I will tell you what you want to know."

"Those creatures are the Ocypete and Aellopus you named to us?" I asked the question. Typically, Jason had fallen to the rear of the hall, as far away from the horrible action as possible while maintaining some semblance of being there, of not deserting the scene.

"Yes, they are the names of the harpies. My bitch of a wife Idaea has summoned them here from Crete, where their mother Dicte reigns as supreme goddess. Idaea has imprisoned my eldest sons and threatens to let her harpies keep tormenting me until I disown them and recognize her infant son as my heir."

"No human being deserves to suffer as you are suffering. Phineus, you have my word we will help you set things right here." It was the firmest command decision I had yet made. Jason cowering in a rear corner of the hall, added feebly one word, "Yes."

We found a few more bits of food that had not been befouled, gave them to Phineus and took our leave to plan our strategy.

Outside the palace, Polyphraxis was awaiting us. "So, gentlemen…you have seen."

"Yes, as horrible as it is, we have seen."

"It has been going on for a year. The king has managed to accustom himself to eating filthy meat and bread or he would have perished long since. He has moved from room to room in the palace, hoping to evade them, but they always find him and carry out their horrible work. He has even tried hiding in other buildings, but…" He shook his head as if to say it was no use.

Argus asked him, "Why do the slaves not clean the palace, at least?"

"All but myself and the three you saw have fled, sir. Half the population of the city has gone elsewhere, convinced that Salmydessus is cursed beyond redemption. Only those slaves remain to serve Phineus his meals…for the little that is worth. Three slaves, and such a large palace… They could never keep pace with the winged fiends."

"But...but the people! Someone must have tried—"

He fell silent for a long moment. "Many have tried. The harpies attack anyone attempting to feed the king—any save those three slaves, three times a day. They have even attacked people in the main square of the city who were plotting against them. And...they are venomous. One bite from their fangs, one scratch from their claws is quite deadly. There is no part of Salmydessus that has not been terrorized. The city has been without an effective ruler for more than a year."

"And your army?"

"We are a city of merchants and fishermen. Our army is small and our soldiers are not much more than armed guards. Even so, a dozen of them have died trying to rescue King Phineus."

It was all too horrible. I asked, "And where is Queen Idaea?"

"She resides in the temple of Dicte." He gestured toward it. "She has her own servants, including a nursemaid for her child."

That was all we could learn. We withdrew to the *Argo* to plan our next move.

* * *

When noon came we had not yet devised our plan, not fully. But it was taking shape. Amphiaraus divined the location of Idaea in the temple and told us she was so confident of her position she had only four guards. Atalanta offered to lead a group of Argonauts to capture her. There was no guard stationed at the young princes' prison door, but it was sealed with three locks; they keys were in Idaea's possession. As for the harpies...

Idmon saw them torment Phineus at his noonday repast. In his vision it became clear to him that like all reptiles they had vulnerable underbellies. And their wings were thin and membranous, like a bat's. They were swift in their movements. We would have to confine them to one room if we were to have any chance of killing or disabling them.

Atalanta was our swiftest runner. We sent her to tell Phineus of our plans. He was to move from the hall to a smaller room. When she returned, there was nothing more we could do... but wait and brace ourselves for the evening to come and its conflicts.

* * *

Sunset. Time for the evening meal.

Atalanta took a group of Argonauts to take Idaea captive. The rest of us, under my command, were to do battle with the harpies. Jason, intrepid leader that he was, remained outside, planted firmly in the causeway among the temples, on the premise that either my group or Atalanta's might need reinforcement. Given that he would certainly have shrunk from any combat, however slight, it was just as well.

Phineus awaited in his bedroom. Everything there was covered with filth, exactly like the dining hall and exactly like everything everywhere in he palace. Kalais, Caeneus, Mopsus, Polyphemus, Polllux and I wrapped our faces in linen and concealed ourselves there, hiding behind various pieces of furniture, upturned tables and such. We brought Phineus a few morsels of food he could eat before the slaves and the harpies came; he ate greedily, like a starving animal.

Meanwhile, Atalanta led a party of a dozen men to the temple of Dicte. We were confident she could capture the queen with little difficulty. As for our fight against the harpies...how could we be certain of anything? We would have to fight them, being careful not to let them close enough to bite and inject their venom. If worse came to worst we could force Idaea to order the harpies away.

The slaves came, carrying trays of food. They spread them before the king. He groped blindly for pieces of bread and meat. The slaves, cowering, bent low lest the harpies descend on them, left quickly. Phineus devoured what he could.

They came. The two of them soared into the room as rapidly as birds of prey. They swooped and dived at the king, knocking the food from his hands.

We jumped out of hiding. Periclymenus transformed himself into an enormous eagle, startling them, sending them off balance. Polyphemus and Pollux took the mattress from the king's bed and held it over the doorway, blocking their escape. The harpies took no notice but went about their foul task, tormenting the king.

Suddenly Kalais, who had been concealed behind an upturned table, sprang into the air and set upon them. He wielded his sword, slashing at them, keeping them from getting too near to him and slashing with their claws. Periclymenus assisted him, forcing the harpies away from him and the king. The harpies, off balance and realizing they had flown into a trap, flew at the door, clawing furiously at the mattress and the men who held it, trying to escape the room. But Mopsus and Caeneus, armed with long spears, kept them from getting too close; their claws slashed only at the air. Kalais flew at them from behind, still slashing at their wings. The harpies shrieked like the hellish creatures they were.

Finally Kalais managed to sever the wing of one of them. She fell to the floor, howling and hissing like the venomous serpent she was, her good wing still flapping uselessly.

I thrust at her sister with my spear and, though she tried to evade me, my spearpoint pierced her side. She tumbled onto her wounded sister, and the two of them lay there, flailing and shrieking and clawing at the air. Mopsus got a length of rope around them and tied them together. And that was that.

Caeneus ran to the main city square to announce to one and all that their king was free and the city's nightmare was at an end.

Phineus had heard but not seen, of course. I walked to him and put a hand on his shoulder. "Eat, Phineus. Eat till you are stuffed. Eat like you've never eaten before."

"You have slain them, then?"

"They are wounded, perhaps mortally. We will take them out to the city's heart and chain them there so that all Salmydessus can see that your torment is at an end. The city has its king again."

"But…but my wife."

"Our people have taken her by now. You may punish her as you please. Jail her, torture her or send her back to Crete. It will be as you wish."

"And my sons, who I love?"

"The keys to their prison will be taken from Idaea and they will be released."

Just then, predictably, Jason strode into the room and planted himself beside me.

Phineus took a deep breath. "I am so deeply in your debt. Let me send tribute to Iolcus and sacrifice to your gods."

Jason bowed to the blind king. "We are most happy to have been at your service, Phineus."

The rest of us glared at him, but he showed no sign of shame or embarrassment.

* * *

The harpies Ocypete and Aellopus were dragged with hooks to the central square of the city. There they were chained to an ancient monument to the city's founder, a monument so old no one remembered the name of the man it honored. The twin monsters were still wounded, still reeking, still covered in slime and filth. They snapped and scratched at anyone who got close to them, but the Salmydessans were canny enough to stay just out of their reach. But sunset children had made a game of teasing and tormenting them.

At noon on the following day Idaea, in chains, was brought to the square and chained alongside them. Phineus, having enjoyed three full meals by then, was led by Polypraxis to the square, where a ceremony was held declaring Idaea's reign of terror at an end. Urion and Podarge were at his side.

The deposed queen's head was unbowed. She glared haughtily at Phineus and told him what a pathetic old fool she considered him.

"Perhaps," he responded, "you should explain that to your flying lizards. They will make a captive audience for whatever proud speech you deign to make. Your infant son, by the way, has been taken to the hills west of the city and left there for the wild beasts to feast on. Should we save the choicest cuts for your harpies?"

Hearing that chilled me. It hit much too close to home. But...but the world is a savage place. No one but me seemed to mind the king's vengeance.

Idaea started to make a retort, but a boy threw a handful of mud in her face, and she fell silent. Even she realized the reality of her reduced state.

After the official ceremony, Phineus invited us to the palace for a feast. There he made a speech of thanks for our help ending the reign of Idaea and the harpies. He instructed Polypraxis to give us the best chart available of the Black Sea. We were delighted to see that it indicated not only islands and mainland cities but ocean currents as well. "I wouldn't count on this being too reliable," he told us. "The currents at the entrance to the Bosporus are known to shift and change often. This is our most recent chart, but do not depend on it too heavily."

The Phineus took Jason and myself aside and told us of Colchis.

"It is a dark, savage place. Hecate is the goddess they revere most."

"And the body of Phrixus?" I asked. "Do you know where it is kept?"

"In the trees. You must seek among the trees."

"What on earth do you mean?"

But he would tell us no more.

The next day we set sail again, heading southward to the mouth of the Bosporus, then east along the sea's coast. The waters we met, thankfully, were tranquil.

Years later I heard that Idaea had grown old and died still chained in the main square of Salmydessus. The harpies, being semi-divine, did not age; they were still chained there and would remain so in perpetuity, taunted by children, laughed at by one and all. As for Phineus. he grew so fat he could barely move. When he died, Urion and Podarge fought a war to succeed him, and both of them were killed in the fighting.

So much for Salmydessus and its royal line.

Chapter Ten
The Seizure of the Fleece

Phineus' people counseled us that the Black Sea was normally calm and peaceful. The waters at the mouth of the Bosporus were turbulent, as much so as the waters in the Bosporus itself and in the Hellespont, but once we were past that point we should have no more troubles—not with navigation, at any rate. When we asked about Colchis itself they were as tight-lipped as their king had been.

We passed the mouth of the Bosporus quickly and with no problem. Tiphys maneuvered the ship so as to take full advantage of the currents and eddies, so we had very little rowing to do to get past that channel. All the signs were that we would have a prosperous voyage from then on.

There were two danger points on our route before Colchis. The first was just beyond the Bosporus—the city of Mariandyne. Phineus gave us letters of introduction to their king, Amycus, which should guarantee us a friendly reception.

But a short way past the city was one of the fabled entrances to the underworld. It was a great chasm. The only mortal ever known to have plumbed its depths was Hercules, who brought the three-headed dog Cerberus up from its deepest part, as one of the 12 labors he performed for his lover Eurystheus of Argos. The hound was still to be seen near the abyss, chained to a massive boulder against which it strained constantly, trying to get back to its infernal home.

Our reception there was indeed friendly. We spent a day relaxing, seeing the sights, enjoying Amycus' hospitality. The black infernal chasm was wider and deeper than anything any of us had ever seen. The sight of it filled us with awe and fear: Dicte, whose priestess we had enslaved and whose daughters we had wounded so grievously, was one of the deities who held sway there. Amycus told us it was not normally dangerous, but from time to time rogue waves had been known to sweep seagoing vessels into it. We were cautioned to make doubly certain the *Argo* was securely moored. We approached it most cautiously and once we had had the chance to inspect its mouth we left it most happily.

After our day at Mariandyne the next potential danger was the Island of Ares. We were advised to steer well clear of it for reasons no one was willing to explain. Argus was not happy about it. "Is every place on the Black Sea a dangerous mystery? We need better information than that." But no such information was forthcoming. There was nothing we could do but set sail and hope the gods were with us.

Yes—I said "the gods." By that point on the voyage I had become at least an agnostic if not actually a believer. A few prayers now and then could hardly hurt.

There was a gentle west wind at our backs. Rather than row, we set the sail and let the breeze carry us eastward. After Lemnos and Salmydessus we deserved a peaceful voyage.

On the third day we sighted an island to the north of us, miles out to sea. It appeared to be substantial, but we were too far away for even Lynceus to make out much detail.

Nauplius checked his chart and announced, "That is the Isle of Ares, which we were counseled to avoid. Let as keep moving eastward as quickly as we can."

Jason took his place in the prow. "Did anyone hear anything specific about this place?"

No one had. Nauplius urged that we go on.

But Jason had other ideas. "Does anyone know why it is called that? Does the god himself reside there, or is it simply that the residents revere him, or what?"

No one had a clue.

"Then let us change course. I want to see the place for myself. Who knows, there might be a more fabulous treasure than even the Fleece."

"Jason, we were warned." It was clear Argus did not like what Jason was suggesting. "We would be fools to—"

"Relax, Argus. I have no intention of landing. I merely want to get close enough to see, that's all."

Reluctantly we acceded to Jason's natural obstinacy, turned north and rowed for the island. Lynceus remained at the prow, scanning the horizon anxiously for the least sign of trouble.

The island loomed larger and larger ahead of us. Most of it was barren and rocky, but there were patches of green on the slopes of the central peak. We moved slowly, fearful lest we encounter more preternatural danger. The sea remained placid, the breeze soft and gentle. It was late afternoon; the sea glistened with flecks of reflected sunlight. Everything was calm.

Then suddenly Lynceus cried out, "Birds!"

We shipped our oars at once. A dark cloud rose above the island and moved in our direction. The cloud, like the waves below it, was flecked with glints of bright bronze, shimmering in the dying sunlight. We watched it, transfixed by the sight.

Argus was the first of us to come to his senses. "Quickly, let us leave this place! Row!"

But Jason countermanded his order. "No, stay where you are, all of you, until we see what magic is coming upon us. We conquered the harpies, the children of hell itself. We will certainly know how to fight this."

Soon enough the dark cloud resolved itself into hundreds, thousands of individual specks. It was soon clear they were in fact birds. But what kind of birds glinted and gleamed in the dying sunlight? We all watched Lynceus; he would be the first to know what we were up against.

The cloud of birds grew and shifted, now stretching horizontally, now vertically: exactly as a large flock could be expected to. It seemed almost a living thing, changing, distorting, distending its dimensions like a jellyfish. No one on the *Argo* spoke a word; anticipation made us more silent than we had ever been. After what seemed like an eon but was only a long, long moment, Jason ordered us to heave about and get away from the island.

"Bronze!" Lynceus shouted. "They are made of bronze!"

We watched. The flock was moving with unnatural speed and purpose. Soon enough even those of us with only normal eyesight could make out individual birds. And yes, they were made of bronze or of some similar metal.

"Get your spears and swords!" Jason cried.

257

We scrambled to do so, all the time wondering what good our weapons could be against metallic flying things. Jason left his command post and helped deal out the weapons.

"We were warned, Jason," I said to him in a whisper. "We were advised not to approach this place. What's the good of seeking out counsel from wiser men, men who know this sea, if you are going to be so foolhardy as to ignore their advice?"

He glared at me, but before he could respond the birds were upon us. The air was filled with their screeching cries, and their wings made a clacking, ringing sound that was almost deafening. We swiped at them with our swords, but to no effect. They swarmed around us, a whirlwind of them, their sharp bronze feathers slashing us, cutting our skin to ribbons.

The tip of one bird's wing slashed Euphemus' left eye. Blood spurted, polluting everyone around him. Bronze claws dug into our flesh. We reached frantically for our shields and moved to make a canopy of them, a protective awning over our heads. The birds flew beneath it and kept slashing us as they flew, clawing at hair, eyes, faces. Pollux hacked a bird in two and it fell with a loud clatter to the deck.

Without thinking, acting purely on impulse, "Quick!" I called out. "Those whose oars are on the lower deck, get down there and row us away from this place! Everyone else, cover the entrance to the underdeck with our shields to protect the towers!"

We combined our defenses and made a protective cover over the entrance to the lower deck. When the men there got to their oars, we felt the ship lurch forward and begin to move away from the island. The wounded crawled to the center of our protective parasol and lay there, supporting one another. Polyphemus and I, side by side, were at the outer rim of our defensive barrier; we slashed at the birds again and again with our spears, hacking off wings, legs, heads. The severed bits fell to the deck and continued writing and trying to maul us. Their screeching was almost deafening.

The swarming birds were relentless. They dove at us and crashed into our shields, splintering some of them. Castor's shield split neatly in two. More blood flowed; more men were cut. We could not get away from that accursed place rapidly enough.

Polyphemus shouted to me, "Stay here and keep fighting. I'm going up to the prow."

"No! What on earth do you think you can do there?"

"I think I may be able to send them back to their island."

"What?! Polyphemus, has their screaming driven you mad?"

A bird managed to fly into the space between our shields. It slashed my forearm with its wing then dug its claws into my hand. Polyphemus hacked at it with his sword. It fell in pieces to the deck and lay there, flailing uselessly.

I could not let him go. "Stay here. Fight with us."

"I may be able to do more at the prow." He must have read the puzzlement in my face. "I know the language of birds, remember?"

"Birds. Yes, real birds. These are… things, not living birds."

"I have to try."

I tried to stop him with my wounded arm, but I was too weak. Before I could say another word to him he dashed out from under our protective canopy and planted himself firmly at the nose of the *Argo*.

In a flash the birds set upon him, cutting his face, tearing at his arms, his thighs. In only a moment he was drenched with blood. Bravely he ignored it and began making sounds like a bird of prey. The bronze monsters held off; they seemed not to know what to make of him. But he continued and slowly, one by one, they backed away from him and from the ship. The cloud of them circled once, then flew back to the island. Polyphemus had done it.

We gained speed, and soon we were leaving the Isle of Ares far behind us. The remaining birds slowly left off their attack and returned to their home. Nearly 20 of us were hurt, some grievously.

Caeneus took charge of tending to the wounded. Euphemus had lost his eye. Atalanta's throat had been slashed, but we got it bandaged before she lost too much blood. Polyphemus' body was covered with gashes. The others who were injured had less serious wounds, cuts, scratches, most of them not very deep.

When we were far enough from the island, when the birds were far behind us, we lay still in the water for a time. The sun had set in the west. Hermes shone, a pure white beacon in the heavens, as if to remind us of our mission.

Now there was nothing ahead of us but open water and, at the far end of the sea, Colchis and the Golden Fleece.

* * *

The birds had not damaged our sail, which as I said had been safely furled. Each morning before dawn and each afternoon before sunset a soft wind arose out of the west to speed us on our way. In between times we rowed, those of us who were able. Nauplius never stopped checking his charts and estimating our position by visual clues onshore. He thought we should reach Colchis in three to four days— long enough, we hoped, for all but the most seriously injured to recuperate.

The Black Sea, as I have said, was quite unknown to us. The only one of our original company who had ever been so far from Greece was Hercules. Without him, every mile we traveled was a new adventure, a league further into the unknown. And of course he had been at least half mad when he was here before. He might not have been of much real use as we traveled to the edge of the world. The passing shoreline was everywhere dense with grasses, trees and a great many flowers; it seemed a most unlikely landscape for him.

Kalais, happily, had not been hurt when the bronze birds attacked us, suffering only a few small nicks; I had done my best to keep myself between him and the birds. He fussed over my wounds like an anxious nursemaid. I will admit, somewhat shamefacedly, that I enjoyed my lover's attentions. Leaning at the rail on the sunset of the second day, I commented to him how beautiful I was finding this new world now. "I was expecting something wild and chaotic, a jungle filled with fierce monsters. But except for those infernal birds..." I left the thought hang unfinished.

"It may not all be like this. We are at the limit of civilization, Acastus. The gods that hold sway here are the gods of blood and death. The people who worship them are apt to make even the Spartans seem cordial."

Glum thought.

He went on. "Hecate dominates here, Hecate and Ares. If Aphrodite has ever manifested herself here, it is as the goddess of uncontrolled lust, not gentle love."

Legend held that Aea, the capital city of Colchis, had been built by the Cyclopes at the beginning of time. It was, or so it was believed, the oldest city on earth. Whether that meant it was also the most civilized, or whether it was civilized at all, time would reveal.

Jason was content for us to make slow, steady progress. For once

I agreed with him. A few days' delay in reaching our goal would mean that more of us were recovered from our wounds and therefore able to fight if it was necessary. I voiced a silent prayer to Aphrodite and Hera that it would not be. But one way or another we had to return home with the Fleece.

* * *

It was on the fifth day that Aea came into view on the far horizon ahead of us. Unlike typical Greek cities it was built on a level plain; there was no acropolis. But there was a well-constructed harbor teeming with ships. Lynceus described them as a mixture of fishing vessels and war ships. As for the city itself, it was a metropolis of grey stone which in the morning sunlight seemed almost white. The buildings were large, even massive, the kind of buildings that might in fact have been erected by the storied one-eyed giants. Beyond stretched lush green fields, and in the farthest distance was a primeval forest. Then finally beyond it all was the largest, most massive building. It had to be the palace. Why it was so remote from the city we could not guess.

From his lookout's post at the prow he announced, "They've seen us. A ship has left the harbor and is coming this way quite swiftly." After a pause he added, "Jason is—"

"I am what?" Jason asked testily.

Lynceus looked at him, then at the Colchian ship, than back at Jason. "Nothing. Nothing."

"It's a very odd nothing that begins 'Jason is.'"

"Nothing, Jason, really."

Jason was going to press him, but before he could Echion took his place at the prow. We would need a herald now, not a lookout. Lynceus went back to his oar, with Jason glaring at him all the time.

It was only a matter of a few minutes till the Colchian ship reached us. She was a two-masted vessel but all her sails were furled. A bank of rowers—one level of them only—propelled her to us. 50 yards in front of us she stopped. Her crew maneuvered her to a halt crosswise in front of us. We were quite effectively blocked. Our two banks of oars gave us a tactical advantage; we could easily have rowed around her. But this was the time for diplomacy, not confrontation.

Their herald announced, "Hail. You are Greeks, are you not? We represent King Aeëtes of Colchis. We welcome you to the land of Colchis and the city of Aea. Please to identify yourselves and your mission."

"Greetings, men of Aea. We are the crew of the ship *Argo*, here on a quest for King Pelias of Iolcus. We assure you our mission is one of peace and amity with the people of Colchis."

A second man joined their herald at their ship's prow. And for an instant I wasn't at all certain my eyes weren't playing tricks. So that was what Lynceus had started to say then caught himself. The man could have been Jason's twin. Same gleaming red hair; same magnificent athlete's build. Even across a distance it was possible to see his bright, clear green eyes. "This," their herald announced, "is Prince Apsyrtus, come to greet you on behalf of his father the king."

Apsyrtus made a courtly bow. I glanced at Jason to see how he was reacting to the man. And he looked positively dumbstruck. I couldn't tell if he was feeling envy, pride, lust… or a mixture of all three.

The exchange of diplomatic folderol went on. If the Colchians were the least bit suspicious of us, they did not let it show. Finally they offered to escort us into the harbor and thence to the palace, where Aeëtes would greet us and make us welcome. Jason indicated we should follow them, all the while never taking his eyes off Apsyrtus.

I couldn't resist trying to learn what he had on his mind. "You don't by any chance have an identical twin brother, do you?"

"Don't be absurd, Acastus."

"How else do we account for him?" I gestured at the Colchian ship, which had hove to and was leading us at a gentle pace.

"It's simple. Once the gods found the template for the perfect man, they could not resist reusing it."

I chuckled. "If Apsyrtus has a colossal ego, I'll be quite certain he's your twin."

Jason grumped, turned his back on me and pretended to go over a map with Nauplius.

* * *

Before long we were safely moored and stepping ashore. Jason left a crew of ten on board for security. Everyone else was free to explore the city. "Be back at the harbor by nightfall, though. Things here seem friendly enough, but we've had too many unpleasant experiences to take anything for granted." We filed down the gangplank and took in the view of the city, what we could see of it. Jason came ashore last.

Aea and its buildings were—the word in unavoidable— cyclopean. Enormous buildings constructed of massive blocks of grey-black stone. It was easy to believe that only the giants of legend could have built them. And something else struck me almost at once. The buildings were all plain block, no decoration, no inscriptions, no ornamentation of any kind. It was the most primitive building style I had ever seen; the most backward Greek islands made at least some pretense of making their structures look amiable. Not here. What kind of people, I wondered, could live in such an austere environment? What ancient secrets might they know and hide?

Apsyrtus was waiting for us on the dock. Now that I had the chance to see him close-to, it was clear that he was younger than Jason and somewhat shorter and slighter of build. In fact it was easy to see he was even a bit younger than I was. And his complexion was quite pinker, the kind known as roses-and-milk, and his hair a shade more blond, of the kind known as strawberry blond. Jason never took his eyes off him; and the expression on his face wasn't hard to read. He was quite rapt, like Narcissus falling in love with his own reflection. I suppose it shouldn't have surprised me; Jason's self-regard was hardly news.

Apsyrtus, on the other hand, seemed quite oblivious to their resemblance. He went about his official duties—welcoming us, probing us gently to find out why we had come to Colchis, ordering servants to see to our billeting and take care of our baggage. He went about it all in a quite businesslike way, no fuss, no, pomposity, no affectation at all. His resemblance to Jason was only physical, it seemed.

"My father will be most pleased to meet you all. Please accompany me to the palace."

A half dozen of us followed him quite happily, Jason and myself, Argus, Kalais, Nauplius and Tiphys. Echion tagged along as well, in case we needed his diplomatic skills. We had known so little of Colchis and had so little idea what sort of reception we would meet there; this charming young prince could not have come as a nicer surprise.

Jason made a point of walking beside him. It was all too plain, to me at least, what he had on his mind, and I didn't want him to do anything that might sour our welcome. I forced my way to the front of the group, got between them and introduced myself. "Your city is quite magnificent, Apsyrtus."

"Thank you. It's quite gratifying to hear you say it. When occasionally in the past Greek adventurers have made their way here, they've had the most amazing preconceptions about Colchis."

I laughed. "We are at opposite ends of the known world, after all."

Jason kept trying to jostle me aside and get closer to his younger, trimmer twin. I held my ground quite firmly and did everything I could to hold Apsyrtus' attention. I admit, somewhat shamefacedly, that my intentions were not completely pure either. The same face and body that had attracted me to Jason when I first met him attracted me to Apsyrtus as well. But I held myself in check; I couldn't let my attraction to him interfere with our mission.

We passed through the city and were dwarfed by its buildings. S always, the people we passed were fascinated by Kalais' wings. And there was something else, something we all noticed, Jason certainly included: A good number of Aea's residents, men as well as women, wore jewelry of amber. Rings, earrings, necklaces, even the hilts of knives and short-swords…the stuff was everywhere. That goal of our journey, at least, held promise.

After a few minutes the buildings began to thin out. We were faced with open cultivated fields and sparse orchards. In the distance beyond them was the palace, surrounded on three sides by forest. Oddly, hanging in the trees were numbers of leather sacks, securely sewn up and swaying slightly in the breeze that blew off the sea. Some of them were being picked at by crows, jays and other birds. Though it was broad daylight, I even saw an owl clawing at one of them. Butes was pleased to see swarms of bees feeding in the fields.

In the distance ahead of us was the most immense building of all. "Is that your father's palace, Apsyrtus?" He told us that it was, then launched into a little dissertation on his country's agriculture. They grew plums, apples, pears…and on and on. Agriculture seemed an odd topic for him.

The large field just beside the palace—quite an extensive one, 50 acres or more—was quite uncultivated, overgrown with weeds and creepers. The rest of the palace grounds were quite meticulously tended. The lawns were well manicured, the shrubs nicely trimmed, hedges formed into neat rows; servants tended them all. Why was that one field so wild, so completely ignored?

I noticed in the distance, at the far end of the field, two brass sculptures in the form of bulls. They were quite oversized, three times the dimensions of living bulls. Their horns must have been at least ten feet long, and their hooves, what I could see of them through the weeds, seemed to be made of iron—a strange choice for statues in brass. Why on earth were they there, and why was the field in front of them so terribly unkempt?

As I watched, I thought I saw one of them turn its head slightly in our direction. The other one exhaled a stream of fire two feet long. I blinked, and they were still again. It must have been an illusion, my mind playing tricks on me. It must have been, or so I told myself.

* * *

The palace was as monotonously rectilinear, as drearily cubic, as all the other buildings, and as dully devoid of art or ornamentation, though its size was quite imposing. I kept wondering if it was an expression of austerity or the result of a lack of imagination.

Apsyrtus ushered us through the corridors, one passage after another of blank, empty stone. Even the servants—slaves?—there were wearing amber. The stuff seemed to be everywhere. That part, at least, of our intelligence about Colchis was accurate.

Before long we reached the throne room. Aeëtes sat in austere majesty, every inch a monarch and every inch a sober one. And there were quite a few inches. Aeëtes was the fattest man I had ever seen. He must have weighed four hundred pounds, if not more. I kept wondering how much marble it would take to do a proper sculpture of him.

His crown was of gold inlaid with still more amber, quite a bit of it. And he was simply dripping with amber jewelry. Things, on that score, looked more and more promising.

As we entered the chamber he glowered at us as if we might be physicians or bill collectors. Seated on a smaller, shorter throne beside him was a rather striking woman, presumably his queen. Needless to say, she also wore jewelry of amber. And beside her sat a young woman of quite remarkable dark looks, a raven-haired beauty who might almost have stepped out of a legend. And her eyes—her eyes were of a shimmering green like the skin of a beautiful reptile.

We paused at the door, and Apsyrtus whispered to us, "They are my father and my mother, Queen Chalciope. The girl is my sister— well, half-sister—Medea."

He ushered us in and said, "Father." He bowed deeply, and we followed suit. Apsyrtus introduced us by name and turned to us. "Gentlemen, this is my father Aeëtes, ruler of all these lands." Lowering his voice to a whisper he added, "And there is enough of him left over to rule many more." Gesturing to the woman he went on, "And this is my mother, Queen Chalciope. With them is my sister, Princess Medea, High Priestess of the Great Goddess Hecate." In another confidential whisper he added, "She fancies herself a witch as well as a priestess. You would be well advised not to displease her."

I decided that I quite liked Apsyrtus.

Aeëtes started to say something but Medea glared at us and cut him off. "My brother, gentlemen, as I'm sure you will have gathered, is quite devoid of the reverence befitting one of his station." Had she somehow heard his whispers, then?

Apsyrtus chuckled. "My sister, gentlemen, as I'm sure you must have noticed, is quite lacking the sense of irony befitting an educated woman."

Their father had not cracked the slightest smirk during this. Indeed he had not moved an inch since we were presented to him. To move all that royal flesh must have taken quite an effort. But finally he spoke. "I welcome you to Colchis, gentlemen. I trust Apsyrtus is making you comfortable and seeing to your needs."

Jason took a step forward. "He most certainly is, your highness. If all Colchis is as welcoming as Prince Apsyrtus, ours will be a happy visit indeed."

"We are most glad to hear it, Prince Jason."

"You must be wondering why we have made such a long and arduous journey to this land of yours. It has been a journey fraught with many perils, and we—"

"Enough! We are most anxious to hear the story of your travels, but court business demands our attention. Please let Apsyrtus afford you all the comforts of our palace. And please bring the rest of your crew and join us tonight for a welcoming feast. That will be the time for travelers' tales—and for business." For the first time he smiled and waved us out of his presence.

We all bowed, made a few more polite comments, and our audience was at an end.

* * *

Aeëtes knew how to give a feast. There was music and dancing. Torches blazed. And there was more food than we could all have eaten in a week. Most of it was on a platter before the king, but there was still plenty for the rest of us. As we dined we were entertained by minstrels and play-actors doing bawdy, blasphemous pantomimes of the gods. Through all of it Jason flirted rather shamelessly with Apsyrtus, and Apsyrtus returned his attentions. We would have an "in" with one member of the royal family, at least. But Medea noticed what was going on between them and did not try to hide her disapproval. Kalais leaned close to me and whispered, "The princess is jealous. I wonder if male love is as honored here as it is in the civilized world."

"Sh."

Over our meal, Jason told the story of our voyage from Iolcus, accompanied by Orpheus on his lyre. The Colchians listened, spellbound. The Lemnian women, the nymphs of Pegae, Phineus and the harpies…they lapped it all up.

At the end of this recitation, Aeëtes signaled for quiet in the hall. "We have our share of wonders here in Colchis, too, you know. But that is for later. Now tell us all why you've come here."

Jason described the haunted condition of Colchis and its king, the decline of the city, and our voyage to claim the Golden Fleece and calm the ghost of Phrixus. Aeëtes listened like the taciturn fat man he was, then announced, "If Apollo of Delphi has decreed you must have the Fleece, then of course you must have it."

The words couldn't have been more welcome. After all the horrors of our voyage, Colchian cordiality couldn't have been more welcome. I could see Jason relaxing for the first time all day.

But our relief didn't last long. The king added, "But of course there will be a price."

Jason, caught off guard, stammered, "A—a price, Aeëtes?"

"Yes, exactly." He looked like a cat with a bowl of cream. "The Golden Fleece is one of the great treasures of Colchis. We could not part with it without some sign of the gods' favor on you. You don't think that unreasonable, do you?"

"N-n-no."

"Phrixus, you may have freely. Out trees are getting much too crowded anyway"

"Your trees, Aeëtes?"

He frowned. "Yes. Our trees. In Colchis we do not bury our dead or burn heir remains as you Greeks do. We have never adopted that barbaric custom. We sew our dead up in leather sacks and hang them in trees, for the birds which are the emissaries of the gods. We bend the corpses into a low crouch, fit them into a sack of the proper size and leave them for the gods. You must have noticed them hanging everywhere"

"Uh…yes, we saw all the sacks. But we hardly stopped to think—"

"There is something, er, exceptional about Phrixus's body. The birds have never touched it. It's so strange…" He shrugged. "At any rate, that is the ancient custom for disposing of our dead."

"Not to do so is the gravest blasphemy" Medea added. "The gods are entitled to reclaim their human handiwork. To deny them that would bring dire catastrophe up on us."

Feeding carrion to birds struck me as a most bizarre concept of a religious act. Still, I supposed our own way of sending our dead to the gods was no less likely.

Aeëtes went on. "But the Fleece is another matter. It is quite precious, regarded as a tangible token of the gods' favor. You must earn the right to take it."

Echion got to his feet. "May we ask how we are to do so, your majesty?"

"It is quite simple, really. You must plow our field. You must have seen the one I mean—the unkempt one by the palace."

Another look of relief came over Jason. "Plow that field? That is all?"

"Other men have tried. None, I'm afraid, have survived."

This was getting more baffling by the moment. I got to my feet. "Plowing your field is deadly, King Aeëtes?"

He laughed again. "Not the actual act of plowing, no. But that field is the home of Hephaestus' oxen. Surely you saw them? Two great, outsized brass beasts with iron hooves? You must yoke them and plow the field."

"Those statues?"

"Statues? Prince Acastus, they are quite alive. Forged by the god himself and given to Colchis. They have claimed that field for their own, and they kill everyone who enters there. No one has ever been able to yoke them, much less plow with them."

Jason was completely out of his depth, and it showed. "What, they gore men to death? A good, stout shield would—"

"They breathe fire." Aeëtes' voice was flat. He was clearly not joking with Jason. And what I had thought I had seen, I really had seen: fire.

Aeëtes went on. "Wooden shields burn, metal ones melt. Men die." He suddenly became animated; evidently the thought pleased him. He laughed and rubbed his hands together like a schoolboy playing a prank. "But you are Greek heroes, are you not? None of it should bother you. I'll expect you at the edge of the field at sunup. Till then." He waved his hands to indicate the feast was at an end. That was that.

* * *

Later, in the room I shared with Kalais, Jason called a little council. He brought Apsyrtus with him; they entered hand in hand. Just behind them came Argus, looking even more unhappy than usual.

Jason sat glumly on the edge of the bed. "Well, what on earth are we to do?"

"We?" I didn't want to make things too easy for him. "Aeëtes wants you to plow the field, not me."

269

"My loving cousin. Are all royal families like this?"

I shrugged. "It seems to be the tradition. At least if you ask the poets." I turned to Apsyrtus, who sat in a corner with his chin on his knees. 'Is what your father told us true?"

"The bulls? Yes, I'm afraid so. The trees around the field are heavy with the corpses of men who've tried to yoke them."

Argus, as usual, turned his mind to the practical matter facing us. "Surely there must be some way around them—some way to immobilize them or whatever."

"Not that anyone's ever found. Jason." Apsyrtus moved to his new boyfriend's side. "You aren't really going to face them, are you?"

Jason took a deep breath and barked one syllable. "No." He jumped to his feet and began pacing the room. "Pelias brought this curse upon the city and the ghost upon himself when he killed my father. Let him find a way to remove them."

I said softly, "Jason, he has. That's why he sent us here, remember?"

He glared at me. "He sent us here, but he didn't give us any hint how to do the impossible. Why on earth should I—"

He was interrupted by a knock on the door, and without ceremony Idmon and Amphiaraus came in. "We have news, Jason, Acastus. From Iolcus." Idmon looked more grave than I'd ever seen him.

Amphiaraus expanded. "We have had a vision. Both of us. We have seen the precise same thing, down to the least detail."

Jason was impatient at being interrupted. "Yes, what is it?"

"It is not happy news we bring."

"In the name of all the gods, will one of you get to the point?"

I asked them both to take chairs. It was clear they had something serious to tell us, something important.

Idmon looked from me to Jason and back again. Slowly, softly, carefully measuring his words, he announced, "Pelias is dead."

"Whether he was killed by the ghost," Amphiaraus added in a hushed voice, "died from loss of blood, or whether his passing was natural, we cannot say."

Idmon took my hand. "We are most sorry to be the bearers of this news, Acastus."

"Don't be. You know Pelias and I were never very close, not as fathers and sons should be. I stopped feeling anything for him when I was still a child. Save your sympathy for Jason, here. He is the new king, or will be once he's crowned." It hit me like a bolt. "He was just telling us that lifting the Iolcan curse is up to Pelias. No more, it seems."

Apsyrtus put his head on Jason's shoulder. "You will have to face the bulls after all? And the Serpent of a Thousand Coils?"

"Serpent?! What Serpent?"

At that point we were interrupted again, this time by one of the palace servants with a message for Jason. Jason read it and dismissed him. Then for the first time all night he broke out into a smile. He tore the note to pieces, crumpled them up and sprang to his feet. "Come, Apsyrtus. Let's get a good night's sleep. Good night to you all."

The two of them left quickly, leaving the rest of us more bewildered than ever. One by one the others bade us good night and left me and Kalais to our bed.

But just before I snuffed out the candles I spotted a large of paper on the floor. It was a fragment of the note Jason received. I uncrumpled it carefully and read:

"—but there is a way. Meet me by the field an hour before dawn. Medea."

And so Jason would have to do the impossible to redeem the city of which he was now king. Kalais and I snuggled, whispered affectionate nothings and made love gently, quietly, restraining our passion lest we disturb my cousin the monarch, who was in the next room with his young double.

* * *

Morning dawned brilliant with sunlight. Neither of us felt like breakfast. We found a temple slave and had her lead us to the field where the bulls held sway. There was already a small crowd, mostly our fellow Argonauts but there was also a fair sprinkling of Colchians. Like people everywhere we went, they oohed and aahed over Kalais' wings.

Aeëtes had had a portable throne set up and sat in all his portly majesty, obviously relishing the death he was certain he would see.

271

Chalciope stood behind him, scanning the crowd anxiously; I couldn't tell what or who she was looking for. Beside them stood a trio of servants with trumpets.

Sunlight blazed off the bulls almost blindingly. Even though they were at the far end of the field and partially hidden by the wild growth, the dazzling reflected sunlight made me look away. I could see alder trees around the field, scores of them, burdened with hundreds of leather sacks holding the bulls' previous victims. The field itself was riotous with weeds, creepers and wildflowers of every description. Thousands of mayflies flitted among them. Leaning against a tree near the bulls was a huge wooden yoke. I wondered how many brave men had perished in a futile attempt to yoke the bulls with it. Not far from it lay a large plow, leaning on its side.

We bade our comrades good day. I had expected to see Jason there with them, but there was no sign of him. At the edge of the crowd stood Lynceus and Autolycus, watching the field intently as if they were studying it. I crossed to them. "You have a newfound interest in wildflowers?"

Lynceus never took his eyes off the bulls but Autolycus turned to me. "Morning, Acastus. Jason asked us to watch them for any patterns of movement we might detect. He has a plan."

"A plan? Jason? That doesn't exactly inspire confidence."

"Shh!" Lynceus hushed me. "I just saw one of them blink."

"A bug in its eye, maybe?"

"Stop it. Don't break my concentration."

I rejoined Kalais. A moment later Apsyrtus joined us. "Hello."

"How was your night with our king and captain?"

"Quite regal, thank you." He grinned and blushed like the schoolboy he was. "Have you seen my half-sister?"

It hadn't occurred to me, but there was no sign of her, not with her father and not in the crowd. I shook my head. "Why? Do you miss her?"

"Don't be absurd. But shh. Things are starting to happen."

Aeëtes struggled to his feet and, looking vaguely up at the sky, made a little speech greeting the sun and intoning a prayer to Hephaestus.

"Your father is looking the wrong way. Hephaestus is one of the earth gods."

He shrugged. "Pro forma piety is pro forma piety."

Kalais nudged me and nodded in the direction of the palace. Emerging from a side door were Jason and Medea. He was carrying a large bronze shield and an enormous iron sword. She in turn had a huge bullwhip. They paused, embraced, kissed. I glanced at Apsyrtus; he hadn't seen them. I suppose brothers and sisters are natural rivals, especially brothers and sisters in royal families, which seem inescapably to be turbulent. Medea rushed to her father's side. Jason joined us.

He was beaming, evidently overflowing with confidence. He bid us a hearty good morning and took several deep breaths of the brisk air. "What a glorious day."

It took me aback. "That's a mighty cool attitude for a man who's facing death, Jason."

He waved a hand in the air casually. "Death? You ought to know me better than that by now. Where there's a will to say alive, there's a way to stay alive."

I shook his hand, firmly and warmly. Despite the dislike that had grown for him, I hardly wanted to see him dead, if only because his death would devolve the Iolcan throne upon me.

He walked over to Lynceus and Autolycus, exchanged a brief few words with them, then crossed to the king and bowed.

Aeëtes bellowed, "Let's not waste any time with this. You know what you have to do."

"Indeed, your majesty. The last thing I'd want to do it put this off."

"You don't really think that shield will protect you, do you?" He could hardly conceal his amusement. "Better men than you have—"

"Why don't you wait till I've finished before you decide they were better men than me?"

Aeëtes shrugged and signaled to his trumpeters to sound a fanfare. A man in the robes of a priest chanted a prayer. Suddenly the bulls in the distance became animated, pacing to and fro, snorting plumes of fire at the sky. They moved stiffly, mechanically, like the creatures of brass they were; yet they conveyed an unmistakable air of great strength and ferocity.

Jason held up his shield and advanced slowly across the field. The bulls caught sight of him and watched him warily, pounding the earth with their hooves, still snorting fire but at the ground, now. A few of the weeds caught fire and sent streamers of black smoke skyward. Jason continued his advance, slowly, slowly, evidently trying to take their measure as he inched forward. I glanced at all the sacks hanging in the trees and wondered what good he thought it would do.

Suddenly he rushed forward, shouting a battle cry and waving his sword. The bulls reared in unison and breathed enormous streams of fire at him. The fire sprayed his shield and was deflected.

From somewhere came a deafening roar. At first I thought it was from the bulls, but no, they were busy making their holocaust. Something—a large dog?—was rushing across the field. In an instant I realized it was Autolycus, transformed into a wolf. He charged at the bulls from one side and leaped onto the back of one of them. Jason was using him as a diversion.

The bull reared and tried to shake him off but he held fiercely on. Its companion breathed a stream of fire at the wolf that was our shipmate. Autolycus' fur took the fire, and he jumped down and ran off into the trees yelping madly in pain. But in that moment, with the bulls distracted, Jason dropped his shield, ran to the tree where the yoke was waiting, lifted it and advanced on them.

He moved more quickly than the brass automata could. In a trice he had the yoke first over one of them, then over its companion. The bulls strained against it and blew flames wildly every which way they could, but he climbed under them and fastened the yoke's bindings. It seemed to me I saw the fire spray him more than once, but it must have been an illusion, for he kept right on with his task. After only another moment of futile straining, the bulls quieted.

Jason called out, "Bring me my whip, so I can teach these beasts how to plow."

Aeëtes looked perfectly glum. Medea ignored him and carried the whip across the field to Jason, walking with a steady, stately gait.

He set the traces, snapped his whip in the air and the bulls became quite still. Jason, laughing, yelled across the field, "Someone bring me my plow. I have work to do."

A pair of temple slaves dragged the plow to him and he harnessed it to the yoke. In only a moment he was steering the bulls in a steady row down one edge of the field. They moved stiffly, the metal of their bodies creaking and groaning, with nothing like the animation they had shown only moments before.

Medea returned to her father's side. "Your field is being plowed. Are you pleased?"

The king snorted like one of his bulls. "You know the answer to that perfectly well. If you had not helped this Greek upstart he would never have succeeded. What did you give him?"

"The blood of a crocus that blooms in the Caucasus. It made him proof against the bulls' fire. But you saw. He would have succeeded anyway."

"I'm not so sure."

"You will give him the Fleece? You did give him your word, Father."

Aeëtes laughed softly. "I said I would let him take it. If he can. He still has to face the Serpent of a Thousand Coils."

I looked at Kalais. "What on earth can that be?"

"Never mind that. Look at Lynceus."

The man was standing apart from everyone else, his face buried in his hands. He glanced up at us. "I told him not to do it. I told him not to do it. We must go to him."

Autolycus. I had completely forgotten about him, what with everything else that had happened. "Let us go find him."

We cut across the rows Jason had already plowed, toward the place where Autolycus had disappeared into the trees. "He will be all right, Lynceus, surely. He is a magical being, after all."

Instead of answering he ran ahead of us, into the woods. We stepped up our pace and followed.

A path of scorched grass and shrubs pointed the way clearly. In a moment we were beside Lynceus. Autolycus lay on the ground, reverted to his human form. And his body was covered entirely with burns and blisters so severe they were bleeding. He opened his eyes feebly and looked at us. In a hoarse whisper he asked, "Did he do it? Did he yoke the bulls?"

"Don't worry about Jason." Lynceus got down on a knee and kissed him gently. He could have added but did not, *Jason isn't worried for you*. Even that light kiss made Autolycus shudder with pain.

"I'll run back and get Medea. She must have something that will ease the burns."

I ran. I found her. She was quite immobile, watching Jason with what appeared to be satisfaction. I glanced at Apsyrtus. He was watching his sister, a dozen emotions crossing his face, none of them good.

I told her we needed whatever healing powers she might possess. "For who?" She did not like the distraction.

"For Autolycus, the man who sacrificed himself so Jason could succeed."

"Oh. Oh, yes, I'll come at once."

She ran into the palace to fetch her medicines. When she returned I had to tug at her again and again to get her to follow me, so rapt was she by the sight of Jason at his plowing.

But it was not Medea's infatuation that concerned me, it was Lynceus' love. Love to no avail. By the time we got back to Autolycus he was quite dead. The bulls had had their victim after all.

Lynceus could not stop weeping over him. It was all we could do to persuade him to return to the place with us. We promised him we would build a pyre and send his dead lover to the gods, Colchian tradition be damned.

We told several of the others what had happened. They helped us build a catafalque to bear his body back to the palace.

Another of the Argonauts was gone. Another survived to mourn him.

If Medea's crocus blood had indeed made Jason immune to the bulls' fire, Autolycus had sacrificed himself for nothing. I meant to confront him when he finished with his plowing, but Medea waylaid him first. They disappeared into the palace together. Lynceus was left to mourn without comfort from his captain. Apsyrtus…well, he would not let his emotions show. But it was not hard to guess what he was feeling.

* * *

Our entire crew helped build Autolycus' pyre at the distant end of the new-plowed field. By mid-afternoon it was ready. The bulls eyed us but, properly tamed, made no attempt to interfere.

There was no priest to officiate properly; the Colchians were quite at a loss. I acted as priest, reciting the prayers I could remember, doing my best to make certain all the rituals were carried out properly. Then I took a torch and lit the pyre.

Lynceus had stopped weeping, but I had never seen a human face so torn with grief. Not even Kalais, when Zetes died, had seemed in such all-consuming anguish. When the ceremony was over he thanked me. Then his closest friends in the crew led him back to the palace. He had told them he wanted to be alone, but several of them lingered by his room in case he should decide he needed them for anything.

During the pyre ceremony I had noticed one Colchian among us: Apsyrtus was there. He looked even younger than he had earlier; I would have sworn he was no more than fourteen, fifteen at the most. Tall and well-built for his age, but definitely young. He seemed a bit puzzled by the ritual, a bit fascinated, and...there was something else, I couldn't tell what. But after the others had departed he approached me and Kalais.

"Apsyrtus." My voice was soft and low. I did not have it in me, just then, to be hearty. "It was good of you to come. I hope your father isn't too upset by our religious practice."

"I don't much care. Can you tell me, please—" He seemed uncertain whether to go on. "Tell me about Jason."

"What can you possibly want to know about him?"

"Is he—is he faithful? I mean, can he be trusted?"

"Can any leader ever be trusted fully? Jason is a born leader, if only in that. You saw the way he used Autolycus."

We walked slowly back to the palace. Apsyrtus took my hand, not in an amatory way but, it seemed, because he needed someone to hold onto. He avoided looking at me directly. "Jason and I—well, we made love last night."

"I know."

"He said—well, he said things about being faithful, about being with him as long as I want to be."

I didn't want to tell him Jason had said those same things to me, back when. That wasn't what Apsyrtus needed to hear.

"And now, my sister—he—he's with her." He stopped walking and looked directly into my eyes. "She's always hated me. She saw that I had him, so she took him."

"Family values are such fleeting things."

"If I—if I come back to Greece with you, do you think he might…well…love me again?"

"I don't know. How could I know that?"

"Love among men is… well, it's never really been accepted here in Colchis. But I've always heard that in Greece you…you…"

"Yes. We do."

"And Jason? Does he… I mean… well…"

"Yes, of course he does. You learned that last night."

Kalais added, "I have the impression he'll make love to anyone who gives him the opportunity. Jason is a king now. Or he will be when we get back to Iolcus. What king has ever been true to anything but his own crown? But listen, Apsyrtus."

"Yes?"

"Our crew is down several men. If you can pull an oar…" Kalais smiled gently.

"And if your father agrees." I said it a bit sternly, I'm afraid. Crossing Aeëtes was the last thing we'd need.

"He never would. But I'll come anyway. He'll never know till it's too late."

We spent some time trying to talk him out of it, to no avail. There was no way we could actually give him permission, but if he were to hide aboard the *Argo* till after we sailed…

I wasn't at all certain I wanted it to come to that. But it was left ambiguous and inconclusive. The boy was feeling first love—and first disappointment—and I remembered what that was like; my own had not been so very long ago. We were walking on eggs, and we made sure he knew it. The rest, only the future could unfold.

* * *

The evening meal was, well, uncomfortable. Aeëtes was clearly not pleased that Jason had yoked the bulls, but he could hardly say so. He was the one who set the task, after all. But he gave us several excuses for delaying our retrieval of the Fleece. None were very convincing; it was clear he was simply temporizing till he could devise more villainy like yoking the bulls.

Apsyrtus sat with me and Kalais. His father seemed displeased when he noticed, then ignored the boy completely.

After our meal we retreated to our rooms for a council. Jason and all our usual group were there, joined by Medea. And Apsyrtus came as well. The siblings sat at opposite ends of the room, she beside Jason, he with Kalais and me. Every now and then she glared at him with undisguised hatred in her eyes. I had never seen anything quite like it; even between royal siblings the animosity she displayed was quite outside my experience. Had that kind of loathing spurred Pelias to kill his brother Aeson?

Jason spoke first, asking Medea, "So what is this Serpent of a Thousand Coils?"

She was quite offhand. "It keeps watch in the Grove of Ares, guarding the Golden Fleece. There is a pond there, the Pond of Hades; it reputedly covers one of the gates of the underworld. The serpent is a great water snake and lives in it most of the time. No one knows if it was set there by the gods or found its way there and settled in for some reason. But many men have tried to take the Fleece, and the serpent has slain every one of them."

"They say," Apsyrtus added eagerly, "it is the longest, largest snake in the world, long enough to wrap the remains of all the men it has killed in its many coils. The ones it does not kill outright it drags under the water to drown. When it emerges it drags them behind itself—and will do so eternally, it is said."

Medea sneered at him with a withering glance. "No one has asked you for help, here, little brother. Mind your tongue."

Cowed, the boy fell silent. I found myself liking him more and more, and disliking his sister. He was so anxious to get back into Jason's good graces, and he was at least canny enough to understand that that would only happen if Jason found him useful.

Medea went on with her little lecture. "The serpent does indeed have many coils, more than enough to enfold the scores of men who have died in the grove. We must go there at first light tomorrow. Phrixus' remains hang in a blackthorn tree there, the same tree as the Fleece. You may get them and the Fleece both at once. I know charms and spells that will lull the serpent to sleep. That will give you your chance. Then we must hurry to the *Argo* and set sail before the palace wakes."

I spoke up. "We? You said 'we.'"

Jason responded for her. "Medea will of course come with us.

279

Once her father learns she has helped us, her life would be worth very little here."

I felt Apsyrtus stiffen, and I did not want to look at him. But he jumped to his feet and pointed at his sister. "You haven't told them about the dragon's teeth. It's why Father has tried to delay."

Jason looked at Medea. She waved dismissively. "It is nothing. One of the treasures of Colchis is a supply of the teeth of the primordial monster Python, which fell here when Cronus slew it. Aeëtes is going to sow the teeth in the field you plowed, in hopes they will grow into new monsters to stop you from leaving Colchis. But they will take days to grow, possibly many weeks. He will try to delay you here till that happens. He has no intention of letting you take the Fleece. But if you act quickly—"

"And why," I asked in the most authoritative manner I could manage, "have you not told us about this before now?"

For the first time Medea looked abashed. "I—I—I didn't think it mattered," she said weakly. "If you move quickly—"

"It matters." I was firm. "We must be grateful that Apsyrtus told us about it. If you are going to counsel us, Medea, it behooves you to tell us the complete truth."

She looked at Jason. "I'm sorry. I thought—"

"Think no more of it," Jason told her resolutely.

And with that our council ended. But Medea paused at the door as she was leaving. "Oh, and the serpent has 50 heads." She turned and went.

I couldn't resist. I sneered at Jason. "Your lady friend has either a most peculiar sense of humor or a very odd idea of the complete truth."

"Don't concern yourself, Acastus. I know women. You don't."

And so we headed to our room and our bed. Apsyrtus curled up in the hallway outside our door and fell asleep there. I wanted to invite him inside, but it would have been most inconvenient. Kalais and I, as always, slept in one another's arms.

* * *

Something woke me in the night. I went to the door and looked out into the hall. Apsyrtus was sitting there, staring into the low flame of a lamp. When he heard me he looked up. "Acastus."

"You should be asleep."

"You're not going to say, 'You're a growing boy' are you?"

"Perish the thought. Are you all right?"

Apsyrtus nodded. "Just sleepless, that's all."

"Perhaps if you take a walk."

He reached up and touched my hand. "Come with me."

I looked back into the room. Kalais was fast asleep. "Sure. Where can we go?"

"I want to see your ship." He got to his feet and slapped the dirt off the back of his tunic. "Show me the *Argo*."

Why not? It was clear enough why he wanted to see it. We walked silently through the palace, through the fields and out into the sleeping city. There was no sign of life anywhere. It didn't take us long to reach the waterfront.

There were sentries posted on the ship's deck and they were quite vigilant. Once they recognized me they let us go aboard.

I showed him everything both above and below deck. He took it all in with a kind of wide-eyed wonderment, like a boy who had never seen a ship before—which he certainly was not. The Colchians were a seafaring people; it seemed so odd. When we had seen everything else he asked, "And where do you and Kalais sleep?"

So I showed him our bunk. And that was the end of our little tour. I had to get back and get some sleep. We would be rising before first light.

* * *

Early morning, well before dawn. Jason, Argus, Idmon, Kalais and I, accompanied by half our men, set out for the grove; among our group was Periclymenus, who had always kept the lowest profile of our men.

"We'll need lamps, Jason."

Medea answered me in alarm. "No! Nothing must betray what we are about."

And so we walked in darkness.

Medea guided us, first through cultivated fields, then through the woods. Apsyrtus followed at the rear of our band. The rest of our crew headed silently back to the *Argo* to ready her for sailing.

It was farther than I'd expected. We must have walked nearly an hour, always on our guard, always vigilant lest the Colchians detect us. I beckoned to Apsyrtus to walk beside me. I did not trust his sister, and I wanted him by me as a check lest she lead us astray.

The sky above us, what we could see of it through the trees, was flecked with clouds. Stars shone through the breaks in them, and a declining gibbous moon scudded its way toward the western horizon. I saw a falling star come off the shoulder of Orion, then a second one, then a third. I hoped it was a good omen. But almost at once the clouds closed.

Trees—alders, blackthorns, dogwoods—surrounded us on all sides, and every one of them was hung with leather bags containing the bodies of Colchians. Owls, ravens and other predatory birds pecked and clawed at them happily. They must have been spoiled from having this food brought to them in such abundance. The owls kept up a constant chorus, hooting and screeching into the night. Their eyes caught the moonlight and glowed at us eerily. If they found our presence alarming, they did not show it but kept on with their grim feast, chewing at the leather sacks, tearing bits from the bodies within. They ate quite greedily, and it was clear they would not be deterred from it. Now and then Medea's raven would leave her shoulder, fly to one of the sacks, tear off a piece of rotting flesh, swallow it, then flap contentedly back to her. Once it wrested a strip of meat from the beak of a young bird which flew off in terror. It seemed an apt pet for her.

At one point a great horned owl, the largest I had ever seen, swooped over our heads, then perched on the limb of a blackthorn and tore into the nearest body bag. When it looked at us now and then I thought I could detect indifferent contempt in its manner. We were in its territory, its arboreal charnel house; we were the interlopers.

At length the trees around us became denser. We had reached the Grove of Ares. A massive statue not of Ares but of Hecate stood among the trees, staring impassively into the night of which she was mistress. It was of black stone, maybe basalt, and its face bore a fierce expression. The leather sacks in the trees were more numerous than before. Apsyrtus told me that they contained the remains of former kings and nobles; to hang here in the grove was a badge of nobility. There were no more owls dining on the corpses. "Birds don't come this close to the serpent's pool."

"Be quiet, Apsyrtus!" Medea shushed him quite firmly, like a schoolmistress or an angry queen which, I assumed, she expected Jason to make her someday soon.

Ahead of us was the Pool of Hades. Its waters were calm—and black as ink. The clouds moved from around the moon, and its light was reflected to us by the water's surface. And in the moonlight, in a dogwood on the far side of the pool we could see a glittering, shimmering golden glow: the Fleece.

Medea pointed to it and whispered, "There it is. The leather bag just below it is the one you want."

"Phrixus?" Jason kept his voice low.

Medea nodded.

Jason took a step toward it and motioned to all of us to draw our swords and follow him around the pool. Taking what we had come for seemed such a simple thing. I looked around for Apsyrtus. He was gone, not that I much blamed him.

Something broke the water of the pool. A serpent's head, large and malevolent, reared up and stared at us. And hissed. Then a moment later a second, then a third, a fourth, fifth, and more. Medea had not exaggerated. Jason gestured to Periclymenus and whispered, never taking his eyes off the serpent's heads. "Now!"

Periclymenus held his arms up to cover his face and bent down into a ball. Slowly, slowly he began his transformation. His body turned black and glistened in the moon's light. It lengthened. It sprouted a second head, a third, a fourth. He was making himself into a mirror image of the creature in the pool, smaller but clearly similar.

Cautiously, he slithered forward inch by inch to the water's edge. The serpent watched him, wary, curious. I whispered, "Periclymenus, be careful! It will see you as an enemy." Jason turned on me with his finger to his lips. "Not now, Acastus. This is not the time to talk."

"We have lost enough of our men." I kept my voice hushed.

As did Jason. "Do you think I don't know that?"

Medea held up a hand, signaling to us both to keep silent.

That horned owl flew above us again, circling the pool and lighting in the tree that held the Fleece. I had a fleeting thought, wondering if it might be Athena's familiar owl, there to protect us.

The serpent reared up out of the water. All of its heads were in motion, dozens of them, all regarding us with unveiled hostility, all of them hissing. 50 tongues darted in and out, sampling the night air. In the still night the hisses seemed almost deafening. The great owl screeched in alarm and flew off into the night. Kalais took my hand, and I was ever so glad to feel his touch.

Periclymenus crawled forward and dipped one of his heads—I assumed not his real one—into the water. His other heads intertwined, coiling and uncoiling in a rhythmic, almost hypnotic manner. The great serpent moved toward him, cautious but apparently fascinated, its heads twining and untwining. It began to crawl up out of the pool then circled him, and its length was so enormous most of its body was still in the water, still concealed there, making the water turbulent. But a dozen of its coils were exposed. Wrapped in them were the corpses of dead men, heroes who had come for the Fleece before us, some of them still holding their swords and shields. Some of them were nearly intact; some were merely bones.

Then Medea stepped forward. Periclymenus had distracted the great beast so that she had the opportunity to move very close to it. She placed a hand on its back and began to chant in a low musical voice. The words were not in any language I knew; they must have been some ancient tongue, some language long forgotten by all but sorcerers. The serpent, without moving its fore-body, curled more and more of its great length out of its aqueous home. Water poured off its scales and off the bones and remnants of flesh it carried in its coils. More and more of it came, 50 feet, a hundred, more, each coil clutching the mortal remains of a man long dead. Its length and size were staggering, as was the spectacle of death it embodied.

None of us moved. The sight of the enormous snake and all those dead men kept us hypnotized as surely as Medea's song had hypnotized the serpent itself.

Then her words and the melody she was chanting changed. She clapped her hands loudly and, impossibly, from them issued clouds of thick red smoke. The serpent reared up slightly but by now it was numb and in her power. Its heads stopped their chaotic twining and froze; its great body, still partway concealed in the pool, became still. Medea's smoke had blinded it, or put it to sleep, or…I couldn't guess. She turned to Jason and softly but firmly said, "Now."

Jason sprang into action. He dashed around the pool and leaped into the lower branches of the blackthorn tree. He gestured at the first sack he reached and turned to Medea questioningly. She nodded, and he produced a knife and cut the cord that cinched it to the tree. It fell heavily to earth. The serpent responded to the thud it made by shuddering. Its entire length trembled, and I wondered if it was shaking off its trance. It reared up, then dropped again and sank its fangs, one set of them after another, into Periclymenus. One head coiled around him and dragged him into the pool. His serpent's body writhed wildly; the water roiled; but he did not return to the surface. Only a brief instant later the serpent was quite still again.

Jason climbed higher into the blackthorn and reached the Golden Fleece. He lifted it from the branch where it hung, slung it over his shoulder and climbed back down to earth. Dragging the bag of Phrixus' remains behind him, he rejoined us.

"We have lost another man, Jason." I could not keep the bitterness out of my voice. For the second time we had had Medea's help and for the second time an Argonaut perished. There had been no need, none at all.

"Not now, Acastus."

"Then when? How many more of our band must die for your ambition?"

"Come," Medea urged. "We must go before the serpent regains its senses a second time."

None of us had to be asked twice. She led us back through the trees. Purple dawn was breaking; the faintest stars were becoming lost in it. The moon was on the horizon and would be gone soon.

"Hurry!" she exhorted. "The palace and the city will be waking soon. We must be gone before they can realize what we have done."

As we rushed past the palace and into the city we saw the lights of candles flickering on. At the harbor the first fishermen were preparing their nets and lowering their boats into the water. One of them, a boy of sixteen or so, stopped his activity and stared at us. He dropped his net and ran in the direction of the palace. The game was up or would be as soon as he could spread the alarm.

Our fellow Argonauts had the ship ready to weigh anchor and sail off.

We had the bones of Phrixus. We had the Golden Fleece.

Chapter Eleven
Apsyrtus

We lost no time leaving port. We had a good, stiff breeze to propel us, and we rowed for all we were worth. It seemed to me we had little enough to worry about. Even if Aeëtes was furious at our seizure of the Golden Fleece, and even if he was angry at Medea's defection, there was little he could do. None of us had any idea of the Colchians' military ability, and Medea was not much help on that count, saying she considered the army beneath her. But we were a crew of skilled, accomplished warriors. Well, all but Orpheus and me, that is.

Argus and two of the others had, er, borrowed a large brass urn from the palace, large enough to hold the mortal remains of my ancestor Phrixus in their leather bag. It was decorated with pictures of the Colchian gods—the gods of death and the underworld, which seemed only appropriate. And we had stolen an ornate wooden chest, again covered with images of the Colchian gods, for the Fleece.

Most of us had left belongings behind in the interest of a quick, secret escape. There had simply been no way to stop and fetch them, not without the risk of being discovered. At least we had all reached the *Argo* safely—all but Autolycus and Periclymenus, the latest victims of Jason's ambition.

20 minutes after we left Aea, I found myself at the command post by the helm. Jason was busy below deck, stowing the Fleece away in its chest. Medea was with him. It told him I wanted to stop for a moment in remembrance of our two fallen comrades, and of all our fallen shipmates, but Medea insisted we keep rowing till we were certain of our safety, and Jason added that the deaths of Periclymenus, Autolycus and the others would mean very little if we

allowed ourselves to be hunted down by a vengeful Aeëtes. There was, as usual, no arguing with him, piety be damned.

When he was back on deck and resumed his command, it was my turn to go below and stow my things, the few I'd been able to bring. "Don't be long, Acastus. We're not safe yet. We need you at your oar."

I made a mock bow. "Yes, your majesty."

Kalais came with me. We straightened the bedclothes on our bunk then put our few things into a footlocker.

Something moved under the bed. "A rat!" I reached for a sword.

"No, don't strike! It's me."

A head appeared from under the bunk, a head full of bright red-blond hair. It was Apsyrtus.

"What on earth are you doing here?"

"Isn't it obvious? Help me out of here. I've been under here for a long time and my muscles are cramped."

We helped him out and pulled him to his feet. Slapping the dust off his clothes, he looked at us and smiled shyly. "You don't mind, do you?"

Kalais helped him smooth his hair. "Mind what? That you weren't honest with us about what you were planning, or about the fact you've put us in peril?"

"Peril?! How?" He seemed genuinely taken aback at the suggestion.

"Listen, Apsyrtus." I tried to make my voice firm, probably without success. To tell the truth, part of me was glad to see him. "Your father will be angry enough at our taking the Golden Fleece. When he realizes we've also taken both his children…"

"Medea is here? She really came?!"

We both nodded. "Still, I suppose there's nothing to be done about it now. We can hardly turn back."

Apsyrtus fell silent, thinking over his situation and, I imagined, ours. The news that Medea was with us alarmed him; that much was clear. He looked shyly away from us. "You must have known what I was going to do, or at least suspected. I did everything but tell you outright. And Medea—I never thought she'd come."

I looked at Kalais. Like Apsyrtus he looked away. "Well, I did have my suspicions, yes. But I thought for certain you'd tell us if you were planning to…to…"

"I'm sorry, Kalais. I'm sorry, Acastus. I thought you were my friends. I thought you'd be glad to see me."

"It's not that, Apsyrtus." I put a hand on his shoulder. "But you've created a very awkward situation for us."

"Awkward, to say the least." Kalais brushed a smudge off the boy's face. "Come on, let's get above. Jason and the others will have to be told. We might as well get it over with."

The three of us went up to the main deck. As we left the hold, me first followed by Kalais then Apsyrtus, I caught a glimpse of our captain and his...what would be the term? Girlfriend? Mistress? Concubine? Witch?

Medea noticed us first. When she realized her brother was with us, something like pure hatred flashed in her reptilian eyes. She said something to Jason and pointed at us.

He left his post beside the tiller and rushed down to us. "Apsyrtus. What on earth are you doing here?"

"I thought... I thought..." For the first brief instant something like hopefulness had shown in his eyes, but Jason glared at him, and it very quickly turned to disappointment. "I only thought..."

"You are your father's son and heir. He will not take kindly to this."

"I'm sorry, Jason. I only wanted to be with—" He seemed to realize that line would not get him anywhere, and he changed tack. Raising an arm, he pointed at Medea. "You brought her."

"Yes, I did. What of it?" He was not going to give an inch to the boy who was so smitten with him.

"I..." He slumped in his disappointment. "I'm sorry. I thought you...we..."

"We can't. We won't. You must find a way to return to your father. We must find a way to send you. We'll set you adrift in a rowboat or put you ashore or something."

"No! Please! He's never loved me. He's never wanted me." The emotions that showed in his face changed from fear to disappointment to sorrow so quickly it was alarming. A boy in that state is capable of anything, no matter how self-destructive.

"Never the less."

I decided to get between them. "Be sensible, Jason. Aeëtes will certainly be following us soon, if he's not already. Any pause, any delay for any reason at all could put us into worse peril."

Jason paused and thought for a moment. "The boy may stay. But keep him out of my way."

He returned to his post and to Medea. Through all of our exchange she had not taken her eyes off her brother, looking at him with undisguised loathing.

* * *

We were making good time. Every available oarsman did his part. Apsyrtus took his place in one of the vacant spots and pulled an oar like the rest of us while his sister stood imperiously, disapprovingly at Jason's side.

Then the wind came around to the north, a stiff, chill breeze that slowed us despite our best efforts. Kalais and I, as always, were side by side. "Why don't you tell your father the North Wind to take it easy on us?"

"Even if he could hear me, I'm afraid we're not all that close. I've told you."

"Well, you've got to be closer that the royal family of Colchis. Look at her." Medea had not stopped staring venom at her brother.

Kalais looked across the deck at the boy. He was trying his best to keep up with the rest of us, but the strain was showing.

The sky was gradually clouding over and the north wind blew ever more stiffly. I prayed we would not have a storm. And I kept looking impulsively over my shoulder; the sea behind us was, happily, quite empty of pursuing vessels. But despite our lead I could not feel secure, not till we reached the Bosporus and maybe not even then. This turn in the weather would give Aeëtes every opportunity to catch up with us.

Medea stood near the helm, as immobile and impassive as a statue—a statue seething with hatred. She was wearing, as always, a long black robe with enormous sleeves; they blew wildly in the wind but she herself was stone-still. Jason tried sweet-talking her a few times, but she could not be shaken out of her loathing for her brother. If even Jason's charm had no effect on her, I told myself her hate must run deep indeed.

A few times I glanced over at Apsyrtus, to see how he was holding up under the strain of rowing, which he could hardly be used to. Something like fatigue was beginning to show, but he gamely kept at his oar.

I moved across to the bench next to him and put a hand on his shoulder. "No one will blame you if you take a break, Apsyrtus."

"No." He kept rowing. "I want Jason to see I'm a man. A man worthy of him."

"Jason is preoccupied with your big sister. Not that it seems to be doing him any good. She is preoccupied with you."

"She hates me, Acastus."

"That much is obvious. But why? Even for royal siblings—"

"We had different mothers. She expected to be father's heir, but when her mother died and father remarried..." He looked at me shyly, self-consciously. "Not that I'd ever have made much of a king—or wanted to."

I understood, and I told him so.

"That was when she turned to the dark gods. She practices their rites with a vengeance—and with glee. I've seen her sacrifice living animals and drink their blood, grinning. I've been terrified of her for as long as I can remember."

There wasn't much I could say. Even a promise of protection was bound to ring hollow. Medea was not the kind to fight fairly or honestly. I kissed Apsyrtus lightly on the temple and went back to Kalais and my oar.

* * *

There were flashes of lightning to the north, the silent kind not accompanied by thunder. Bursts of light illuminated the horizon then quickly vanished. The wind died down a bit and we were able to make some time again, but the sea was still wildly turbulent.

Suddenly Lynceus cried out from his post. "Behind us! Look!"

I jumped to my feet ad scanned the horizon behind us, but my eyesight was no match for Lynceus'. I went to the helm. Jason was quizzing him about what he saw.

"A ship, one of the great ones from the harbor at Aea."

"Aeëtes!" Jason barked. "He is after us, and if he's any kind of king he won't rest till he catches us."

For the first time Medea seemed to emerge from her self-absorption and notice the rest of us. She looked from one of us to another as if she were waking from a trance and did not understand how she got on board the *Argo*. The ship pitched and she reached for Jason to steady herself. I wondered for a fleeting moment if she had somehow summoned her father—if she had led us into a trap.

She reared herself up and pointed at her brother. "Give him the boy."

Apsyrtus froze.

"You are mad, Medea." I had to speak up for him, and for all of us. "Your brother is not the only thing we took from Colchis. There is the Fleece. There is Phrixus. And there is," I said as pointedly as I could, "you. We could just as easily return you to your father."

"No." Jason sounded more like a commander than I had ever heard him. "That is out of the question."

"My father has lost a great deal today." Medea's coolness was perfectly astonishing. "As you yourself have reminded us, Acastus." She turned back to Jason. "He will be happy enough to get his heir back. Apsyrtus is the only bargaining tool we possess."

I looked back. The Colchian ship was now well in sight, a large black spot on the horizon making good time despite the rough water."

The wind kicked up again. The waves were growing more and more treacherous. Jason ordered our sail hauled up. Our oars were useless in the churning water. Our progress stopped cold.

"You're supposed to be a sorceress, Medea. Do something to aid our escape." I kept looking at Aeëtes' ship, which was looming closer and closer. "Calm the sea and whistle up an east wind for us."

"My powers," she said coolly, "do not extend to control of the sea and the weather. We must wait till my father catches up with us then offer him the boy."

"How on earth is he making progress while we can not move?"

"These," she said calmly, "are his waters. This is his sea."

Jason kept looking from Medea to the pursuing ship and back. His growing anxiety was not hard to see. "Please, Medea, if you can do something, do it now."

She shrugged. "As I have said, this is beyond my power. You must bring the boy to the stern and show him to Aeëtes. He will have no way of knowing Apsyrtus came voluntarily. He must be assuming you kidnapped the boy as a hostage, for just such an event as this."

Her logic seemed unassailable.

We were stopped dead. How the Colchian ship was making such good time advancing on us while we sat helpless in the waves was more than any of us could fathom. I could not escape the suspicion that despite her protestations Medea was somehow behind it. At any rate, Aeëtes' ship was upon us soon enough. She shipped her oars and sat abaft of us, her crew brandishing swords and spears most ominously. Worse yet, another trio of Colchian ships appeared on the horizon, making swift time in their pursuit of us. We were outnumbered or soon would be.

Aeëtes sat on a throne in the prow. He got heavily to his feet and walked to the rail. Facing us, he bellowed. "You have breached our hospitality most egregiously. Return what you have stolen."

Jason moved amidships to face him. "We have stolen nothing. We only took what you promised us, Phrixus and the Golden Fleece. Your daughter and your son came with us of their own free will."

"I am the king." Aeëtes was not about to be placated. His ship pitched and two of his attendants rushed to steady him. "Their will does not matter, only mine. They left—you took them—without my leave. Return them and the other things at once or none of you will leave this sea alive."

Their exchange went on for some minutes with neither side yielding any ground. The other Colchian ships were now plain to see in the far distance. It was obvious we were heading for a confrontation worse than just verbal. Argus and I passed the word for our men to start dealing out weapons as quietly and unobtrusively as possible. Apsyrtus stayed by my side, obviously looking to me for protection. We were all of us expecting things to come to blows.

But suddenly Medea stepped to the rail to confront her father. "Aeëtes, we are on the high sea now, not in your domain. You have no right to issue orders to anyone here."

"You are my daughter, a member of my household, a member of the royal family of Colchis." He was not about to be deterred. "Each of those facts gives me the right."

I felt the boy take my hand and tighten his grip.

We were standing eight feet or so from Medea; Apsyrtus was hiding behind me, out of his father's sight. I hoped he did not think that might be able to save him.

Medea left Jason's side and walked deliberately over to us. Suddenly, quick as a cat, she acted. She caught her brother by the hair and started to drag him back to where she had been standing. Apsyrtus fought against her with all his might but he was tired from rowing. Screaming in protest, he had no choice but to go with her. She wrapped an arm around his throat to hold him there.

"Here is your son, Aeëtes," she announced. "He was as anxious to escape you as I was."

Aeëtes glared but said nothing.

"Take the boy and go back to Aea."

Still glowering, he turned to Jason. "Return my son. Return my daughter. Return the Fleece. Take the rotting corpse you have purloined and go."

Jason looked to Medea then back at her father. "Your daughter is a free woman who came with us freely You may not take her."

"My ships will be here momentarily, Greek. You will be outnumbered and out-manned. There is no way you can prevail."

He was right. There was no way we could win this confrontation. Or so it seemed.

Medea lowered her voice and said to Jason, "There is a way. We discussed it. We can quite ensure Aeëtes will have no choice but to let us go."

This was unexpected on my part. I didn't know why, but it sounded alarming. "What do you mean, Medea? How can we—"

But Jason cut me off. "Now! Do it now!"

From the sleeve on her free arm Medea produced a knife. Before any of us had time to react she plunged it into her brother's throat. Blood spurted out and polluted her and the Argo's deck.

"No! For the love of the gods, what have you done!" I cried it and rushed to help Apsyrtus, but before I could reach him he fell lifeless to the deck.

Medea looked at her father. "Your son is dead, Aeëtes. If you want his remains, give us your word you will take them and let us go in peace."

"Never! You will pay for this abomination—all of you!"

Without responding, Medea got down on one knee beside her brother's corpse. She took her knife and began cutting pieces from his body.

It was too much for me. I screamed at her. "What are you doing now? What foul thing?" I tried to pull her off his body, but Jason caught me by the collar and pulled me away.

She ignored me and called out to Jason. "Get down here and help me before Aeëtes recovers his wits."

He did so. The two of them worked quickly and sliced Apsyrtus into ever smaller sections. Limbs, fingers, hands, finally the boy's head. Then she got back to her feet, wiped her hands clean on her gown and began scattering the pieces into the sea. The choppy waves carried most of them quickly away from the *Argo*.

Aeëtes let out an anguished howl. "No! Not my son! Not this!" He shouted orders to his men and they lowered boats into the water and began trying to retrieve the pieces of their young prince.

It was all too clear to what Medea was doing. She had told us on our first day in Colchis: Their gods required them to offer up their dead and to do so properly, according to custom. Not to do so would bring calamity. If even so much as a toe were lost, the wrath of the gods would be rained down upon them. Aeëtes' men would be occupied for hours gathering up the remains of Apsyrtus. We would have more than time enough to escape, unhampered by our pursuers.

And escape we did. The Colchian ships were stalled in the angry waters of the Black Sea, doing their duty by their king, their dead prince and their gods. We rowed for all we were worth. So intent were we on escaping, none of us had time to stop and ponder the awful fact that our captain, the new king of Iolcus, had been complicit in a ghastly crime. It was a crime that saved our necks, yes, but it was a crime nonetheless. Much less did we have time to contemplate the horrible woman he would make his queen.

Chapter Twelve
Idmon

Jason and Medea made no secret of their mutual affection, to the point where Jason ignored his duties as commander of the *Argo*. It fell to me and Argus to assume command.

Idmon seldom took his eyes off the man he loved; his dejection at the sight was impossible to miss. He never said a word; his silence was more eloquent than any utterance. Jason was aware of it, and it was plain he didn't like it at all. He obviously thought that the moment he was through with his lovers they should be through with him as well, and he let his impatience with Idmon show. But Idmon could not seem to help himself.

The storms grew steadily worse and did not let up for days. Guiding the ship through the Bosporus and the Hellespont was the greatest challenge I ever faced. I relied on Argus and Nauplius to advise me on the safest course. The winds buffeted us, the rocks clashed against us—happily without doing too much damage.

When we finally reached the Aegean again, we put in at Samothrace to make repairs. Our welcome there was as warm as it had been before; we were initiates into their mysteries, after all. Much was made of us. We and the Golden Fleece were paraded through the streets like heroes returning from war.

The priests invited us—those of us who weren't preoccupied repairing the ship—to witness a prophetic ceremony.

"Tragedy awaits. One will not survive the bronze. Tragedy awaits." So warned the oracle. None of us knew what to make of it.

* * *

Once we left the harbor, favorable breezes blew us south and west. Then, quite abruptly, more storms arose. Like the winds in the Black Sea they raged for days. Mad currents formed in the sea, spinning us around, leaving us quite disoriented. Our supplies ran low; food, water were nearly exhausted.

When, after five days the storms finally died, we found ourselves facing land. It was a green place, covered in trees, flowering shrubs, flowing springs, all fronted by broad sandy beaches. "What is this place?" I asked Nauplius. "Where are we?"

He checked the sun's position and rustled through his charts till he found the one he was looking for. "I believe this is the north shore of Crete."

"No! The storms have taken us miles too far south."

Worse yet…it was not just any island, it was Crete. Land of the death goddess Dicte. Home of the harpies. The sense that we might be in mortal danger spread quickly through the crew. Were there more of the winged fiends? Was that the tragedy the Samothracian oracle had warned us of? But…bronze. The oracle had said bronze. What…?

Danger or no danger, harpies or none, we had no choice but to put ashore. We needed food and water, and Crete offered both in abundance. We all kept our eyes on the sky, awaiting the avenging harpies, and our weapons were always at hand, ready for the fight. But Argus was worried about something else. "Crete is guarded— famously so. In the days of King Minos, the inventor Daedalus created a guardian, a giant man of bronze, fifteen feet tall."

"And you have seen this bronze man?" Jason scoffed.

"No, but the stories about him are many and consistent. Daedalus built Talos large enough for a fire to burn in his stomach. Priests keep the fire burning each day. The bronze of his chest glows red hot. He holds men to his chest till the intense heat fries them to death."

Jason laughed. "Piffle."

I was appalled. "After all we have seen on this voyage, how can you laugh at this new peril?"

"Even if this Talos exists, he is only one. And if he is made of bronze he will move slowly, like the Colchian bulls. It will not be hard for some of us to distract him while the rest gather the food we need."

So we put ashore at the widest, purest beach we could find. One by one we went down the gangway, watching the skies above us, watching the land around us.

* * *

Idmon had withdrawn into himself quite completely. Of all our crew he was the only one neither excited nor alarmed by our situation. "Bronze," he told me. "A bronze man, a giant. This is what the oracle meant."

"The oracle was not specific. They never are. You know that."

"I told you many months ago, Acastus. I saw my end, and I told you."

"Don't dwell on it. Come ashore with the rest of us, Idmon. We need all the hands we have. If we work quickly, we can be gone again before any danger can materialize."

"Yes."

So we went ashore; Idmon and I were the last to leave the *Argo*. His mood, unlike most of us, was one of sad resignation. We filled our water casks, loaded up baskets with fruit. I kept a cautious eye on the sky as did all our crew, and there were no harpies. Medea stayed by Jason's side, apart from the rest of us. I remembered a poem of the Hebrews my nurse read to me as a child, and one line seemed especially apt: "They toil not, neither do they spin."

Then suddenly one of our men cried out, "There, up the beach! Talos!"

The bronze man was there, advancing on us more rapidly than I would have thought possible for a thing of metal not flesh. He darted along the beach quick as a rabbit and got between us and the *Argo*. His metal body gleamed in the sunlight—all but his chest and stomach, which glowed red-hot, almost white-hot due to his inner flames. And he was indeed a giant, taller even than Argus had believed, as tall as three men.

"There you are, Jason. So much for your prediction he'd move slowly." I had no idea how we could battle a foe of bronze. "What can we do to fight metal?"

"There must be a way." He pounded his fist against a tree trunk. "There must be a way. We cannot be stranded here to die."

"Perhaps you should ask Medea." I pointed a finger at her. "She has your full attention, it seems. Maybe she can lull the giant to sleep."

Both he and Medea glared at me.

Talos pursued one of our men after another, running after us with what seemed to be glee, or as close to it as a man of metal could come. He caught Pollux by the foot and lifted him into the air. Pollux's sandal slipped loose and he fell to the ground and scrambled away.

Our men threw spears and rocks at the bronze giant, and they bounced off him harmlessly. But they came at him from so many directions he seemed not to know how to react; he just kept flailing at the air, quite fruitlessly. It seemed we might get the best of him after all.

Jason, typically, stood watching. Then he pounded a fist into the palm of his hand. "That's it! We need someone to keep him distracted while the rest of us gather our food and water and return to the ship."

Distract—that seemed to be the only strategy he knew. He had used it against the brass bulls and the great serpent, each time resulting in the death of one of our men. I could not think of a reason why only one of us should have the job of distracting Talos, and I said so. "A group of us can do the job more safely."

"Don't argue with me, Acastus. Go and fetch Idmon."

"Idmon?"

"Yes. You heard me. He will have the task of keeping the bronze man occupied.

"No, not Idmon. He is fast, Jason, but he's far from our fastest runner. Atalan—"

"You heard me, Acastus," He barked. "It will be Idmon's job."

There was no arguing. I went and found Idmon. He was filling a basket with lemons, and I interrupted him to give him his orders.

"Jason wants me to—? But why? Our men are holding their own against Talos."

It was only too clear to me why. But I could hardly bring myself to say it. I put a hand on his shoulder. "Run and dodge as fleetly as you can. Stay alive."

And so he ran and took his place at the forefront of our men. "Go and help the others gather food," he shouted. "I'll keep him busy."

It was all too predictable. Our crew gathered more than enough food and water for weeks of sailing. Meanwhile Idmon ducked and feinted, and the bronze giant snatched at him repeatedly, and repeatedly missed. Jason stood apart and watched it all with a steady eye, waiting for the inevitable. Medea stayed by his side, holding his hand.

And finally it happened. Talos caught Idmon by an arm, lifted him into the air, then pressed him to his red-hot, burning chest.

Late at night, when sleep will not come—and sometimes, even, when it will—I can still hear his agonized screams. And I can still smell the horrible aroma of seared flesh, which seemed to fill the air everywhere around us, so thickly there was no escaping it.

Jason ordered us to board the *Argo* without collecting Idmon's poor remains, no burial rite, not even a prayer uttered aloud for the man. His sad ghost must still haunt the shore of Crete, pining, weeping over his love for Jason—and the bitter reward it reaped him.

As we left, we could see Talos still on the beach, playing with Idmon's corpse, tossing it, catching it, tearing off limbs and throwing them into the air. It was like watching a cat tear apart the body of a dead mouse. I ordered the men to row as fast as possible to get us away from the horrible place.

Chapter Thirteen
Iolcus

The remainder of our voyage home was, thankfully, uneventful. Nauplius was able to plot our course quite easily, assisted by Argus, who was quite familiar with the route. The sea was tranquil, the weather fair and the islands on our route hospitable. There were no more storms, no more monsters.

When at last we sighted the great lighthouse before dawn one morning. it was with a sense of enormous relief; all the horrors of the voyage were behind us. The great metal goddess with her flame held high promised life and love not death. The morning star blazed in the east, accompanied by a narrow crescent moon.

It was too early for all but a few fishermen. There was no one to welcome us—not that they'd have had any way of knowing to expect us. We disembarked quietly, each of us preparing to go his own way. I offered all the crew housing at Argo House for as long as they'd need or want it, an offer they gladly accepted.

A few fishermen recognized the *Argo* and came to greet us. "Acastus!" One old sailor embraced me. "We are so glad to have you home again. But...but..."

"Yes?"

"You have returned to a troubled city. Your father is dead, and Iolcus' troubles continue unabated. The population shrinks more each day. Have you...have you brought the Golden Fleece?"

"Yes, we have, and the remains of Phrixus." I pointed to where the chest containing the Fleece was being carried down the gangplank. "The city's fortunes are sure to take a turn."

There were tears in the man's eyes. "You believe that? No one else does. Not any of us who are left here."

This was not the homecoming I had hoped for. But I put on a brave face. "We must all trust the gods to help Iolcus back to prosperity. We have done the bidding of the oracles. The gods will smile on us."

The old man's tears were flowing freely now. He told me he hoped I was right, then went back to his fisherman's nets.

* * *

Over the next day's life returned to something like normal. Jason assumed the duties of kingship as if her were born to them. I suppose in fact he was—at least if he really was who he claimed to be; my early doubts had never quite been allayed, and now that I was home again they returned full force. Still, I was grateful not to be king myself.

Jason sent heralds to all the cities of Greece announcing the successful end of our expedition. To those cities that were home to the men who had fallen on the voyage he added special messages praising their valor and fortitude. The fact that they might still be alive but for his ambition went discreetly unmentioned.

Castor and Pollux were the first to leave Iolcus. Pollux thanked Jason and me for inviting them to share our adventures. Castor, typically, was less gracious. "We have given you the means to save your city. See that you do not squander them."

"Odd, I thought Medea had done that. But we'll do our humble best, Castor." I couldn't hide the fact I was glad to see the last of him.

By ones and twos the others left over the next few weeks. Acting for Jason, who was preoccupied with administrative affairs, I bid each of them a good farewell and thanked them for their service to Iolcus. The few I had become close to, Argus, Atalanta, Amphiaraus and some others, I was especially emotional with. Friends part, sometimes forever.

* * *

The best part of my homecoming—well, one of the two best parts—was seeing my sculptor's workshop once again. I had instructed the servants not to disturb anything while we were gone and, happily, they followed my instructions quite faithfully. There were still blocks of stone waiting to be carved; there were still chips of granite littering the floor. My tools, like everything else in the room, were covered with dust and cobwebs. The group of Zeus and Ganymede, half-finished, was waiting for me. A pair of elderly slave women said they were anxious to clean for me, but I wanted to do it myself, I wanted to feel home again.

Staring at my Zeus and Ganymede I could not help but remember Hylas, how perfect his body was and how willingly he posed for me. Well, there were other boys. None of them were so perfect, but... And my Zeus was barely formed out of the stone. On reflection I decided to scrap the project, move on to something else.

I had my sculpting again. And I had something equally wonderful—more so, even. I had Kalais.

Of all the Argonauts he was the one who chose to remain in Iolcus. To remain with me, in fact. Days we walked the city, and the people soon came to adore him almost as much as I did myself. "Our winged godling," they called him, and they loved to see us walking hand in hand, arm in arm. The pair of us were welcome all throughout Iolcus; the people took our love as a sign of the city's prosperity, which they were sure would return now that Pelias was gone and the Golden Fleece had returned home. Myself, I wished I could be so certain.

On clear moonlit nights Kalais carried me to the sky and made love to me there. The stars and the planets and the comets and the meteors were our companions, our co-conspirators in romance. I sometimes heard Iolcans refer to us as "celestial acrobats." It was so very, very good to be home again.

* * *

I suppose the people needed us, needed something to believe in. In the months since we had gone all the ills of the city only worsened. Crops had failed; herds had thinned of healthy animals but swelled with sickly or deformed ones. Temples and other public buildings slid into disrepair. Even the death of Pelias had not stopped the decline; the curse was on the city not merely on him.

There was of course a new king. Not long after our return Jason conferred with the priests and civic officials and fixed the date for his coronation. Perhaps the new monarch would bring prosperity back. I know I wasn't the only one to hope so.

And of course with the new king would be a new queen. Medea was to be married to Jason on the day of his coronation so that they could be installed on the throne together.

* * *

A great pyre was erected, taller than any building in the city, and Phrixus' remains were placed atop it with great ceremony. The pyre was so tall and so unstable it threatened to topple. Thankfully it never did. It towered over the city for days while Jason and the priests planned and prepared for the cremation and attendant ceremonies.

Children played around it, even climbed on it as if it were a real hill. The pyre was precarious; soldiers had to be posted to keep the children away, for their own safety and the safety of the city. A handsome young captain named Epigonus was placed in charge.

Amid much religion and much civic pomp Phrixus' remains were finally given the cremation decency and tradition required. With great fanfare the pyre was lit. Smoke rose to the heavens, carrying to the gods the last of the sad boy whose father had tried to kill him.

People hoped it marked a turning point in Iolcus' fortunes. Sadly, they were right. Horribly so.

* * *

Then the next important day came. The twin ceremonies of coronation and royal wedding were carried out with all the pomp a dying city could muster. Flower girls strewed the way from the palace to the temple of Zeus. Choruses of boys sang hymns celebrating the city and its new monarchs. Priests burned incense. It was all quite impressive or would have been if the city could have afforded it.

Jason carried the Golden Fleece with him, declining to let any attendants do it for him. With great ceremony, accompanied by choirs, trumpeters and drummers, he hung it in a place of honor, a shrine beside the statue of Zeus in a shrine within the god's temple. He had commissioned the shrine immediately on our return, especially to hold the Fleece. In a more prosperous city it would have been fashioned of solid gold; all Iolcus could afford was gilded cedar. A series of priests blessed the Fleece, blessed the shrine, blessed the city, blessed Jason, blessed this, that and the other. It was such a blessed event.

Then came the coronation. I had a place of honor at the temple with Kalais at my side. Jason, freshly arrayed in white garments trimmed with gold, looked perfectly magnificent. The priests, masters of stagecraft that they were, had arranged the lights inside the temple so as to illuminate Jason's golden-red hair; it glowed like a halo or an aura, almost as brilliant as the Fleece itself. Placing a crown atop it seemed almost redundant. A quintet of priests did just that, though, each trying to jostle his way to the front of the queue and the king's right hand. The effect was unintentionally but quite definitely comical. Jason seemed not to notice.

Kalais leaned close to me and whispered, "Kingship seems to become our captain. He seems more composed and serene than he ever did in the face of danger."

"My cynicism is rubbing off on you, Kalais." I put on an impish grin. "Good."

Once Jason was officially king he and the priests were joined on the dais by Medea. She was dressed in a crimson gown with gold trim, red as the blood she had spilled, not her usual black. The effect was to make her dark complexion seem dirty. I told Kalais, "Red's not her color." The choristers launched into a new hymn, this time to Aphrodite, imploring her to bless the royal union and the city. The five priests were joined by two more, and the low comedy of jostling and elbowing one another aside was repeated.

Next came the wedding. A priestess of Hecate conducted the ceremony, not the customary votary of Aphrodite. Medea had insisted on it since she herself was a devotee of the death goddess. Kalais and I can't have been the only ones to find it...incongruous, to say the least, perhaps even ominous. But for once we both held our tongues.

The ceremonies complete, Jason and Medea took their places on a large palanquin, decked with flowers of every imaginable kind and draped with fabric of spun gold. An octet of soldiers shouldered it and began a long procession through the city, from the temple ending at the lighthouse. "Soldiers," Kalais commented drily. "Doesn't he claim to be intimate with the centaurs?" He looked around in an exaggerated way. "Why aren't they the ones bearing this precious royal burden?"

"Where are they, at all?" I smirked. "Perhaps there's a horse race somewhere."

Jason obviously expected cheering crowds on every street and there were some, but the show met largely with indifference—very pointed indifference, it seemed to me, with a definite sprinkling of animosity. Here and there along the route people shouted things like, "Why don't you use all that gold to buy us food?" Medea had a look on her face as if she were wondering what she had gotten herself into—as if she had expected Iolcus to be as happy and prosperous as Athens or Thebes. It had never occurred to me that Jason must have been as dishonest with her as he had been with all his other lovers.

But it was not the occasional jeers that troubled me. It was the people themselves. The crowds, sparse crowds, were sprinkled heavily with people showing obvious deformities. Armless onlookers waved their stunted limbs. Legless men, women, children limped along on their beggars' carts or crutches behind the marriage procession. Eyeless people stared sightlessly as we passed, their gaze guided by friends, relatives, perhaps strangers. A boy, plainly excited to see his new king, waved and cheered at us. The puppy in his arms had no front legs, no eyes; it licked its young master's cheek with desperate affection. Despite our return, despite the Golden Fleece, Iolcus was still Iolcus.

At any rate, despite the cheers in the streets, muted though they were, and despite all the misbegotten Iolcans, there did seem to be a glimmer of hope abroad in the city. I uttered a silent prayer to the goddess that their hope was not misplaced. But every time I closed my eyes I could see again what Medea did to her brother. Hardly the most propitious way to begin a marriage or restore grace to a city.

* * *

The city's misfortunes did not stop, but over the next year they seemed to slow. The number of people leaving dwindled. Crops grew healthier than they had in years. Flocks and herds fattened, and the number of misbegotten births—both human and animal—decreased.

305

The fishing fleet brought home bigger hauls. That winter was milder—less hard on the people—than any I could remember. Perhaps the return of the Fleece and the coronation of a new king and queen had made a difference after all.

I continued to live in the palace, with Kalais at my side. Kalais proved useful as a diplomatic messenger when the need arose to communicate quickly with other cities.

My workshop and all my tools were still where I had left them, as were a number of sculptures I had left unfinished when we embarked on our voyage. I went back to work on them, and I was more than gratified that my talent had not seemed to diminish in the time we were gone. On reflection I decided after all that I had to complete Zeus and Ganymede—Argus and Hylas—and they took beautiful shape; I gave Ganymede's features a sense of sadness, of impending tragedy. Kalais thought it the best thing I had ever done.

"You truly are a brilliant artist," he told me. "How could I not love you?"

"Is it because I'm an artist or because I'm so completely irresistible?"

"Well, it's certainly not because of your modesty." He laughed. "But you are hiding your light here in Iolcus. Why not move to a better, more prosperous city where your talent will be properly acclaimed?"

I appreciated his confidence and told him so. "But there is something I want to do—something I feel a great need to do. I want to do sculptures of all the Argonauts." I kissed him. "Starting with you. I have to do it now and here, before my memories of them fade too much." I rummaged through a sheaf of papers. "I still have the sketches I made on our voyage."

"You would actually waste a block of good marble on a statue of Castor?"

"He was one of us, wasn't he? Besides, I can make him appear to be the smug jerk he is. Or better yet sculpt him and his brother locked in loving embrace."

"Do all artists have sex on their minds so much?"

"Lie down on my bed and I'll tell you."

I told him. Often and enthusiastically, every chance I got. His kiss, his embrace, the feel of his wings enfolding me meant more and more to me each passing day. All the ardors and all the horrors of our voyage soon drifted into that safe, pleasant place men call history. Now and then, when official duties kept Jason from officiating at this function or that one, I would go in his place, always with Kalais beside me. And the people of Iolcus loved and accepted us as the lovers we were.

"You see, Kalais, how the people here honor us and our love? There are cities where that would not be the case."

"Acastus, your fame as a sculptor—"

"—is growing across Greece. Perhaps more slowly than it would if I were in Athens or Argos, but it is growing. We have a home here, Kalais."

* * *

I decided to do a sculpture of Apsyrtus. He deserved that kind of monument, at the very least.

Kalais warned me, though, not to make it too easily recognizable. "Jason would hardly relish a reminder his wife is a fratricide. And who knows how she herself would react?"

He was right, of course. But I had to do it. The statues of the Argonauts would have to wait while I carved the likeness of the boy whose death had ensured our lives. I planned to keep it in my workshop. Medea and Jason came there only rarely, and only on brief official visits. None the less, I made the boy's features vague enough that I could plausibly claim it was a representation of Hylas, or of some other anonymous boy altogether.

* * *

For their part, Jason and Medea seemed as happy as Kalais and I. Six months after their wedding Medea announced she was pregnant. Jason doted on her like a mother hen. She kept insisting she was more than healthy and capable of seeing to her own advancing maternity, but Jason kept fussing and clucking over her anyway. If it annoyed her she did not show it.

Her growing belly, to my surprise I admit, seemed to soften her. She smiled at Jason, smiled at me, smiled at the people of the city in the sweetest, most endearing way. It was almost enough to make me forget her murder of Apsyrtus. Almost... I only hoped childbirth would bring out her loving, human side even more.

* * *

That winter was cold and stormy, but not excessively so. Everyone in Iolcus could remember worse ones. There were even days at a stretch when the fishing fleet was able to leave port; and they returned with opulent hauls.

Spring came. Everyone kept a watchful eye on the flocks, hoping for a rash of normal births. And our hopes were rewarded. Sheep, goats, cattle dropped more healthy offspring than anyone could recall. Even the stray dogs and cats gave birth to healthy litters. Jason and the Golden Fleece were bringing prosperity and normality back to Iolcus.

In early summer Medea came to term. The midwives, the same women in black who had haunted our palace for as long as I could remember, barred everyone from the birth chamber. Not even Jason was permitted to witness his wife's delivery. He paced and fretted like a schoolboy not a king.

At length Anticleia, my old nurse, emerged from the chamber, hobbling on her crutch, to give us all the news. "I bring tidings of great joy," she announced. "The queen has given birth to healthy twins, a boy and a girl."

Jason caught her by her shoulders. "Which is the elder?"

"They will both survive. They are as strong and robust as any newborns we can recall."

"But which one was born first, woman, the boy or the girl?"

Anticleia's face darkened. "Does it matter? There are ways of ensuring the continuity of the royal house."

I remembered the shrine in the forest and the fate of my infant brother. Perhaps the day was not as happy as I had thought. A twin girl would be...superfluous at best. The path to the shrine of Hecate was well worn. And even the foxes must be bearing healthy young.

But my fears for the young princess were, happily, unfounded. Once Jason got a look at his newborn children he fell in love with them, instantly and totally. I got the chance to see them not long after he did. The little girl, who was given the name Eriopis, was dark-haired and dark-complexioned like her mother. The boy, Pheres, was golden-haired and rosy-cheeked like Jason. Pheres took hold of my finger and would not let go; he would be a strong, vibrant prince. The future of Iolcus was assured. I only hoped the two of them would get along as they grew. Royal murder, like Athams' attempt on the lives of his children, or Pelias' slaughter of his brother Aeson, was not a thing the city needed to see again.

* * *

One by one as I finished my sculptures of the Argonauts I sent them to their native cities with the request that they be dedicated in the temple of Aphrodite. Most cities were glad to receive them and even gladder to comply with my suggestion. The statues of Kalais and Zetes I chose to keep for myself, though. I did not think Kalais would ever leave me; we were that happy together. But the Fates are fickle and not at all merciful; in the event circumstances ever compelled him to go, I would have my handiwork to remember him by—him and our love.

Everyone said the pair of their renderings were my finest work. Even Jason, ever the most practical and self-absorbed of men, commented how real they looked, how warm the stone, how soft and living every line of them seemed to be. "I have never appreciated your talent, Acastus. You must certainly have been touched by some god when you crafted these." But I knew it was not a god but the goddess Aphrodite. Love guides the hand of even the feeblest of artists.

Eriopis and Pheres grew into lively, happy, energetic and well-behaved children and Jason doted on them as thoroughly as any father. It was not unusual to see him adjourn some important meeting on the city's affairs to play with them, give them a new toy or spoil them in some other way. They ran and played in the palace's many corridors, always laughing and smiling. It hardly seemed the same palace as the one where I'd spent my own childhood. And Jason hardly seemed the same man as the one who had sacrificed other men to his own ambition.

Everyone in Iolcus seemed to love them. When they appeared in public at some official event or other, the people doted on them, cheered their presence in much the same way they had me when I was a child. Even the priests, who were normally so dour and serious about everything, melted into blind adulation when Pheres and Eriopis were near. I remember seeing the priests of Zeus let the children play with the Golden Fleece; Pheres loved to wear it like a cape or cloak and the priests were all too happy to let him. It always struck me as one of the surest signs of the city's recovery that the mere presence of those children brightened things so.

But as for Medea, well, she was not exactly a warm loving mother. She tolerated her children, no more, bearing with cold patience their whims, needs and caprices. Her son and daughter, with the happy optimism of childhood, never seemed to notice how little she cared for them even though she barely concealed how annoying she found their games and even their affection. When they hugged and kissed her she tolerated it but it was clear how little she relished it. The seemingly all-consuming love of their father was enough for them.

The women among our household servants also spoiled the pair of them quite shamelessly, sneaking them sweets all the time, preparing their favorite dishes—even ones Medea didn't like— pampering them, catering to their every wish. Even old Anticleia, crippled though she was, adored the children and did everything she could for them. In their turn, they loved her as well, helping her get around the palace and affectionately calling her "Mum-mum."

All in all it was as idyllic a life as I could imagine for royal children. The fact that it was so very unlike my own childhood bothered me not at all.

* * *

One evening by accident I overheard an argument between Jason and Medea. I was walking down a hall that passed their bedchamber when I heard their voices raised. At first I thought nothing of it. All couples have their disagreements; even Kalais and I squabbled now and then. But as I drew closer the cause of their dispute became clear. He wanted more children. She would have none of it.

"I've given you a son and heir. And if some accident or childhood disease should take him from you, you have a daughter as well. Be content with that."

"Women do not reign in Greece, Medea. Eriopis can never be queen in her own right. You know that. I want more boys. The city wants, needs and deserves more boys."

"Not from my womb. Two squealing brats is enough."

Brats. She called her adorable children brats. It seemed incredible to me—till I remembered Apsyrtus. Some parents are simply not loving, and some royal parents are even less loving then most. At any rate I did not wish to eavesdrop on their marital dispute. I crept quietly away and listened no more.

* * *

When the twins were five I was working in my studio one day; a commission from Sybaris wanted a sculpture of the Three Graces. Since I had never sculpted them before I was only too happy to accept the commission. Three young girls from the city were my models.

It was, I remember, a gorgeous spring day, bright blue sky, bright white clouds, calm hospitable sea. Kalais had I had been together all those years and had grown more and more close with the passing time. Everyone in Iolcus acknowledged us as lovers— *committed* lovers—and respected us as a couple.

Kalais had taken up painting and was up on the palace roof sketching the harbor. I had always believed he had an artistic side and I had prodded him again and again to begin exploring it. At first he was reluctant but he soon took to it eagerly. Our rooms quickly became filled with his paintings and sketches.

I had not quite worked out the expressions for the Graces' faces. I made sketch after sketch trying to find the right one, but none satisfied me. Something was missing, I could not decide what, and it was infuriating me. I told my models to get dressed and come back the next day.

"Are we doing something wrong, sir?"

"No, no, if anything, I am. Be patient with me. I'll figure out what to do eventually."

There came a knock at the door. Pheres was there, carrying a huge armful of flowers. "Uncle Acastus, I brought these for you." His manner was tentative, uncertain. "I've always thought the Graces should have flowers in their hair. I hope you don't mind."

"Pheres! Flowers! Come in! No, of course I don't mind." I rushed to greet him, shook his hand and took the flowers. "Here, girls, weave these into garlands for your hair. Prince Pheres has proved still again that he is more of a Grace than the Graces themselves."

The boy blushed. At five he was tall and handsome with a rosy complexion and the same red-blond hair as Jason. His eyes were the most brilliant green anyone had ever seen—not the reptilian green of his mother's eyes but green like bright jade—and he moved with the easy elegance of a young stag. He had been hanging around my studio more and more and had even asked me to teach him how to sculpt. "But promise me you won't tell father, okay? He And Uncle Epigonus say I should be exercising with the army and not doing anything else. They say I'll have really nice muscles someday."

"Uncle who?" He had caught me off guard.

"Uncle Epigonus. You know—in the army."

"Oh." I remembered him—the captain who had guarded the pyre of Phrixus. "Of course. I didn't know who you meant at first."

"Promise you won't tell them."

"I promise, Pheres." Like everyone else in Iolcus I could deny him nothing.

And so I had started teaching him—slowly, on the sly, so neither Jason nor Medea would suspect. He learned how to hold the chisel and other tools as if he were born to it. At five, he was not yet quite properly in control of his body, his muscles, but that would come. How Jason would react when he discovered he had an artist for a son, not a warrior, I did not want to know. But loving uncles are supposed to be subversive, aren't they?

Loving uncles... like "Uncle Epigonus?" I wasn't at all sure why, but the boy's mention of the man left me vaguely unsettled.

* * *

One afternoon a few days later I joined Kalais on the palace roof; he had sent a note by one of the slaves asking me to join him there. It was another fine day; since our return from Colchis there had seemed no end of them. I wanted to enjoy the sunshine and the warm Aegean breeze. Kalais embraced me and kissed me as if he hadn't seen me forever. When I finally pulled free of him I couldn't stop smiling. "Now that is the kind of welcome an Argonaut deserves. I can't wait to see what comes next."

"Control your raging psyche, Acastus. I am glad to see you, but for a reason."

"Yes?" I narrowed my eyes like a suspicious lover, which I suppose I was.

"I'm bored with doing landscapes."

"And you thought putting your tongue in my mouth would break the monotony."

"Not exactly. Stand over there and let the sun shine full on your face."

I did as he told me. "What is this about?"

"Everyone says my drawing has improved greatly. It's time for me to try my hand at portraiture."

"And you want me to pose?! No! Absolutely not!"

"Fair's fair, Prince. You've made everyone in the palace pose for your sculptures, including me."

"True, but beside the point. I have things to do. I have a commission to work on."

"'I have things to do' has never been a good enough excuse for Acastus the sculptor. It won't work to get Acastus the artist's model off the hook either."

"But Kalais—"

"But nothing. Stand still and let me make a preliminary sketch. Try to look thoughtful and intelligent."

"Bitch." He had me. I resigned myself to posing for my lover. He set to work with his charcoal and I stood patiently, studying the palace grounds and the city below. The lighthouse was gleaming brilliantly. Fishing boats were pulling into the harbor. Just below the palace the army was drilling—there had been word of another Spartan force on the march. One particular soldier caught my eye; he was talking with Jason and the two of them seemed awfully friendly. "Do you have any idea who that is with Jason down there?"

He glanced away from his sketch. "That captain? I think his

name is Epi-something. Epidoxus? Epimetheus? I'm not quite certain."

"Epigonus?"

"Yes, that's it. Epigonus. I've met him once or twice. Very handsome man. *Very*. He looks a bit like you, now that I think of it, except for his brown hair. Why the interest?"

"Oh, nothing. He and Jason seem, well, mighty friendly, that's all." I didn't add that they were friendly enough for Jason to have his children call Epigonus "uncle." "Besides, I think I should keep an eye on anyone my lover finds so very good-looking."

"'Mighty friendly'? Is there some reason why they shouldn't be?"

"No, I suppose not. Hurry up with that damn drawing, will you?"

"And you call me a bitch. Hold your tongue and be still. Art takes time."

* * *

Over the following weeks I saw Jason with Epigonus quite often, so frequently I began to be sure they were something more than just captain and king. As my curiosity grew, I determined to meet the man. Early one evening I hung about near Jason's rooms; I could hear two male voices inside. The other man simply had to be Epigonus.

When he came out into the hall I pretended to be looking for something I had dropped. "Oh, excuse me. I didn't realize there was anyone else around."

"There's nothing to excuse. Can I give you a hand with something?"

"Oh, it's nothing. A button fell off my tunic, that's all. I'll have one of the serving-women sew another one on." I straightened up. "I'm Prince Acastus, by the way."

He shook my hand. "Yes, I know. I'm Epigonus, captain of the king's bodyguard."

"Odd that we haven't met before. Iolcus is as peaceful a city as I can imagine. I'm surprised Jason feels the need for a guard."

"We're a new unit. If our army actually has to face the Spartans it will be our job to encircle the king so he won't be captured. Jason saw my unit exercising a few weeks ago and decided to form a bodyguard on the spot. Funny, isn't it? But kings are kings, I suppose."

Yes, and Jason was Jason. Epigonus was indeed a handsome man, tall, muscular and athletic with a hairy chest and legs, an easy manner and a most ingratiating smile. It was impossible not to be cartain that Jason's interest in him was something more than official. "Well, I need to see about that button. It was nice meeting you."

In the six years since our return from Colchis I had never known Jason's affections to stray from Medea. To judge from their behavior in public they were still quite in love. And he certainly doted on his children almost to the point of obsession.

Medea was a dangerous woman. How she would react to her husband's new infatuation—if that's what it was—was something I hoped never to learn. I had faced monsters; I had come face to face with the old gods on Samothrace; but the thought of facing Medea's wrath had me almost paralyzed with fear.

Kalais thought I was being silly. "I've never heard of a king who didn't have a 'favorite' or two. Why should Jason be an exception?"

"Very few other kings are married to witches—and jealous, murderous ones at that."

"You're worrying over nothing, Acastus. Come look at my sketch of you."

"Must I?"

"Don't be a stick. You're a much more experienced artist than I am. I want your opinion."

So I looked. It was, well, okay, no more. I told him as diplomatically as I could that he should stick to landscape drawings and architectural renderings.

* * *

The seventh anniversary of Jason's marriage to Medea was approaching. It marked an opportunity to celebrate the city's recovery from its dark years (even though as yet the recovery was only partial and tentative), and there were plans to make it a big civic celebration. Temples, the palace and other civic buildings were to be ornamented with flowers and banners. The fishing fleet would be likewise bedecked. There were to be parades and pageants; a troupe of actors was coming from Athens. The city had commissioned me to make a sculpture of Nike, the Goddess of Victory, to be erected in the heart of the commercial district. I gave her Medea's features.

I wondered how wise it would be for Jason to trumpet his marriage anniversary when he was to all appearances carrying on an affair with one of his captains. Not that most people would mind, of course; Greeks understood such things and even revered them. But Medea was not a Greek; she was an easterner with a different set of cultural values and expectations. We had not stayed in Colchis long enough to know just how bloodthirsty a race they might be, but we certainly knew that they were barbarians—which is to say not Greeks. And I remembered Apsyrtus telling us that male love was not accepted among his people.

Equally to the point—if not even more so—she was a sorceress, and one with a jealous nature in the bargain. It was possible, I suppose, that her murder of her brother Apsyrtus was strictly a matter of expediency, a ploy, however horrible, to give us time to escape her father. But I had seen her unmistakable loathing for him and her rage at his dalliance with Jason. Killing him as a way to facilitate our escape must have seemed all too convenient to her. If she was as much of a witch as she claimed she could have whistled up a windstorm to delay her father's ships, or a fogbank to stop them dead. Instead...she did what she did. We escaped, and she was rid of her rival for Jason's amatory attentions.

All those years later, the murder of Apsyrtus still haunted my dreams as surely as the ghost of Phrixus had haunted my father's.

* * *

The day of the celebration arrived. All activity in Iolcus was suspended—all but rejoicing, that is. Every part of the city was decked out with flowers, roses, hyacinths, poppies, violets; the colors were perfectly riotous. Commercial activity was put on hold; workers and merchants alike drank, ate, caroused through the streets.

At noon a triumphal procession formed at the palace gates and headed down to the city. A brigade of our finest soldiers, in spanking new uniforms and armor, led the way. Next came a band of trumpeters and drummers, marking the cadence. Civic officials and priests walked, or were carried in litters behind them, all in the best finery, all taking outrageous pleasure at all the attention. People lined the route, cheering and whooping good-naturedly. The city's new prosperity was on display for everyone to see and celebrate.

Next came Jason and Medea, accompanied by Pheres and Eriopis, all four borne in sedan chairs. The children were growing into perfect models of their parents, Pheres golden and radiant, Eriopis dark and brooding. The two of them seemed not quite to know what to make of all the festivities. The royal son and daughter more than anything else represented a hopeful, prosperous new beginning for Iolcus and us all. Kalais and I followed, the only other members of the royal family not to have been married off to other cities (like most of my sisters) or confined in madhouses (like the rest of them).

The procession made its way through street after street; we passed through every quarter of the city. Everywhere along the route people marveled at Kalais' wings, as they always did when we appeared in public. As frequently as we had gone among the citizens, you'd have thought they'd be used to the sight, but they never were. Kalais had been my partner even longer than Medea had been Jason's wife, after all. But "Lift Acastus to the sky!" they would cry out, or "Show us how you can soar!"

The end point of the parade was the temple of Hecate. It struck me as an odd place for the celebration of a royal marriage much less the city's prosperity. Why the goddess of death and not the goddess of love? Or Plutus, the god of wealth, for that matter? But Medea, Hecate's priestess, had insisted, and Jason either saw no reason to argue or lacked the strength to do it. I suspected the latter.

The crowd around the temple was especially thick. People wanted to see us all enter and leave again. The litters were put down by their bearers. We all got to our feet and moved toward the temple.

But there was a beggar near the base of the temple steps, an old woman so withered and decrepit she didn't look like much more than a heap of rags. She called out to everyone in sight, begging for alms. As Jason and Medea passed her she cried out to them in a feeble voice, asking for whatever largesse they chose to give. Jason began to reach into his purse for a coin, but Medea elbowed him aside, then kicked the old woman. "Out of the way, crone!"

"Medea! There is no need for such vehemence." Kalais was suitably appalled at her behavior.

The old woman persisted. "Alms, alms! I beg you." And as Medea passed her she reached up and caught the hem of her gown.

Medea pulled away, but the beggar woman clung tenaciously. "Alms for a poor old woman. Have mercy."

Medea raised an arm and pointed a finger at the women as if accusing her of something. What happened next happened so quickly I was never quite certain what it was. Something—a bolt of lightning, a column of fire—shot from Medea's outstretched arm and struck to the woman. In an instant she was consumed in a ball of flame.

Her shrieks, loud terrifying howls of agony, echoed through the city. People many streets away heard them and stopped their jubilation.

In only a moment where the old beggar woman had been there was only a pile of smoking ashes.

* * *

The official party continued into the temple and the ceremony solemnizing the marriage continued as planned. Incense burned, torches blazed, the voices of a children's chorus filled the sanctuary. The priests intoned their customary flummery.

But outside, word of the beggar woman's death spread through the city. When we all emerged, we were met with stony silence and faces as grim as if the event were a state funeral. Jason looked at me, an expression of obvious concern on his face. Medea walked a step in front of him, unperturbed by the general silence, perhaps even oblivious to it.

Festive events had been planned throughout the city for the rest of the day, but no one seemed in a celebratory mood. The few events that went off as planned were sparsely attended. Most petered out and ended without reaching their planned conclusions. Medea's wrath had cast a pall over all Iolcus.

* * *

"I don't understand what could have come over her." It was late afternoon. Jason paced in my studio, grinding one fist into the other.

"It's not like her at all. She's never done anything of the like before."

I stared at him impassively and held my tongue. Reminding a king his wife is a fratricide is… well, impolitic. But I glanced across the workshop at the image of Apsyrtus. Jason had not noticed it. Following my glance he muttered, "You and your damn statues, Acastus. I'm talking about something serious."

"What do you expect me to say? She's your wife. You know her better than I do, or could—or could possibly want to."

"You've never liked her, have you? Why?"

"You don't really want me to answer that."

He stopped pacing. "No, I suppose I don't. But I have to do something. The whole city is unhappy about what happened."

"Unhappy or angry?"

"What difference does it make? I'm the ruler. I have to do something to quell this unrest. Even the priests in Hecate's temple are grumbling. Donations have been down."

I sat on a stool, put my knee up on a block of marble, leaned back and cupped my hands behind my head. "Have her make a public apology? Humble herself before the city?"

"You have to know she'd never do that."

"Send her back to Colchis, then."

"Will you be serious? This is a crisis."

"Yes, a crisis of Medea's making."

He sat down glumly. "You're right."

Pheres and Eriopis came into the room. Pheres ran to my side and greeted his Uncle Acastus. Eriopis had never visited me before; she gaped at the various sculptures in the room as if they were magical things made stone by one of the gorgons. Neither of them said a word; the pall that covered the city seemed to have affected them too.

I lifted Pheres onto my knee. "So, how did you enjoy the ceremony?"

He looked to his father as if he was not sure what to say or whether to say anything at all. Jason nodded, and the boy turned to me and said, "I wanted to see plays and dancers. They were all canceled."

Pheres had always enjoyed the drama; it was no surprise he was disappointed. So had I and so was I, for that matter. I started to commiserate with him. But just then a gust of wind blew into the studio. My sketches fluttered in it. The room was in an interior part of the palace; I couldn't imagine where the wind might have come from. The children looked to the doorway with expressions of alarm on their faces. But nothing happened and no one appeared there, and they both relaxed.

Just when I thought it had died another, stronger gust filled the room. Chips of marble clattered across the floor. Papers danced in little eddies of wind. The gust was strong enough to make me sway on my perch. "What on earth is happening?"

No one answered. The children looked to the door again, and this time Jason did as well. Then they ran to their father's side. He put his arms around them protectively and kissed each of them on the brow, and they cowered beside him.

Then Medea strode into the room, her black robes billowing in the wind. The cause of their fright became clear in an instant. That she really was a witch I had never doubted, at least not in the figurative sense. That she really could whistle up the wind, conjure it from nowhere, had always seemed much too improbable to credit. But there she was in the midst of this windstorm out of nowhere. She glared at her daughter and son. "There you are."

Jason spoke up. "Yes, they are here with me. Do you want them for something?"

"I have called and called them. And they heard me. I know they did. I saw them running away from me."

The situation was too uncomfortable for me. "They are children, Medea. They were playing."

"I am their mother!" Her voice thundered and even seemed to echo. "When I call them I expect them to come."

"I'm sure they meant no disrespect, Medea." Jason seemed almost as cowed as the children. He kissed each of them on the brow as if to reassure them. I repeated the sentiment to back him up.

But she ignored both of us. She strode to Jason and grabbed the children by their necks. "When I call you I expect you to come."

They were terrified, and it showed. Pheres put a protective arm around his sister.

"Medea!" I shouted at her. "They are only children!"

She thrust them both toward the door and told them to wait for her in the hall outside. Then she turned on me. "You would be well advised to stick to your statues, Acastus." She raised a hand and pointed to the statue of Apsyrtus. It exploded, shattered into a thousand pieces.

Without saying another word to either me or her husband she left.

Jason was plainly abashed. He was king in Iolcus but not in his own palace, it seemed. For the first time since he came to the city I found myself feeling a bit sorry for him. In the early days of his marriage and fatherhood he had never seemed anything but happy. Now...

I crossed to him and kissed him on his forehead as he had kissed his children. "It will be all right, Jason. She'll get over it."

"I wish I could believe that. She has been having more and more of these angry outbursts. I'm...I don't know...when she's like this I have no idea how to react or what to say or do."

"It will pass, Jason. It must."

He was finding the conversation more and more uncomfortable. He jumped to his feet. "I must be going. The army is drilling out in the Field of Mars. I should be with them. Epigonus wants some advice on military tactics. Later, Acastus."

"Shouldn't you make certain the children are all right first?"

"The army needs me."

The Iolcan army had never amounted to much, but he had made up his mind and he left. Given his wife's mood, going to Epigonus hardly seemed the thing to do. But Jason was Jason, and he had never listened to me. And the man who had quailed at facing the harpies was hardly likely to take decisive action against the Colchian witch.

I gaped at the empty doorway after he left. How could he go and leave his children to Medea's anger? Even for Jason it seemed...well, cowardly. I had grown fond of them, especially Pheres. I simply had to go and make certain they were all right.

The halls weren't very busy. A few servants made their way here and there but otherwise the palace was deserted. I stopped one young slave, a boy who sometimes tended to Jason and Medea. "Do you know where the queen is?"

The question alarmed him, and it showed. "Q-Queen Medea? N-n-no. Why?"

I caught him by the sleeve. "Where is she?"

"In—in her chambers, I think."

I let him go and he rushed off down the hall.

The wing with the royal residences was even more deserted than the rest of the palace. As I approached Medea's rooms I heard screams. "Mother! No!"

The children. I rushed. As I approached nearer and nearer the screams grew louder and more agonized, more terrified.

Unannounced I dashed into her anteroom. Pheres and Eriopis were cowered in a corner, crying hysterically; he again had a protective arm around her. Medea was lashing them with a small whip. A horde of snakes had materialized from…somewhere…and were crawling over them. "Monsters! You do not run from me. Not ever. When I call you, you come." With each word she beat them harder and harder, more and more furiously.

"Medea! Stop!" I ran across the room and tore the whip from her hand. "They are children. They cannot withstand this kind of treatment."

She rounded on me. I had never seen such blind fury in a human face, and it was a sight I'll never forget. "Acastus! I have warned you. Tend to your own business or you will feel my wrath too!"

I tried to remain calm. "You will find it is not so easy to intimidate an adult. These children are precious, and not just to me. They are perfectly sweet children, and they are the heirs of the throne of Iolcus. Harm them and you will have the wrath of the city to face." I got between her and the children and drew them to myself; she would not be able to beat them again, not while I was there. They were still crying; they could not stop. The snakes had vanished.

"Princes have died before now, Acastus." Medea said the words calmly and coolly.

"Yes, but not any at the hands of their own mother. Are you threatening me or Pheres?"

"Mark my words well. You can hardly understand the peril you are flirting with."

"I understand perfectly well. I knew your brother, remember?"

She glared. I saw the expression that crossed Pheres' face. I should not have said it in front of him. Then again, they had to know the kind of creature their mother was.

322

"I am taking the children with me now, Medea. Compose yourself, and think about what you have done here."

Taking them by their hands, I led them from the room and back to my workshop.

Pheres asked me, "We had another uncle? Mother had a brother?"

"When you are older, Pheres, I promise to tell you all about it."

"Please, Uncle Acastus."

"No. Now is not the time. Both of you find someplace to curl up, and take a nap. You've been through a lot. Be careful of the marble chips on the floor."

Eriopis climbed into the arms of a statue of Athena. Pheres found a corner with a mat where I sometimes slept when I had been working late. In a very short time they were both asleep. And even in their sleep they were still crying.

* * *

Iolcus was not the only place in Greece with troubles that summer. The Spartan army was on the march again. They had invaded Corinth and captured and deposed—according to some reports executed— their king Heracleion. They were making a bid, and a good, solid one, to control the isthmus that joined mainland Greece with the Peloponnese. It would make them effective masters of most of the country's trade. The rest of us had good reason to be concerned.

Elsewhere unrest was widespread, perhaps fueled by concern about Sparta. City-states made war on other city-states; leagues formed among them, leagues both defensive and offensive. Every city of any size or longevity had its share of treasures, and plunder is always an enticement to war. For as long as I can remember the cities had squabbled among themselves; war was a way of life in Greece. But war was more rife than ever that year.

And there were internal disturbances everywhere as well. The citizens of Athens were fomenting rebellion against the tyrants that had ruled the city for generations. Similar revolution was in the air in Thebes, Tiryns, Argos and even Olympia itself. Reports of like unrest came to us from as far across the sea as Ephesus and Pergamum. But the revolutions, such as they were, were vague and formless. Oust the rulers and what could possibly replace them but more rulers?

But all the talk and most of the news were of war not politics. Not for the first time we found ourselves preparing against a Spartan invasion. Jason, with Epigonus as his lieutenant, drilled the Iolcan army tirelessly. The two of them were quite inseparable. There was a long tradition in Greece of military bands formed pairs of lovers, of course; no man wants to be embarrassed or seem cowardly in front of his lover. Jason and Epigonus were part of that tradition. It would have taken a particularly obtuse observer not to realize they were lovers, not merely general and subordinate.

Was Medea that obtuse? It seemed unlikely. Would Jason be able to withstand her wrath indefinitely? And would he—or more likely, I—be able to protect his children from their witch-mother? By that point I was quite convinced of the existence of the gods. Each night, in bed with Kalais, I prayed. For myself and my lover, for Pheres and Eriopis, for Iolcus itself. One of the gods, at least one of them, must hear my prayers.

Each day Kalais and I made our way through the city to the temple of a different god or goddess to make sacrifice, to seek the counsel of the priests, and to pray. Kalais often told me I was being a more responsible king than Jason.

"I don't know, Kalais. Do the gods really answer our prayers? Does your father Boreas answer yours? At least Jason is preparing us for a possible Spartan invasion."

"There is always a 'possible Spartan invasion,' Acastus. I can't remember a time when there wasn't."

"That is useless fatalism. The king of Corinth must have told himself that same thing. Now he's in prison—or dead. Jason will not let that happen here, not without a fight."

"Yes, because Jason himself is king here."

"For all your heavenly aspects, Kalais, for all your wings and flying, you are more cynical than I am. That takes some doing. I'm hopeless at military matters, and you know it. The city needs a king, not a sculptor."

He took hold of me and kissed me. "You might at least admit it needs both. What would Iolcus look like without all the beautiful art you have graced it with? Would you really want it to look as bleak as Sparta?"

* * *

And so the army drilled long and hard every day, exercising and engaging in mock battles. I used to stand on the palace roof and watch them when I was taking a break from my sculpture. Kalais usually joined me there, sketching the soldiers as they marched, fought, wrestled. There were men of every conceivable description, and they had beautiful bodies; sweat and muscles glistened in the sunlight, and as his skill grew he captured them perfectly.

Late each afternoon, when their drills were finished, they would strip and make love, frequently in the open on the Field of Ares. Different groups of men each day, but they would embrace, kiss and more. And they were often led by Jason and Epigonus. From our vantage point many yards above them their erotic passion was quite palpable. And it was catching. It was not uncommon for Kalais and I to be so enflamed by the sight we would end up withdrawing to our rooms to, er, worship Eros, or even now and then to do so right there on the roof.

One afternoon I was there alone. Kalais had flown off to a nearby forest to practice sketching trees and wildlife. I watched the soldiers' embraces, first martial then amatory, quite absorbed. And I felt myself, as nearly always, having an erotic reaction to what I saw. I reached down idly and began caressing myself through my tunic.

Suddenly I realized I was not alone. A figure in heavy black robes was standing at another corner of the roof. It was Medea. When she knew I had seen her she moved close to me and spoke. "Look at them. They call themselves an army. They call themselves men."

I decided to be wry. "What would you call them? Their sex is easy enough to see."

"Look at them," she repeated. "My own husband and the fool he calls his lover. My father would have them all executed. Or at least drummed out of the army and banished in disgrace."

"I don't remember Colchis having much of a military reputation."

"Laugh if you will, Acastus, but men cannot behave that way without consequences. Men are meant to be husbands, not catamites."

"Meant by who? By you, Medea? You've been here for years. It's really time you adjusted."

She turned on me. "Cities die from things other than invasions, Acastus, and faithless husbands have learned to regret their actions before now." Again I saw that burning, all-consuming hatred in her eyes, and it left me momentarily speechless. The gods only knew what she might be capable of. Before I could formulate a response she turned and left.

I looked down at the army again. Lips pressed against lips; limbs entwined, sweaty bodies made love. And it was all colored by the reptilian green of Medea's eyes.

* * *

"She watches, you know." It was late evening. Jason and I were alone in the council chamber. "She stands on the roof and watches you and Epigonus and the rest of the army. And she positively drips with loathing."

Jason was offhand; he tossed an apple casually from hand to hand, leaned casually against the council table and said, "Shoo her away, then."

"I'm serious, Jason. You saw what she did to that beggar woman. You have brought a dangerous creature into the heart of Iolcus. We have always known her nature but now, with you flaunting your affair with Epigonus…"

"She's in Greece. She must learn to adjust to our ways."

"You really think Medea capable of adjustment? How long has she been here? How long do you think adjustment should take?" In my frustration I began pacing the room. "You know her. You certainly know her better than I do. Sharing is not in her nature. Send her back to Colchis, Jason, before she—"

"Before she does what? And what on earth makes you think she would submit quietly to being dismissed?" He took a bite from his apple. "Would you send Kalais back to his father if I asked you to?"

It was too frustrating. "That's not the same thing and you know it. Kalais is a demigod, but he is not a murderous one."

"Really? What do you know of his life before you met him? Besides, Medea is the mother of my children. Should I send Pheres and Eriopis to Colchis with her? You know how much I love them."

He had a point. It seemed the first valid concern he had raised.

326

Would she leave her children behind in Iolcus? Would she go at all, for that matter? More to the point, would Jason ever find the strength to stand up to her?

* * *

Things came even closer to a head a few days later. Two messengers arrived from Corinth, one after the other in short order. The first one brought word that the Corinthians had managed to expel the Spartans from their city. This was excellent news; it was the first time anyone had managed to best the Spartan army, and it held out hope for us that we would never have to face them in battle.

But their king Heracleion was indeed dead. He had been held prisoner, but the Spartans, when they realized they were being routed, slaughtered him. And now the people of Corinth were confronted with the problem of replacing him.

Then, two days later, came the second messenger, a herald bearing a formal invitation. Someone there had remembered that our family had distant ties to their royal house. Their herald brought a request for Jason to assume the Corinthian throne. He was promised full access to the city's treasury, a royal investiture and carte blanche to rule as he saw fit.

There were two dozen of us in the throne room when the herald read his message. I could see Jason's appetite for power growing even before the message was finished. The confirmation that Heracleion was dead was enough to set the wheels turning in his mind. Corinth was a larger, wealthier city than Colchis. Any ambitious man would have salivated at the prospect.

Jason thanked the herald and sent him back with a firm promise that the King of Iolcus would consider their offer for all it was worth, but he begged a month's grace to weigh the pros and cons of it. Wealth and power to one side, Corinth was much closer geographically to Sparta, and it stood on the isthmus that separated her from mainland Greece—and therefore from her ambitions there. Accepting the Corinthian kingship would mean, almost inevitably, that Jason would have to face the Spartans in battle sooner or later. Not a pleasing prospect for a man with his penchant for, shall we say, caution.

That evening at the dinner hour he summoned Kalais and me to

327

attend him in the throne room. When we got there we were surprised to see it was only the three of us. The chamber was lit by only two torches. Our voices echoed eerily in the near-empty room. Jason sat on the throne with one leg over an arm of it, plainly lost in thought.

Even before he spoke it was easy to see the conflicting emotions plaguing him. "Thank you both for coming."

"What is on your mind, Jason?" I asked as if it weren't simple to guess.

"Please don't be coy with me Acastus. I need your advice."

"About?"

He sighed. "You do not play dumb at all convincingly, Acastus. Please stop."

I glanced at Kalais then back at Jason. "Fine. You want to know whether you should accept the Corinthians' offer."

He looked from one of us to the other, obviously expecting us to give counsel freely. We stared back at him. Finally, testily, "Well, should I?"

Kalais chuckled. "How can we say? You alone know what's best for you and your family."

"You are the last of the Argonauts remaining here, the last of my comrades in arms."

"An accomplishment," Kalais whispered to me.

"You know my strengths and weaknesses better than anyone."

"Yes, Jason," I said impatiently, "but there is no way we can know your mind."

Again he sighed. "Think, Acastus. My decision will affect you, too. If I leave here, you will be king."

"If I live that long." I was wry.

"Stop it. Please stop it. I have visited Corinth, but I hardly know the place. What would they think of me? Of my children?"

"And of your wife." Kalais made it sound as ominous as he could—quite fittingly.

"That," he said firmly, "hardly matters. I have decided to do as you suggested, Acastus, and send her back to Colchis. One way or the other, she will not be my wife much longer. Aeëtes and Colchis can have her."

I looked at Kalais, who was looking at me. We couldn't have been more surprised. It took me a moment to gather my wits, then I asked him, "And how does she feel about that?"

"She doesn't know yet."

"She must have some idea, surely. She has seen you with Epigonus often enough. You hardly try to conceal what exists between you."

Oddly he broke into a smile. "Epigonus. Yes. The bond between us keeps getting stronger. He is from a village on the Corinthian isthmus. He would be a huge help to me."

"Then perhaps he is the one you should be consulting." This was making Kalais uncomfortable; he did not want this audience to go on any longer, and he didn't try to hide it.

But I had to press. "And how would Eriopis and Pheres feel about becoming abruptly motherless? Would Epigonus be of help there, too?"

"Neither of you is taking my quandary at all seriously. Why didn't I expect that?"

Kalais took a few steps backward; he was ready to leave. I wasn't; I reached back and caught his hand. "Jason, it sounds as though your mind is made up and you merely want us to confirm your decision. I'm afraid neither of us feels qualified to do that. But at the very least you should consider the twins more seriously than you seem to have done."

"Medea can hardly want them. She has never loved them, never. I'm quite certain she only bore them because she understood it was her duty to me and the city. You will have noticed she hasn't given me any more. And she knows I would love it if she did."

"You brought her here. You chose her. Unfortunately it is the rest of Iolcus that must live with her."

He glared at me, daring me to go on. But I was not about to be silent; he had asked me for my counsel. "You are king here, Jason. In a very real sense the city is part of you—an extension of you. If she decides she wants to hurt you..."

Kalais added, "We hardly need to remind you how vindictive she can be."

This was not going at all the way Jason wanted it to. We hadn't told him one thing he wanted to hear. He sighed still again, then snorted to show his frustration. "Fine. Go, then. Thank you for coming—for what it has been worth."

"Jason, think." I pressed. "You are behaving as if whatever

decision you make will affect you and you alone, as if it matters about no one else. No decision is ever that narrow, certainly no decision by a king. You wanted the throne. I remember just how much you wanted it."

"Go, I said!" His voice thundered in the room.

We went, obedient subjects to the king. As we were leaving the room he jumped up and began pacing and muttering to himself.

* * *

For months I had been avoiding meeting Epigonus. We had passed in the halls a few times, exchanged a few cordial "hellos" but never more than that. Finally it became inevitable.

In late summer Jason's birthday was to be celebrated as a public holiday. I couldn't remember the king's birthday ever being celebrated publicly before, but then the only previous king I had known was Pelias, and nothing about him was very celebratory. Jason's birthday was another matter. The city had prospered under his rule as it never had under Pelias. A delegation of priests and magistrates imposed on him to permit a public celebration; Jason was only too happy to go along with it. Moreover he agreed to permit the twins' seventh birthday, which was coming up in early autumn, to be celebrated as well.

Every public official in the city was invited to attend, and even though I did not have an official title other than "prince," I was expected to be there. On top of that I was commissioned to do a bust of him. I told the priests there was not enough time for a proper job and that it would be impossible to get him to pose for very long, but apparently the city had a yearning need for a marble Jason. So I warned them that the likeness might not be very good and set to work.

The central square was to be decked out with ribbons, streamers and lanterns, and a huge feast was planned, open to everyone in the city. Jason, typically, and even though he was flattered by all the attention, found a reason to complain: It was all being paid for out of the public purse, which was to say *his* purse. I listened to his grousing with considerable amusement. "Jason," I told him, "it's your birthday. Try and be a little gracious."

He grumped on.

Finally the day came. The lanterns, it turned out, had been a good idea. It was overcast, not quite dark but decidedly grey, and there were occasional rain showers. There were flashes of lightning far off on the eastern horizon. But despite the weather everyone was in a festive mood. Food was abundant; wine flowed freely. A military band played fanfares and marches, and choruses sang bright hymns in front of all the temples. Kalais and I enjoyed the crowd, the music and the food, and people greeted us as if it were our day not Jason's.

The only one not enjoying all the festivity was Medea. A portable throne had been set up for her and Jason on a dais at one side of the square. He was happy to circulate among the people, with the children beside him. She remained seated and glared at it all. Or rather at *us* all. A slave took her a plate of food, and she waved him away without a word.

Epigonus was there in his official capacity as head of the Iolcan army. He kept trying to catch my eye but I had no intention of hobnobbing with him. As slight as my fondness for Jason had become over the years, I had at least a bit of sympathy for him; yet I had no desire to become entangled in is marital affairs. But finally the captain managed to corner Kalais and me.

"You are the sculptor and the bird-man, are you not?" He laughed; he had been drinking. A lot.

Kalais spread his wings and flapped them. "Are all army officers so astute?"

He ignored this and shook my hand energetically. "Jason keeps telling me I should get to know you."

"He thought you needed someone to make snide remarks to?"

"You are his brother, are you not?"

"Half brother."

"Close enough."

I looked him up and down; it was the first time I'd actually had to pay attention to him. And he was indeed a splendid man physically—taller than me, with magnificent muscles, wavy black hair and deep blue eyes. Jason certainly had an eye for male beauty; there was no denying that. I glanced across the crowd at Medea; she was staring daggers at us.

"Oh, cheer up, Acastus." Epigonus had not stopped laughing;

whether it was at us or a general drunken laughter I couldn't tell. "I'll be part of the family soon, your brother-n-law in every way but a strictly legal one. The twins love their Uncle Epigonus, and you ought to, also."

"I already admire you, Epigonus. All that energy."

"Energy? What do you mean?"

It was my turn to laugh. "Well, you drill the army every day and Jason every night."

He glared. Kalais tried to get between us. He looked around the square quite pointedly. "I keep wondering if Jason's old friends the centaurs will show up."

Epigonus didn't stop scowling at him for a moment. "You two really ought to work on your diplomatic skills."

"All in good time, I suppose." I took Kalais by the arm. "Come on. I see and old friend from the fishing fleet."

That was the extent of our interview. But a few moments later Eriopis ran up to us through the crowd. "Uncle Acastus, Uncle Kalais, have you seen Uncle Epigonus?"

"Not for ages."

"It's time to unveil your statue of daddy, and he wants Uncle Epigonus with him."

"I see. And what about your mother?"

"She says she's too tired to get up."

"Ah. Well, Epigonus disappeared into the crowd a while ago. Your father might do well to go it alone."

"Okay, I'll tell him." She scampered happily off into the throng.

We just had time to refill our cups before the unveiling ceremony. Jason stood proudly beside the covered bust. We took our places beside him, and a row of priests and magistrates lined up beside us, led by Kallicrates and Melicanthus, who kept jostling each other aside for pride of place. Just as things were beginning Epigonus elbowed his way between me and Jason.

Speeches were made, more hymns sung, more fanfares blasted. Finally amid a flurry of drum tattoos, Kallicrates stepped forward, pulled a cord and the veil fell off the bust. It sat on a red granite pedestal five feet high. I had carved the thing so quickly, and Jason had been so reluctant to pose, I was surprised how closely it resembled him.

Medea had not budged from her elevated throne. Suddenly I saw her raise her left hand in a menacing gesture. And at once the square was filled with wind. Violent gusts, tearing streamers from the buildings, extinguishing lanterns and sending everyone scurrying for cover. Kalais had trouble keeping his balance in it and held onto me.

A torrential rain squall blew up. And a stroke of lightning parted the clouds and struck the center of the square. Terrified Iolcans ran for their lives. Then another lightning bolt shot out of the sky and struck the bust of Jason, shattering it and sending the fragments flying in every direction.

When I looked at the dais again it was empty. People later said Medea vanished in a whirlwind, or rode away on it. I discounted the stories. It seemed too improbable, even for her.

* * *

There was, for the first time in years, unrest in Iolcus. People had a growing fear of Medea. There was more and more pressure on Jason to set her aside, for the good of the city if not his own well-being. And the pressure was beginning to come from priests and other civic officials. He had quietly let it be known, off the record of course, that he intended to do that, without ever making a formal announcement or mentioning the offer from Corinth.

Every night without fail, arguments erupted between the royal spouses. Voices were raised, and they echoed through the halls of the palace. Threats were shouted, on both sides. On many nights the children came to Kalais and me, terrified of the hateful passions raging between their parents. Many more times than once they cried themselves to sleep in our arms. Kalais suggested once that we take them and leave the city. But we had no right to do that, absolutely none. And the people of the city loved them, and us. Taking them would hardly have been wise.

Jason came to me—never to Epigonus, it seemed—and complained. "She is threatening to take the children and return to Colchis. She despises them; she knows how desperately I love them and she's only making the threat to torment me."

"Head her off. Take the children and go to Corinth. Or hide them someplace where they'll be safe from her. Send them to the centaurs."

333

"I wish I could. She'd follow me, or she'd find them."

"Then have Epigonus arrest her and confine her to the dungeon."

"What good would that do? You've seen her at work. You saw her destroy the bust of me. She'd whistle up a whirlwind and topple the palace to free herself."

"I don't know what you want me to tell you then, Jason. I love them too; you know that. But she is your wife, after all, and their mother."

"I know it, Acastus." He buried his face in his hands and began crying. I never thought I would see the day when Jason wept, but there in my workshop he broke down and cried. "May all the gods help me, I know it."

* * *

One afternoon not long after that I decided to take a walk in the forest for the first time since returning from our voyage, for some exercise and fresh air. There were several well-traveled paths; I chose the northernmost one. It was a beautiful late summer day, brilliant sunshine, puffy white clouds. Birds sang in the trees; squirrels and chipmunks chased each other in merry play.

I had the eerie feeling I had been that way before. The path took me over a rise and I remembered: It was the path where I played as a child, the one that led to the shrine of the death goddess Hecate. The one where parents exposed unwanted infants, the deformed or sickly ones. The place where the foxes came for easy meals. Was the shrine still in use?

At first I had trouble finding it; several side-paths led me off my intended route. It had been so long since I'd been that way. The shrine and the awful sacrifices left there had shaken me so much when I was a boy, I had never returned there. Till now.

When, after an hour of searching, I finally came to the place, I stopped cold in my tracks. Someone was at the shrine, worshipping there. Incense was being burned. Prayers were being chanted; I was sufficiently far away that I couldn't hear the words, just the monotonous tone suppliants used when they addressed the gods. I had never heard of this, or any other forest shrine, being used for formal worship; the temples in the city served that purpose. Why would someone be there?

It was a woman praying. She was tall and slender, and she was wrapped in a cowled black cloak like the one my nurse Anticleia always wore. A widow's cloak; a witch's cloak. I scanned the ground around her, hoping I would not see that she had abandoned an infant there. There was none, and I let out a sigh of relief.

Whether it was that sigh or some movement that gave me away I couldn't tell, but something betrayed my presence. Slowly the woman turned her head to face me. And I knew her at once. It was Medea. A slow smile came other lips. That smile chilled me to my very heart. Then she turned back to the shrine and went on with the prayer she was intoning. I might not have been there, for all the further attention she paid me.

When I got back to the palace I was on edge. Medea...why was she there? What did she hope to accomplish? I told Kalais what I had seen and he brushed it lightly aside. "I wouldn't make too much of it. She comes from a barbarous land, remember. For all we know praying at forest shrines may be strictly required of her."

I tried to put it out of my mind. But that night my childhood nightmares returned.

The day came for the celebration of the twins' seventh birthday. Jason decided the ceremony would be held on the palace roof. It would be an easier space to guard.

It was a bright blue morning with brilliant sunshine, and the weather was warm and sultry. Slaves were on hand to fan the attending dignitaries. Birds were singing in the trees around the palace; I had never heard them chirp so boisterously. There were even butterflies; a score of them flitted about playfully, reminding us that their name was the word for "mind."

A ring of soldiers lined the perimeter of the roof, all of them carefully at attention, all of them watchful lest anything happen to mar the festivities. Epigonus commanded them personally, and he was tireless walking the perimeter, prodding them to stay alert and on guard. No one mentioned Medea, but it was clear the soldiers were a precaution against her.

The roof was hardly large enough to accommodate everyone who wanted to see the children on their birthday. The Camp of Ares, below the palace, was thronged with people from the city who wanted to see their little prince and princess on their special day. It was planned that at the appropriate moment Jason would walk to the roof's edge and hold the twins up so everyone could see them.

A pair of ornate canopied thrones had been set up under an awning at one end of the roof. When Kalais and I climbed to the roof Jason was already seated on his. Despite all the precautions he looked bored, as if this were nothing but another tedious official duty; but underneath his boredom it was possible, at least for one who knew him, to detect a sense of foreboding. A pair of smaller, plainer thrones had been erected for us; we dutifully took our seats. There was no sign yet of Medea.

I glanced down at the crowd. Their mood was patently festive, yet they were relatively hushed, expectant. Soon enough the royal heirs would be confirmed in their place in the dynasty, and the city's future would be assured. I was the only one who knew Jason was planning to leave, except possibly Epigonus. Or so I thought.

Jason had opted for relatively little fanfare or ceremony. There was a small chorus from the temple of Aphrodite and a sextet of trumpeters to play the appropriate fanfares. Pheres and Eriopis would be blessed by the high priest of Aphrodite, Jason would then show them to the crowd and formally proclaim them his heirs, and the ceremony would end. It was simple and straightforward, in keeping with Iolcus' nature as a practical commercial city.

The twins, like their mother, were nowhere in evidence. I buttonholed Epigonus and asked him where they were.

"Medea is bringing them. She wants to present them on their special day."

It seemed harmless, even obvious, but it left me with an uneasy feeling. She had never disguised her lack of interest in them, not to say her active contempt for them. Why should she be so solicitous now? Kalais asked him, "Is that wise, Epigonus?"

He shrugged. "Jason fought with her for hours about it. She finally wore him down. Excuse me, I have to check my men."

He moved on, and Kalais and I exchanged glances. We were obviously feeling the same misgivings. I told him, "Wait here. I must have a word with Jason about this."

But before I could go to him, and quite suddenly, everything went quiet. The trumpeters lowered their horns; the choristers left off their hymns. Even the birds became still except for a few short, random chirps. I did not have to look behind me; I knew perfectly well what it meant: Medea.

Slowly, being careful to wear a smile, I turned. She was there with the children, holding each by a hand. Her robes as always were black and heavy with full billowing sleeves, warm weather be damned. The expression on her face was as stony and impassive as a statue, and not a particularly graceful one. The children looked uncertain what to expect and, eve, vaguely frightened. They had been carefully prepared for the day's events, but their mother's baleful presence served to dampen any high spirits they might have felt.

"Uncle Acastus! Uncle Kalais!" Pheres tried to break free of his mother and run to us, but she tightened her hold on him, squeezed his hand so tightly he winced and cried out in pain.

I crossed to them. "Really, Medea. It is their birthday. Let them enjoy it."

She ignored me, as she nearly always did, and crossed to Jason, pulling the twins behind her.

"Proceed." Her voice seemed to thunder. "Let us get this over with."

"Pheres, Eriopis, come to your father. Sit on my knees and listen to the beautiful hymns."

"They will stay with me, Jason." Her eyes warned him to obey her. Her jaw was set and her voice was like ice.

He did not want to make a scene in public, did not want to mar his children's day, and it showed. "Very well, if you insist."

Instead of seating herself on her throne she stood beneath the awning and glared at the crowd. She had not loosed her grip on the children.

Jason nodded at the singers and they resumed their hymns, one after another for the next ten minutes. Medea tapped her foot impatiently. When the singing was over Jason moved to the edge of the roof and proclaimed a day of celebration throughout the city in honor of his children who—he told us as if we didn't know it quite well—he loved more dearly than words could express. Medea did not move, speak, or release the twins from her grip.

Jason went on speaking, telling the crowd that as the children had attained the age of seven and were healthy and robust, he was proud and happy to declare them his heirs. His voice carried clearly to the crowd below, and they erupted in thunderous cheers. Someone shouted, "Where are they, Jason? Let us see them!"

Kalais nudged me and nodded toward the west. I followed his glance, and the sky there was clouding over, with the blackest, heaviest clouds I had ever seen. I tried to get Jason's attention, to signal that he should move things along and finish as quickly as possible. But he was caught up in the crowd's enthusiasm.

Medea took the children to the roof's edge. "You want to see them?" she said to the people. "Here they are."

The crowd applauded and cheered, but in a more subdued way. Medea's presence had that effect. Jason moved to pick the children up onto his shoulders, but Medea pulled them out of his reach. "People of Iolcus," she intoned, "you are here to celebrate the declaration of two royal heirs. Let me tell you what the Fates have in store for them."

I watched the western sky. The clouds were growing, billowing, rolling toward us at an alarming rate and the sky was darkening even faster. Streaks of lightning leaped from them to the ground below. Soon enough they would be overhead, and they threatened a horribly violent storm. I saw a fire lit in the lighthouse. There had to be a way to get Jason's eye and prod him to speed things up.

"These children," she bellowed, "will never rule this city."

"Enough, Medea." Jason lunged to get the twins away from her, and again she pulled them out of his reach. "Medea, for the love of the gods!"

But she ignored him and went on addressing the crowd. "Today is their seventh birthday. They will never see an eighth."

She drew a long curved dagger out of her sleeve, and before any of us could react she drew it across the children's throats, first Pheres then Eriopis. Blood gushed, and the twins fell lifeless. The people below let out a collective cry of horror. The ones nearest the palace had been spattered with the children's blood.

It formed pools around their little bodies, spreading more and more. It did not seem possible that two such small children could have had so much. Medea stood in the blood and glared at us, an expression of triumphant joy on her face.

"Noooo!" Jason's agonized cry echoed across the city. Animals in the distant woods must have heard it and wondered at it. In a moment he recovered his wits and shouted, "Epigonus, seize her! Kill her!"

The storm clouds were just above us now, a broad, thick, roiling mass of blackness. Streaks of lightning leapt from cloud to cloud and from the clouds to the earth. I saw several of them strike the lighthouse, and it swayed as if in an earthquake.

Another bolt hit a corner of the palace. Large chunks of stone tumbled to the ground, sending the panicked crowd fleeing in terror. The soldiers who were stationed there fell to their deaths. A torrential downpour hit us as we rushed for the stairs into the palace, large, heavy drops of rain and even larger pellets of hail. The last thing I saw as I ducked into the stairwell was a streak of lightning striking the temple of Aphrodite. The pediment shattered and fragments flew every which way. Jason was just behind us as we tore down the stairs.

There came a deafening crash, and the earth trembled beneath us. We rushed to the palace door and stopped there to look down at the city and see what was happening. It took us a moment to see clearly amid the storm swept city, and another even longer moment to realize what was happening.

The lighthouse was swaying wildly. Bolts of fire from the sky struck it, one after another, and the earth shook with the sound of thunder. Before our eyes the great sculpture of Aphrodite broke into fragments and collapsed, causing the earth to quake even more. People at the harbor were trapped under it and crushed. Large pieces of bronze tumbled into the sea; other pieces rolled and rocked menacingly in the storm. Where its base had been there was nothing but a pile of debris and mangled bodies.

More and more pillars of fire from heaven were striking the city, toppling buildings, shattering monuments and temples; more and more thunder made everything tremble violently. We watched, horrified, as dozens of streaks shot from the sky and destroyed building after building. Despite the driving rain, fires were springing up everywhere. Terrified people ran this way and that, scattered in every direction in their frantic efforts to find safety. We saw men, women and children engulfed in flame. One by one they tore through the streets then were still.

Torrents of rainwater and hail flowed through the streets, flooding one district after another. People caught up in it swam for their lives; we saw many vanish in the flood waters and never reappear.

Jason was still inside, slumped in a corner, weeping madly. Some of his soldiers and various servants and city officials were scattered about the room, huddling together for protection. I ran across the room to him. "My children" he cried. "My beloved children."

"For the love of the gods, Jason, she must be stopped! We must find a way to stop her! We must make her stop this storm or Iolcus is lost!" He was too numb to move.

We tore through the palace trying to find her. The thunder was deafening, and the ground shook with it in a way that made it nearly impossible to stand, much less run. But we knew we had to find her. In room after room there was no sign of her, so we dashed outside and ran, panicked, around the palace trying to find her. But there was no sign of her. Kalais caught my arm and cried, "She must still be on the roof."

I craned my neck to see. And there she was, standing at one corner of the building, her arms raised, calling down more and more thunder and lightning, more and more hail and rain.

"Medea!" I shouted. "Stop this! For the love of all the gods stop it!"

She either couldn't hear me through the storm or ignored me deliberately.

"Let us go up again. We have to try and stop her." We ran back inside, out of the driving rain and hail. Jason was still slumped in his corner, still weeping. I pulled him to his feet. "Come, Jason. Medea is on the roof. We must stop her."

Jason looked up at me. "Where is Epigonus? We need soldiers."

Someone—one of the soldiers, I think—shouted, "He is dead. I saw a blast of wind carry him off the roof and he landed on a jagged piece of masonry."

Jason caught the man by his collar. "Are you sure? Are you certain it was him?"

"Y-yes, Jason."

"No! Good god, no!"

I took him by the arm. "Come on, Jason. We have to stop her."

Pulling him behind us, Kalais and I climbed back up to the roof.

Medea was still there, on the opposite corner, her robes blowing wildly in the wind, calling to the sky in some alien tongue, the language of Colchis or the ancient tongue the devotees of Hecate speak. A huge gap had opened in the roof, separating her from us.

"Medea," I shouted, "stop!"

She looked at us, a mad, wide smile on her lips. She raised and arm and a bolt of fire shot down and struck the palace roof between her and us. More of the roof collapsed into the building, and from below us we heard the cries of people crushed under it. The gap made it impossible for us to reach her. Another bolt struck the Camp of Ares. She was not going to stop; nothing would stop her.

Kalais took me by the arm. "I can reach her. I can cross that gap with no problem."

"No! It—she—is too dangerous. I won't let you do it."

He laughed, "Try and stop me!" and spread his wings to take flight.

"Kalais, no! You can't fly properly when your wings are wet. You know it!"

Before he could even try to fly a blinding bolt of lightning shot out of the sky and struck the building between us and Medea. It knocked both of us back against the battlement; Kalais felon top of me. The thunder that accompanied it was deafening—literally so; it was several moments before I could hear anything again. When I came to my senses Kalais was kneeling over me, stroking my cheek. "Are you all right?"

"I—I think so. Where is Medea?"

We looked, and she was still standing at the same spot, her arms upraised, robes billowing wildly in the wind. All around us more and more lightning was striking the earth. Below us the city was in flames, and still the fire from the sky struck again and again.

Helped by Kalais I got to my feet. "Medea, you must stop this," I shouted. What on earth do you want?"

She smiled at me, the same evil smile I had seen her wear at the shrine of the death goddess. She raised an arm high over her head. "See!"

Above our heads the thick black clouds parted at last. For a moment I let myself believe her awful revenge on Jason, on all of us, on the city itself, was at an end. But then something appeared in the gap between the clouds, something black and formless. I looked back at her. "What are you doing? Haven't you had enough?"

She laughed at me. "Behold!"

I looked up again. The black spot between the clouds became two, and they grew larger and larger.

In a matter of moments their nature became clear: dragons. Two black dragons were soaring down from the sky. And they were pulling something behind them.

Kalais and I looked at one another. Something like terror showed in his face. In all the time I knew him and through all the horrors of our voyage I had never seen its like. My lover, the demigod, the son of the North Wind, was alarmed, perhaps ever terrified. And he communicated his fear to me. I took hold of his hand and squeezed it as tightly as I could.

"I have seen them before, Acastus. They are the most fearsome beasts in creation."

I watched as they flew nearer and nearer. Something…there was a spark of something, a shaft of light or… Then I realized. They were breathing fire, enormous, long shafts of it as they descended on us. And they were pulling…what? A wagon or a litter or…

I heard Medea's laughter. "Watch, sculptor!"

The dragons flew in tandem over the city, breathing more and more shafts of flame, sparking fires in the quarters where none had started already.

"Medea, stop, please stop!"

She laughed and raised her arms skyward again. The dragons, as if on cue, stopped circling the city and flew toward the palace, toward us. I could finally make out what they were pulling. And it was a chariot, a jet black chariot trimmed with silver. They flew to the side of the roof where Medea was waiting for them and hovered there. She stepped into the chariot, clapped her hands and they rose into the air again with their fiendish passenger.

"I can stop her," Kalais cried. 'I can clasp her in my arms and bring her back."

"No. Kalais, no."

Without saying another word he spread his wings and soared into the air in pursuit. I could tell he was struggling, his wings were so completely soaked. Despite that, he flew more quickly than he ever had; in no time at all he would overtake her. Soon they were all hundreds of yards above me.

But just as he was about to pluck her from her chariot one of the dragons craned its neck and turned its head to face him. Fire shot from its mouth and struck him. His wings took fire and he began to fall. I watched in horror as my lover plummeted from the sky, a horrific fireball. Before he struck the earth he was totally engulfed. I ran down from the palace roof—what was left of it—to the place where he landed. There was nothing but a pile of smoking ash. I collapsed, crying wildly, and rubbed the ashes over my face.

My city was a ruin. My lover was dead. Medea had vanished into the sky and the black clouds had closed behind her, never to be seen again. Perhaps her dragons took her back to Colchis. Perhaps they carried her to the depths of Hades.

There was myself, and there were ashes, and there was the rain. That was all.

Epilogue

All of that was—how long ago?—70 years. Iolcus died that day. Our dynasty ended as it began, with the slaughter of children.

There were survivors, myself, Jason, some of the soldiers, some of the citizens and even some slaves. It took us six days to extinguish all the fires and nearly a month more to gather up the dead. Kalais and the soldiers we built pyres for and sent to the gods. The rest, scores and scores of them, we buried in mass graves in the countryside; it took weeks to cart them all there and weeks more to dig the graves, it was arduous and it was the most horrible job I have ever done. When I laid Kalais' remains, such as they were, on the pyre and lit the flames I cried uncontrollably, cried like the saddest infant the world had ever seen.

The dead were everywhere. People had huddled together against the wind, the rain, the lightning, the fire, then died in one another's arms. Every street, every alley, every open square had its dead. Some were burned, some crushed by falling stone; some cut their own throats in a terrified attempt to escape the holocaust.

The harbor was choked with floating bodies. Fish dined on them. If there had been a fishing fleet left they would have had a fat season.

A crew of soldiers rolled the remaining pieces of the lighthouse into the sea. In other times they would have clogged the harbor, obstructed the fleet, brought trade to a standstill. Now it hardly mattered.

When all the awful chores, all the cleaning up and burying, were finished the survivors began to leave, one by one, for other places. Some of them headed north for Argos, others for Athens or Thebes, still others to try where the Fates would lead them. Others simply…went, anxious to believe there were places where the likes of

Medea could not harm them. I could never find it in myself to blame them.

Jason was hardly his old self; he had been shattered at the loss of Pheres, Eriopis and Epigonus. He helped dutifully in the rites for the dead, but he was numb, nothing like the cocksure yet cautious man he had been. Once we finished all our work he announced he was leaving for Corinth. "You are more than free to come as well, Acastus. Corinth needs sculptors, civic art, just like every other place."

I wasn't sure whether he was making fun of me in his grief, but I thanked him and refused his offer. He left a week later, taking the last of the soldiers with him.

I have to make a constant effort to remember how long ago all of it was, how many decades. In my mind it could have been yesterday. Sometimes it seems like that. But then my aged body, racked with all the ills that plague earthly flesh, reminds me it has been much, much longer. At least my poor fingers can still manage my sculptor's tools.

* * *

Here among the ruins of my city I have lived all this time, the last of the Argonauts. Going elsewhere was never an option for me. One wing of the palace was spared; I found a good, dry room and took my bed there and slept there these thousands of nights.

I have learned to mill my own flour and bake my own bread, even make my own wine. The vineyards and fruit trees in the countryside give me all the food I need; even untended they are bountiful. There are flocks of sheep and goats, tame enough and slow enough for me to catch easily, but I can never bring myself to slaughter them for food. Drawing the knife across their throats would remind me of Medea and her children, and this place has seen enough death.

There is plenty of stone. Whatever else Medea did, she transformed Iolcus into an inexhaustible quarry—inexhaustible in my lifetime, at least. Fallen temples provide marble to me, and of course there are the ruins of the place. Working alone I cannot move the heavy fragments, so I work on them where they fell. The streets of Iolcus—of what once was Iolcus—are ornamented with statues of my shipmates from the *Argo*.

My Zeus and Ganymede, locked in loving embrace, face Athamas across the marketplace. Another Argus stands in the harbor, gazing eternally out at the vast blue Aegean. Castor and Pollux wrestle as they did when I first saw them. Atalanta runs fleetly down what remains of the market square. And all the others are here with me as well.

Most of them I have carved more than once, some of them many more times than once. Autolycus is here in both his aspects, man and wolf. Caeneus is both man and woman. Hylas in stone is the boy we met in Delphi, seated so seductively on his tripod. Hylas the older boy is locked in embrace with Hercules, who he loved and who loved him in return. And Jason and Idmon are here, and Periclymenus, and on and on. Periclymenus in his many forms adorns a dozen or more quarters of town. I have even made sculptures of the harpies and Talos. It is, now and always, my passion and my worship. The Muses have blessed me with ever-growing ability to bestow life on the stone.

* * *

Occasionally visitors come to Iolcus. Some are mere curiosity seekers. Some knew the city before Medea came, the beautiful harbor, the magnificent lighthouse. Some come as emissaries from other cities to implore me to move there. Sometimes they bring news: this one of the Argonauts or that one has died.

Jason governed Corinth for long decades, and his last words on his deathbed were the names of his children. All of the city's visitors comment on my work, my tribute to my shipmates and the renewed life I have given them.

They line the streets, gazing expectantly down byways, across squares, into the hills around Iolcus. They make the entire ruined city into a cenotaph. When the moon is full its light makes them seem like ghosts populating this ghost of a city.

But there is one who makes my lonely life sweet. Even ghostly in the cold moonlight he smiles at me lovingly. I have sculpted Kalais many, many times. He stands, wings outspread and waiting to enfold me, in all the places I visit most.

And late at night when I am fast asleep his ghost comes to me in my room, covers me in his downy wings and makes love to me once again. Then he clutches me and carries me high into the sky. We touch the moon, we dance among the stars, we make love amid the planets, which are the souls of the gods. Whether he really comes or it is merely an old man's dream does not matter at all. He is here.

I know that my beloved Kalais will be with me throughout my life. And when my life ends he will be with me forever in the hereafter. The goddess always smiles thus on the ones who love her most.

About the Author

John Michael Curlovich is a freelance writer based in Pittsburgh. His gay-themed fiction includes the dark fantasy *Blood of Kings* series: *The Blood of Kings* and *Blood Prophet*, both to be reissued by Riverdale next year along with a new title, *Blood Music*; his short story "Reflections on Death," a part of that mythos, will be included in Riverdale's *The Morris-Jumel Mansion Anthology of Fantasy and Paranormal Fiction*. He is also the author of the acclaimed gay-themed Arthurian fantasy *Mordred and the King*. Additionally he has published fiction in a number of other genres including horror (as "Michael Paine"), mystery (as "J.M.C. Blair"), and erotica ("Jon Jockel"). Riverdale Avenue Books will publish his "Jon Jockel" novel You Must Remember This, an erotic retelling of Casablanca, next year for that film's 75th anniversary

Other Riverdale Avenue Books Your Might Enjoy

Mordred and the King
By John Michael Curlovich

/

The Tattered Heiress:
Volume Two of the Charlotte Olmes Mystery Series
By Debra Hyde

/

Of White Snakes and Misshapen Owls:
Volume One of the Charlotte Olmes Mystery Series
By Derbra Hyde

/

Menage a Musketeer: A Novel of Sword and Debauchery
By Alexander Dumas and Lissa Trevor

/

www.ingramcontent.com/pod-product-compliance
Lightning Source LLC
Chambersburg PA
CBHW072026020726
47501CB00006B/1976